*The Thousand Year Man:
Book of Prizom*

by John Harasimo

ISBN   978-1-63393-163-3

Published by

In Association with
köehlerbooks™

The
THOUSAND YEAR MAN

Book of PRIZOM

JOHN HARASIMO

A THANK YOU TO THE READER OF THIS BOOK.

I wrote this book as a form of entertainment for the mind. My sole purpose was to elicit a smile at least once during your reading of it. If you do smile, then I have succeeded!

The story told here is just that, a STORY. It was not intended to influence or insinuate ANYTHING as to personal beliefs. These are just settings for a tale that I hope you find interesting and make the book hard to put down.

I truly hope that you find value from your purchase of this book.

Thank You,

John Harasimo

CHAPTER 1

Exposing A Dream

She awoke from a deep sleep and realized that, once again, her husband of nine years was not in bed. A quick look proved that he wasn't in the bathroom either. Tying her robe around her as she exits their bedroom, she wonders where she will find him tonight.

After checking the usual places - den, office, kitchen - she looked out a window and saw him sitting on the patio by the pool. He sat motionless in a deck chair, never noticing her approach. There was no acknowledgement to the noise of her dragging a chair to his side.

It was hard for her to see him like this. Once he awoke from this dream, he would leave the bedroom and sit in this strange trance for almost an hour. She placed her hand ever so gently on his, and tried to get his eyes to focus on hers.

"John? Are you ok, John?"

"Yeah, just thinking," he finally replied. This had become his nightly answer to what always seemed to be her first question.

"Same dream?" she asked, even though she knew it was.

He nodded yes slowly. "Same one."

"John, we need to talk to somebody about this. It has been happening every night for almost five months now. Every night, it is the same thing. This has to stop. I'm really getting worried about you. You never get a good night's sleep."

"Who we going to talk to, Barb? A shrink? I'm not crazy. I just have to find a way to deal with this dream." He turned to her and continued.

"It's the same every night. Same cave, same book, and the same feelings. It must mean something. There are lots of people who believe our dreams mean something."

"So you think you have to find this book and cave?"

"I have no clue where either one could possibly be. I don't get the feeling I am supposed to look for them. It just seems that somebody needs to tell the big guy to open the book. I don't know how to do it, but I think that is what I need to do. Maybe a letter?"

He rolled his eyes and smiled at his wife. A chuckle arose from his throat as he added.

"You think he would read a letter sent from a Baptist?"

John found himself looking into his wife's eyes. He has to be the luckiest man alive to have married such a woman, he thought.

"What?" she asked, having noticed his stare.

"It's 3:30 a.m. and you look so beautiful. How do you do that? I lie down for just two minutes and look like the fat, balding man I am when I get up. But you? You get up looking like an angel." He paused for a moment before joking, "Must be your superior genetic makeup." They both smiled and held hands as they rose to walk back into the house.

After the usual kisses and good nights, she lay there thinking. There must be somebody to talk to, but whom? This was the big question she had not been able to answer these last few months. Then she remembered.

Mathew Cobleir was a Catholic priest. His friends all called him Matt, and that was how he was introduced to her. She recalled how patient he had been while trying to teach her to pronounce his last name correctly.

"No, no, no. Say it like this. Cob, like corn cob and Leir, like a Lear Jet. Now try it again."

"Mathew, I'm a Southern girl, and I'll *never* be able to pronounce it right. Just let me call you Mathew and be done with it."

She hadn't spoken to him in several years. Could she really take such an odd issue to a man she'd met at a party, and had only spoken to three other times? Also, not only does she not attend church, she's not Catholic.

She decided that any embarrassment she might face was greatly outweighed by her concern for her husband's health. That's it. His number was still in her cell phone. She would call him tomorrow.

~ ~ ~

The alarm woke them both as usual at 5:30 a.m. Their morning routines were executed with a comfortable precision that most married couples achieve. The only difference this morning was that Barb finally had a plan on how to deal with her husband's persistent dream. She was actually excited and anxious about John's departure for work. After a kiss at the door, she watched him back out of the driveway, and then dashed to find her cell phone.

She sat staring at the phone, wondering what this simple phone call could lead to. Her finger pushed the button, and Mathew's picture came up. All she had to do was touch the little screen on the phone. What was she waiting for? Why was she hesitant? She loved her husband very much, and this conversation could lead to her husband finally getting some relief – and a full night's sleep. She should call right now!

The ringing of the phone startled her so much that she actually fell off the couch. Her eyes darted back and forth, trying to see where the phone had fallen to. There it was.

After snatching it from underneath the sofa, she saw it was her husband calling.

"Hey, what's up? Forget something, honey?" she said as calmly as she could.

"I left a folder on the kitchen counter. Be a peach and bring it out to me. I'll be in the driveway by the time you get it."

Once off the floor, she bolted to the kitchen, grabbed the folder and headed to the front door.

John was pulling into the drive as she walked down the porch steps. She noticed the small scratch on his front bumper - the one she'd accidentally put there when her foot had slipped from the brake pedal while sitting in the garage. She had hidden the damage to his toolbox with a black felt tip pen, but the bumper was way beyond her abilities to conceal. Still, John had never mentioned it to her, so maybe he thought he had done it.

"You know, I think you forgot this just so you could get an extra off-to-work kiss this morning. Didn't you, big boy?"

"And I thought I was being so slick this time! Do I still get that kiss, even though you're on to me?"

With the kiss over and John backing out of the driveway again, she was off to make that phone call. Fishing the phone from her pocket, she didn't hesitate at all and touched Mathew's picture. As it rang and rang, her mind began to race with question after question.

What if he has a different number now? What if he's been transferred to another church? How would she find him now? She was so focused on these questions that Mathew was on his second 'Hello' before she realized that he had answered.

"Hi, it's Barbara Parson. Used to be Barbara Hadley when you and I met. Remember me?" Oh please remember me, she thought.

"Of course I remember you, Barbara. How have you been?"

"I've been good. I got married right after the last time we talked. Can't believe it's been so long!"

"You know, I think I remember you telling me that you were about to get married. I am so happy for you both. I don't believe that I met him, did I?"

"No, but I was kinda hoping to get you and him to talk."

At this point, she didn't care if this was an awkward way to get into the real reason for the call. She wanted to talk about it, and now they were talking.

"Barbara, are you two having troubles?"

His voice was so smooth and non-threatening. She smiled as she thought he must be a very good priest.

"What? Oh, no, no. That's not what I meant at all. We are fine. Well, things between us are fine. We aren't, you know, fighting or anything."

"I'm glad to hear that. So what would you want me to talk to your husband about?" He hesitated.

"Wait a minute. I didn't think that you or your husband were Catholic. Are you?"

"Well, no. But before you make up your mind, please let

me explain."

"Barbara, you don't have to be Catholic for me to talk to you," he said with a chuckle. "I consider you a friend and would be glad to do anything I can to help."

"Mathew, this is going to sound too crazy over the phone. Can we meet and do this?"

"Of course we can. Would you feel comfortable meeting me here at the church, or would you rather I meet you somewhere else?"

"The church would actually be more appropriate, since it kinda concerns the church. Kinda."

"When would you like to come over?"

"I can be there in 20 minutes. Will that work for you?"

"Great. Please pull around to the back parking lot. I'll be standing outside the third door."

"See you in 20."

Where did she leave those car keys? On the upstairs nightstand. Of course, they were always on a different floor of the house than she was.

Her legs seemed to fly up the stairs. Grabbing the keys, she spun to run out to the car. She caught a glimpse of an open book on John's side of the bed. He's been reading it more and more every day. She slowly walks around the bed to his nightstand. Looking down at the Bible, she feared this holy book did not hold the answers he was so desperately seeking.

As she stepped down into the garage, she wondered if she had enough gas to get to the church. At this point, she decided she'd go straight there, even if she ran out of gas in the parking lot. She just wanted this conversation to happen, and happen now. Unlike the phone, there was no hesitation as she started the car and backed quickly into the street. A shift into Drive began a blurred trip towards an uncomfortable conversation.

As she pulled into the church parking lot, she thought this had been the most apprehensive 20-minute drive of her life. It was a wonder she hadn't had a wreck. She couldn't even remember driving down Main Street, and this was morning rush hour.

Looking up, she saw Mathew standing where she couldn't miss him. She locked the car and tried not to seem like she was running as she hurried up to greet him.

Should she hug him? Well, maybe, once they're inside and out of public view. She extended her hand to him, only to have him put his big arm around her shoulders and give her a friendly squeeze. She had forgotten how tall he was. His hair was full of grey where it had been dark brown. His smile was just the same, though, and those blue eyes, still gorgeous.

"I can't believe you thought I had forgotten you," he said as he held the door for her to enter the church.

"Well, it was a long time ago, and we really did only talk three or four times, you know."

"Let's go to my office. It's the fourth door on the right."

The walk to his office was so short that neither one said a word. Mathew motioned for her to enter first.

"Let's sit around the table. Those big chairs are really comfortable. I just made some fresh ice tea. Would you like some?"

"We Southerners can never turn down ice tea. I'd love a glass."

"I'll be right back. Just make yourself comfortable."

Mathew turned and hurried off down the hall. Barbara looked around Mathew's office. A desk and two chairs were on one side of the room. The small round table Mathew pointed her to was surrounded by four leather-padded chairs. Two large bookshelves were nudged into the corner behind the table. She laughed to herself at how much she'd worried about having this conversation. This office was very relaxing. She was ready to talk.

The echo of footsteps in the hall signaled his return. She was still wiggling into a comfy position in her chair when he placed her tea on the table in front of her. Now was the time, and she felt good about it.

After sipping the tea, she said, "That is good! Thank you." Using both hands to gently place the glass on the coaster, she continued.

"Mathew, I hope you don't mind, but I can't bring myself to call you 'Father'. I don't mean any disrespect, but...".

She stopped speaking as she saw Mathew smile and raise his hand like a traffic cop.

"I remember our first conversation. You said the same thing." He smiled while shaking his head. His shoulders shook as he laughed. "I agree that the old rules between us still apply.

No Father."

Barbara giggled as she remembered their first conversation. Sixty seconds into it, she began explaining her personal rules on talking to clergy of any faith. She wasn't going to treat them any differently than anyone else. They were just people of faith and not due any other social advantages in a conversation. Though she admired them for their helping others, they were no better than her and didn't have any more insight to life than she did. Now that she thought of it, it was a wonder they'd ever had a second conversation.

"Well, I don't really know how to begin. More to the point, where to begin."

"Wow, no chit chat. Right to it. You seem like a person on a mission," he said with a smile.

"I'm sorry. This has just been such a crazy past few months. I can't tell you how much it means to me that you're willing to talk to me."

"I have fond memories of the conversations you and I had. I wish more people were as direct as I remember you being. Please, just start in."

"Ok. Here goes."She wiggled one last time to get a little deeper into that very comfy leather chair.

"My husband John started having a dream a few months ago. Actually, five months ago. He has the same dream, and he has it every night. He hasn't had a full night's sleep since this started.

"Every night it's the same thing. He dreams, then he wakes up. He gets out of bed and slips away to some private place in the house, and he just sits in the dark. He goes over that dream in his mind, over and over and over. Finally, he gets tired again and comes back to bed." Barbara stopped to sip her tea.

Mathew asked, "And this happens every night?"

"Yes, every night for the past five months!"

The rise in her own voice caused her to sit back a little further in her chair. She gestured with open hands, looked at the ceiling and let out a muffled sigh. "I'm sorry. I guess it shows how tense I am. This whole thing is just... I don't know."

The look on Mathew's face showed that he was intently listening to her. He must be a very good priest. Again, she responded to his gentle demeanor, and her tension drifted away. *Do they teach this to priests or was he just a natural? Either way, he was very easy to talk to.*

"The last few weeks, I've been waking, for some reason, myself. I find him gone, so I go looking for him. He tries to act like it's nothing, but I can tell he's getting run down by this. Badly worn down."

Though Mathew's face showed puzzlement, his demeanor was still very friendly.

"I'm not sure if I'm qualified to help with dreams."

Barbara was about to speak, when Mathew continued.

"On the phone, you mentioned this concerned the Church somehow. Is the dream about the Church?"

"No. Well, not exactly."

She cleared her throat and realized that she was stalling. It was time to get it out.

"In the dream, my husband sees a book in some kind of a man-made rock cave. The general gist of the dream is that somebody needs to be told to open the book. Somebody you know."

Another sip of tea and quick assessment of his facial expression allowed Mathew to say, "I know this person? Are you saying I'm in this dream?"

"No, no, no, you're not in the dream. What I meant was you will definitely *know* who he is when I get to that part."She rolled her eyes and smiled.

"Ok, what is this book? Does your husband know why it is in the cave?"

"I don't know all the details, just the highlights so to speak. I was really hoping you would help me get my husband to sit down and tell everything to you. Maybe if he did, then the dreams would stop."

"Oh, I get that. I've read about people working through their fears and dreams. Facing them or acting upon them, to get them to stop."

"That's what I was thinking and why I called you."

"But I still don't see what this has to do with the Church," he said. He looked quizzical, with one eyebrow slightly lower than the other and his eyes locked straight on hers. He sat waiting for her to continue.

If ever she had experienced an awkward moment in a conversation, this was by far the worst one she could remember. The few seconds it took for her to sip her tea again and glance at his face, seemed like an hour. She knew now was the time. *What the hell, Barb, spit it out*!

"The one that needs to be told is, well, uh, the Pope." She quickly scanned the expression on Mathew's face to see just how crazy he thought she was. To her surprise, he sat calmly for a few seconds before asking.

"And just what book does he need to open? Was there a name? How is he to know what book?"

"My husband has told me this many times, so I have this memorized. He says that at the end of the dream, he always hears a voice clearly say, "Let him be told, it is time to open the Book of Prizom".

"The Book of Prizom? I've never heard of such a book. I assume it must be of a religious nature. Perhaps it is one of the forgotten books, and your husband is just getting the name wrong. But then again, sometimes a specific manuscript is referred to by more than one name."

"Forgotten books? I guess this is where you find out that I never really paid that much attention in church as a child." She said this with a sheepish grin.

Mathew continued, "A lot of writings were considered for inclusion into what we now call the Bible. A few years ago, somebody had compiled and printed some of them. They were selling them on TV. I actually had several members of our church come to Confession wanting to know if they were sinning by reading these books they had purchased. Still, I don't recall ever hearing that name in regards to these forgotten books."

As Mathew rose from his chair to scan the bookshelf behind him, Barbara took another nervous sip of her tea. Then a calm rushed over her with the realization that he was taking her story seriously. He didn't laugh and say she was nuts. No, he was actively looking for something. She had been right. Talking to Mathew was exactly the thing to do.

"I have a reference book somewhere," he said as he looked on the top shelf. His left hand lightly slid left to right along the books until he snatched a small gray one from its home. He flipped through the front of the book as he had done on so many occasions. With his eyes fixed intensely on the pages, he spoke without looking up.

"This little book has been my best friend for many years now. It lists every known religious manuscript ever found. If this book from your husband's dream really exists, it should be listed here."

After flipping a few more pages, he slowly closed the book. "But it's not listed. Perhaps your book was found after this one was printed." Pointing the book in her direction, he told her, "I've been meaning to buy a more current copy of this."He slowly put the book back where it came from.

"Well, there's no reference to any book named Prizom here in my small library. So, let's check the computer. If it exists, we'll find it."

"Sorry, but you're about to waste your time. My husband and I have searched the Internet many times and many ways. Never found a thing."

"Ah, but you didn't have access to a Vatican search engine like I do!" He smiled and motioned for her to join him behind the computer on his desk.

He pulled one of the leather chairs next to his office chair behind his desk. Pushing the power button on his monitor, he looked up and grinned.

"Time to play musical chairs. Let's go a' huntin."

She slowly peeled herself from her chair. "But this one is warm. Now I'll have to start all over".

"Come on, young lady. This is going to be fun!"

Shaking one leg, humming and wide-eyed, Mathew looked like a little boy on a secret mission. This was a side of him she'd never seen. But then again, she had only seen him four times, and that had been over nine years ago. After all of the worrying that Barbara had done, Mathew had not treated her like a crazy woman, and now appeared to actually be having *fun*. She felt so foolish.

Barbara squeezed between the desk and the big leather chair Mathew has positioned by his own. As she settled into its soft leather, she felt vindicated by the cold seat. She said, "I was right. This one's cold!" and bumped his shoulder with hers.

There were the usual sounds of typing. "I'm almost in, just one more key and there we are. I always forget my password on here. Now, we want to search for the book of, how would you spell that? Prizom?"

"Well that's how John and I were searching for it. John would get in a hurry sometimes and type prison by mistake," she said, laughing. "Then he would just sit looking at the screen shaking his head and say 'What happened?'".

She noticed Mathew looking at her quizzically. She added, "Trust me, at 4:00 in the morning it seemed funnier."

"Well, there's no hit on the word Prizom. Could be that it needs to be spelled a little differently?"He sat there for a minute, and then said, *A Ha!*" before leaning forward again to type.

"I know what we can do. They just added some new search techniques. One is a 'Sounds Like' search method. I think the email said that we could play with it, but it wasn't fully debugged yet. I just need to remember where it is. I saw it the other day, but didn't have time to play with it."

Mathew was typing so fast and the screens were flashing by so quickly that Barbara said, "Stop typing so fast, I'm getting dizzy. Are you really reading that fast, or are you just trying to impress me?"

She noticed that Mathew had stopped typing and was just sitting there staring at the screen. "Don't tell me. You typed in prison didn't you? Admit it, you did!"

"Here we go," he said calmly. There on the screen was a question.

Barbara reads the one lonely line out loud. "Possible match in secured section. Access yes or no."

"Well, we seem to be onto something here. I'm just not sure about this secured section it's referring to."

"Maybe we should stop. I don't want you to get into trouble on my account. Let's stop."

"No," he said slowly. "The email said they wanted us to play with it. To help them work out the kinks. Let's say yes." He hit Enter.

"It's asking for my password again". Again, there was typing.

Mathew said, "Access Denied."

He tried to log in two more times and got the same response.

He slowly leaned back in his chair, put his hands behind his head, and looked at the ceiling.

"What's wrong?" Barbara asked.

"Well, I think we just triggered something here. This could mean that there is more to your husband's dream than you thought."

"Triggered what? What do you mean by triggered?"

"When I did a search on Prizom just now, the system asked me for a password. In all of these years I've had access to this, I've NEVER had the system come back and ask for another password."

"What kinda system are we on?"

"This is a special search engine that the Church provides for us to research sermons and anything else we are working on. Supposedly, the wealth of religious knowledge that the Catholic Church has accumulated over its entire life is at my fingertips. Of course, this would just be the translated manuscripts."

"So are you saying that there may be information out there on this book in John's dream? But you just can't get to it?"

"Seems so." Mathew was obviously deep in thought. His responses to Barbara's questions had a completely different tone from just a few moments ago.

"You know, Barbara, I think we've gone just about as far as we can for now. I have a friend I need get a hold of."

"No problem. I know you're busy."

"No, I think he can help me get into this."

"Please Mathew, don't do anything that will get you into trouble."

"Don't worry," he said with a smile. "I assure you that I will *not* get into any trouble over this."

"Well, I need to run some errands anyway before I go home."She started to get up from her newly warmed chair as she continued, "Thank you for not making me feel like a complete idiot about all of this."She walked to the table, picked up her purse, and headed for the office door.

Mathew followed her out into the hall and escorted her silently to the door that led to the parking lot. As she stepped into the bright sunlight, Barbara stopped at the top step and turned to face him.

"I really want to thank you for doing this. I can't tell you how much this means to me."

"No problem. I love doing research like this. When I find out more, I'll call you."

"Thanks again, Mathew," she said as she turned to go down the steps. The walk to her car was relaxed and much slower than when she had first arrived here. When she reached her car, she pulled her keys from her purse, inserted the key and opened the door. A quick glance over her shoulder and she saw Mathew waving from the back of the church.

Mathew watched her drive out of sight before turning and walking back to his office. After putting Barb's chair back by the table, he once again sat behind his desk, only to see 'Access Denied' on his monitor. *This is so strange, but very exciting*, he thought to himself. Every priest wondered if the rumors were true. Does the Catholic Church, the oldest religious powerhouse in the world, really have secret books that it hides from the masses? If so, why? And was this book of Prizom really one of them?

His curiosity was piqued as his electronic phone book appeared on the computer screen. He began turning the mouse wheel with his finger, while the cursor on the screen searched for his friend's name. Ah, there it was.

Father Latanye had been a guest speaker at Mathew's seminary school. The subject of his talk was "Ancient Manuscript Research and Translation", and the Father headed one of three teams commissioned by the Pope himself. How impressive was that?

Mathew recalled how Father Latanye had struck up a conversation as they turned out the lights and left the conference room together that day.

~ ~ ~

"So you are in your last year here, right?"

"Yes. I still remember my first day. I can't believe how fast these years have gone by."

"Time is one thing that continuously sweeps us along to our destiny, and I am being swept back to the Vatican in the morning."

"Father, having a last name as I do, I know that many people have difficulty pronouncing last names. I would like to know that I am pronouncing yours correctly."

"And you are a very thoughtful young man to ask. It is very simple. Latan, like the word Latin and Ye, like 'Yeah, we won'.'"

"That will be easy to remember. I like how you did that. I'll start doing that when helping people pronounce my name from now on. Thank you."

"Well Mathew, have you given any thought to ever coming to Rome?"

"I've been to Rome before as a child with my parents. I really only remember bits and pieces of it, but they are very fond memories."

"If you ever come to Rome again, call me. We have many beautiful things to see there. It would be my pleasure to show you around. Please don't hesitate to call me if there is ever anything that I can help you with. Anything at all, Mathew."

~ ~ ~

Mathew grinned as he recalled his visit to Rome the following summer, and how Father Latanye had insisted that he call him Rick. Though there were many years between their ages, the two men shared a real love of research. Mathew's method of research was mainly through computers, and he had often thought that was what Rick was really interested in. Whatever the reason, the two had become very good friends, and they never lacked for subjects to discuss while together. The clock in Mathew's office read 1:05 p.m. Since Rome was seven hours ahead of Dallas, he realized it was 8:05 p.m. there - a perfect time to call. Rick would have finished his evening meal and prayers.

As usual, Rick answered the phone before the third ring. He was definitely sitting in his favorite chair and looking out his bedroom window. He had spent many hours sitting in that chair and pondering his day's translations.

"Rick, it's Mathew."

"Mathew, my friend! It is always such a pleasure to hear from you. Are you well?"

"Of course, and you?"

"Yes, I'm fine as well. Still have the daily aches and pains of a 77-year old man, but I have no complaints. Nothing that keeps me from my work or my God."

"I have a favor to ask."

"Finally, after all these years, you FINALLY have something I can help you with. This is a good day!"

"Nonsense. You've helped me hundreds of times in the past."

"Well, what is it, my friend. Don't leave me waiting too long."

"I suppose you still have never used your computer to search for things. Have you?"

"Mathew, the Pope continues to bless me with young apprentices. They all know how to use those computers very well. Why should I deprive them of feeling like they are really helping me?"

"Just as I thought, you still haven't tried to do any of the things I've shown you. Why do I waste my time on you?"This was a game that Rick seemed to truly enjoy. He would ask Mathew to show him something, knowing that he would never do it himself.

Mathew had no idea that Rick was a lot more computer-savvy than he was letting on. Rick had actually experimented with everything Mathew had ever shown him; yet, in the end, he still chose to let his assistants do the computer research.

"You show me, because we are friends. I don't use it, because I have helpers. Now that we have this straight, again, what can I help you with?"

"Anyway, I was trying out a new search method on the Vatican site. I was searching for references to a book."

"Mathew, you have my total attention now. What book? Is it an old book?"

"Well, I really don't know anything other than the name of the book."

"And the name is?" Rick loved taunting his young friend.

"Prizom, it's called the book of Prizom. Ever heard of it?"

Rick was completely intrigued now, because he had never heard of such a book.

"I am afraid that I've never heard that name before, Mathew. It doesn't sound like a title for the type of old documents I deal with. It isn't the name of any religious sect that I'm aware of either, ancient or current. Where did you hear this name?"

"I didn't think so either the first time I heard it. A personal friend of mine came to see me today. She has an interest in this book, or actually her husband does. Anyway, I ran a computer search and got the strangest response from the Vatican system."

"What response?" Rick was really beginning to get excited. He loved both research and mysteries. This could be a sweet new project to fill a lonely old man's spare time.

"It came back with a message saying, there may be a match in the secured section. Then it asked if I wanted to access it or not."

"I take it you said yes. What then?" Rick was sitting on the front of his chair now, his elbow on the reading table, eagerly awaiting Mathew's answer.

"I did, and it came back wanting a password. I thought that was odd because I had already signed on with my password. Why would it ask for it again? So I typed it in and hit Enter. I was immediately given an 'Access Denied' message."

"Secured section? What is the secured section?"

"Well, that is something I had hoped you could help me with." Mathew was now wondering if Rick could help him at all.

"We both know that I work with many documents the Church deems sensitive. But I've never heard anyone refer to any of our areas as the secured section. Plus, I'm aware of every manuscript that is in my department and both of the other two as well. That is, unless something is being hidden from me. I can certainly check that tomorrow."

"That would be great! Would you prefer I call you again tomorrow night, since you are computer illiterate when it comes to email?" This was Mathew's only dig at his friend.

"Mathew, etiquette requires that you call me. I am older, and also the one doing a favor for you."

"Same time, tomorrow night it is!"

"As always, Mathew, I look forward to your call."

The sound of a dial tone signaled the end of the conversation. Mathew began to shut down his computer and straighten his desk in preparation for leaving. He was going to visit a sick member of the church and then going home. He already knew that he was going to have a hard time getting to sleep tonight. The events of the day would surely make it hard for his mind to drift off to the peaceful oblivion called sleep.

As he continued to straighten up his office, Mathew realized that the 'Access Denied' message would probably show up on a security access report somewhere. He wondered if he would get a call about it. What would he say if he did? As a priest, of course he would tell the truth. Where are these feelings of dread coming from? He is a Catholic priest, not a spy.

Why should he be nervous? After all, he is a priest helping a friend with a problem. A problem with obvious religious overtones. He is definitely on high moral ground here. Besides, who is ever going to know? If he did appear on an access violation report, it would be months before anyone reviewed it. Even then, his entry would be one of many.

Standing in his office doorway before he turned out the light, he said aloud to himself, "No one will ever know."

CHAPTER 2
The Vatican Knows

We have a problem," said a network security analyst in the Vatican's main office. He was standing in the office door of the new Vatican Network Security officer, a single page in his hand.

"What's the problem?" asked the man behind the desk.

"Well, sir. As you know, the new security software rollout was two days ago and now, security violations are automatically routed to our department. I was logged in and working when this level one popped up on my terminal."

With a little agitation in his voice, Mr. Spreck finally looked up at the young man. "Of course I'm aware the rollout was two days ago! Who do you think authorized it?"He motioned for the young man to give him the paper he was holding.

"What is this? I don't recognize this type of message." He sat upright in his chair, pulled himself tightly against his desk and reached for a light blue folder. After thumbing through it quickly, he tossed it back on his desk. As he looked up, he saw a now obviously nervous man standing in front of him.

"This wasn't generated by our systems. I wonder where it came from. And you say it just popped up on your terminal?"

"Yes, sir. I had never seen one like it either, so I screen-printed it to run it by you. I started a scan of the transaction log for that terminal ID, but my PC froze, and I'm rebooting now.

I thought maybe I should come on and show it to you instead of waiting."

"I know that I ride you civilians really hard at times, but just so you know, you did the right thing here. Is this the first time your PC has locked up?"

"No sir, and it's the second time in the last three hours. When are they going to replace that router?"

"They promised me it would be done this morning. Now they are saying tomorrow, of course. When you're back up and the scan finishes, grab Rebeca and bring the printout in here."

"Yes, sir. Right away, sir." The young man practically sprinted out of the office.

"And stop calling me 'sir' so much!" he yelled at the fleeing analyst's back. He sighed. "Civilians. This job is going to kill me."

The young man returned to his desk to find his PC fully booted up. In a few seconds, he had logged back in and started the scan again. *Please, run this time*, he thought to himself. He watched the screen as the I/O counters were continually updated, indicating how many records have been read. He keeps looking over his shoulder and trying to see what Mr. Spreck was doing. Is he watching him to see what is taking so long?

Rebeca was working in the next cube and heard the young man muttering softly "come on, come on" to his monitor. She finally rolled her chair out of her cube, across the floor and into his cube.

"Tim, why do you let him get to you like this?"

"I'm the new kid on the block. This is only my third week and I don't think he likes me at all."

"I don't think he likes anyone that isn't ex-military," she said with a grin.

"Well, he likes you. He always wants you included in everything that goes on around here. Point in fact, I'm supposed to grab you when I get this printout and we are both to go to his office."

"I don't want to go to his office! What did I do?"

"*A ha*! So he gets to you too! Doesn't he?"

"Not the same way he does you, silly. If I go in there, I'll walk out with something else to do. I still haven't finished the last three things he gave me yesterday. That router keeps hanging up my PC, and then I have to re-input everything again. They really need to replace that stupid thing."

"Spreck just said it's not getting replaced until tomorrow."

"Tomorrow? Yesterday they said it would be today."

"That's it. The scan finished. I'm routing it to the printer now, let's go."

She twirled her chair seat around, put her feet on the back of his chair, and with a somewhat hard push, propelled herself all the way back into her cube. The chair was still moving as she stood up and grabbed her coffee for one last sip.

Looking around, she saw Tim had already been to the printer and was hurrying towards Spreck's office. She had to practically run to catch him as he rounded the corner of the last filing cabinet.

"Would you *please* slow down?"

Tim stopped just to the right of the door to let Beca enter first. She wrinkled her nose at him as she breezed by.

"You're such a gentleman, Timmy."

"Cut the flirting you two, and close that door," Mr. Spreck barked as he too, took the last drink of his somewhat cold coffee. "And I thought the Navy had bad coffee. This stuff is all over the board. Weak yesterday and so much caffeine today, I've typed 20 pages in the last three minutes".

"Well, are you going to give me that printout or do I have to guess what it says?"

Rebeca chuckled as Tim stumbled on the trash can as he tried to step around it to hand Spreck the pages.

"What's with you, son?" He displayed a serious scowl towards Beca, then continued. "And you, stop laughing! This is serious stuff we do here. So someone did some kinda search for a word. What is this Prizom thingy?"

"It's a book title. If you look up five or six lines, you'll see he scanned once for 'Book of Prizom'. That's when he got the message saying a possible match was in the secured section."

Mr. Spreck glanced up at Rebeca, who was rocking back and forth on her heels with a very smug look on her face.

"A book. Somewhere, someone, is trying to find a book, and we get a high level security access error? What the hell is going on here?"

Realizing where he worked now and that his remark was not really appropriate here, he shook his head. "I know, I know. But I'm getting better! That's the first one in over an hour, right?"

"More like 25 minutes." Rebeca said. "Remember what you just told Marty by the coffee pot?"

"Are you keeping score or something?"

"Well, you *did* ask us to help you clean it up. You said you didn't want your colorful words to embarrass the department, remember? Or did you not really mean it?" Rebeca earned a very stern look for this comment.

"Rebeca, you've been here the longest. Any idea what this secured section is referencing? I can't find anything on it in either of these Vatican Departmental Security briefings I was given when I first came here."

"I would say we start with Father Latanye. He heads a department that does something with old documents. I had to go there once to show his assistants how to do some things. Of all the Vatican departments that I've been to, his was by far the most secured of them all."

"Sounds good. I'll give him a call. Tim, get me a name of the person scanning for that book. And I'm warning you, if you say 'sir' to me once more today, I'll throw you out the window. Now get to it."

"We don't have any windows in this department," Rebeca said with a smile.

"And you, Miss Wise Guy, Wise Girl, whatever. You stay seated."

Tim stood, turned and looked down at her. He wrinkled his nose at her before exiting the office.

"So, what do you want me to do now?" she asked.

"I'm just curious. Why did this message only show up on Tim's screen?"

"Well, it's complicated."

"Enlighten me, *please*!"

"With the rollout, we all were given some new filter parameters to handle the newly automated security violations. To cut paper costs and streamline the process, they were to start streaming directly to our screens. The software phased in at 4:30 a.m. the day before yesterday. By the time we all got into the office, we each had several hundred error messages showing on our PCs. We knew this was not going to work, as 99% of them were stupid line faults or fat finger hits. So we just turned them all off, since the original memo said there would be a class next week to discuss controlling this very thing."

"Well, this sounds more like the Navy, all right. Let's roll out some new software and then give a class two weeks later on how to use it!"

He reached for that coffee cup again, but stopped short. The last sip was cold and awful. He needed a fresh cup.

"So did I miss the part about where you actually answer my question? Why did Tim get the message if you all deactivated the new software?"

"Well, Tim is so paranoid about you." She drew out the word 'you', as to make a point. "He refused to just turn off the new security hooks. He sat over there on his lunch hour and figured out how to eliminate all the trash messages. Now he only gets the ones with Severity Code three and above."

"And he did this without a manual of any kind?"

"Yep!" she said while grinning and tilting her head. "See, I told you he was smart. Young and naive, but *smart. Very* smart."

"Yeah, yeah, yeah. So, why didn't the rest of you set your filters up like his?"

"Remember the memo? It said that the clerks who currently check the violation reports were going to continue checking them as long as they are being printed. It also went on to say that they will be printed until the week after we all finish our training on setting up the filters."

"Oh," said Spreck. After staring at her for a few seconds, he said, "So, get out of here! Go do some work."

She slowly got up and left the office. She motioned as if she were going to close his door.

"Don't," is all he said to her, as he turned to continue what he was working on.

At the end of the day, Spreck turned out his light and locked his office door behind him. Walking between Tim and Rebeca's cubes, he said, "You two need to get out of here now. I have a feeling tomorrow may be a late one for all three of us."

As they both turned to face each other, Rebeca said, "See

what I mean? Now I'm going to get another 'Got to have it NOW' assignment". Tim just stared at her, sitting there making quotation marks in the air with the fingers on both hands. "And this is ALL your fault! If you had just left the filters off like the rest of us, nobody would ever have seen that violation message."

"But isn't this what we get paid for? Stopping people from seeing things they aren't authorized to view?"

"It was a book inquiry! You said it yourself. Somewhere there is a priest wanting to see some book. Not a spy trying to steal Vatican secrets." She logged off from her workstation. "Come on and walk me out, spy baby."

They began to put on their warm coats as they headed to the door. Tim mumbled, "I'm not a baby."

Rebeca locked her arm in his, pulled hard and forced him to get in stride with her. He was a nice looking guy. Tim killed the lights as they passed through the door. The sudden darkness sparked a thought. She wondered if she could ever kiss him. Would it feel creepy, like kissing a brother? It didn't really matter. He was taken.

~ ~ ~

Mr. Spreck flipped the switch. The lights snapped on to reveal an empty department. As usual, he was the first to arrive. In the 25 years of his naval career, it had become a habit to be the first one on the floor. It had been a hard decision to leave the Navy. Little things like this seemed to ease his transition into civilian life. The pay here was better, and there was still some special prestige in working for the Vatican. He wasn't a pure civilian. Not really.

He wasn't halfway back to his office when he heard the electronic door lock snap open again. Continuing on his way, he heard two voices say, "Morning, boss."

After dropping off their coats, they all met in the break room. Tim was busy rinsing out the coffee pot, while Rebeca was carefully selecting the flavor of coffee for this first pot of the day. "Dark roast OK with you two?"

No response came, so she tore open the pouch and poured it into the filter basket. The machine started gurgling as it heated the water and they both turned towards the boss. He was standing behind them, cup in hand.

"I wanted the breakfast blend."

Rebeca patted his arm. "I know. That's what it really is".

"You can't bribe me, you know. You're not getting a raise."

Tim said, "I don't think she deserves one," as he noticed that the empty coffee packet in the trash said 'Dark roast'.

"So, it's off to see this Father Latanye this morning. I made a call to the front desk and it seems that he arrives exactly at 7:45 a.m. every day. He has a short meeting with his staff, first thing each morning. So, I'll give him a call at 8:30 a.m. Either one of you know anyone on his staff?"

"I know a Cindy who works for him," Rebeca said.

"Good. While I'm talking to him, I want you to chitchat with her. We'll compare notes after we get back up here."

"Oooh, sneaky. I like it." Rebeca saw some interesting possibilities with this side of Mr. Spreck. Things could really liven up around here.

"Enough yakking. Get to work." And Spreck lumbered off to his office with his hot cup of coffee.

It's hard to get much done when you know you are about to depart on a secret mission. Rebeca sat in her cube, thinking about what she was about to do. How was she going to casually extract information from her unsuspecting friend, Cindy? Wow! It dawned on her that Tim's spy paranoia had taken hold of her, too. She glared at his back from her cube.

"Psst. Psst. Tim." She whispered, "You find that spy's name yet? The one looking for that book."

He turned and rolled his eyes at her. "Quiet! I'm working on it".

"Want to borrow my gun? You know, in case he's dangerous?"

"Very funny, Beca."

She noticed that Spreck was returning to his office with a second cup of coffee. The department clock showed 8:05 a.m. That meant that Father Latanye was here, and in the middle of his morning staff meeting.

"Good morning, everyone!"

"Good morning, Father."

"Does anyone have anything for the group before we start our day?"

The silent, blank faces told him that they did not. It was time to find out if any of them knew anything about Mathew's book. Some of his people had already turned to go to work when he stopped them.

"I have a question for the group. Have any of you ever heard of a 'Book of Prizom'? I know our group has never been assigned such a book. Anyone?" He paused and looked around the room.

A voice from the back asked, "Did you say 'prison', Father?"

"No, Prizom," and he spelled it out.

Cindy raised her hand slightly.

"Cindy, you have heard of this book?"

"No, Father. I was just wondering if you want me to check with the other two teams."

"No, thank you. I have to speak to them anyway. Have a productive day, people."

"Cindy. A moment please." He motioned for her to join him by his office.

"I have some things to attend to this morning. Please see to it that I'm not disturbed until after lunch."

"Certainly, Father." She returned to her station to begin her day's work. Watching from her desk, she saw the Father slowly walk to his office. This was odd, since he never stayed in his office very long. In the seven years she had worked with him, he had always spent his day jumping from one station to another. It wasn't that he didn't trust them; he just really loved every aspect of their work.

Everyone on his team was thankful for this and loved his being so involved. He had so much knowledge to share with them. A better mentor could not be found - not in this very specialized field of work. He was a world-renowned scholar of ancient languages and obscure dialects. People from all around the world applied to work for him every time there was a rare vacancy. Of course, very few people left his employ. Yes, these jobs were cherished positions.

"Father, what should I say if someone asks to see you?"

"Just say I can't see them today. Ask for their name and phone number, then tell them I'll call them back as soon as I can."

"I will, Father."

As Father Latanye closed his office door and forwarded his

phone to Cindy's desk, he thought to himself *'Nobody ever calls me at work, ever'*. He faintly heard the ringing of a phone, but paid no attention to it.

"Hello? Document Translation Department, Father Latanye's office. Can I help you?"

"Yes, I'd like to speak to Father Latanye."

"I'm sorry, but the Father is not available. May I take a message?"

"This is Maxwell Spreck. I'm the Vatican Network Security Officer. I really need to speak to him. I know he's there."

"Well sir, he is in, but he is not available. If you leave your name and number, I assure you he will call you back when he's free." Once he had left his phone number, Max wondered why a man that heads a research department couldn't take a call. Maybe the Father had a crisis on his hands ... or was he avoiding him for some reason? But why would he do that? He finally concluded that whatever it was, it had nothing to do with this Prizom book.

"Hello William, this is Father Latanye. Do you have a few minutes to talk?"

"Ricardo, I can always take time to talk to an old friend. Especially one who is my superior."

"William, those are titles bestowed upon us by the Church. We are friends of many years, and that is what truly matters."

"How can I help you, Ricardo?"

"I have a personal and private issue to discuss with you."

"You have a secret request? Ricardo, your secret is my secret." The Father was elated that his good friend had chosen to trust him with a personal matter.

"Thank you, my good friend. Have you ever heard of a 'Book of Prizom'?"

"Not a name that one would forget, but I'm afraid not. It's an odd name for our line of work. Have you found a reference to it in your work?"

"No, I am helping a friend who is searching for any information on it."

"Have you asked Father Peterson yet? Although I do not think he is working on such a book either. He and I just had dinner together last night. We discussed our respective team projects in great depth while enjoying some very tasty veal. It is a new place called Marizio's. Have you heard of it?"

"No, I called you first because Father Peterson is in Accounting this morning. They had questions about the chemical usage on his current project. I asked him to meet with them this morning on my behalf."

"I understand completely. He is a better bean counter than either of us!" His jolly laughter echoed on the phone.

"I will ask him when he is free. And I expect an invite to share a meal at your new eatery soon, my friend."

"If I stumble upon anything about your book, Ricardo, I'll call you immediately."

"Thank you my friend."

If William had no knowledge of this book, there was no need to ask Father Peterson. Although he was among the world's best at restoration of brittle and degraded parchment, he had never shown any interest in the actual search for the documents they worked on. Of course there would be a purely political call placed to Father Peterson, just to maintain a good working relationship between the three teams.

Rick now knew that he must involve a very special friend if he was to find out anything about Mathew's Book of Prizom. A powerful friend who could tell him what this 'secured section' really was. But this would not be by phone. A couriered message to the depths of the Vatican would result in a very isolated meeting. He would have to leave the department to start things rolling.

The sound of his office door opening attracted Cindy's attention. She sprang to her feet to take the note to her boss.

"Father, you've had a call. Should I place it on your desk?"

Holding out his hand, he said, "I'll take it, my dear." He stopped briefly to read it.

"Maxwell. Network Security Officer? I met this man when he was first hired. Did he say what he wanted?"

"No, Father. Just that it was important he speak with you."

"I should call him before I go out." Turning around, he re-entered the office he had just left. He found it amusing that he had entered this office more times today than he had all last week. Wondering what this security officer wants with him, he dialed the number on the note.

"Hello, Maxwell Spreck here."

"This is Father Latanye. I'm sorry that I missed your call."

"No problem, Father. I would like to come see you, if you have a few minutes for me."

"I have an errand to run and am on my way out now. I will be back in less than an hour. Would you like for me to stop by your office?"

"Father, I would rather come to you. I have a small question, and was hoping to use it as a pretense for a little tour of your area."

"Of course I would love to show you around. We are very proud of our department. I will call you when I return."

"Thank you, Father. Till then."

Max was proud of himself and how he had dodged a bullet. He really did want a tour of their area, because it was one of the few he had not seen since being hired. It was also important that Rebeca have an opportunity to speak to this Cindy on the side. This was working out just as he had planned. His self-admiration was broken by the sound of tapping on metal. Without even turning to look, he knew who it was.

"Tim, have I ever told you how annoying that is? Why, *yes*, I do believe I have. Several times! Now, what?"

"I have that scan, sirrr, sorry." Tim couldn't believe he called him *sir* again.

Max sat, staring at a young man who was probably the brightest he's ever worked with, but also one who could irritate the dead.

"Again, I suppose you want me to guess what?" Tim finally handed him the pages he'd brought with him. Being a very fast reader, Max finished the three pages in less than two minutes.

"So it's a PC assigned to a priest in Dallas, Texas. You gotta be kidding me! Name is Father Mathew Cobleir. What kinda name is that? French?"

"I think so, sir," and having said the 'sir' word again, Tim immediately tightened his lips while jerking his head. Of course he didn't have to look. He could feel the boss staring at him.

"This report is a little light, don't you think?"

"Light?" Tim said, with a baffled look on his face.

"Yeah, light. I like the info on the church name, location, etc. etc., but I want other things like, does this Cobleir guy rate a private office? If so, who has access to his office and thus the PC? You know, just because it was his PC, it doesn't mean he did the search. Got me?"

"I didn't think of that. But how do I find that out?"

"You call them and ask."

"Just like that. Ask?"

"Look, knucklehead. Call him and tell him you work here in the Vatican Network Security office. Every Catholic office in the world knows we just upgraded our security software. Say that, as part of the new software rollout, he is one of fifty people that were chosen to participate in a survey. Then you ask things like, did the rollout cause him any down time? Has his PC hung up any, blah blah blah. Things like that."

"Then mix in the questions we need to know. Is the PC in an office? Is it his alone to use? How secure would he say it is? Does he have his password written down where somebody could find it? Of course, if he says, 'Yes', then jump his ass. Sorry."

This time Max was the one who tightened his lip and jerked his head. "Don't mention that slipup to Beca. Ok, buddy?"

"I don't tell Beca everything I hear. Why do people think that? It's her, she just needles me and needles me. Pick. Pick. Pick, until you let it slip and then, HAH! Everyone thinks you told her." Tim was cut off by a louder voice.

"Wow, Hot Rod! Slow down. Hit the brakes, will ya."

"Sorry." Tim was embarrassed and tried to recover. "I think I got it. I'll find out what I can."

Shaking his head and taking exaggerated steps out of the office, Tim headed back to his desk. Once in the safety of his cube, he began to go over how Spreck wanted him to get this information. It was pretty cool how he came up with all that on the spur of the moment. Tim wondered if the rumors could be true about Spreck having actually been a spy.

He heard a phone ringing. It was coming from Spreck's office.

"Hello? Maxwell Spreck here."

"Mr. Spreck, it is Father Latanye. I have returned to my office. When would you like to come over?"

"I can be there in 15 minutes. Is it OK if I bring someone with me? She works for me, and says she has a friend in your area."

"It must be that pleasant young woman with the lovely red hair. I know she and Cindy have lunch together from time to time. I believe her name starts with a B. No. Her name is Rebeca and Cindy calls her Beca. Of course, bring anyone you wish. I look forward to meeting you again in person."

"Thank you Father. We're on our way."

Quickly placing the phone on the hook, Max jumped to his feet. One last sip of coffee. Empty? What timing. Walking quickly, he went straight to Rebeca's cube. She was standing, probably needling Tim again. Max wondered if the kid had cracked.

Beca heard him coming and turned to look. Catching her eye, Max simply motioned with his head towards the door and walked right past her.

"Hey, wait up will ya," she said as she raced to catch up with him. He was already holding the door when she added, "What is it with you guys? Always walking like you're on fire. Doesn't anyone ever stroll anymore?"

Max waited until she was about to pass between him and the open door, then he said, "Stroll? What are you, 90? Nobody says *stroll* these days."

"I was being polite and trying to use words your generation understands."

Max mockingly glared at her, while thinking she really did have some red hair. With the door closing behind them, he said, "My generation, huh. Remember this morning's coffee room chat, the raise? Could be years and years and...".

"You love me," she replied with an exaggerated smile.

The office banter continued right up to the sound of Rebeca pushing the speaker button outside Father Latanye's department. First a low crackle and then a voice said, "Can I help you?"

"It's Maxwell Spreck to see Father Latanye. He's expecting me."

After two attempts, the buzzer released the door and allowed them in.

Father Latanye was just inside and immediately began to apologize for the door sticking.

"I am so sorry. I've called every week for a month about that door. They were supposed to fix it yesterday, but now they are saying today."

Max was quick to comment. "We have a router like that."

The Father first shook hands with Max, and then Beca. "I hope you have been well young lady, since our last encounter."

"Yes, thank you, Father."

"Cindy, you have a visitor," and he turned back to face Max, "as do I."

Motioning towards his office, Rick said, "Again, I must apologize. We do not allow beverages of any kind in here, so no coffee."

"I understand completely, Father. I would think that liquid would not be friendly to the items you have in here."

They entered the office and sat down side by side in front of a massive wooden desk.

"This thing is beautiful. Makes mine look like a card table."

Blushing from embarrassment, Father Latanye said, "I was fortunate to be its home of last resort. They remodeled the floors above ours last year." He leaned towards Max as if trying to keep a secret. "Some very important people up there."

"I'd like to rescue one like this someday."

Max was gingerly rubbing his hand on its ultra smooth surface while actually eyeing the stacks of papers on the desk. Though mainly papers, there were many open books sticking out along one side.

"I see you have taken notice of my rather bizarre filing system."

"I wouldn't say bizarre. If you saw mine, you'd know we probably took the same course."

There was a light-hearted laugh from each man, but they both had been sizing up the other. They now knew that the other was equally observant.

"What was the question you had for me today?"

"Father. Should I call you Father?"

"Ricardo, please."

"Max," he reciprocated. "I trust you appreciate the sensitivity of what I'm about to ask you."

"The word 'security' is in your title. Of course I understand your need for secrecy."

"Father, Oh, Ricardo," and Max smiled, "this will probably turn out to be nothing, but an attempt to access some information was made recently."

"What type of information? Did it concern me?"

"No, I assure you it has nothing to do with you. There are two pieces to my question. There was an inquiry about a certain book, a 'Book of Prizom'. I was wondering if you knew what it was."

He strategically paused long enough to watch for a reaction of any kind on the Father's face. None came.

A less experienced man would have completely exposed his astonishment at the mention of the very book he was himself seeking information on. Recalling the question asked of him in this morning's meeting, he said, "I'm sorry, did you say 'Book of Prison'?"

Chuckling, Max continued. "No, Prizom." He spelled it out slowly.

Having bought some time to think, the Father responded carefully. "Not the type of name we hear in reference to the documents we work with. What was the other part of the question?"

"The scan for this book title triggered a second tier password challenge. It mentioned a 'secured section' as if it were a department inside the Church. Only thing is, I can't find anyone that knows of any secured section."

"My assistants do the computer work for me. You should talk to them. As far as a secured section, we are secured. We are even sometimes held prisoners by that door, but I have never heard my department referred to as the secured section."

"Well, I've taken up enough of your time, Father, uh, Ricardo."

"It was my pleasure, Max. I'm sorry I wasn't of more help. Would you like me to make some inquiries for you?"

"Yes, I'd really appreciate anything you could find out for me."

"And I'll be discreet, just as you asked."

"Good day, Father."

The office phone rang as Max stood to leave. He motioned to the phone and said, "Please, I'll show myself out."

Cindy and Rebeca had just stepped through the door into the

hall when Max caught it. "Ladies."

"Hey, boss. Cindy is taking me for a pastry. Did you know they have a new vendor in the lobby?"

"No, I'll see you back upstairs," he said, as he opened his eyes wide and nodded towards Cindy while whispering, "Anything?"

She smiled. "Nada."

"Same here. The old man has never heard of the book."

"Sure you don't want a doughnut?" she asked as she rejoined Cindy.

"Try not to fall into a sugar coma!"

Max slowly began his stroll back to his office. His gut told him that there was something that Father Latanye is hiding, but what? As with most things in life, it would just be a matter of time before something gave. Nothing was going to happen very quickly. He was sure of that.

"Hello, Father Latanye speaking."

"Rick, it's me, Mathew."

The Father was shocked. The sound of Maxwell Spreck's voice was still in his ears, and now Mathew was on the phone. He realized that this whole situation was escalating rapidly. A security officer had just asked him a question, and he had chosen to deceive the man. To make matters worse, this officer was still in the office when Mathew called. How could this be happening?

"Hello? Rick. You there?"

"Sorry, Mathew my friend. I am somewhat speechless at today's chain of events."

"You and me both! I just had a call from the Vatican Network Security office."

"What? I can't believe this. The head of Network Security was sitting at my desk when you called."

"You got to be kidding me! What did he want?"

"He asked if I had ever heard of the 'Book of Prizom'. Of course I managed to change the subject without really saying. What did they want from you?"

"Well, on the surface, it seemed very innocent. They are supposedly doing a survey about the new security software they rolled out a few days ago. Problem is, my PC had such an old operating system it could not be upgraded to the new software. I received an email, saying that my PC was flagged in their system for a later upgrade. They were waiting on a patch from the vendor before my PC will work with their new software. I was cordial on the phone, but after I hung up, I knew something was wrong. If my PC was flagged on their system, seems to me they would not be calling to see how the upgrade went. I almost didn't call you because I felt foolishly paranoid. But now I'm sure there's something going on here, aren't you? "

"Well Mathew, we may not understand what is going on here, but we do know one thing."

"What?"

"This 'Book of Prizom' must exist and somebody doesn't want its existence known. By the way, I have enlisted the help of a very powerful friend to help us find your book. If the Church has it or knows about it, he will know."

"At this point, I'm not so sure that's a good idea. All I did was an online search for a book name, and look what has transpired in less than 72 hours? If another, more senior individual starts asking questions on your behalf, this whole thing could fall right back in your lap. Hard! If it does, I expect you to tell them the truth. Tell them that I started this. Me."

"I appreciate your concern, Mathew, but I can't believe that there is anything sinister going on here. The existence of a book is in question. So what? It's a book. All they need to say is Yes or No. We may not get the answer we want or the information we seek, but there *will* be an answer and this will be over. Isn't that all you were after to begin with?"

After a slight pause, a calmer Mathew said, "This is why I hold you in such regard, and am so proud to have you as a friend. You're calm when those around you are nervous, like me. You see things so clearly, right to the heart of the matter. I pray to become more like you, my friend. I have gotten all worked up for nothing. I should have more faith in my Church. You are right. It is just a book."

After their goodbyes and a mutual promise to speak again tomorrow night, Rick sat alone thinking. Though he has managed to soothe his young friend's worries, Rick knew the treachery that could be dispensed from inside these holy walls. Still, what he had set in motion was now in motion. The more this mystery unfolded, the more intrigued he became. This whole issue had brought some long-sought spice to an old lonely man's life. He wondered what would happen next.

"It's about time you get back. Hey, what's your hurry?" Tim said, as Rebeca sprinted past him to lay her pastry on her desk without even looking at him. She was almost to Spreck's door before Tim finished saying, "That's it, just ignore me."

Not stopping to knock, she just hurried to the side of his desk. He had stopped typing but still had his hands on the keyboard. She leaned on his desk with both hands.

"I take that Nada back. You aren't going to believe this. Cindy made a comment about Father Latanye acting different today."

"Different, how? And so what if?" is all that Max could say before being cut off by Beca shaking her head and saying, "No, No, No, that's not the important part. He asked the group this morning if anyone had ever heard of the 'Book of Prizom'. I thought you said he had never heard of it."

"He what?" Max's eyes were locked on hers while his hands began fumbling around for his misplaced cup of coffee.

"Damn it! Where's my cup?"

Rebeca scooted it over to his hand, and didn't even take the opportunity to point out that he just cursed out loud.

"I knew he was hiding something. It didn't show on his face, but I could tell there was something he was hiding. You know, every priest I've ever known could look right through you and not show any emotion on their face. They must learn that in school!"

Rebeca leaned a little closer. "Focus. Can we?"

"Don't get smart! Why did she think he was acting funny?"

"She said three things were odd this morning. First, he never goes into that office. She said he spends his entire day going from one person to the next. All day, every day. He helps them and moves on. But today, he told her right off the bat that he was going to be in his office and she was to hold his calls."

"That's when he put *me* off. I knew it! God, I'm good!" he said as he smirked at her.

"And I thought your head was already too big. You should be careful. It could explode."

"Cute! What were the other two things?"

"Well, she said he never leaves the department from the time he gets in till he leaves for home. He never goes to eat or to run errands, never. But this morning, he was on the phone a couple of times and then went out for almost an hour."

"Yep, I knew about that too. I wonder where he went. Go on."

"Lastly, she was kinda bent out of shape about him not letting her call the other two teams. Seems she is always the one he asks to pass info and questions between the teams. But when she said she'd ask them if they knew anything about this book, he said he would do it himself. I don't know if she was being paranoid, or just had her feelings hurt."

"Hum, this whole thing is very odd. Why would he deny ever hearing of the book?"After pausing for just a second, Max added, "You know, he never really said he had *not* heard of the book. How'd he put it?"

While Max tried to remember the Father's exact words, he was waving his hands slowly and staring blankly into space. With a snap of his fingers, he remembered.

"'Not the kind of name we hear about the documents we work with'. That is what he said, or something close. Either way, it was an answer that didn't answer the question."

"Maybe he's a retired politician?" said Beca.

"I think it was a subliminal slip."

"A what?"

"Look, Beca, people slip up and give away clues to what they're hiding. The trick is to be able to spot the slipup. Since he asked if any of his people ever heard of this book, we know he's looking for it too. "

"So what's the slipup?"

"Beca, do I have to spell it out for ya? He doesn't think the book is something like what they usually work with. He probably didn't even call the other teams because he already knows they won't know anything either."

"So that's why he didn't let Cindy call the teams, right?" Rebeca said, her finger pointed at him.

"You're getting it. But he is also a very sly fox, this one. I bet he did call each head of the other two teams, just for show. He then went to see someone that could help him find this secured section. That's the errand Cindy saw him leave to do."

"I gotta hand it to you, Maxy," she said with a pseudo look of admiration on her face. "You make a pretty good detective."

"Yes I do!" He said before leaning towards her to say, "and don't call me Maxy. In 25 years of Navy life, only one guy ever called me that."

"And you threw him overboard. Right big guy," she said playfully.

"They never found him."

A tapping on the office doorframe made both of them exhale exaggeratedly before saying in unison, "Come in, Tim."

"I talked to that priest who did the inquiry on that book, and…" is all he gets out before being cut off by Rebeca and Max.

"The priest knows." Beca was cut off by Max, who was standing now and finished her sentence with "Father Latanye".

Tim looked first at Rebeca, and then at Max. "Obviously I've missed something, as usual! See how you guys are. Always leaving out the new guy. Never fails. First you ask me to…" but Max stopped him by holding up one hand.

"Tim, I'll fill you in later." Rebeca said with a big smile.

"You'd better."

He turned back to Max and said, "So, boss, we about to blow the lid off this thing?"

"No, we still don't know enough. Besides, this whole issue is out of our area of responsibility."

"But somebody needs to know about this."

"Beca, when I know more, I'll take it to my boss. That's all we can do. Then it will be up to him to decide what to do f rom there."

"So now what?" asked Tim.

"We wait, young man. We wait."

Rebecca had already exited the office on her way back to her desk. The two guys heard Rebeca yell "Tim!" They looked at each other and Max shook his head.

"You ate her pastry. Dead man."

CHAPTER 3
Talk With a Dreamer – Part One

The soft sound of a door being gently closed was just enough to put her mind on the path back to consciousness. Barb's repeated blinking ended when she was fully focused on John sneaking back into the bedroom. Obviously, he'd had his nightly dream and was already returning from his solitary meditation.

It had been three days since she had spoken to Father Cobleir about her husband's dream. Since their talk, she had been so relaxed and slept so deeply, that she had slept through John's nightly routine again. This was the first night in three that she had even been awakened by John's returning to the bedroom. She felt badly for having these restful nights of sleep, while her husband was still being haunted by his dream.

"John, I'm awake. Please come back to bed."

"Just want to splash some water on my face and I'll be right there."

His face was still damp as he slipped back under the covers. "I'm sorry I woke you. I was trying not to."

"Don't be silly, I just can't believe I didn't wake up when you got up."

"You were actually snoring." He paused, then added, "God, I envy you. I can't remember the last time I slept straight through till morning."

"Well, I can. You haven't been able to sleep all night for over five months. I'm really worried about you."

"Before you say it again, the answer is still *no*. I'm not going to talk to your friend the priest. NO!"

"John, why not?"

"I can still get a few hours of sleep before it's time to get up. Please, can we just drop it?"

He was right. She knew that her talking would deprive him of the little sleep he got each night. Once he had done his penance after being awakened by the dream, John usually fell asleep immediately, never moving a muscle until the alarm went off.

"I'm sorry. I'll shut up."

"Barb, I love you. I didn't tell you to shut up."

"Really?"

"Yes, really. I love talking to you. Just not now, and not about this."

She leaned closer to kiss him ever so gently on his lips before lying back on her pillow. The last step in getting comfy, she snuggled up close to his side. As usual, he was so warm. Why are men always so warm? Though her feet would be warmer resting on his, she skipped this part of her nightly routine. John was already snoring and she didn't want to stir him.

~ ~ ~

The alarm had come and gone, followed by John's usual frantic pace of getting showered, shaved, and dressed. A few quick sips of coffee and he was out the door to work. They had performed their normal morning activities without discussing the issue on her mind. There was only a brief mention of it as John was picking up his briefcase.

"Gotta go. I'm late."

"Late? You're the owner! You can't be late."

"I have to set an example for the crew, don't I?"

She snuck up behind him and wrapped her arms around his waist. Her grip was just loose enough for him to spin around so they're face to face. Looking into her eyes, he said, "I know what you're up to. Please, don't ask it."

"Ask what?" she said shyly.

"I know you very well. You aren't fooling me, Barb".

"If you know me so well, then you know I'm just worried about you."

"Noted. Now I have to get."

He gave her a quick kiss. Breaking from her grip, John picked up his case and dashed out the door.

Barbara slowly walked to the front window and watched until he had driven out of sight. Why won't he talk to Mathew? What is he afraid will happen? These thoughts were swirling in her head as she poured a cup of coffee. Caffeine in hand, she made her way to the sunroom that overlooked their patio and pool. This was her favorite place to sit and think.

Sipping on the coffee, she replayed their conversation in her head: the one they had the evening after she had talked to Mathew.

~ ~ ~

"That was absolutely delicious! I've never had chicken like that before. Loved the sauce."

"Thank you!"

"So, what did you do today, besides cook this wonderful meal?"

"Well, I went to see an old friend. Actually more like an old acquaintance. I really only talked to him three or four times, and that was right before we got married."

"Wow, been awhile. You say you went to see him? Who is he? Do I know him?"

"No, you've never met him. I called him and then went to where he works."

"Why? Where's he work?"

She hesitated long enough for John to become suspicious. Her nervousness must have shown on her face because John continued.

"What have you done, Barb? Spit it out."

"He's a priest that I know. Now before you get upset...", John cut her off.

"A priest? A Catholic priest? I can't believe you would do something like this without talking to me first. Did it ever dawn on you that I don't want anyone knowing this is happening to me? How could you?" He stood up quickly and left the table.

She had never seen him like that before. He'd always been so calm about everything. It was one of his traits that really drew her to him when they first started dating. Could this reaction have been from lack of sleep?

Following him into the living room, she sat down beside him on the couch. He never looked at her. His eyes were riveted to the fireplace.

It had never crossed her mind that he would react like that! Be a little upset perhaps, but not like *that*.

"I'm sorry. I just wanted to help."

"You don't help by parading my problem in front of a complete stranger! He must think you married a nut case."

"What? Come on. He's a friend who happens to be a priest. He was the perfect person for me to talk to. Can't you see that?"

"No!" He hesitated. "Uh, well, maybe. It just gets me that you didn't mention this to me first."

"So you could talk me out of it? Is that what you're saying here?"

"No, I just think you should have said something to me first. It's done now. Can't be undone."

"Besides, I think you're going to like what happened."

"Really?" His expression changed from angry to suspicious. "What happened?"

"Well, first of all, he never acted like any of this was crazy. Don't you think I was nervous about how he would view me, too? But he listened and we talked. It was nice. He made me feel so comfortable."

"You didn't convert to Catholicism, did you?"

"Don't be silly." She had said this with a little smile.

At least his sense of humor was back. Another trait that she has always admired about John was his ability to joke about things, even during very depressing situations. He always took things in stride and moved on. She hoped the rest of her story would cheer him up.

"Mathew said he had never heard of the 'Book of Prizom'."

"Well, that's not good!" John replied.

"Wait, will you. Stop interrupting me. Trust me. You want to hear the rest of this."

"Ok, go on." And he sat way back on the couch with his arms

folded across his chest. If he had a pair of glasses to peer over, he would have looked just like the perfect angry old school teacher.

"As I was saying. Mathew hadn't heard of the book either. So, he checked the personal library that's in his office."

John interrupted her again. "His office? You went to his church?"

"Yes, I thought it would be easier on me to do it face to face. Remember, I said I was worried about him thinking I was crazy."

"That's what I've been trying to tell you. Anybody hearing this will think *I'm* crazy! Get it?"

"Oh. Yes, I see your point. But anyway, he didn't. He has a book that lists every old religious document or book found to date. But it wasn't in there. But he has access to some kinda special Vatican search thingy on his computer, so he tried to find the book on that. Then something weird happened."

"What do you mean weird? How weird?"

"Well, I don't really understand this part completely, but he had a strange message come up on his computer. It said something about a possible match in the secured section."

She noticed that John had suddenly become very interested. He had relaxed somewhat. Both hands were now in his lap, and the tense expression had vanished.

"I told you this would interest you."

"It actually said 'secured section' on his PC?"

"Yes, and *he* was very interested in it too."

"So, what happened then?"

"It wanted another password, and when he put his in, it didn't work. He got a message saying he was denied or not authorized, something like that. Anyway, he couldn't get past it. He said he would try to call somebody he knows that could help him with it. He's supposed to call me if he finds anything out."

"So, have you heard from him?"

"No. It's been three days now. You think I should call him? I've been dying to, but afraid at the same time. This whole thing is making me nuts."

"I'm sorry, Barb. I have been so focused on this dream that I didn't even consider how it must be affecting you too."

"Well, you haven't had much sleep. It's no wonder you can't see anything else. John, I've been so worried about you."

"I know you have baby, and I hope you know that I do appreciate you looking out for me. I love you very much."

"Me too." She leaned over and put her head on his shoulder. He had slipped his arm into hers. They both sat there quietly for a few minutes.

"Do you think I should call him now?"

"Well, I would like to know if he's found out anything yet. But, you know, he said he'd call you if he found out anything. Since he hasn't called, I guess he hasn't found out anything. No, let's just wait till he calls you."

~ ~ ~

Sitting in the sunroom, sipping her coffee and remembering their conversation, it was clear that John would not be happy with her if she called Mathew. She wanted to, but John was right. Mathew had said he would call if he found out anything. Since it had been three days now, she had begun to doubt that he would call. If he called and said there is no book, what else could she do to help her husband? There was nothing to do but wait.

The phone ringing snapped her back to the present. Without thinking, she flipped open her cell phone and said, "Hello. This is Barbara".

Mathew's voice shocked her into sitting upright in her chair.

"Hi Mathew! I was just thinking about calling you. Have you found out anything?"

"Good morning, Barbara. I'm sorry it took so long for me to call. Is your husband still having that dream?"

"Yes he is. Every night. So, find anything out?"

"Yes and no. Still haven't found if the book exists or not, but did find out something interesting. Very interesting actually."

"Good or bad?"

"Who knows? But what I do know is that we are not the only ones interested in this book's existence. How exciting is that?"

"Really? You mean somebody else is looking for this same book? Who?"

"No, it's not that anyone else is looking for the book. What is interesting is that somebody has taken an interest in my inquiring about the book."

"On no! I told you not to do it. If you get in trouble over this,

I'll just die."

Mathew was laughing when he said, "I told you in my office, I won't get into trouble over this."

"Are you sure? Then why are they interested in you looking for that book? Who's interested?"

"Yes, I'm sure they're interested. I'm not sure exactly *why* they're interested, though. It could just be following up on me trying to sign into an area I wasn't supposed to access. But..."

He paused. Should he tell her in detail what was happening or not? Barbara's impatience brought him back to the conversation.

"But what? If not that, then what are you not telling me?"

Mathew decided it would be a big mistake to give her any more details than he had to. It would probably make her more paranoid than she already seems to be. But now, he really wanted to talk to her husband. He was very curious to hear more about this dream.

"What I'm trying to say now is the same thing that I said to you three days ago in my office. Remember? I told you that this book may really exist, and if it does, your husband's dream may have some reality to it. I'm not sure how or what, but this is definitely the most interesting issue I've ever had to deal with."

"I'm so sorry I got you mixed up in this, Mathew. I was looking for answers and now I've messed things up for you too. I'm so sorry!"

She was not sure why she felt like crying. A woman she was, but not one who cried at just anything. Yet here she is, actually feeling that she could cry.

"Don't be! I'm glad you involved me, for many reasons."

"Name one." Her voice was starting to choke up on her. What was wrong with her, she wondered.

"Barbara, please listen to me. I can tell by your voice that you are getting emotional over this. You told me yourself that you are very worried about your husband. You also said this has been going on for five months. That is a long time to be worrying about someone you love. This pressure is obviously taking a toll on you. You have to believe me. Nobody is in trouble, nor will they be. We need to focus on helping your husband. As odd as it sounds, your husband may actually be dreaming about a real book. Unfortunately, it looks like it is a book that is being hidden from public view."

"Ok, but why would it be hidden from the public? What's it about, and why is my husband dreaming about it?" She had managed to regain her composure a little.

"Ah, but the real question in my mind is, how does he know about it in the first place? Is anyone in his family Catholic? If so, are any of them clergy, by any chance?"

"I don't think so. At least, none that I know of. Though we don't attend church very often, we were both baptized in Southern Baptist churches. He's an only child, but I have heard him speak of an uncle who is still alive. Both his father and this uncle were mechanics. Didn't I tell you that John owns a big paint and body shop on 10th Street? He's opening a second shop next month on Indiana Avenue. I don't know how he continues to focus on opening this new shop, with all that is happening to him because of this dream."

"So Barbara, when do you think your husband is going to talk to me?"

"Mathew, I really hate to tell you this, but John doesn't want to talk to anyone about this."

"Really? But you - " and she jumped right in talking.

"Again, I'm sorry. I didn't tell him I was coming to talk to you until after we had already met that day."

"So what happened when you told him?"

"Well, to be honest with you, he had more of a reaction than I was prepared for. I've never seen him get that upset in all the time we've been together. It really caught me off guard. The bottom line is that he said he is not going to talk to anyone about it. I don't know what to do now."

"Do me a favor. Please let him know that I called you today. Tell him everything we discussed, and that I would really be interested in talking to him."

"I'll do that, but I don't think he will change his mind. He can be very stubborn at times." This was another trait of John's that she had come to notice over the years. Not a good or bad trait; just an accurate observation of her husband.

"Let me know what he decides. Barbara, please be safe and blessed."

"You too, Mathew. Thanks for calling."

She remembered that it was grocery day so she had better get cleaned up. As she took her empty cup to the kitchen, she wondered how she could convince her husband to speak to Mathew.

"When John says no to talking to Mathew, how am I going to get them together? They have to talk, even if John gets upset again. They just have to talk."

Sitting in his office, Mathew hung up the phone and thought about what to do next. If John wouldn't come to him, he would have to go to John. This would mean going to Barbara's home one evening, unannounced. Most people would find this to be tricky, but he had spent a year doing cold calls on homes from a list provided by the Church. Never knowing what to expect, he would knock or ring a bell. Then he would talk about the Church with whoever opened the door. If Barbara didn't call tomorrow to arrange a meeting, he would just go to her home that night.

He knew he could do this. More to the point, he knew his curiosity would drive him to do it. This situation was more than a little intriguing. A non-Catholic man has a dream about an unknown book that may well have been hidden by the Roman Catholic Church. If this book does exist, and Mathew is almost positive that it does exist, what is in it? Why was it hidden? Who is hiding it?

Then he remembered something that Barbara had told him during their talk. She said that her husband was supposed to tell the Pope to open this book. If the book was real, could the rest of the dream touch reality as well? It felt like the weight of the Church was crushing his soul as he said out loud, "The Pope could have this book."

~ ~ ~

Mathew's next day was routine and uneventful. Each time his phone rang, he hoped it was Barbara calling with good news. But each time, there was a depressing drop in his mood as he realized that the caller was not her. The only bright spot in his day would be his three favorite weekly visitors to his confessional.

The three women were in their late seventies and had been friends since they were four years old. Each of them, having grown up in this very church, now looked to Mathew for their spiritual guidance. He looked forward to their weekly visit, as he was always stunned by the revelations they brought to him. They always arrived together, were very punctual, and it was that time.

Margie was as full of life as most 10 year olds. She was slender, well-kept and led a very athletic lifestyle. She had buried three husbands in her collective 51 years of marriage. She was still attractive and her confessions always concerned sex. Having had her last husband die right in the middle of the act, she was hopelessly paranoid about being damned to hell if she killed another one. These were her words, not his.

Linda was a more robust woman with a real talent for cooking. She was known by every parishioner in this Church as "The Cookin' Mama". Every pot lunch drew a crowd of parishioners eager for a taste of her culinary brilliance. Her confessions always pertained to her husband's snoring, and what she dreamed about doing to him to make him stop. It was very hard for him to restrain his laughter at some of her proposed solutions to this monumental problem.

Mildred was a meek and exceptionally sweet lady. Never having been married or having traveled farther from home than Oklahoma City, she was the most naive individual he had ever met. Her weekly confessional was always about the same thing. She was afraid that her two friends' constant talk about sex and muffling a snoring partner were going to cause her to snap someday. Her dreams of having sex with unknown men always ended with them dying from her stuffing a sock in their mouth. Mathew couldn't help but watch Mildred with concern whenever he saw her chatting with any of the older gentlemen in his congregation.

With the melodrama of their confessionals over, Mathew hurried to his office. It would take him about three hours to finish his next sermon. Once completed, he met Father Milo for their monthly dinner at Marinzio's restaurant. Though Mathew alway looked forward to this meal, he knew he would find it hard not to seem anxious about visiting Barbara's home afterward.

Having finished dinner with Father Milo, Mathew made a very graceful exit before fumbling for his keys and almost running to his car. Once inside, he told himself to settle down. His mind was sorting through a multitude of possible conversation starters, hoping to find that perfect one. He arrived at Barbara's street before he knew it. As he pulled to a stop in front of her house, he wondered what was going on inside at that very moment.

~ ~ ~

"Well Barb, I don't know where you are getting these recipes from, but they are absolutely delicious. You must have worked all day on dinner," John said as he began helping her clear the table.

"You would think so, but they were actually very quick and easy to do."

"Where did you get them, anyway?"

"From a web site called 'The Cookin' Mama'. There are over 100 meals out there."

"And I think we should try every one of them," he said as he placed the last of his dishes in the washer. He spun around, wrapped his arms around Barbara's waist, placed his head on her shoulder and pulled her tight.

"Stop! You're going to make me drop this." She wiggled free so she could put the last of the dishes in the washer.

"You know, honey? I have a feeling that tonight is going to be a *good* night."

With his words still in the air, the doorbell rang and they both looked towards the front door. John said, "I'll get it," as he bolted from the kitchen.

He turned on the porch light and opened the door. There stood a priest, and John knew immediately who he must be. With a forced smile, he slowly opened the door and motioned for him to come in.

"Come on in. I'll bet your name is Father Mathew."

"Please call me Mathew." He extended his hand once he was inside.

"Call me John."Their handshake was thankfully cut short by the sound of glass breaking in the kitchen.

"Barb, are you ok?"

John's call for his wife's status, was quickly answered with a very loud "Yes, just dropped a glass. Who is it?"

Of course, she already knew. Hearing Mathew's voice was

why she dropped the glass. Her peaceful evening with her husband had just been transformed into one of nervous apprehension. Though she knew John would not be rude or cause a scene, he was definitely going to assume she'd planned this.

"I apologize for arriving unannounced like this. I hope I'm not interrupting any plans you may have."

"Not at all, we just finished supper. Please, have a seat." John led Mathew into the den.

"Would you like some tea? Or we can make some coffee if you prefer. Only takes a few minutes."

"I'll have whatever you are having. Thanks."

John nodded and turned to walk to the kitchen. Barbara was just sweeping up the last of the broken glass and putting it into the trash.

"It's your friend the priest." He brushed past her, looking her in the eye. "Did you know he was coming over?"

"No. I haven't talked to him today."

"Well, we both know why he's here," he said as he filled a glass for their guest.

She blocked John's exit from the kitchen. "I know how this looks, but I really didn't plan this. Really!"

After looking at her for a few seconds, he asked, "Really?"

"Really. Maybe he has found out something and he just couldn't wait to tell you?"

John slipped around her and spoke while walking away. "Let's find out."

Mathew accepted the tea and took a long, slow drink. He had already drunk five glasses of tea at the restaurant with Father Milo, but he used this to give John and Barbara time to sit on the couch across from his chair.

"You have a beautiful home. This is a very nice area."

"It's quiet. We like it." Barbara commented.

"Well, I know you're both wondering why I'm here, so if you'll allow me, I'll get right to it."

John nodded and motioned with his hand for Mathew to continue.

"First of all, John. I took it upon myself to come see you. Barbara didn't know I was coming and again, I apologize for crashing your evening." He paused to sip his tea while quickly trying to get a feel for John's mood.

"I know this is a very personal issue for you and I understand your not wanting to talk to someone you don't know. I also understand that my being a representative of a different faith from you, makes it even harder for you to feel comfortable talking with me. So I was hoping that we could just talk as two individuals that have a common acquaintance." He motioned towards Barbara. Moment of truth as Mathew paused to allow John to react.

John took a deep breath. He pushed his hands along the sides of his head and locked his fingers together once they were behind his neck. Closing his eyes, he slowly exhaled. He began to speak before opening his eyes.

"I know that both of you have the best intentions here. My wife, because she *is* my wife. You, because of the nature of who you are - what you are. And, yes, you're right about it being awkward for me to talk to you since I'm not Catholic. But that said, I'm afraid I still don't want to talk about this."

John shrugged his shoulders, but left his hands folded behind his neck. The short pause was broken by Mathew.

"I understand. I do. If I may, I would like to touch on some things that I'm sure Barbara has already told you about." He sipped his tea slowly. With no reaction from John, Mathew continued.

"When Barbara told me about this book from your dream, I did a search on my PC for its name. It appears that there may very well be such a book. I have contacted a friend who actually works in Rome for the Vatican. Due to his curiosity, he too has now enlisted a friend to help in the search. I was hoping to ask you some simple questions, but I'll understand if you would rather I not ask them."

John noticed that Barbara was nodding her head towards Mathew as a gesture to say, 'Go on. Tell him it's OK'.

Looking at her for a second, he slowly turned to Mathew. "Ok. Sure."

"Great. Please feel free to stop me when you've had enough." He chuckled in an attempt to lighten the mood.

"Barbara said you've been having this same dream for the past five months and that it is always the same. I was wondering if you had any idea what started it?"

"That's a good question," John said, and he takes another sip of tea. "I've asked myself this same question. But..." and he shrugged his shoulders.

"Ok, let me ask you this. Is the dream vivid or hazy like most dreams?"

This time, John didn't hesitate. "Oh. It's vivid all right! I can see it clearly in my mind all day. As if it were imprinted on my brain. I can't seem to get away from it. It's always there."

John stopped talking and just sat silent for almost a minute, looking down at the floor. Then he ever so slowly looked at Mathew. "I'm afraid that I really don't want to talk about this anymore. I'm sorry, but this is just not comfortable for me."

Mathew immediately smiled. "John, I appreciate your talking to me at all. I have to admit this whole thing has been very intriguing for me. Unfortunately, I now see that my curiosity is causing you distress and I am very sorry for doing this to you. Please forgive me."

"It's all right. I know that, from the outside looking in, this would be especially interesting for you." John smiled for the first time since Mathew's arrival. "I am very impressed that you would go to the lengths that you have in order to help a friend." John glanced at his wife. "I know nothing of the Catholic religion, but it seems to me that the people in your Church are very lucky to have you."

"Thank you." Mathew responded. "Well, I thank you for the tea, and it's time for me to let you two get on with your evening."

Mathew readied himself to leave. As he starts to get out of his chair, Barbara asked, "How did you find our house?"

Mathew sat back down. "Oh, that was easy. Ryan, you know, your next door neighbor."

"You know Ryan McGowin?" John asked.

"Yes, I met him when I first came to St. Mathew's."

"Ryan goes to your church?" Barbara's face displayed a comical shocked look.

"I'm sorry. It never dawned on me that you didn't know that. When he mentioned that he had given you tickets to the Museum, I assumed you knew that I knew him."

Barbara's eyes widened. "That's right. Ryan is the one that

invited me to the party where I first meet you. But he wasn't the one that introduced us. Some lady did."

"Yes, that was Linda. I doubt you would have known this, but she was the one that cooked all the food for that party. You may not remember how delicious it was, but it was. Great cook, that one. She actually has a website now called 'The Cookin Mama'. You should check it out sometime."

Now John's eyes opened wide. "What?" He turned to his wife. "Isn't that the name you just told me about after dinner tonight?"

They all are smiling now, realizing that they're already much more closely connected than they had previously known. Their fates had been intertwined for a long time, and only now was it coming to light. John was smiling from ear to ear when he asked Mathew, "This is just too weird. How can we all be so, so, *connected* like this?"

Mathew seized the opportunity.

"John. These things happen for a reason. I feel strongly when I say this to you. What is happening to you, this dream, it's all part of a plan. No matter what your faith, things like this should be proof that God has a plan. We are free to travel the path as we see fit, but the path is sometimes pre-ordained. I don't want to push you, really I don't. I would love to hear more about your dream. But only if you are truly comfortable with it."

John paused before speaking. "You know, I really would like to talk about it now, and it seems that you are supposed to be the one. Or does that sound nuts? Yeah, that sounds nuts." He began shaking his head.

"John, please, it's not nuts. Even I feel that there is more going on here than any of us know."

"Mathew," Barbara started, "you knew that Ryan gave us tickets to the museum. Right?"

"Yes, he even told me that John got sick that first night you both went. I believe he said you both left too quickly to have gone past more than the first few displays." Mathew looked towards John before adding, "I even remember him saying how glad he was that you had come back alone to view something again. Like me, you must love being that close to ancient artifacts."

"Why would you say that?" John said with a questioning tone in his voice. He almost sounded defensive about it.

Mathew cautiously answered, "Well, Ryan said you came back several more times and always went directly to the same display. Said you spent a lot of time just looking at something. I do the same thing. Most the time, I couldn't tell you why I'm drawn to one piece of an exhibit while I ignore all the others. You must be the same way."

"I didn't know you went back to the museum." Barbara was now looking directly at John, a questioning look on her face. "Why didn't you tell me you went back? And more than once?"

"I guess it never occurred to me that you would want to go as well. It really wasn't a big deal."

"Of course I would have gone with you. We always go together to these things." She paused for a second. "You didn't want me there, did you? Why would you not want me there?"

John sat motionless for a few seconds. His eyes were focused on the ceiling as he searched for the right thing to say. Being a priest these past years had helped Mathew to hone the skill of paying attention to a person's expressions and gestures. He knew that John did not want to answer his wife's inquiry. So now was the right time to score points with John, get him on his side. He decided to rescue John by changing the subject.

"In all fairness to John, it was five months ago. He probably can't remember why."

With Mathew's words still hanging in the air, Barbara's face came alive as she said, "Wait a minute. That was just a little over five months ago." She was about to continue when Mathew said, "This sounds like another connection."

At that very moment John looked first at his wife, and then at the priest. "Wow. I never thought about that."

With all three of their minds in hyper-drive, they each sat there quietly for almost two full minutes before Mathew broke the silence.

"Excuse me, but are we all thinking the same thing here? I take it that your dream started around this time."

John did his usual thing with his hands, and they ended up behind his neck with his eyes on the ceiling. A short exaggerated breath heralded a revelation.

"The exhibition's last day was that Thursday. My first dream, *that night*."

CHAPTER 4

Talk With a Dreamer – Part Two

Without warning, John suddenly dropped both hands from behind his neck and loudly slapped them on his thighs before proclaiming, "I need coffee. Anyone else?"

The unexpected noise startled Barbara so much that she nearly spilled her tea on their new $1,100 couch. "John, what in the world?" she protested, but he was already halfway to the kitchen.

"Sorry, love," he said.

Mathew snickered. "Well, my heart's pounding! I'm not sure I need any coffee after that!"

They both began laughing as they moved the conversation to the kitchen, where John already has both coffee and water ready to brew. He plugged in the pot and turned to ask, "How many cups?"

Mathew had taken a position on the opposite side of the kitchen and was leaning on the counter next to the refrigerator. "You know, coffee *does* sound good. I'll take a cup."

"Make it three," Barbara said as she pushed down the lid on the trash can. In her haste to join the earlier conversation after clearing up the broken glass, she had left it open.

John actually seemed happy as he retrieved cups and saucers, placing them on the breakfast table. He and Barb often sat here talking while sharing a cup of coffee after dinner. The pastel flowers on the wallpaper pleasantly clashed with the slightly tinted table top. It was a picturesque setting nestled into the bay window overlooking the hot tub and pool.

Mathew commented, "I know that I said this earlier, but you both have a very lovely home. This is all so peaceful looking."

"Yes it is," said John before adding, "but I really haven't been able to enjoy it like I used to."

"Speaking of that, John, how much sleep do you lose a night, any idea?"

"Well, on average, about an hour and a half."

As he lifted the pot from the machine, the other two eagerly migrated to the table. Mathew stood until Barbara sat down, and then accepted John's gesture for him to do the same. With the efficiency of an experienced waiter, he poured all three cups of coffee and returned to the machine. One hand placed the pot back on the hot plate, while the other picked up a small basket with the usual mix of sweeteners, creamers and coffee stirrers. He had a youthful spring in his step, one his wife had not seen for months.

As he approached the table, Barbara took the basket and told Mathew, "We also have milk or half and half if you like."

"Black will be fine."

John slipped behind Barbara and sat down, his back to the wall. "I know tea has caffeine too, but I just have to have this stuff."

Everyone was feeling much more at ease.

Mathew said, "Do you usually drink much coffee close to bedtime? It could be helping to keep you up, don't you think?"

Barbara answered him before John could put his cup down. "We discussed this several times. But John is one of those people who can drink an entire pot of coffee, lie right down and sleep for eight hours straight. I've seen him do it time and again."

"I'm afraid you're going over the same things we have, Mathew. Barb's right, the caffeine is not a factor here." Another sip, then John looked straight at Mathew and said with a grin, "For some reason, I'm feeling kind of talkative. Ask whatever is on your mind."

Mathew, leaning forward, didn't hesitate. "Of course I want to get back to the museum exhibits, but I just have to know about this dream. Please describe it to me."

John took yet another sip, placed his cup on the saucer and stared at it for a second before starting in.

"It's one of those dreams that start right in the middle of you doing something. Know what I mean? All of a sudden, I'm walking. I don't know where or why. Just me, alone, walking through a hall of some kind. The hallway is dark. Not totally dark, more like shadowy. There are strong beams of light shining through a doorway on my left and striking the wall on the opposite side.

"I walk to the edge of the light and lean my head in just enough to see into the room beyond. Now you know how dreams are scrambled some? I'm in a hallway, like a building, but I'm looking into what appears to be a man-made rock room. Kind of like a handmade cave, chipped out of solid rock.

"The door has a regular frame on the hallway side. But I always notice that the rock side of the door appears to be a big circle. I can see the shape because I'm looking in at an angle."

Barbara looked at John. "You've never told it like this to me." She turned to Mathew and repeated herself. "Not like this, not to me."

John continued. "Like I said, for some reason, I feel kinda chatty tonight. Anyway, the room is small, about 10 by 10 feet. There is something like a bench, a rock bed I guess, built into the back wall's right corner. In the middle of the room is a pedestal, and it's also made from rock. And it's obviously still attached to the floor. I take this to mean that it was made at the time the chipping out of the room was done. I always notice these things before I focus on the book."

At this point, Mathew had pushed his belly tightly against the table's edge. It was a subconscious attempt to actually get into John's dream. He was so enthralled by what he was hearing that he couldn't take his eyes off John. A loud clank from cup meeting saucer was the result of him not looking.

"Sorry, my bad."

The other two giggled like three year olds.

In the past few months, neither of them had been this free from the tension. Barbara was happy to see the man she loved coming alive again. This was more like the man of so many months ago. She realized that her decision to visit Mathew had been the right thing to do. John had held the details of his dream inside for so long. Maybe he'll sleep tonight, she hoped.

"I've always wondered about this next part. The book is floating just above the top of the pedestal. And it's kind of transparent, like a ghost. I can see through it. It's just a book, about 10 inches square and maybe eight inches thick. It's closed. The edges of the pages aren't clean-cut and flat like our books are today; they're jagged and wavy. They weren't flat like our paper."

Mathew blurted out, "I know why. It's the way they made parchment paper back in ancient times. It's actually made from animal hides, I think. I've actually seen real parchment paper that preceded Jesus' life by hundreds of years. I have a friend who works exclusively on translating these very old documents." He turned to Barbara.

"Barbara, he's the one I told you I would call. He is also the one that has now involved one of his friends in the search for this book."

Having realized how excited he must sound, Mathew tried to make light of it. "Maybe I don't need any more coffee".

Again, the other two giggled like children until Mathew finally joined them.

After the laughter died down, Mathew wiped the tears from his eyes. "I'm sorry, John. Please continue."

John was really enjoying himself now.

"Well now, before I was *soooo* rudely interrupted, I was saying." His expression changed slightly as his thoughts returned to the dream.

"The book is, well, I don't know how to explain this. It's in the room, but not really. It is almost like when a picture is superimposed over an existing picture. You know what I'm saying?"

Barbara interjected, "It's like it was put in by a computer?"

John nodded. "Yeah, something like that. Anyway, that's when I hear the voice."

Mathew shook his head as if he couldn't believe what he's just heard. "You hear voices too? Is it in English? What did it say? Do you get a feel for who it is?"

Once more, John snickered. "You want to make a list there, buddy? So I don't miss one?"

Embarrassed again, Mathew smiled and shook his head no.

"Let me answer them in order. Yes, Yes, I'll tell you in a minute and **no**!" John sat back, took a big gulp of coffee and smiled big. "Did I get 'em all?"

Barbara reminded Mathew, "I told you he heard a voice telling him to open the book. Remember?"

John quickly corrected her. "It didn't tell *me* to open the book."

Mathew recalled what she had told him, and asked John to continue.

"I only hear the voice at the very end of the dream. Right before I wake up. It must be English, because I understand it. It says, 'Let him be told, open the Book of Prizom'. By the way, I don't have a clue whose voice it could be. Just that it's loud and it's clear."

John took one more swig of coffee. "And that's it. I wake up."

Mathew's eagerness to investigate was apparent. "Why do you get up after you wake?"

"Well, that would be too hard to explain. You know, to put into words. All I can say is that it always leaves me with some raging emotions, and it's just easier to go sit alone to work through them. I'm not going to talk anymore about that."

Mathew began to stand up. "I'm sorry. I had five glasses of tea before I rushed over here, and now..." but he was interrupted by John.

"I completely understand. Down the hall, first door on your right."

As she watched Mathew disappear around the corner, Barbara was first to speak.

"I'm so proud of you, John. You amazed me with how you described your dream in such detail. I can see now why you're always so wide awake after it happens."

"Yeah, I'm sorry that I never talked more in depth with you about it. I still can't believe I'm doing it now. You know, he's very easy to talk to. I think I really like him."

John's comment about Mathew made her smile, as she recalled thinking that same thing herself. Mathew had *always* been very easy to talk to. Barbara noticed a change in John's expression, and knew that Mathew must have reappeared from the hallway.

"Well I'm back. Thank you. I feel much better now." Mathew sat down.

He wasn't finished. "So ... do you feel like chatting about the museum for a minute?"

John nodded slowly. "Sure. Why not?"

"I was just wondering. What exhibit did you go back to see each time you went back to the museum?"

Clearing his throat, he began. "It was a royal Roman scepter of some kind. There were a lot of jewels encrusted on the top knot. The whole thing was about three feet long and displayed in a glass case. It looked like a long stick with a softball stuck on the top end."

Barbara's eyebrows rose. "I remember seeing that... hey, wait a minute. That is where you got sick. It was only like the third exhibit inside the door."

Mathew was, if possible, even more intrigued.

"John. I know this may sound odd, but do you think that scepter had anything to do with you getting sick?"

John glanced slowly from Mathew to Barbara. He was struggling to formulate an answer. They both sat watching him as he rested his chin on the folded fingers of his left hand. His eyes appeared to be focused off into the dark void of their hallway, as he slowly began to speak.

"All I remember before I got sick was that I was laughing with Barb right before I stepped in front of the case. Then..." He paused again, and covered his eyes with his fingers. He appeared to be shielding his eyes from a bright light. Nobody moved until he began to speak again.

"It just hit me. This awful pain came out of nowhere. At first I just felt it in my stomach, but it quickly spread across my back. My head started to pound something fierce. I thought I was going to hit the floor."

"That's right. I grabbed your arm. Remember?"

"Not really. I just felt that I needed to get out of there, but I couldn't take my eyes off what was in that case. Finally, I just knew I had to leave. You know, get out of there."

Barbara took over for him. "You hardly said ten words all the way home. I thought you might be having a heart attack. But you said there was no way you were going to the hospital. I ran three red lights getting home. Put you right to bed and you were out in two seconds.

"I was a nervous wreck that whole night. You tossed and turned all night long. You kept mumbling words I didn't understand. Sounded like Italian or Spanish maybe. Whatever it was, it wasn't English. Since it was Friday night, I thought you would sleep in late the next morning. I was shocked to wake up and find you gone before 8:00 a.m."

Mathew pushed his empty cup to the center of the table. Barbara began to reach for it so she could refill it, but Mathew motioned that he'd had enough.

"So John, why did you go back?" Mathew's continuing curiosity led John to continue.

"Well, I don't really know. I called Ryan to see when they opened on Saturday and made sure that I was there when they did. I walked slowly up to the case this time." John smirked then continued. "Like I was sneaking up on it. Anyway, nothing happened. I just stood there."

"So you thought that the scepter was somehow responsible for the way you had felt. Didn't you?"

Looking down at the floor, John nodded. "Yes."

"You knew," Mathew repeated.

"Yes. As crazy as it all seems, I knew. So anyway, there I am. Standing and staring at this thing. Everyone else just saw a white staff with all these jewels on it, but I was getting these images."

John stopped without completing the thought. His shoulders were visibly tense and he just stared down at the table. His posture resembled that of a small child who had realized he'd just said something he shouldn't have.

"John. Were you seeing visions? I mean like, did it feel like a dream with your eyes open?"

His response was sharp. "I may not be Catholic, but I know what visions are."

Almost as soon as he said it, John regretted his outburst at the priest. Barbara was staring wide-eyed at him.

Biting his lower lip and slowly waving his open hands towards Mathew, he said, "I'm sorry, I didn't mean it that way. It's just that ... well ... I *did* see things. Several scenes would flash in my mind, then just stop. Then there would be another series of scenes, and they'd stop. It almost made me dizzy, it was happening so fast. I must have stood there for over an hour. I just stood right there in front of that case, not understanding the things that I was seeing in my mind."

With his most sincere and softest voice, Mathew slowly asked, "Do you think you know who it was you were seeing in these visions?"

There was a simple answer given. "Yes."

"But you aren't going to say, are you?"

Another one word response. "No."

"Ok. Let me ask you this. Do you think what you were seeing were scenes from the present, or the past?"

"It was all from the past. They were definitely from the past."

"Tell me. Each time that you went back to the museum, did you have the same visions?"

Finally, John's demeanor lightened and he smiled. But once again, he only uttered one word.

"Yes."

"Well, why did you go back so many times if you always saw the same thing?"

"To understand."

"What do you mean?"

"They were very clear. Like watching a movie or the TV. I even heard the sounds."

"You heard them speaking? Did you understand what they were saying?"

"Not all of it. Just the parts that I think I was supposed to. Look, I can't and won't tell anyone but him."

"Him? Him who?"

With John just sitting silent, Mathew glanced quickly at Barbara as if silently asking her to come to his aid. She shrugged her shoulders and raised her eyebrows as if to say 'Don't look at me'.

"Ok, uh, I got it. Is it the same person who is to open the book?"

"Yes."

John leaned forward onto the table, as if he were trying to meet Mathew in the middle. Then, with a look in his eyes that sent shivers up Mathew's back, he declared, "Now do you think

I'm crazy?"

Mathew now had so many thoughts to comprehend and scenes to analyze that he realized he too was dizzy. Perhaps this is exactly what John had felt like. He had to get a grip here. So many questions were fighting to be asked first.

He finally blurted out, "I gotta take a break." Then, as he stood to stretch his legs, he said, "John, I don't think you're crazy at all. I think you have been chosen." He motioned towards their back door and asked, "May I step outside and collect my thoughts for a moment?"

Barbara was quick to respond. "Please do, it's always so peaceful out there. At least we think so."

"Thank you." He walked outside to the patio.

~ ~ ~

Having taken advantage of Mathew's stepping outside, John was returning from his trip down the hall. As John rounded the corner, he saw that his wife was still sitting at the table. Approaching his chair, he asked, "Is he still out there?"

She was looking out the window, and John's eyes followed hers. There in the dark, Mathew was pacing back and forth on the patio, hands in his pockets and head down. He was taking short steps while dragging his heels.

"I wonder what he's thinking?" John asked.

"He said he needed some fresh air and to clear his head. You and I have been dealing with this for months, him just an hour."

John put his hand on Barbara's shoulder and bent to kiss her softly on the lips. Looking into her eyes before standing up, he said, "I love you. You did good here. This was just what I needed."

He lovingly put his hand on her cheek. She cupped her hand over his, and leaned her head into his hand.

This was the picture Mathew saw when he looked up into the house. The bay window beautifully framed a scene of two people who were most definitely in love. As he stood there in the dark, observing his friends, the magnitude of this entire experience just deepened his own belief in God. What was happening here was in no way simply a series of coincidences. His faith had been shaken at points in his life. He had doubted his calling to lead others to Christ. But he felt closer to his Creator now than at any other point in his life.

He bowed his head. "Please Lord, grant me the strength to fulfill whatever role you have planned for me in this. I have doubted many things of late, and I am truly sorry. Guide us all, especially my new friend John, that we can walk the paths you have chosen for us and fulfill all that you desire of us. Amen."

As he opened his eyes, Mathew saw them both still at the table. He waved and hustled back into the kitchen.

"So, ready with some more questions?"

Now it was Mathew's turn for the one-liners. "Yes."

Mathew pulled his chair closer to the table and began. "Just to be clear, are you saying that you think you have a message for the Pope?"

"Not really a message. Actually, I think that mentioning the book's name is all that is necessary to get him involved. As crazy as that sounds, I think it is that simple."

"But, what about all of your visions? Are you to pass them on to him?"

"No. They aren't really for him."

"Do you know who they are for?"

"Me."

Mathew was bewildered by this last response. Why are these visions for John? What are these visions telling him? Since John seemed very willing now to tell his story, what is stopping him from telling them what the visions were?

At this point, Mathew knew that John's part in this affair would not end with the Pope becoming involved. What cosmic role has John been chosen to perform? Mathew's soul quivered as he realized that he could be sitting with a man who could have a profound effect on the world.

"I wonder, was there a book of any kind in the museum exhibits?"

"No. That same thought had crossed my mind too, but the exhibits had already moved on to another town. I still had the exhibit's pamphlet from the museum, but it made no mention of a book either. So, I had to call Ryan and ask him. He checked for me. Nothing."

"Did you mention the book's name to Ryan?"

"No, I didn't. But I did get him to find me some reading material on that staff. I have spent a lot of time on the internet reading about that thing. Interested?"

Mathew nodded yes.

John continued, "Well, there are many differing opinions from the living experts. But the fact is that the Roman scepter I saw has been dated based upon some of the writings on the shaft. Want to venture a guess as to the timeframe?"

Mathew was nodding now. "I'm going to go out on a limb here. Would it be anywhere close to when Jesus is thought to have lived?"

"Give this man a prize. The real kicker here is that most religious historians believe that it was made right after the death of Christ. There are some writings on the shaft that have been partially destroyed over time, so it's not clear cut as to what it says."

John stood up and retrieved a folder from his briefcase. Opening it and sifting through the pages, he pulled one out and began to read.

"Though most of the inscriptions on this royal Roman scepter have been destroyed over time, a prominent Vatican researcher has translated what is legible. It is his opinion that this relic was created shortly after the crucifixion of Jesus Christ."

Mathew extended his hand across the table. "Please, can I see that?" His eyes rapidly scanned the page for the name of this researcher, and there it was. The name of his friend, Father Latanye, practically leapt from the page. "You guys aren't going to believe this."

Barbara quipped, "Let me guess. Another big connection."

"Yes! Very big. This researcher is the friend I called about your book."

Not even the sound of their breathing could be heard for several minutes, as they sat there staring at one another. Then they all began reading the various pages that John had accumulated in his folder. The large picture of the scepter was passed around the table several times. Each of them eyed this photo for some clue that they felt must be in front of them. Barbara was the first to rekindle the conversation.

"John, this is a lot of research here. It must have taken you days to gather all of this. I don't remember seeing you on our laptop that much. When did you do this?"

"At the office, of course. I couldn't get it off of my mind. So, I just sat in my office and poked around on the PC. I've been doing it for weeks now and several hours a day. Sometimes, I'd do it all day and never do any work at all."

"You know, I always wondered how you were able to concentrate on the shop with so little sleep. I just thought that you were working really hard on opening your new shop. Sort of a way to keep your mind off the dream stuff."

"I know you did. You mentioned it to me several times, and I just let you think that."

"Why?"

"I was too embarrassed. I didn't want anyone to know how totally consumed I had become by this whole thing."

Mathew spoke up. "So you even thought yourself that you were becoming consumed with this?"

"Yes. Very much so. I realized how consumed, when I started wanting to take a trip to see that exhibit again. By the way, it's in Chicago right now. Then it leaves this Sunday to go to New York for two weeks. After that, it's headed home to Rome." John had a twinkle in his eyes as he finished with, "Sound consumed now?"

Barbara commented, "Home to Rome? What a rhyme."

John had a confident grin on his face. "It's just one more thing that is falling into place here."

Mathew rubbed the back of his head and looked down at his watch. "Oh my, it's very late. I'm sorry to have kept you both up so long. I had better be going. But before I do, I am just wondering." Looking directly at John, Mathew said, "I get the feeling that you seem more relaxed than you were earlier. Is it because you now know me better, or is it just that you have talked about it more?"

With the friendliest smile he possessed, John said, "Of course it helps to know you now, but I really think the talking has helped. I don't feel as tense as I have all these past weeks. In fact, I actually feel quite relieved."

Barbara immediately joined in. "It would be great if you could sleep now that this evening has happened. Maybe you will get some much deserved rest."

"John, I agree completely with Barbara." Mathew held out

his hand to John, who grasped it firmly. "It has been a pleasure to be a guest in your home. I will pray extra hard tonight for you to get some peaceful sleep as well."

John and Barbara walked Mathew to the front door. As Mathew walked to his car, he turned to wave and say, "Thanks again for the coffee, it was delicious!" He disappeared into the darkness.

They watched from the open door as his inside light came on briefly, then dimmed out. The sound of the engine drifted off into the night, and they closed the front door.

Still holding hands inside the sanctity of their own home, she pulled herself against his chest and laid her head against him as he held her. He let his hands fall to her side and then slipped them around her back.

"I'll clean up the kitchen. You go on and get ready for bed. I think tonight you'll sleep all the way through. At least I really hope so."

Turning towards the hall, they held hands until the last second. Barbara was so happy that she found herself humming as she moved all the dishes from the table to the dishwasher. The events of this evening had left her feeling as if she were floating on clouds. Soap in the washer, door closed and the sound of the water beginning its cycle was all that she heard as she turned out the light.

~ ~ ~

Mathew's mind was still in high gear as he drove away from their house. His problem was that he wasn't remotely sleepy. Was it the caffeine from eight glasses of tea and two cups of coffee he'd had during the course of the evening? He knew it wasn't. He wanted to do some research of his own on that scepter.

Although he'd have loved to do it on his personal laptop in the comfort of his own bed, he knew he would have to go to his office to access the Vatican search engine. The security system used the BIOS chip's ID from the computer to bounce against an access table. No match, no access.

He was too excited not to go. He drove back to the church building.

What if someone else was there? What could he say? It's

simple. He's working on his sermon and just wanted to get out of the house. No, that would be a lie. He looked into the rear view mirror and saw his own smiling face. Do other people fret over such dilemmas? He doubted it.

Pulling into the parking lot, he was relieved to see that there were no lights on in the church. Dilemma solved. He can't wait to get on that PC. If somebody had been watching his fast pace, they would have thought he was afraid of the dark.

Back door locked, he switched on the hall light. His mind was still mulling over what John had said, as he entered his office. He was on his PC in a flash and began looking up the scepter.

"I think I'll try the Internet first," he said aloud to himself. He remembered the title at the bottom of the big picture from John's folder. After typing in the words 'Royal Roman Scepter of Arenia', he pressed Enter. There are hits, but none of them had the information he was looking for. Again, he spoke out loud, "Let's try just Arenia," and hit Enter again. Still no direct hit.

Wait a minute! How did John find all the stuff he had in his folder? What could he have used to look for it? Well, he had the pamphlet from the museum! Of course! He looked up the museum, but there was nothing listed for this. Well, of course not - the exhibit tour had concluded. They had obviously taken it off their website since it moved on. Where did John say it was now? Chicago! That was it.

With the Chicago museum's web page up, he looked for the exhibit's name. There it is! A click of the mouse and one more click, there was the picture that John had. There was only one page of information about the scepter. He had also read this page earlier, as it had been in John's folder.

Sitting and scratching his head, he realized now why John had spent so much time trying to find information on this scepter. The fact that John had found all that information meant that he was just very determined, or a very good research analyst. Maybe even both.

Mathew decided he wasn't going to waste any more time on the open Internet. This is why he had come into the office anyway.

Switching to the Vatican search engine, he again typed in 'Royal Roman Scepter of Arenia', but paused before hitting the

Enter key. "If this thing gives me another reference to the 'Secured Section', I'm in trouble." Hearing his own words out loud, he laughed and hit Enter. He didn't see the infamous message, but instead he saw seven references.

The first one was about an obscure Roman city that had been destroyed by a mysterious fire. He wondered to himself, 'How can an entire city be destroyed by a fire, when there was no mention of an act of nature or a battle?' Was that why it was considered mysterious?

The next five hits took him to pictures of the scepter from different angles. He found himself looking very closely at each. One was very similar to the photo John had in his folder. The second showed the other side of the staff, including the markings that his friend Rick must have been asked to interpret. He saw where some of the writing had been worn down, and in some cases, practically erased from the surface. Then there were two pictures of the opposite sides of the jewel-encrusted ball atop the staff. The fifth and last picture was taken from above, looking straight down onto the top of the ball.

Again he talked to himself aloud. "I'll bet John would love to see these." While his printer was busy rendering them for his friend, he wished he could blow up the pictures a little bigger on his screen.

Reaching inside the lap drawer on his desk, he took out a very impressive magnifying glass. It had been given to him as a joke by one of the secretaries. She had told him that somebody of his age would need it. That reminded him, he still has to get even with her for that! But then again, here he was using it. Maybe she was right. So what? She was expecting him to retaliate, and it was all in good fun.

He quickly picked up each picture as it came off the printer. He rapidly scoured each one with his newly-found tool in an attempt to keep up with the printer. Why was he in such a hurry? He decided to give each one a closer inspection. After spending a few minutes with the glass on each picture from the printer, he decided to move on to the last entry.

This appeared to be a report of some kind. It discussed in great detail about what was readable on the staff, and made inferences to the partially obscured writing. This report must have been written by Rick.

After 20 minutes of reading and re-reading the report, he realized he was very tired. Looking at the clock, he was shocked at how early in the morning it was.

He was just about to sign off when he stopped. Sitting there and staring at his PC, he was tempted to inquire about the book name again. He knew that Vatican Security were monitoring his PC, so why not rattle their cage again? Or, is he pushing this when he shouldn't? He may be a priest, but he is also human. Typing the book's name, as he had done with Barbara during the day of her visit, he doesn't hesitate to press Enter.

To his complete surprise, it doesn't come back with anything. Did he type it in wrong? He tries it three more times, still nothing. He said to himself, "They've taken it out of the system!"

He logged off and shut down his equipment. As he rose from his desk, he again looked at the clock and hoped that John was getting a much-needed night's sleep. Standing in his doorway, Mathew thought, 'Well, at least they've stopped looking at me.'

CHAPTER 5

The Vatican Still Sees

So what do you think we should do?" Tim asked Rebeca. "What are you, 12?" she said, with the palms of both hands up and a little shake of her head. "You have to tell him. You did all this work and he'll want to know. By the way, it's not *we*. It's *you*. I'm not going with you this time."

She rolled her chair backwards, smiling as she exited his cube and entered hers. The back of her chair collided with the edge of her desk, and brought her trip to a sudden end. Sitting there for just a few seconds, her eyes still locked on his, she simply said "NO!"

With a quick push of her foot, she spun quickly around, and the sound of typing began the moment her hands touched the keyboard.

"I'm not 12." He stuck his tongue out at her back.

"If you just did what I think you did," she added, "then you might only be ten."

His tongue snapped back into his mouth and he wondered how she knew. His mom always knew, too! He was glad he ate her pastry.

Grabbing the folder with his research, Tim reluctantly rose from his chair and started the dreadful walk towards Spreck's office. Over her cube wall, he heard her say quietly, "You better not be glad you ate my pastry either. And don't tap on his doorframe.

It drives him crazy."

He wondered how she always knew what he was thinking. Was that her giggling? *She's spooky*, he thought to himself.

He raised his hand and extended one finger to tap, but was stopped by a gruff voice. "Don't. Just get in here."

Tim stopped short of the front of Spreck's desk and just stood there. Max finished what he was writing before looking up.

"You have something for me, young man?"

"Yes. You asked me to keep an eye on that priest in Dallas."

"Ah, him. What has our mysterious Father been up to?"

"I set a permanent trace on his logon ID. I started to just do it on his PC's ID, but then I thought he might use somebody else's PC."

"Smart! I like your thinking. So what'd he do now?"

Tim stepped to the side of the desk, cautiously looking for that trash can, and placed his folder in front of Max. Opening the folder, Tim flipped to the third sheet before pointing to the middle of the page. Max's eyes zoomed in on the line showing Mathew's attempts to scan for the Book of Prizom.

"So? He's still trying to find that book. So what? We know he's looking for it. Hell, we're looking for it! As far we know, the Pope's looking for it. So what?"

Max finally looked up and saw Tim staring wide-eyed at him. Then it dawned on him what he'd just said. That's two curse words in the same sentence as the word 'Pope'. Well, at least Rebeca didn't hear it.

"Bet you didn't think I heard that, right?"

Rebeca stood in front of the desk. Both men's heads snapped to face her.

"You know, I don't think you were serious at all about cleaning up that language."

After a blank stare at Rebeca, Max turned to Tim and flipped his right hand in small circles. "Ignore her and tell me what I'm missing here."

"Well, sir, look what happened when he inquired about the book name this time."

Max looked at the paper for a few seconds. "That's odd. It didn't give him that message about the secured section. How'd you get that to stop?"

"Uh, I didn't. It wasn't one of our messages, remember?"

"Oh, yeah," and he sat up a little straighter in his chair. "That *is* odd, isn't it?"

Rebeca joined the conversation. "Come on, Tim. Show him the rest of it."

"Show me what?"

Tim leaned down and began turning pages again. "If you go back to the first page ... here it is. Look what he was looking for *before* he searched for the book name again."

Max said out loud, "Royal Roman Scepter of Arenia. What the..."

This time he caught himself and stopped, looked at Rebeca, then continued.

"What in the world is this thing? Wait a minute, so he's doing research, so what? You don't know that this scepter has anything to do with the book. He could have been getting ready to quit and just typed in the book search again because he's an idiot."

Rebeca chipped in. "Well, but we do know that this scepter is somehow tied to the book. Timmy Boy looked it up, and guess what he found?"

This time, Max didn't know who to look at for his answer. During the somewhat long pause, he looked back and forth between the two of them several times. But neither answered.

"Ok. I'm getting dizzy here, one of you spit it out."

After a look from Rebeca, Tim said, "I did the same search he did. It gave me seven hits. The first one was about the city this thing was supposedly made in. Then the next five are just pictures of this scepter from different angles. But the really interesting thing is this seventh hit, which was a report."

Again, Tim flipped through the pages in his folder. Rebeca snickered as Max turned his head in a small half-circle with every page that Tim turned. If he wasn't dizzy before, he will be now.

"It's a report by a Vatican researcher that discusses interpreting the writings on this thing. There, see that name." Tim was pointing at the author's name just above the bottom of the page.

Max's eyes became as large as plates. He snatched the paper from the open folder.

"I'll be damned! Father Latanye was the researcher on this."Max looked directly at Rebeca. "And I *meant* to say that one. This whole thing is just, just, out there!"

"We thought you'd like this," Rebeca said, smiling at Tim.

"This is amazing. You two did good. I'm impressed. I want to read through this myself, so make me a copy of everything you have so far. Is there anything else?"

Tim hesitated and Rebeca coughed to get his attention. Of course, Max was looking right at her as she motioned for Tim to explain.

"Well, there is one more thing. I hope I didn't go too far on this one. But I think I found somebody who had something to do with removing that original message, or at least knew about it."

Max was really impressed with Tim now. It showed both in his smile and his voice. "You what? But how? Wait!" He held up one hand in Tim's direction. "Do I really want to know how you did this?"

He looked directly at Tim, only to see Rebeca standing behind him, shaking her head and silently mouthing 'no'.

"Ah then, let's leave it there for now. I think there are some secrets that you two need to keep to yourself."

Now Rebeca is shaking her head but silently mouthing 'yes'.

"Look Tim, just give me the highlights."

"Well, it turns out that the day after you talked to Father Latanye, a certain Cardinal sent an email to what looked like a 'No Reply' address. At least that's what I first thought."

Max interrupted Tim. "Wow. What Cardinal, and what is a 'No Reply' address?"

Rebeca stepped back and slowly shut the office door. It was obvious that she didn't want the closing of the door to trigger the 'gopher effect'. A rush of colleagues' heads, popping up simultaneously above their cube walls, would give them an audience that they didn't want. With that done, she began to explain.

"First. A 'No Reply' address is one that is used to communicate information out only. You have gotten them before. They always say something like 'Please Do Not Reply to this email address'. That's because they are not monitored and the system just flushes all incoming emails. This is standard in the industry."

Max nodded. "Ok, go on."

"The problem is that if you *do* reply, your email is just trashed, because you were already told not to reply. But this one didn't just reply. It replied every time the Cardinal replied."

"So? That's it? And the big deal is?" Max obviously didn't see where she was going on this.

"The big deal is that the fine print on the bottom of the email changed each time there was a reply. Which means an automatic message generator was not doing it. Also, Tim noticed that behind the scenes, the internal message format was that of a regular email packet and not that of a server error message format."

Max began nodding his head. "And you said there was fine print changing on the bottom of the replies? What about the bottom of this Cardinal's emails?"

Tim took his cue from Rebeca and spoke up. "What struck me as odd at first, were two things. The Cardinal continued to send messages to this 'No Reply' address and what he was saying didn't make any sense. They were just odd statements like 'Having a good time. Wish I was there'. Things that he could have put in any email.

"Then, when I noticed the whole thing with the networks' internal formats and codes, well ... I knew something was going on. That's when I went back and really looked at everything on the email. Then I found it.

"The fine print was mixed in with some supposed routing info at the bottom of the page. It changed every time on every reply."

"And it said?" Max asked, becoming impatient.

Rebeca interjected. "Don't downplay this, Max. I still can't believe that Tim caught this. It's incredible, to say the least. And then how he broke this code, was really cool." Her eyes led Max's eyes back to Tim.

"Code? What code?" Max's entire naval career had centered around codes and the breaking of them. His eyes were glued to Tim as he continued explaining what he'd found.

"The fine print was changing, but it was just a mixture of upper and lower case letters, mixed in with symbols and numbers. I knew this was nothing to do with routing info, so I cut and pasted this print from each email for both the Cardinal and the 'No Reply' box. Then I ran them through a decipher package that

I've been toying with."

Max stood up. "A decipher package *you toy with!* Where did you ever learn about ciphers?"

Rebeca held out both hands, motioning for Max to sit back down. He reluctantly returned to his seat before Tim continued.

"I was kinda in this hackers' club in college. Nothing major. No big deal. Kid stuff, like pranks mostly."

Rebeca shook her head. "Your college buddy, Randy, told me you hacked the Pentagon once. That's your idea of nothing major? No big deal?"

Again, Max was out of his chair. "You hacked the Pentagon? As in the US Defense Department's Pentagon? What kind of cyborg PC hack wacker are you?"

Tim hung his head like a child in trouble. "Well. They never knew." He raised his head and looked first at Rebeca, then Max. "They never knew. Really!"

"Boys, we're getting off base here. Tim, tell him what that software package of yours found."

Tim pulled a folded page from his shirt pocket and began to spread it out. After clearing his throat, he began.

"Cardinal, secured messages are visible. Box, suggest we remove completely. Cardinal, concur with that, completely. Box, can re-mask entry point later. Cardinal, sounds good, how long. Box, two days but must hold for four days. Cardinal, why four days? Box, must be hidden within next system updates, four days."

Max sat motionless for almost a minute before motioning for both of them to sit down. Tim appeared hesitant but Rebeca pinched his arm and whispered, "Sit."

Once both were seated, Max rested his forehead onto his clasped hands with his elbows on the desk. It gave him the appearance of sitting in prayer. He sat there for a few moments before looking up at them. He began to speak very slowly.

"So," and he sighed a heavy breath. "Without telling me *how*, tell me about the Cardinal that was sending these messages."

He looked at them but neither spoke up.

"Well?"

Tim looked at Rebeca. She nodded, and he began speaking.

"It was Cardinal Mortello. You know who he is, don't you?"

"I'm new, but I'm not stupid. Of course I know who he is." Max looked straight into Tim's eyes with a stare that neither of them had seen before. "Are you very sure?"

Tim slowly nodded. "Yes. Very."

Looking back at Rebeca, Max asked, "Is it true that he is favored by the Pope?"

"Yes. Rumor has it that Cardinal Mortello could be the next Pope."

"I've heard that he is a very straight arrow. One of the truly good guys." Max thought hard while he looked over their heads into space. Eventually, his focus returned to them.

"I want to tell you both that I am extremely impressed with your work. Seriously! You have both gone so far above and beyond my expectations, that I feel you have a right to know what I'm going to do. This whole issue is beyond the mandate for this department; however, we stumbled onto it, and we have followed it as far as we should. You may not like it, but I'm going to take all your hard work and kick this upstairs to my boss.

"So I'm keeping this folder, and I'll need that paper you read from your pocket. The moment I do this, I can't promise you that I'll be able to tell you what happens. However, I will promise you that I will tell you everything I can. Due to the sensitive nature of this issue, you are not to talk to anyone about it. I don't want you two talking about it between yourselves either. Doyou understand?"

They answered in unison. "Yes."

Tim asked, "Should I continue to monitor the priest in Dallas?"

"Yes, for the time being. But keep a lid on it. Again, good work. I mean it. Now get out of here and go back to the boring part of your normal jobs." Max had the friendliest smile they'd ever seen on his face. "As much as it pains me to do this, I need to take this next step now. Please close that door on your way out. Thanks."

Once the door clicked shut, Max dialed his boss's number. After negotiating an appointment time with Bishop Westin's secretary, he began to read the entire contents of Tim's folder. His appointment with the Bishop was in 30 minutes, which only gave him 20 minutes to become more familiar with this subject.

~ ~ ~

Having explained everything to his boss, Max calmly observed the Bishop as he stood looking out the office window. The
Bishop, hands clasped behind his back, had been motionless for
almost five minutes now. He was a young man, but well-known
for his political savvy. This one trait had been instrumental in
his being appointed to this office. It was also the real reason that
Max wanted to bring this to his attention. Finally, he turned and
slowly settled back into the chair behind his desk. With his usual
soft voice, he began to speak.

"Max, I appreciate you bringing this delicate situation to
me and instructing your people to be discreet as well. You are
extremely fortunate to have such resourceful talent in your department. For you and your people to have put this all together,
well, it is very impressive. The way forward from here will require
some careful navigating. I'm sure you can appreciate this."

"Yes sir. I've always known that my forte was the tracking
down of information. The interpretation and use of it, well, I've
always left that to others."

"When I hired you, Max, I must admit that I had reservations
about letting you assume such a docile managerial position. I
understand your motivation for a slower pace than what you
experienced at the CIA. Yet, I felt that your natural talents would
surface when presented with a challenge. A challenge like the
one we have before us here.

"As with any large entity, the Church has many secrets that
require many levels of protection. Though I accepted the title of
'Head of Security', I knew that there would be some levels that
even I would not be aware of. Your findings have just proven my
assumption to be very true. The reality is that Cardinal Mortello
is a party to something that I've only become aware of by accident. His close proximity to the Holy Father means that the activities you've discovered are most likely known by him. Thus, I
do not believe that these activities are detrimental to the Church
and therefore, do not warrant any further investigation."

Though Max' face was expressionless, his mind was racing.
He had always suspected that, in some ways, the Church would
be very similar to his last master. Now he realized that it was a

huge organization rife with power players who built small kingdoms of personal influence. There were also figureheads that accepted their limited roles, despite their lofty titles. He was somewhat disappointed by what he'd just heard. It appeared that the Bishop did not want to challenge this hidden pocket of power. This information was about to fall into a dark hole and would never see the light of day again.

But then the Bishop sat for a moment longer and then completely amazed him.

"Max, I've changed my mind. It's not my place to decide what to do with this information. Since I am not involved with whatever is being protected here, I think that those who *are* involved should be made aware that their secret has been discovered.

"Of course, I will personally eliminate any references as to how and by whom I know of these things. I fear that the common knowledge of your professional background will make it easy to surmise that you were involved. However, it should be our shared and utmost responsibility to protect the identity of the two that work for you. Agreed?"

"Yes, agreed."

"Good. So, with your permission, I'd like to keep this folder." Bishop Westin had one hand on Tim's folder, and was looking straight into Max's eyes.

"Of course," Max quickly replied.

"Good, that's good. I trust that none of the pages in this folder offer any clue to who actually gathered this information."

"That's right. I went through it twice myself before I brought it to you."

Though a little hesitant, he decided to ask anyway. "What do you think they will do?"

"That is a very good question. I think they will be nervous at first. To have what you thought was private, suddenly thrown into the sunlight. Well, that is going to be a shock. I usually stray far away from the head on approach, but they need to know that they are visible. If they were tasked by the Holy Father with the safekeeping of whatever this is, then it is our duty to His Eminence to point out its vulnerability."

Max realized that this meeting was drawing to a close, so he asked one last question.

"What should we do now? Back to our regular daily work?"

"Yes, but I'd like for you to continue to monitor that priest in Dallas, Texas. I have to admit I'm very curious what he and Father Latanye are looking for."

"As you wish. Would you like regular reports, or just whenever we have something of interest?"

"I would rather only receive a report when there is something of interest, but I'll leave it up to you."

"Just one more thing … should we actively seek information, or truly just monitor?"

"At this point, my friend, I think we should keep an arm's length from both of them. I would like to know if they inquire about anything else. I wonder what they are looking for?"

"So monitor it is." Max stood and walked towards the door. With his hand on the doorknob, he heard the Bishop behind him.

"Max, my door is always open to you. I look forward to our next meeting."

Max smiled and closed the door behind him. He liked Bishop Westin, but he had always been a little nervous around his own bosses. He's relieved that he is not the one who will take this up with Cardinal Mortello. It was a conversation that could destroy a person's career quickly. But if anyone could pull it off, Max knew that the Bishop could.

~ ~ ~

Bishop Westin sat at his desk and slowly read each page in the folder that Max had given him. Though his eyes were reading the lines, not all of his thoughts were on these pages. His mind was shuffling different scenarios for the conversation he would now have with Cardinal Mortello. This would obviously require an extraordinary amount of focus; more than had ever been required of him. He had known the Cardinal personally for several years. Still, he was not sure how the Cardinal would react to the news that his secret endeavors were known by others.

The ringing of his phone interrupted his challenging thoughts. A quick glance at the phone showed it was the Cardinal returning his call.

"Cardinal Mortello. I apologize for interrupting your busy schedule."

"Paul, you are not interrupting at all. In fact, I should thank you for giving me an excuse to get out of a very boring meeting. Of course, that is just between you and I."

The Cardinal's laughter on the phone eased Paul's apprehension about their upcoming discussion. "I have a very urgent need for some of your time."

"Urgent? Sounds serious. I'm free now, if you would like."

"Yes, that would be excellent. I'll be there in, say, five minutes."

"It is always good to see you Paul. By the way..." The phone went silent.

"Hello? Cardinal?"

Once the phone was securely in the cradle, he found himself sitting and staring at the folder. He was instinctively breathing deeply to calm himself. He rose from his chair, picked up the folder and walked to his office door. The abrupt ending of the phone call had brought back those feelings of uncertainty from a few minutes ago. He hoped that the walk to Cardinal Mortello's office would give him a few more minutes to organize his thoughts.

Paul had his head down as he opened his office door, and ran right into the Cardinal.

"Cardinal Mortello! I'm so sorry. I should have been paying more attention."

"Easy, my son. It was my fault."

"But how are you here so quickly? You were just in your office. I saw your name on my phone."

The Cardinal smiled. "I have a new feature on my office phone that allows me to make calls from my cell phone without identifying its number. Instead, the caller ID indicates that I'm in my office when I make calls, but I can be anywhere."

"Our phone call just ended all of a sudden. I wasn't sure what happened."

"My cell phone loses its connection in certain hallways. I was just about to tell you I was close to your office when the line went dead. So you see, it was my hurrying to your door that caused our collision!" The Cardinal's laughter could be heard throughout the hallway.

"I thought we could just meet in your office."

"Certainly."

Paul backed through his office door and stepped aside for the Cardinal to enter. He motioned towards a couch and chairs that were strategically placed directly in front of his windows.

Sitting down with his back to the window, the Cardinal began. "So, Paul, what is so urgent?"

Paul had hoped to tell the Cardinal an eloquent story, but now it was time to ad-lib. He began by slowly telling the Cardinal the same story that Max had told him earlier this afternoon.

The Cardinal was silent throughout the entire telling. When he was finished, Paul felt he'd covered the subject very diplomatically. The Cardinal's eyes had remained focused on the contents of the folder, but he had never asked a question. Having completed his narrative, Paul sat back slowly in his chair and waited for the Cardinal's response.

Cardinal Mortello sat motionless for several minutes. He would gently clear his throat, look out the window for a moment, then focus on the folder before him. This nervous pattern was repeated three times before the Cardinal sat up straight and leaned towards Bishop Westin.

"I want to let you know that I appreciate you bringing this information to my attention so quickly. As you can imagine, it is quite a shock to know that something so secret has been detected. I trust that you have already moved to ensure discretion on the parts of those that know of this."

"Of course. The fate of this information is totally your decision. My sole intent of this conversation was to let you know that your efforts were visible to others. I intend to leave this folder with you, and will accept your guidance without question."

"Paul, you are a good man. I believe you are sincere in your motivations. I also have no doubt that you only seek what is best for the Church. I think that what I'm going to tell you may confuse you at first. So, please bear with me a moment. I actually believe that we could use your help on some very delicate issues. Issues the Holy Father is very much aware of. But first, I'd like to address something that I'm sure you have already wondered about. As head of Security, you may feel that you should have been made aware of secrets such as these."

"Cardinal Mortello, please believe me. I knew when I took this position that I would not be made aware of all the Church's secrets. It makes complete sense that certain information would be secured through other channels."

"You are a very wise young man, Paul – one of the reasons I suggested you be offered this position."

"It was you? I had always wondered who had been behind my being considered for this office. I hope that you have not found cause to doubt that decision."

The Cardinal smiled before saying, "I have never doubted you. In fact, I have reveled in the realization by others that I was so very right about you."

"Thank you. Now, how can I be of service to you?"

"Well, let me give you a little insight to this situation from my point of view. I can't tell you everything, but you do need to know a lot more than you do now."

The Cardinal shifted around in his chair as if trying to get more comfortable, but Paul knew he was trying to decide where to start. His smile slowly left his face as he began to speak.

"It is well-known that the Church does acquire ancient writings and artifacts. We allow scholars from all countries to view these beautiful reminders of mankind's past. However; there are a few that we have chosen not to share, or even to acknowledge their existence. I can't divulge why we have chosen this path for these items, but I do ask that you accept that we have very good reasons for doing so."

When the Cardinal paused, Paul reminded him, "As I stated earlier, I will accept your guidance without question."

"Well, I will tell you as much as I can while I explain how you could help us. As you already know, we have secured items that are only known of by a few. The location and description of these items are not important to this conversation. Please do not let your feelings be hurt by this. The mere fact that I have confirmed the existence of these things should be viewed as a great honor."

The Cardinal tried to emphasize his next comment by pausing and looking directly into Paul's eyes. "You are one of a *very* select group that knows these things exist. Of course, you are not to avow this to anyone."

Paul immediately sat upright. "Your trust will not be broken by me."

"I know that, my son. Now, where was I? Oh yes. We know about Father Latanye and Father Cobleir inquiring about a certain book. We also know that they are good friends and have been so for many years. We also know what sparked their curiosity in this book."

In the short time since his meeting with Max, Paul had wondered about this very thing. Max and his people had not been able to ascertain the link or purpose in regards to the book. Paul was an astute diplomat and did not display any signs of curiosity, or of eagerness to know more. It was second nature to him, and the Cardinal was impressed with Paul's reserve.

"Before I tell you more, I would like to ask you a question."

"Cardinal Mortello, please ask me anything, anything at all."

"I noticed that you have never mentioned any names in reference to this information you have brought to me. It was also apparent that you did not want to divulge the number of people involved in the gathering either. I appreciate your loyalty to those on your staff. However, I must ask you if Maxwell Spreck was involved."

Paul hesitated before answering.

"Yes. He was. But I assure you he was merely following a logical path, having been presented with a security anomaly."

"I have no problem with Mr. Spreck's activities. In fact, I wish to further his involvement."

The Cardinal paused long enough for Paul to ask, "You do?"

"See, I knew I would confuse you. Do you think he would be interested in taking this further for us?"

"I am positive he will do whatever we ask him. Within reason, of course."

"Before we continue, I have a personal curiosity about Mr. Spreck leaving his former employer. It was the CIA, correct?"

"Yes it was."

"I understand that he had worked there for many years and had a very impressive career."

"Yes, he was there for 21 years and received eight commendations."

"So this is all true. However, I heard that he left after something went very wrong. I heard that there was a loss of several lives."

"That is also correct. I don't know the real details of the matter. The general gist is that he had warned his superiors that a certain situation was getting out of hand. He tried to convince them that there was a breach and people had been exposed. They ignored every suggestion of proof that he offered them. Finally, he took it upon himself to go out and physically bring them all in. He managed to find and save only two. The others were tortured and killed. He himself was wounded in an attempt to extract a third person. He resigned while still in the hospital. I have never asked him anything more, and he has never offered more information than this. Though he is somewhat of an unpolished gem, he is definitely an honorable man."

"So, would you say that he left on bad terms with his prior employer?"

"Actually, I happen to know that they have tried to entice him back on two occasions since he came here. Each time, he has respectfully declined their offer."

"I'm just curious about his Navy career and his CIA career. How does that work?"

"He was an officer in the Navy. And I believe that his naval career was actually a cover of sorts for his role in the CIA. I'm not sure how it worked."

"Well, I am more certain than ever that we would like him to work with us on this. As his superior, you are OK with this?"

"Of course Cardinal. Exactly, what is to be done?"

"Basically, we would like to send Mr. Spreck to Dallas, Texas."

"Where Father Cobleir is?"

"Yes. We want to know more about the relationship between Father Cobleir and a man named John Parson. It is this man who has prompted Father Cobleir to first search for the book, and then to involve Father Latanye. We don't know anything other than this. Our desire is to know more about Mr. Parson and how he came to know the name of this book."

"Excuse me for asking this, but why have Max investigate this man? I would think that the Church has made inquiries about people in the past, before he was appointed. So, why use Max now?"

"That is a very good question Paul. Yes, of course we have other avenues to inquire about people. It's just that Mr. Spreck is already involved to some extent. But mainly, because we really need to keep this entire affair within the Church. No outside personnel can be involved. It is of utmost importance that no one else learns of the existence of these especially secretive artifacts. Above all, we do not want it known that they are in the Church's possession. I cannot stress enough, the Church's need to have these things remain unknown. Unfortunately, I can't tell you why. I have to hope that you will understand."

"I do understand. Would you like me to set up a meeting between you and Max?"

The Cardinal was quick and firm in his answer. "No. I think it would be far better if there is no direct contact between Max and myself. Of course, you can confirm that he is acting on my request. Later today, you will receive everything that we know of the situation and the participants involved. I will attach a personal note from me to Max, thanking him in advance for his service. This should solidify your role and his."

"May I suggest that we cover his expenses under his current computer security upgrade project?"

"Yes! That is an excellent idea. Paul, you have our complete trust in this matter. We will back any decisions you make in regards to this task. As far as reporting your findings, please have them delivered to my office."

"Thank you. I will."

"Well, now. I think that you may have some questions for me. Though I may not be able to answer them completely, I will tell you what I can. Please feel free to ask whatever is truly on your mind."

Paul had so many questions he would have liked to ask, but he understood that he should not reach too far at this moment in time. "Well, the obvious question would be about this book. I take it that it does exist."

"Yes, Paul, it does. Unfortunately, I can't tell you much other than there is such a book."

"I understand, Cardinal. I did not mean to put you on the spot."

"Paul, please. I can't tell you more, because that is all that we know."

"Oh, so you only recently acquired it?"

"Not at all. We have had it for a considerable time now. For reasons that I can't explain, we have not been able to have it translated."

"Cardinal, I'm confused. Father Latanye has inquired about the book. Therefore, he has never seen it. If you can't translate it, why have you not used his expertise to do so? I would think that he is most trusted by the Church."

"He is. Completely. Again, there are circumstances that have limited how we involve him. I am not at liberty to discuss these circumstances with anyone, but I can tell you this. We have presented some photocopies with writings from the book to him. He was never told from what manuscript they came. He is not even aware that they are from a book. To his credit, he never questioned why we limited his access to only those copies. Just like you, he loves the Church and was very happy to do whatever he could to help."

"I take it that he could not translate it."

"That is correct. He still has the photocopies, and I know that he will continue to attempt a translation because of his professional tenacity. But to date, he has no idea what language it is, where it could be from, or who could have authored it. He has stated that there is always a chance his other activities may, one day, provide the key to interpreting these copies. This is where we have been for some time.

"Then, out of nowhere, we have inquiries about the book. Though it is odd how things have materialized, we need to pursue these opportunities in hopes of learning more about what we have in our possession. This is why we must learn more about Mr. John Parson. It is a huge mystery here, as to how he even knows the book's name."

"Cardinal, this is a lot to take in all at once. Do you know if Mr. Parson is a book dealer or a literary researcher?"

"Well Paul, this is where things become even more curious. It appears that he is an auto mechanic of some kind. Owns his own business there in Dallas, Texas."

After a few moments of pondering by both men, Paul said, "Then perhaps he is a book hobbyist who has just stumbled upon the name. Yes, that could explain it."

The Cardinal was amused as he watched Paul staring out the window, obviously lost in thought. While Paul sat with his thoughts, the Cardinal had his own thoughts, but they were not about the book any longer. His thoughts were about finally acquiring some trusted help in solving this mystery.

Ever since that first inquiry about the book, he had felt so totally alone when trying to figure out what had been happening here. Due to the secrecy surrounding a book that only a few even knew of, the Cardinal had felt very isolated by not being able to involve anyone else. Paul didn't understand how small of a group it truly was.

Cardinal Mortello's memories took him back to the day he informed the Pope of the inquiry on the book's name. His stomach still tensed when he thought about it, but not because of the conversation. It had been the look on the Holy Father's face as he heard and processed the news. In the many years that they had known and worked together, he had never seen anything affect the Pope's demeanor as profoundly as this revelation had.

Though His Eminence had not been pressuring the Cardinal, he inquired almost daily as to any news on the matter. Yes. His prayers for help had finally been answered, and this fine young man would be instrumental in finding a solution. The Cardinal now realized that he could and should share more of his knowledge with Paul.

"Paul, I would like to share several more things with you. I doubt that Mr. Parson is any type of book enthusiast. Even if Max finds that he is, it will still not explain how he came to know the title of this book."

"Again, Cardinal, I'm afraid I don't follow you. Why would that not be possible?"

"Because, my friend, the book's name was given to it by our previous Pope. Remember that only a handful of us know of its existence, and even fewer know of the name it was given."

Paul had a quizzical look in his eyes as he asked, "The book was named by the Pope himself? Of course, without being able to interpret any of it, then someone would logically call it by something. But why the Pope himself?"

"Perhaps it would help for you to know how few are aware of the book. The man who found the book had worked for the Church. After turning the book over to the Holy Father, this gentleman died from some mysterious ailment. He had been married, but his wife had died in an auto accident. He was the last of his family tree. He worked alone, and none were with him at the time of his great discovery. All of his notes are preserved along with the book.

"During the ongoing work to translate it, the Pope began using the name that we now call this book. The previous Pope had delegated oversight of this work to a young Cardinal who is now the current Pope. I, in turn, have been delegated that same oversight.

"So, you see, only two living people even knew of the book's name. Now you can fully appreciate our astonishment when this inquiry was made."

"And no others know about the book?" Paul's face was awash in confusion. "No one?"

"There are two priests who guard the book in a very obscure location, but they have *never* known it by this name. It is always intentionally referenced to, and by them, as "The Book". They merely watch over it."

Paul appeared spellbound by the Cardinal's revelations. Suddenly, he sat up so quickly that his movement caused the Cardinal to flinch.

"I have it! Obviously some computer technicians developed the online access system. The one that issued the ill-fated error message and opened up this Pandora's box. They must be your leak!"

He studied the Cardinal's face for a sign of agreement with his hypothesis. Though his insides were quivering with excitement, his outward persona was his usual: calm and collected.

"A very deductive suggestion! I am very encouraged by your display of intelligent and logical thinking. You're definitely the man I want helping me with this. Regrettably, it can't be the answer."

Upon hearing this, Paul's face fell. He again seemed confused as he retreated to the comfort of his chair. After a few seconds of looking at the ceiling, he quietly said, "Again, not possible. Huh."

"I'm afraid not. Though we know nothing of what this book says, there are attributes of it and its discovery that led us to take extreme precautions when involving outsiders. We had a system created, as you know. Forgive me for only being able to provide you with a layman's explanation of how it works. I am truly a novice with computers. So many buzzwords and acronyms. They boggle my mind."

Paul laughed as he noticed the sheepish expression on the Cardinal's face. "I understand completely, Cardinal. However, one of my degrees is in computer science. I will understand. Please continue."

"It was designed to function with a 'cipher key'. I believe that is what it is called."

Paul nodded. "That is exactly what it is called. I did a thesis paper on this very program."

"Good, I had that right. Anyway, only I have this. And it was I that actually input the items into this system. No other eyes have ever seen the list. Of course the book is one of the items in this archive. We also discontinued using the people who designed it for us. It is unfortunate for them and us, for they did an excellent job. But it was felt that this would isolate and protect the system even more.

"Next, we used an internal source to insert and maintain our little computer project. They do not know what they control, as we play it down as a minor list of Church assets that are kept off the books for accounting purposes."

Paul shook his head. "You are to be commended. It seems that you have diligently thought this through and construct- ed an extremely secure system. Not to sound condescending, but speaking as someone with a computer science degree, I am most impressed."

The Cardinal perked up. "Thank you! I tried to do my home- work on this, and it does me good to hear someone compliment my work. Sadly, I must admit that I was responsible for that er- roneous error message ever being issued."

"How so?"

"When this special system was implemented, I had insisted that my computer inquiries would first search the common base of information and then search my special base of information.

It had always worked just fine, until this big security upgrade the Church just went through. Does this make sense?"

"Cardinal, I think I know what happened. They created a search string for your personal login. One that would search the main databases first. If nothing was found, then it would search your secured database. This would easily have been limited to your login information by your personal security settings, and the settings assigned to your special database.

"During the security upgrade, the settings on your special search string must have been lost. This meant everyone's inquiries were being bumped against your secured database. However, the security settings on your physical database files were still in place. That is where Father Cobleir's 'Access Denied' message came from."

The Cardinal was mesmerized by Paul's ability to tie all these things together so quickly, and to come up with the exact scenario of what had occurred. Again, he was very glad that Paul was now involved. To a layman, Paul's explanation was easier to understand than the one given to him by the computer technicians. Yes, this was shaping up to be a very good day.

"I assume that Max should be informed immediately?"

As the Cardinal began to stand, he said, "Yes. There is nothing more pressing than this. Though I find myself wanting to stay longer and discuss this more, there are three people waiting in my office by now. I'm sure they're all wondering if I plan to attend a meeting that I called!" There was a pleasant gleam in his eye; an endearing attribute to all who met him.

Paul rose to accompany the Cardinal to the door. He halted as the Cardinal reached out to shake his hand. With both men having a firm grip of the other's hand, the Cardinal said, "Paul. I can't express enough how happy I am that these unfortunate events have brought you to my aid. I want you to know, that His Eminence will be completely aware of your contribution towards resolving this whole affair."

"I am so happy to help in any way that I can."

With that said, Paul hurried to hold the door for the Cardinal. He left the office after a nod and a smile.

Paul watched him lumber down the hall and around the corner. He thought to himself that he had just shaken hands with the second most powerful man in the entire Church. One who would surely influence his own future ... the one destined to be the next head of the Church.

CHAPTER 6

The Dallas Triangle – Part One

The speaker on Flight 426 crackled to life. A monotone voice recited, "This is your cabin attendant, Judy. The captain has turned on the seat belt sign. Please return to your seat at this time. Stow all your loose items in either the overhead compartment, or under the seat in front of you. In preparation for landing, close your tray tables and bring your seat backs to their most upright position. We will be making one last pass through the cabin to collect any trash or empty beverage containers."

Many passengers were awakened by this well-rehearsed routine that the attendants had performed countless times before. But it did not find Max asleep. He had been wide awake throughout the entire 13-hour flight to Dallas. Max had spent this time productively creating a game plan. The folder of information that Paul had given him was now covered with scribbled notes. These writings were very calculated steps he intended to follow. Each step was designed to provide him both a cover and access to gather the information that Cardinal Mortello had requested.

After carefully placing these valuable maps of deception back into his satchel, he locked and lowered it to the cabin floor. He slipped the shoulder strap around his foot before sliding it under the seat in front of him. He smiled as he wondered how many times he had done this before to prevent a bag from being snatched away while traveling. It was an old habit from his CIA days in the field.

Having been a CIA field operative for over 15 years, Max had a wealth of knowledge and personal experiences to draw upon. He would utilize all of his talents to achieve what the Church had sent him to do. They wanted information, and he had always been very good at gathering it.

Once the plane was securely docked at the terminal, he made his way to the baggage claim area. He was pleasantly surprised at the speed with which he passed through Customs and reached his designated pickup point outside. Perhaps it was a sign indicating how smoothly this trip would go. His old CIA partner pulled up in front of him in less than two minutes.

Tom Wilson was a stocky man who stood barely over six feet tall. He jumped from behind the wheel and moved quickly to the rear of the car. A beep, and the trunk swung upward. Max joined him behind the car. Each man lifted and lowered a bag into the trunk, before they faced each other with a smile and a handshake.

"How have you been, Max?"

"Very well, Tom. How's Becky and the kids?"

"Fine! Just fine! It's really good to see you, Max."

The two men took their positions in the front seat. Wilson maneuvered the car into traffic and headed for the north airport exit. He noticed Max looking around at all of the new construction inside the airport.

"You know, I was very shocked to hear from you, Max. It really is good to see you again, old boy."

"Same here, Tom. I really appreciate you helping me with this."

"Max, we both know that I will be in your debt for the rest of my life. Actually, I *am* in debt to you for my life."

"You would have done the same for me, my friend."

"I would like to think so," Tom said, as he glanced over at Max still looking out the window. "A lot has changed since you were here last."

Finally turning to face Wilson, Max said, "It's changed a hell of a lot! I'm glad you're driving. By the way, where we going?"

"A small parking lot just two miles down the highway."

"What did you get me?"

"It's a late model. Dark blue I think. One that will blend in so well, you'll probably lose it."

"You're never going to let me forget that, are you?" Max lightly tapped his clenched fist on Tom's right shoulder.

"No, of course not! You have to admit, that was pretty damn funny." Tom's laughter was stopped by Max smacking his shoulder again, harder this time.

"Funny? I was being shot at while running around, looking for that stupid rental of yours, and where were you? Kneeling down beside some old red pickup and laughing your ass off! "

"Well it was funny!"

"Tom, I actually thought about shooting you."

"Nah, you love me bro, and I know it!"

Their laughter could be heard by the toll gate person as they drove through. It took several moments before they both regained their composure. Not another word was uttered until they pulled into a parking lot and Tom had squeezed the car next to a totally black vehicle.

"I thought you said it was dark blue?"

"Hey, so sue me."

"I may shoot you yet."

There was more laughing as they both made their way to the rear of the car. Again, the trunk sprang to life preceded by that beep. Max noticed that Tom was pulling an envelope from his coat pocket. "For me?"

"Yes. Exactly as you requested. Here are the keys and your IDs. I tried to get them to take off a few years from that picture you emailed me, but they said you were too ugly. I was going to get a second opinion, but these guys are professionals, so I figured they knew what they were talking about."

"Ha ha. You know, your humor hasn't changed much, but your hairline has!"

"Good one. Now the car has California tags just like you wanted. So does your license, registration and insurance card. There is one credit card with a $3,000 limit. So don't go overboard. I'll need a check from your boss to reimburse my agency account once you get back home. Oh, and that info on John Parson is under your seat. Not much, I'm afraid. He seems like a straight arrow, that one."

"Tom, this license has my old address."

"Yep. We never took you out of the system. I submitted the paperwork once right after you quit. It was rejected. It was all returned to me in a Manila folder with a note saying, 'Three year hold for possible repatriation'.

"That figures. You know they've contacted me twice in the last six months."

"In Rome?"

"Yes. Two different phone calls. Each preceded by an email. Can you believe it?"

"Yes, I can. They really didn't want to lose you."

"Obviously they didn't realize how serious I was about what happened."

"You are aware they furloughed Peterson after you left?"

Max's eyebrows tensed when he heard this declaration from Tom.

"No, I did not know that. What happened?"

"Well, your quitting sparked an investigation. Didn't take long after they saw how much information, and how often you had given it to the idiot. He's lucky they didn't yank his pension."

"It is all in the past. Can't bring back the dead."

Max squared his shoulders to Tom's and extended his hand. Tom faked a handshake, but grabbed Max in a big bear hug. With his mouth next to Max's ear, he whispered, "Every time I hold Becky and the kids, I only get to do it because you came and got me."

He stood back, hands still on Max's shoulders. Looking straight in his eyes, Tom said, "I owe you my life, buddy. If you need anything else, *anything*, you have my number. Oh, and by the way. Just leave the car anywhere and forget about it when you're done. It's jacked so we'll find it."

Max said nothing. He just smiled and nodded. He knew that when he saw that look in his old friend's eyes, there was something else on his mind.

"Ok, dummy. I know you're about to drop something else on me, so get it over with."

Tom snickered and said, "I love you bro, but this is one time that I'm not going to cover for you. She wants you to come by, and you better not disappoint Becky this time. She is expecting you for dinner one night before you leave. If you don't show, she'll shoot us both!"

Max patted his friend on the back as Tom turned to walk back to his car. Neither looked back as they drove away.

~ ~ ~

The traffic on the highway was light, and Max continued to marvel at all the construction. It had only taken him 35 minutes to drive to his hotel. Pulling into the parking lot, he found a spot just three slots from the front door. This was good.

So far, today, things were going like clockwork for him. If his luck held, he could actually meet Father Cobleir in person before this day is up. It would be nice to get the first little piece of his plan accomplished before the day's end.

After registering at the desk and getting his bags into his room, Max took time to read the information Tom had given him about Mr. John Parson. Tom was right. This man appeared to be an average guy with average activities. Nothing stuck out as a possible warning sign. All Max needed to do now was to find the connection between the two men.

He unzipped one of his bags and pulled out a sack with a very special gift. One that provided him with a reason to stop by the parish where Father Cobleir ministered. He placed it conspicuously beside the TV, so he couldn't forget to take it.

The next task on his list was to get a phone listing for a pizza place in Plano. A quick call from his hotel phone, and he checked off one more of those scribbles on his plan.

Now he just needed to wait for the car rental company to deliver his secondary ride to the hotel. The wait was but a few minutes. His cell phone rang. "Yes. This is he. Great, I'll be outside in one minute. Thanks!"

His alibi in hand, he exited his room and heard the sound of a heavy hotel door falling shut behind him. Once in the car, he typed the address of the church into his GPS device. The sound of a female voice droned, "Please drive to the highlighted road."

His mind swirled with memories of past missions that he'd been assigned as a young man. Realizing he is wearing a considerable smile, he knew for sure that part of him missed his old life. It was obviously a dangerous one that kept him on the move, but, it was an exciting one as well.

Max reached into his pocket and retrieved his cell phone. With a quick flip of his wrist, the phone opened. He dialed 5 without even looking. It took a few seconds for the long distance number to ring, and then he heard Tim's youthful voice. "Hello, boss."

"I'm close to the church. Is he there?"

"Yes, he's online right this minute."

"Thanks. I'll call you if I need anything else."

Max held down the red button on his phone until he heard a swoosh sound as it turned off. This was one of his scribbled notes; one that he hoped will gain him access to Father Cobleir's cell phone. The sound of his phone closing preceded a view of the church appearing just a few blocks away. He slowed and turned into the parking lot. Again, there was a parking spot virtually in front of the door. Though luck was obviously still with him today, his instincts led him to ignore any concept of luck. Luck was something one referenced after the fact. Planning and focus were what were needed now to achieve his goals. Once the gift was firmly in his hand, he got out of his car and walked to the church door.

He was unchallenged as he entered the church and began to stroll around. Finally, a priest appeared.

"It's a glorious day to be in the house of our Lord. May I help you?"

"Yes, I'm Maxwell Spreck and I'm here to see Father Milo Balgoni."

"I am sorry to tell you this, but Father Balgoni left for Austin this morning. I am Father Wilton and I've been waiting for you to arrive. Father Cobleir is waiting in his office for you. He is in charge until Father Balgoni's return. If you will follow me, please."

The priest led Max to an office at the rear of the church. After a brisk walk through some badly lit hallways, Max stood in the doorway of Father Cobleir's office.

"Father Cobleir, this is the gentleman you've been waiting for." Having said this, the priest turned and left the office, closing the door behind him.

Father Cobleir stepped around his desk and extended his hand towards Max. "It's a pleasure to meet you, Mr. Spreck. Please call me Matt."

"Thanks, call me Max. So, looks like I missed the man I was supposed to give this to."

"Father Balgoni was invited to attend a meeting in Austin today. He was looking forward to meeting you in person and talking about Rome with someone who actually lives there. He was just a boy when his family moved here, but I believe he misses his homeland very much. He was somewhat saddened by the news that you were arriving today and he would not be here. Please, sit down." Mathew motioned for Max to sit at the table in the corner.

As Max made his way to the table, he saw a cell phone on the priest's desk beside an open book. After placing the gift on the table, he slid into one of the large leather chairs. It was very comfortable. He remarked, "Wow, this is really nice. I wish my office had a few of these."

"Would you like something to drink? I believe Father Wilton just made some fresh ice tea."

"Yes, by all means, I'd love some ice tea. I've been craving it ever since I made up my mind to visit my sister. You know, after living in Europe these past several years, I still find it odd having to ask for ice in a drink."

Mathew smiled. "I have the same issue every time I go over there myself." The two men laughed.

Max strategically waited until Mathew was in the doorway before asking, "Excuse me, but may I ask a favor?"

Mathew stopped and turned to face Max. "Of course, how can I help?"

"I was wondering if you would mind if I borrowed your cell phone and stepped outside to call my sister. She and her husband are running some errands. I talked to her while I was driving here, but my phone died right as she hung up. I just need to see how close they are to home now."

Mathew didn't even hesitate. He stepped back to his desk, scooped up his cell phone and handed it to Max. "You can talk here if you like. It will take a few minutes for me to get the tea. But if you just want some fresh air after your long flight, the door at the end of the hall is unlocked and gives you a great view of the surrounding neighborhood. It is very relaxing. I find myself out there a lot, when I'm stressed or just need a break."

"Thanks! You know. It was a long flight, and the fresh air sounds great."

Max stood and followed Mathew into the hallway. As Mathew turned and went one way, Max turned the other and headed outside. He immediately opened Mathew's phone and went to his contact list. There must be a phone number for a John Parson in here. His eyes rapidly scanned the list. Ah, there is a 'Parson', but it is a 'Parson, B'. Max is confused at first since the man's name was John Robert Parson. Then he recalled the info that Tom had given him. His wife's name was Barbara. The priest knew John Parson's wife.

There was one more thing to do before returning to Mathew's office. Max called the pizza place in Plano. The phone's memory would help hide his deception, should Mathew become curious and check to see what number had been called. Even if the priest was curious, he would not have any leads as to the identity of Max's supposed sister. Max didn't have a sister or a brother. He chose a mythical sister, because the priest wouldn't find a Spreck in the Plano phone listings if he decided to search her.

Max hurried inside and was barely seated when Mathew's footsteps could be heard coming back to the office. Mathew returned with two tall glasses of ice tea. Max eagerly extended his hand to accept his glass of tea, so that Mathew could join him at the table.

After a short sip, Max closed his eyes and swallowed. A low utterance of delight is heard before he opened his eyes and smiled. "Tastes like heaven. You know. I almost bought a soda can of tea on the plane, but I decided to wait and get the real thing. So glad I did. This is truly delicious."

"I know what you mean, Max. When I first moved to the south, I really didn't understand this southern infatuation with ice tea. However, after living here so long, I find that it is a very captivating drink."They both smiled, then each sipped again before placing their glasses on the table.

Mathew noticed that his cell phone was there on the table

also. "So, how close is your sister to being home?"

"Well, I still don't know."

"She didn't answer? You can try again before you leave."

"Well sir, I feel kinda foolish. I thought I knew her number, but I got a pizza place instead. You know. I'm so dependent on my cell phone that I don't remember numbers once I put them into it. How sad is that?"

Mathew picked up his cell phone, looked at it as if he were examining it, and laughed. "I do the same thing! It's sad that we've become so dependent on these little machines. They rule our lives more than we're willing to admit, and we actually pay for the privilege." Both men laughed again.

Max sat up and slid the package across the table to Mathew. "Well. This is the reason I am here. There is a card attached."

"Do you mind me asking who it is from?"

"Of course not. I'm sure it is no great secret. It's from my boss, Bishop Westin. I'm not sure how they know each other, and I'm not sure what it is. I was hoping to see it when he opened it. Oh well, some things are not to be known."

Something about the Bishop's name had Mathew wondering who he was. "It seems I've heard the Bishop's name, but I can't place it."

"He is the head of Security for the Church."

Mathew's eyes betrayed his thoughts to Max, who immediately asked, "You know him?"

With his composure recovered, he said, "No, but I've heard that name before." Mathew's mind was in overdrive. He wondered if this was no accident. Could this be a follow-up to the supposed phone survey about his satisfaction with the recent church-wide computer security upgrade? If so, then was it somehow tied to his searching for that book? Who is this guy? What is his real purpose here?

"So you say he is your boss?"

"Yep. He's the one that hired me too." Max reached for his glass again. "I don't have much cause to deal with him, but he seems like a nice guy. Gave me a job when I needed one."

"So you are in security, too? Who or what do you protect?"

Max knew for sure that the priest was fishing for a hidden agenda here. Mathew had already lost the game, but Max would string it out a little longer; just enough to make sure that the priest was convinced there is nothing suspicious in his visit.

He will intentionally say things that play into Mathew's suspicions, and then he will explain them away. A typical infiltration technique he'd used many times. First you feed their fears, then prove those same fears are not true. The end result is that the subject you are dealing with feels silly for ever having suspecting you, and they chalk it up to just being paranoid.

Max faked choking on his tea. "Protect? Not me, buddy. You misunderstand. Yes, the Bishop is over all of security, but I'm just a department head over PC network security. They just folded us under him, so we wouldn't report up through the data processing department. I think it is a kind of 'Separation of Powers' type of deal." Max set his glass on the table and sat back in his chair. "At least that's what I think."

Mathew was now convinced that he couldn't trust Max. This guy is probably responsible for that phony survey call. Yes, that's it. He's here on a fact-finding mission. They didn't get what they wanted over the phone, so here is the head guy. Mathew decided to just go for broke.

"So it was you guys who were doing that survey about the upgrade?"

Max was an accomplished liar when the situation required it. He looked quizzical. "What survey?"

"You know, the phone survey after that big church-wide security upgrade. Someone from your department called to ask me how satisfied I was with the upgrade."

Still appearing confused, Max asked, "The big upgrade? My department doesn't deal with end users like you. We only deal with those managers that assign security levels to their staff. They forward request forms to us and we set up their personal security records. Besides, the upgrade was done by the computer data center. They install software packages. My department is only a user, just like you. If you were contacted about a satisfaction survey, it would have been from them. It was their project."

Max paused for a second, intentionally looking down as if he were lost in thought. Finally he added, "That's odd about this survey call. I don't recall ever hearing about any survey. I mean, it makes sense that there would be one, but the entire rollout isn't even over yet. I would think that a survey would come later. I know they never called us to see what we thought about it.

"God, I hope they don't call while I'm gone. It had some adverse effects on my staff. There was a little overtime and a lot of headaches that first week. If they call anyone on my staff, they might just get an earful of something they really don't want to hear. I'm glad you mentioned this to me. But this really could be bad if they do call us. You think I can make a long distance phone call from your land line?" Max smiled as he chuckled. "I hate to say it, but some of my staff can really be vocal at times. I had better nip this in the bud before I end up having to explain it away later."

"Of course. You can call from my desk. I'll give you some privacy and go get us both another glass of tea."

Here is where Max will completely win Mathew's trust.

"If you don't mind waiting while I make this call, I'd like to walk with you and stretch my legs a little more. I promise. The call won't take two minutes. I just need to talk to Rebeca. She is in charge while I'm away, and is very aware of the ones I'm thinking of."

Mathew nodded 'yes' and motioned for Max to move behind his desk. Then he said, "You need to dial '9' to get an outside line."

Rebeca answered and was talking very loud, just as Max had instructed. The plan was for the priest to hear most everything being said. Max went over the story line with Rebeca. After he repeated the tale that the priest had told him, she practically screamed, "And you are just now warning me about this?"

Her voice could be heard in the hall and Mathew actually leaned away from the phone as if trying to escape. Max put his hand over the phone and whispered to Mathew, "And I left her in charge because she is one of the *calm* ones!"

With the phone call over, Max looked sheepishly at Mathew. "I'm sorry you heard that. She is a really nice lady, but obviously a little high strung. Very good at what she does, but well, you heard her."

Mathew smiled and shook his head. "Is she Italian?"

Both men rose to get another glass of tea. Max said, "No, she's American, but I think she's been there *way* to long!" Their laughter faded as they disappeared down the hall.

There was the usual mixture of small-time chitchat all the way to and back from the church's break room. Both men took their turn to relate stories of people who they'd worked with in the past. Once back in the office, they quickly retook their seats to drink their tea. It was a much more relaxed conversation that had nothing to do with the Church.

Max had accomplished what he had come for, and decided it was time to leave. With a quick look at his wristwatch, he exclaimed, "Wow, the time. She has to be home by now. I was enjoying the conversation so much, I forgot about the time. I really need to get going. I'm sure you have more important things to do."

Mathew stood to escort his guest to the front door of the church. Again, they exchanged stories of the colorful work companions they'd met over the years. One would finish his tale, they would both laugh, and then the other would start another story.

Max drove away, happy to have this first piece of information. The priest was a friend of Mr. John Parson's wife. He would have to adjust his plan based on this new information. This was normal in these types of endeavors. He was also convinced that the priest had accepted his visit as just a chance encounter.

Once Max's car was out of sight, Mathew re-entered the building and proceeded to his office. He picked up the two glasses from his table and started down the hall to return them to the break room. There is a little extra spring in his step because he was no longer a prisoner to the thought that he was being watched. The phone survey wasn't part of a sinister plot. As for Max, he couldn't be up to anything. He never asked a single question. Mathew felt so foolish. Looking back on everything, he realized that he had just been paranoid.

<div align="center">~~~</div>

As Max drove back to the hotel to switch cars, he mentally reviewed the next item on his agenda. Though his next target was Mr. Parson himself, now was the time to set things in motion regarding his wife. With the revelation that the priest was actually friends with Mrs. Parson, Max knew he needed more information about her. More details than he'd found in the folder supplied by his CIA buddy Tom. How was he going to get to talk to her? She was a stay-at-home wife, so a diversionary home sales call might work. There was no mention of outside activities. She rarely went to see her husband during the day. That only left the mundane daily chores outside the home like shopping, which weren't conducive to a lengthy conversation.

The file included a mention of her personal grooming habits, noting that she frequented a salon each week for her hair and nails. Perfect! That would be his way in. The key to learning more of her involvement would be found at the salon. Almost all women discussed their personal lives with their hairdresser and manicurist.

With the car back in the hotel parking lot, he hurried to his room for a quick wardrobe change, and to pick up his props for his visit to Mr. Parson's garage. First things first. Max wanted to make sure that Mr. Parson was in his office. He dialed the number to his garage, only to find that Mr. Parson had gone for the day. Max was a little disappointed that he would have to wait until tomorrow to chat with the main character regarding this mystery. But this gave him time to develop a plan on dealing with Mrs. Parson. Plus, Max knew that Tom would need time to gather information on the employees of the salon she frequented.

As Max lay on his bed thinking, he realized that he could possibly accomplish two things at once by taking Tom up on his offer to come to dinner. Yes, tonight would be a very good time for them all to get together. Max had a plan, but it would be tricky to make Tom think it was his idea. After making arrangements with Tom and agreeing to be there at 6:00 p.m. sharp, it was time for a well-deserved nap. He quickly fell asleep after having completed one of the tasks that brought him to Dallas.

~ ~ ~

The drive to Tom's house took Max right past the auto garage owned by Mr. Parsons. Max thought this was a good sign, an omen of sorts. He was in Tom's driveway shortly after passing the garage. Max was just about to ring the door bell when Tom's wife swung the door wide open, stepped out and gave Max a warm embrace befitting an old friend. She had been a secretary in an office next to Max's at the agency. After much prodding by Tom, Max had been the one that introduced them. They had dated for only a few months, and had been happily married for over six years.

"Max! It's so good to see you again. I have thought of you often. Come in, come in." Never releasing his hand, she pulled him inside. "Tom is upstairs with the boys. They saw you drive up. You are not going to recognize them. They have both grown so much since you saw them last."

"Becky, I'm so sorry I didn't take the time to come by before I moved to Rome. It was a crazy time for me."

She stepped closer to him and looked up into his face. "We all understood. You needed to get away after that mess. But you should have at least called us, once you got there. We were very worried about you."

"I know. The truth is that I needed to stop thinking about anything that would remind me of what happened. So I guess the job was just a way to hide out, but it worked. It helped me to put things into perspective and move on." He smiled at her.

They both turned towards the sound of the boys roaring down the stairs.

The boys ran to him yelling, "Uncle Max!"He let them pull him to the floor and they all wrestled like they used to long ago. Tom finally cleared the last step and walked over by Becky to watch the melee.

"Boy's, don't hurt your uncle. Remember, he's an old man now." Tom said this with a smirk on his face.

The boys pulled back and Max stood up. "Old man?"

"Older than me!"

"Ok, you two. Don't start!" Becky was smiling as she began to herd them all into the dining room. "The table is set, so let's all take our seats before it gets cold."

The dinner was excellent and the conversation reminiscent of days gone by. Max learned of all the boys' sports activities, and how they were doing in school. It was wonderful to be with his friends again; people he had shared many experiences with over the years.

After the meal was done and promises made to the boys for games to be played upstairs, they happily ran off to their rooms.

Max began a dialogue that he hopes will result in the recruitment of his best friend's wife.

"Becky, that was absolutely delicious. I can't believe I let this scoundrel steal you from right under my nose!"

"Steal me?" Becky said playfully. "As I recall, you practically forced me to go out with him!"

"Forced you to go out with me? As I recall you practically threw yourself at me."

"Down, you two." Max said with a warm smile on his face. "I merely pushed two people who were destined to be with each other. You both did the rest."

They laughed a little more before Tom noticed that Max's eyes had that intense look that meant he wanted to talk shop.

"Hey buddy, you want to step outside and stretch your legs a minute?"

Becky noticed the men looking at her, and then each other. She said, "You two look like you need to talk, so get out of here and let me clear the table."

"Becky, this is not company business anymore. You are more than welcome to sit with us while we talk. That is if you don't mind, Tom?" A quick glance at Tom, and Max saw the confusion on his face. "Becky, I always wondered if you felt left out when we would wander off to discuss business."

"Max, you sweetie, I never gave it a second thought. I'm impressed you ever thought that, but it wasn't necessary then and it isn't now either. Really!"

Tom looked questioningly at Max. "What are you up to, Max?"

Max motioned to Becky to rejoin them at the table. He waited until she had retaken her seat. "Well, I meant everything I just said, but I do have a reason for wanting you to sit in on this one. I'm in a bit of a time crunch here, and I would like to get a woman's perspective on this."

Becky chuckled in Tom's direction. "See, Tom. He wants my opinion. You should learn from Max."

Max continued. "I have to find out something about a certain woman. My best play appears to be through her beauty salon."

"Well, I do know a lot about this. How can I help?"

"I know that men tell their barbers everything. I am hoping

that women are the same with their hairdressers."

Becky perked up, excited. "I'll say they do! You can learn all about the life of a woman in the next chair just by joining in their conversation. You'd be surprised what I've heard from total strangers on the other side of the room."

Tom is fascinated by Becky's enthusiasm. "Really? How'd you get them to talk?"

"Get them to talk? You don't have to do anything but ask. Before you know it, every woman within earshot will be adding her two cents."

Max leaned towards Becky and her face took on a blank look as she noticed his stare. "But Becky, what I need to know would be something probably very personal. Things that are only discussed with her husband. Things that they may not discuss with others."

Becky smiled and reached out to pat Max on the hand. "Honey, you have no idea what I've told the girls about Tom boy here."

Tom looked shocked. "And exactly what have you told the *girls* about me?"

"You two can get into that when I leave. Becky, how would you go about getting the conversation started?"

"Well, it would depend on what you are wanting them to talk about."

"Allow me to throw some things out here. Then you tell me what you'd do."

Becky was squirming in her chair with excitement at the thought of doing what these two men had done for so long - be a spy. This did not go unnoticed by either man. Tom was not smiling any more as he listened to things unfold.

"I need to know what ties a Catholic priest to a man that owns a garage not far from here. Actually, I already know that the Catholic priest is a friend of this man's wife. I also suspect that this priest wants to talk to this man, or he may already have spoken to him. It has something to do with an old book."

"What garage around here? Are you talking about the Auto Correct garage?"

"Yes. Do you know these people?" Max asked eagerly. If she did, this could be a lot easier than he could have ever hoped.

"No, but our neighbors take their car there. I've driven Margie to pick it up after it was worked on."

"So, do you have any ideas on how to initiate a conversation that would lead to this?"

Becky had both elbows on the table, her hands cupped in front of her mouth. One of her forefingers was lightly tapping her top lip as she stared blankly across the table.

Watching her do this reminded Max how cute she looked doing it in the office. She would be trying to get the words just perfect on a letter, and she would tap her lip while she was thinking. He really liked her, and had always wondered if he should have made a play for her himself. But in the end, he knew his friend Tom would make a much better husband. He liked them both and that is why he set them up on that first date.

Finally, she dropped her hands and spoke.

"Yes. I think I have it. Well, at least a rough way to start it off. All I would have to do is ask if anyone knows a good mechanic. One that could be trusted. A good hairdresser knows what every one of her customer's family members do for a living. She would immediately offer up this lady's husband as someone to try."

Max saw where she is going. "That's simple and straightforward. I like it. I would think at some point you could mention something about old books. Bring that into the conversation and see what is said. But you..."

Tom interrupted Max.

"Wait a minute here. Sounds like you are asking Becky to do this. If you are, then I'm not comfortable with this conversation any more. She's not an operative. She's my wife and mother of my children."

Both Max and Becky were caught off guard by Tom's sudden serious tone. Here is where Max knew it was time to turn this around and make it sound like Tom's idea.

He remembered Becky telling him many times that she had always fantasized about going on a mission as a spy. She told him this several times a week before he ever introduced her to Tom. Hopefully, she still had those desires. If she still did, Tom would only be able to question her safety while doing this. However, there was no danger from a church-sponsored fact finding mission. Tom would not be able to give Becky a rational reason not to do this. It was safe, it helped her very good friend, and it was something she had wanted to do for a very long time.

Max could see it in her eyes. She was hooked. Now it was time to corner Tom.

"Tom, I never suggested anything along those lines. I was merely asking for a woman's perspective on this. I need a plan and now I may have one thanks to Becky. Once I had one, I planned on asking you another favor though. Can we get one of your female field agents to do this? Say tomorrow sometime?"

Tom's shoulders had dropped, and his more relaxed composure showed on his face. But before he could say anything at all, Becky chimed in.

"Wait a minute. I can do this. This would be a piece of cake. Really."

Max knew he would win or lose with his next statement.

"I really appreciate your offer Becky, and I apologize if I gave you the wrong impression here. Tom is right. It is better to be safe than sorry."

Having said this, Max could only watch and listen as the inevitable discussion between a husband and wife unfolded. The husband will be trying to talk the wife out of doing something. But the wife wants desperately to live out a lifelong fantasy. If this is what happens, then Tom will have already lost the argument, because Becky knows that it is something to do with the Church. So how dangerous could that be?

Becky's eyes moved from Max to her husband. She was obviously going to fight for the opportunity to do this.

"Wait. Just wait. Why can't I do this? First of all, Max works for the Church now. He doesn't work for the company anymore. This can't be dangerous. No way!" She had employed her beautiful bedroom eyes and softened her expression. Here is where she will execute every female tactic she has ever learned. Tom will see it her way. She is sure of it.

"Honey, we are talking about going to a salon. Something I do all the time."

Tom looked at his wife, then at Max. "And you are absolutely sure that this thing is safe?"

Max referenced Tom's own background data by saying, "I'm positive. Besides, remember what your report said. They are good citizens. I have never thought otherwise. I just need to know about some old book they're looking for."

Once again, it was time to try and talk them out of it. Max would accomplish several things by doing this. Tom would ultimately be convinced that Max never intended for Becky to do it. Becky would fight even harder to get to do it. And poor Tom will have to admit that he was the one that brought it up.

"Becky, it is obvious that you want to do it, and I'm flattered. But I have to admit that my gut still says no. It may be a holdover from when I was still with the company, but it is ingrained in my soul, no family."

"Tom, I want to do this. It would mean a lot to me."

With her gorgeous eyes fixed so unwaveringly upon him, Tom chuckled and began slowly shaking his head. "Well, it was me that brought it up." With a quick look at Max he added, "And I know you'd never put my lovely wife in any danger. So, why not?"

With the realization that she was about to do The Spy Thing, Becky let out a small squeal to the amazement of both men. She rose from her chair and flew around the table to lay a big kiss on her husband. While her mouth was near his ear, she whispered, "You know, I've always wanted to do something like this. I can't wait till I get you upstairs."

Max shocked both of them back to the conversation by admitting he had heard what she just said. "Before anyone takes anyone else upstairs, let's go over this several times. Just so we all agree on the basics of this plan."

Tom and Becky both visibly blushed at Max's announcement. Becky thumped Max on the back of the head as she returned to her chair.

Tom had already had many conversations with Becky about her fantasy of being a spy on a mission. He decided to give her the full experience, as he's certain that Max will play along.

"I think Max is right. We need to really go over this just like we would with one of our field agents before they go out."

Both men took great pleasure in watching Becky's inner child soaking up all the instructions they gave her. The professional Do's and Don'ts of the trade. Having helped her enjoy her fantasy even more, Max realized it was time to go. Once again, he had accomplished what he sought. He needed sleep now, so he would be alert tomorrow when he approached Mr. Parson himself.

Tom and Becky both watched from their front door as Max drove out of sight. As the door clicked shut, she pushed against him so hard that they both fell against the wall.

"Honey, I can't tell you how happy I am. I know I've told you how I dreamed about doing this all my life, and now I am! This is so exciting. When I worked at the agency, I always envied those agents that I met. This is a dream come true. It is so odd that this is happening, isn't it?"

She began to kiss him more passionately than she had in a while. He wanted to get her upstairs soon, so he lifted her up in his arms and carried her up to their bedroom. Something she said was reverberating in his head with every step he took up the stairs.

As he laid her on the bed, she began kissing him again, but he pulled away for just a second. "When you worked at the agency, did you ever mention this spy dream of yours to Max?"

Becky was still straining to kiss him again, but Tom was offering just enough resistance to keep her mouth free to speak. "I don't know. Maybe. Yeah, I must have at least once or twice. So what?" That's when Tom knew he had once again become a victim to one of Max's plans. Then she locked both arms around his neck and used her weight to pull him down to her.

Before drifting off to sleep that evening, Tom's final thoughts were, "Yeah, he did it to me again. But hey, tonight was worth it!"

CHAPTER 7

The Dallas Triangle – Part Two

The alarm rang just seconds before the phone did. No great surprise to Max, who had been awake for over 30 minutes now. He hit the alarm and snatched up the phone to hear 'It is 5:30 a.m., and this is your complimentary wake up call.' It was an automated call, so he just hung up and went back to thinking of the day's activities he had before him. Today, he would actually meet the man himself. Yes, Max would be face to face with Mr. John Parson.

Max would not allow himself to picture the conversation with his target. No, this would leave conversational expectations in his mind; expectations that could keep him from being alert enough to notice the small nuances in a conversation that might dictate he adjust his plan accordingly. If you over-think an upcoming conversation, you may try to force that conversation to follow how it played out in your mind. To Max, this did not facilitate a 'natural' conversation. A normal conversation evolved and flowed from one participant's comment to the next.

Yes, you must keep in sight what you are after and help guide the conversation along. But if you already have an idea in your mind of how it should go, then even the best actor could come across as a little stiff, or unwilling to let the conversation drift a little. This is what usually made a target sense you are after something.

He had always found that it was best just to have a few small talking points, phrases or comments in mind. Inject them into the conversation and see where they lead. You could always repeat one later in a conversation, just to get back on track. The reality is that you want to find out what they know, not get them to say what you thought you'd hear.

Max slowly rose from his comfortable bed. Anyone who saw him would never know how much he actually hurt when he first got up in the morning. They would see him making fluid movements and appearing to move like a 20-year old. But if they listened closely, they would hear his bones creaking as they began to loosen up. His face never showed it, but he hurt as he forced his body back to life each morning. All the falls, the wounds, the fights, jumping from perfectly good planes and having good planes shot out from under him. These and many more reasons were why his mornings were becoming ever more of an ordeal. It was the life he had chosen. A life he loved. But, damn, it hurt more and more as he got older.

Dressed in his old running attire, he slipped the room key into his armband. Again, there was that sound of a heavy hotel door swinging shut behind him. He made the quick walk to the hotel gym and was relieved to find no one there. His usual 30-minute run on the treadmill would loosen him up. His pace increased from a walk to a run while his mind worked hard to ignore the pain from his stiff joints. As the minutes ticked off the clock, he was thinking of what he planned to do during the day. Before he knew it, his morning routine was complete, and the beeping of his jogging watch signaled a reprieve.

Machine turned off, he was out the door and back to his room in seconds. The shower felt good. Fully dressed now, he bent to pick up his little conversational decoy. A small, dirty white piece of luggage that held the old books he planned to dangle in front of Mr. John Parson. Old books that had the smell of thousands of hands that had turned each page many times. He was off to go fishing, and this was his worm. It was time to see if he got a bite.

He placed the special book bag in the trunk of Tom's loaner car. The drive to Mr. Parson's auto shop was uneventful. With all the daily auto crashes during the Dallas rush hour, Max was amazed there wasn't one along his route. Again, he wondered if this was an omen of how well this day would go. At last, on the right, there was the shop.

As he pulled up to the first open bay door, one of the mechanics strolled over to his open window and said, "Morning, sir! You can just leave her there and the office is right through that door. The manager's there and he'll help you."

"Thanks." Max walked in to find he was the first customer of the day.

The man in the office was busy straightening up the waiting area on the customer side of the counter. Hearing the door open, he immediately stopped what he is doing, turned and greeted Max. "Morning, sir! I'm John Parson. How can we help you?"

Max was standing face-to-face with Mr. John Parson himself. He seemed to be a very friendly person. Not just because he was a businessman. Max could already sense that John was a very likable guy.

"Morning. I'm Robert Phillips. I'm on a business trip, and the car just started acting funny when it's in Drive. It doesn't seem to want to go. Oh, and it sounds odd when you put it in Drive. To be honest, I was told that I needed to have the transmission flushed. But I forgot about it and hit the road two days ago. I really hope I haven't done any serious damage to it."

"Well sir, I'll get one of the guys to do a quick check and we'll see what's going on. Are the keys in it?"

"No, I have them. I'll bet I locked it, too. I have some rare books in the back seat. It's a habit. If you don't mind, I'd like to bring the case in with me, so I can do some paperwork myself."

Max started to turn and walk out to get the case when he heard John's voice.

"Rare books? You a collector or a salesman?"

Max knew he had him on the hook. He could tell by the new expression on John's face. It was more serious, and his smile had fallen to half-mast. Yes, Mr. John Parson wanted to talk books and Max was going to let him.

"Oh, heavens no! I'm not a salesman. I'm a collector of sorts. I'm not an authority on anything, but I have been collecting old, old books since I was ten years old. It's a hobby that I have indulged these past thirty years while I did my real work. But now I'm retired, and it gives me reason to travel around the country."

Max pulled out his keys and pointed to the mechanic standing by his car. "Do I just give them to that guy?"

"Yes, that's him. You are in luck. He's my best transmission technician."

Max turned and walked back out to his car. He opened the door and reached into the back seat to get the dirty white case with the books in it. Items in hand, he turned to the mechanic and handed him the car keys. Before Max could say anything, he heard John call out, "Hey Bill, take a look at the transmission. He says it's sluggish."

John held the shop door open as Max walked back from the car. Once inside, John said, "Well, Mr. Phillips, I can pull one of those end tables over by a chair for you to use if you like. Oh, by the way. Would you care for a cup of coffee? It's fresh. Just made it two minutes before you drove up."

"Thanks! Both would be great!"

There was a loud metallic sound made by the end table being dragged to the chair in the corner. Once in place, John spun around and headed behind the counter.

"Do you take cream or sugar, Mr. Phillips?"

"No sir, just black. Thank you."

Max bet himself that John would come over and sit down with him to see these books. To make sure, he placed the case on the end table and opened it up. He pulled one book out along with a paper tablet full of notes. John was back with the coffee and offered one of the cups to Max.

"Here you go, Mr. Phillips." John was obviously curious about the books in the case. He noticed that one book was wrapped in heavy brown paper.

"Why is that one wrapped up?"

Max extended his hand into the case and placed his open palm on the paper wrapped book. "This one is very special, and is the reason I'm here in Dallas."

"Is it very old?"

"Yes, very. I had a friend send me this all the way from Rome."

Max was looking straight at John's face now. He didn't want to miss any change in expression. John's eyes were fixed on the book under Max's hand.

"Rome? You say it came from Rome?"

"Yes. I haven't had this one very long. I only got it two weeks ago. You seem very interested in old books, Mr. Parson. Would you like to see it?"

What John said next completely confused Max.

"Nah, I would hate to get grease or coffee on it."

Why doesn't he want to see it? He was obviously interested in seeing the old books. What has changed? Then John asked something else.

"I am curious about Rome though, Mr. Phillips. You said you had a friend who got it for you."

"Yes."

Bill, the mechanic, interrupted the conversation.

"John, the transmission is a little low, nothing serious. It doesn't have a leak. I checked it over real good. But the fluid is extremely dirty. Definitely needs to be flushed out."

Max chipped in. "That is what I thought. I'm not a mechanic, but I was hoping that was all it needed. Go ahead and do it, please."

John smiled and nodded at Max before saying, "Ok, Mr. Phillips, but it will take awhile to do it. You mind waiting?"

"Not at all. I don't have to be anywhere until 6:45 tonight."

John nodded at Bill, who said, "On it, boss," before disappearing into the garage bay again.

"So what about Rome is of interest to you, Mr. Parson?"

"Oh, I was just wondering if you or your friend had ever heard of a "Book of Prizom.""

Max's jaw almost hit the floor as the book's name rolled off John's tongue.

"Well sir, I don't think that I've ever heard of a book by that name. How do you spell it?" Max pulled a pencil from a pocket inside the case, and held it above the small table. He looked at John to signal he was ready to write it down.

"Well, I think it is Prizom, but I'm not sure."

"Well, what do you know about the book?"

"Just that it is very old."

"Well, I had noticed that you seemed curious about the books in my case until you actually saw inside. You appear to have an idea of what size it is, perhaps."

"Oh, yeah. I know how big it is. It wouldn't fit in your case there."

"So you have seen it? Where?"

After hearing this question, John's expression changed drastically. He tipped his head and said, "No, not really. But I do know it wouldn't fit in that case."

Max sensed that John wanted to pull back from the conversation. He had to find a way to keep John interested.

"Well, sir, I could email my friend if you like. He usually answers very quickly."

John's facial expression was positive. Before he uttered a word, Max already knew he had hooked him into talking a little longer.

"Well, Mr. Phillips, I can't ask you to go to any trouble on my account."

"Sir, I look for books all the time. That's how I found these and why I'm on the road. Believe me. It is no trouble at all."

John smiled and added, "You're welcome to use my computer on the desk."

"No need for that. I have one of these new fancy phones that does email. I was a little nervous about it at first, but my nephew set it up for me and showed me how easy it was to use. I don't really know how all this stuff works, but it does."

With that said, Max turned and sat down. He began punching random buttons just so John would hear beeping.

John stood there watching him for a few seconds before saying, "I really appreciate you doing this for me, Mr. Phillips. When you get ready for a little more coffee, just holler at me and I'll come freshen up your cup."

Max glanced up at John and nodded. "You're welcome. I'll probably take you up on that extra cup in a few minutes."

John heard Max's phone beeping with every key that he punched. He walked behind the desk and around the corner into his private office.

Once seated in his well-worn chair, he sat there thinking to himself. *Why do I feel so funny? Is it the thought that another piece of this puzzle could be filled in by a stranger that happened into the shop?* Just when John thought he had control of things, this book popped up again.

Max typed a little more before hitting Delete and saying out loud, "It's on its way!"Then Max began thinking about what had just been said.

Mr. John Parson does know of the book, but he seemed either confused or hesitant to say much about it. Max was really curious to find out how John knew what size it was. He must have seen it! He obviously didn't want to say how.

This was odd. It was time to restart their conversation.

Max pushed the button on his phone that made it vibrate loudly. Then he stood up and walked to the counter.

Leaning his head over to see around the corner, he said, "Hello! Sir?"

John popped out of his office and walked to the counter. "Yes, sir?"

"Well my friend just texted me back. He's never heard of a book by that name. He is curious about your inquiry. Seems somebody else has asked him about the same name within the last two weeks. All they could tell him was the name, but he was very interested in how big you say this book is. I told him I'd get some more information. So tell me again, how big is this book?"

John looked like somebody who had just woke up. His eyes were a blank stare. He began to tap the counter top with a pencil he had in his hand. As he began to shake his head, he sighed a little and finally spoke.

"It's about ten inches square and around eight inches thick. It's not a book like we see nowadays. Remember, I told you it was a very old book. I really didn't see it, so I can't be any more descriptive than this."

Max was really getting into playing his part as a book dealer. He recalled how Father Latanye had referred to the old documents in his department as manuscripts. He decides he should show some excitement at this news, so he smiled and leaned a little closer to John as if whispering y a secret.

"This sounds like a very old book. Maybe not even a book, but an ancient manuscript of some type."

John's face came alive. "Somebody else told me the same thing. They called it a manuscript, too."

"Well, sir. Give me a minute to email my friend back with this info. If I know him, he'll have a lot to say now!"

Max turned and walked back to his chair. He made his phone beep just as he had earlier. After he typed for a while, he again hit Delete and looked up at John to say, "Well, it's on its way again. It's things like this that keep me interested in this hobby of mine. I don't want to pester you, sir. But I'm very interested in how you know the size - yet you say you haven't seen it?"

John wanted desperately to get out of answering this question.

"Well, Mr. Phillips, you'd think I was totally crazy if I told you how I know. But I really need to go talk to my guys in the shop for a few minutes. Sorry." And with that said, he turned and quickly disappeared.

Max heard the sound of a heavy metal door shutting. As he sat and waited for John to return, Max was beginning to realize that he was not going to get much of anything from him. John wanted to talk about it, but something was really holding him back. Max was at a loss as to how to continue this conversation.

John intentionally stayed in the garage bay for almost 20 minutes. He finally realized that he was distracting his guys from their work, so he reluctantly headed back to his office. Max heard that metal door again, and he knew that John had come back. He pushed that button again on his phone, and it again vibrated very loudly. John heard it, and knew he might as well go back to the counter and see what news there may be.

Max heard John's footsteps and made sure that he had his head down as if he were reading a reply from his imaginary friend. He stood and approached the counter.

"Well sir, he is excited all right! He says he's going to keep looking and that your description will help, but he doesn't have any answers for you now. Sorry."

"I want to thank you for contacting your friend. Here, take one of my cards. If your friend does find out anything, I'd really appreciate a call. My personal cell number is on that card. Call me any time, sir. And by the way, your car will be ready in about 30 more minutes. I have a ton of paper work to get done. So I need to get to it. Again, just holler out when you want another cup of coffee, Mr. Phillips." With that said, John retreated once again to the safety of his office.

Max sat back down to wait for his car. The day's findings hadn't added up to much. But he had learned more about the physical appearance of this mysterious book. Max's thoughts quickly changed to how Tom's wife was doing on her undercover mission at the salon this morning. Hopefully she would find out a lot more than Max did.

After Max heard the sound of that metal door opening and closing a few more times, John reappeared at the counter.

"Mr. Phillips. Your car is ready."

The two men went about concluding their business in regards to Max's car. John thanked Max again for contacting his friend, and Max promised to call if he found out anything about the book.

As Max pulled out of the parking lot, his curiosity overwhelmed him. He decided to call Tom. "Hey buddy, hear anything from your wife?"

"No, not yet. If she doesn't call soon though, I may have to alert SWAT to go in and get her out."

"Well, those salons can be dangerous!"

Both men laughed a little before Max continued, "I'm headed back to my hotel. Just give me a call, and I'll run by so she can tell us what she found out."

"Max, I'm at home. Come on over and wait here. The kids are in school, so you can fill me in on living in Rome."

"Sounds good Tom. I'll be there in five minutes."

Max pulled in front of Tom's house, locked the car and began walking towards the house. Tom opened the door just as Max's foot hit the first step.

Tom was about to close the door when they heard a car horn being hit repeatedly and growing louder. Becky's car came speeding into view, and the tires screeched as she slid to a stop in the driveway. She was waving her hands as she jumped from the car. Her purse strap caught on the car door. The sudden restraint spun her halfway around before she caught herself. She quickly freed the purse and practically ran to the front porch.

In her excitement, she brushed past the two men and into the front room of the house. She had been talking very fast from the moment she got out of the car, and all the way into the house as well. The two men stood looking at each other, then her, and then back at each other. Tom stepped towards her and gently placed his hands on her shoulders.

"Slow down there, Super Spy. Take off your coat and sit down. You really need to calm down."

"Calm down! I *am* calm." Becky finally noticed that both men were smiling and staring at her. "Ok, maybe I need to calm down a little. But Max, I have to tell you some things. You are not going to believe this."

Now it is Max's turn to try to settle her down. "Please Becky, sit down. I assure you I want to hear everything you have to say. But you have to slow down so I don't miss any of it."

Becky quickly removed her coat and tossed it over the back of the couch. She was the first one seated. She looked up at the men.

"I thought you wanted us to sit down? I'm seated. Aren't you two going to sit? If you want to hear this, and I'm telling you that you DO, then you boys need to sit too. So SIT!"

Having now been scolded, they both took a seat.

Becky looked at each of them, one at a time. With one hand pointed at each of them, she began to talk.

"Now get this. It's a dream."

Tom immediately interrupted her with, "Yes, dear. We both know that this has been a long time dream of yours. Now you..."

She cut him off by making a one-handed axe movement in Tom's direction.

"No, no, no. Not my dream. It's *his* dream. The guy is having a dream. This all comes from a dream."

Max was really confused and shaking his head when he said, "What do you mean it's his dream? Whose dream?"

Becky stared at both of them. "You guys NEVER listen. I told you as I walked into the house. It's his dream. The guy who owns the garage. John Parson is having a dream about this book. Get it?"

Max felt like he had just been hit in the face with a shovel. Her words were ringing in his ears as his mind tried to catch up with what she'd just told them. Tom had already got it, and he turned to Max with a very quizzical look on his face.

"You came all the way from Rome because some guy is having a dream about a book?"

Max looked a little embarrassed.

"Hey, this is the first I've heard about a dream. We didn't know how he knew about the book. The trip is all about finding out how he even knew of it." Then he turned to Becky and continued. "You sure? A dream?"

"Yes, I'm sure! I just spent two hours listening to four different women spill this whole story about this dream."

"Ok, this is obviously going to take some time. Tom, what do you say we all have some coffee at the table? Becky, you take a minute to collect your thoughts a little better. Then I want you to start at the beginning and tell us everything that was said. I mean it, every little thing that was said. Ok?"

Becky was so keyed up that she practically leapt from her chair, said "I gotta pee," and then disappeared around the corner. Her quick exit left the guys looking at each other in silence. They slowly rose and made their way into the kitchen where Tom set about making the coffee. Max was the first to talk.

"You know, Becky shouldn't have any coffee. As wound up as she is, the caffeine could kill her. She might have a heart attack!"

Tom chuckled. "I know what you mean, but we don't have any decaf. You know, I've never seen her so excited. She used to be like this a lot, before the kids came along. I had forgotten how cute she is when she is like this. I guess being a mom changed her a lot more than I thought."

"She's still that perky little cutie that you married. I've always thought you were a lucky guy."

Becky arrived in the kitchen with a much calmer demeanor. She walked over and gave Tom a hug. "I'm better now. Sorry, guys. It has been a VERY interesting morning."

Tom poured three cups of coffee and they each picked one up. Seeing Tom pick up the coffee pot, Becky snatches up a potholder to place under it on the table. They each took a seat and their first sip of coffee before Max said, "So. Let's hear it from the beginning. Slowly, please."

By now, Becky had calmed down completely and she began telling what she has found out. Max and Tom listened intently as she related the story of the dream, the book and the priest. Though she talked for over 30 minutes, the men never interrupted her. They were both busy making mental notes of the entire tale.

She finally came to the end of the story and said, "That's when I paid and left."

She looked directly at Max for some sign of how well she had done on her mission.

"That's very good, Becky. Very thorough on your part. I'm impressed. Really. I just don't get this dream thing. It kinda sounds farfetched to me."

"Several of the women said the same thing. But I had the same beautician that his wife uses. She told me she didn't believe it either at first. But when the priest became involved, that's when she started believing it. And that computer thing. Wow, that was really cool too!"

Max picked up on this immediately. "What computer thing? You didn't mention any computer thing."

Realizing she had skipped that part, she said, "When his wife went to talk to the priest, he got on his computer. Some kinda special search that priests have. They are hooked up straight to the Vatican. He typed in that books name and got this weird message about a 'Secured Section'. The wife was sure that the priest was going to get into trouble."

Hearing this, Max knew that Becky's information must be valid. It didn't make sense to him, but he had collected lots of information over the years that didn't make any sense to him. He had accomplished what they sent him to Texas for.

"Becky, you have exceeded my expectations by miles. I can't tell you how much this means to me. Between what I found out and what you just told me, I have what I came for. I just need to get my flight moved up. If you two will excuse me, I'll go in the other room and see if there is an earlier flight."

Max was up and out of the room quickly. Becky and Tom heard him talking to the airline reservationist. They clearly heard him say, "10:00 in the morning? That would be great. Thanks!" The sound of his flip phone closing barely preceded his return to the kitchen.

"So you got it changed to 10:00 in the morning?" Becky displayed a fake little pout.

"Yep, I did. So I have one last night here in the Big D. You guys want some company for dinner?"

Becky stood and walked over to give Max a big hug.

"We would love to have you for dinner again. We want to spend as much time as we can with you, Max. Who knows when we'll see you again?"

~ ~ ~

As the plane taxied to the terminal, Max realized that he was actually glad to be back in Rome. During the flight, he had shocked himself by telling a stewardess that he was headed HOME. He found it odd to be referring to Rome as home. He hadn't lived there that long, but it was his home now. He found himself looking forward to interacting with Beca and Tim again. Had he missed them? Nah, he was just being silly. So he rationalized these new feelings away as just a symptom of getting old.

With his baggage in tow, he was quickly picked up by a taxi and headed straight to his boss's office. During his phone call from his Dallas hotel, Bishop Westin had seemed very anxious to discuss his findings the moment he returned.

The Bishop's secretary smiled as Max entered the office.

"Hi, Max! Good trip?"

"Yes, but it is such a long flight. You know, the older I get, the harder it is to do these long flights and come on in to work once I get here."

"You're not old, Max. Just well worn. He's waiting for you. Go on in."

Opening the door slowly so as not to interrupt his boss, he saw him seated behind that big desk. The Bishop looked up and a huge smile spread across his face. "Max! Come on in, please."

He began to stand and motioned for Max to take a seat at the table by the window. Max rolled his luggage up against the wall by the door. Then he draped his overcoat across the parked bag and took the same chair he had used the last time he was in here.

The Bishop slid quickly into the seat opposite Max. "I trust your trip went smoothly?"

"Yes, very."

"So tell me everything you found out. Take your time and let me hear it again from the start."

Max had only given the Bishop the highlights over the phone.

So he began to go over every detail from the beginning. The Bishop sat with his hands folded in his lap while the story of the dream, the book, and the priest were presented in chronological order without any emotion or interpretation by Max. As his CIA training had instilled in him, he recounted the facts and did not offer any interpretation at all.

Once he had recited everything he had learned, he stopped and waited for the Bishop to speak.

"So this Mr. Parson is having a dream? He sees a book in this dream. A book he could not have possibly seen in real life. Yet he also knows the private name that this book was given by our previous Pope. He also hears a voice in this dream that says the Holy Father should be told to open it. And this man is not even Catholic? How can this be?"

"Bishop, if I may. I have a hunch we need to focus on this description of the book."

"The description of the book? Why so?"

"When he spoke of it, he was absolutely sure of the book's size. But what also struck me odd, was how he described the book as 'Not being like modern books'."

Max paused to survey the Bishop's face for a sign that he agreed. The Bishop was a blank page. "Go on, Max."

"Well sir, I remember seeing something similar in Father Latanye's department. The Father referred to them as manuscripts. When I mentioned the word 'manuscript' to Mr. Parson, his face lit up. He even remarked that he had heard that word also from somebody. He did not say who."

"So what do you suggest we do now, Max?"

"I believe it is time to have a sit down talk with Father Latanye. I'll bet he won't even be shocked. He may even welcome the talk in hopes he'll find out more about the book himself."

The Bishop was ever so slightly nodding his head 'yes' as he said, "I tend to agree with you. It is inevitable that we have this discussion with him. There is just one thing that still concerns me. How did Cardinal Mortello know so quickly that somebody was inquiring about the book?"

This was another reason why Max liked the Bishop. They both thought alike.

"That has crossed my mind too. I'll bet that the Cardinal

is the one that Father Latanye went to see that day he left his department. Remember, I told you that even the people in his own department found it extremely odd for him to leave in the middle of the day. Then that very evening the Cardinal emails that fictitious 'No Reply' email address. And BOOM, that error message disappears from the system."

The Bishop suddenly sat completely upright in his chair. He placed his elbows on the table and clasped his hands together, fingers intertwined.

"That also explains why the Cardinal was right outside my office after you left me that day. You know, the day you informed me of all this. He was right there. I always thought that it was odd he would be in this building, and then to be on my floor as well. This is way beyond coincidence."

Max watched as the Bishop sank back into his chair before saying, "But I had better run all this by the Cardinal first. We really need his blessing before we talk to Father Latanye. Plus, I told you there were things I couldn't share with you Max. And because of this, I'll need the Cardinal's input on how to handle the conversation."

Max nodded 'yes' without saying a word. He understood completely. He also now knew that the Bishop was skirting something that Max already believed to be true. Max now knows for sure that the book exists. The Bishop himself just said so without even realizing it. He also felt that both the Pope and the Cardinal were the ones hiding the book for whatever reason. Max even thought that the Bishop was now fully involved in hiding the existence of the book.

"Max, you have done well. I know you must be very tired. Today is Thursday. Take a long weekend and relax. I'll talk to you sometime next week."

"Thanks. I will." And Max rose to collect his coat and bag before exiting the office.

~ ~ ~

Cardinal Mortello sat silently in his office chair. The chair was slightly turned to one side. He was leaning back with his head laid on the high back of the chair. His gaze was upward towards the ceiling, but his eyes were wide open. Bishop Westin was seated in a chair in front of the large office desk. He had just finished relaying all that Max had found out on his trip to Dallas. The Cardinal had his left hand on his desk, silently tapping one finger while he thought. Without even looking at the Bishop, he began to think out loud.

"A dream. A book. If it weren't for him knowing the exact name of the book, I'd write this all off as a hoax." He finally sat up and swiveled his chair back towards the desk, so he faced the Bishop. "And you are absolutely sure of his description of the book?"

"Yes, he gave it directly to Max."

"I don't mean to sound as if I doubt Max's report." He began to run one hand through the thinning grey hair that only existed on the sides of his head.

"Cardinal, I take it that the description is accurate."

With no hesitation, the Cardinal said, "Yes. I do not understand how, but it is extremely accurate. I have witnessed many miraculous things in my 42 years of serving the Church. I have uttered the words 'God moves in mysterious ways' more times than I have hairs on my head." He smiled and motioned to his thinning hair before continuing.

"If we are to believe that this is happening by God's own divine hand, then we must follow this to whatever end it leads us. It appears that our way forward will soon require the full cooperation of all that are involved in this event so far. The planning and implementation thereof will be delicate, to say the least. I must seek the guidance of His Eminence, the Holy Father himself."

"Do you have any further instructions for me or my staff at this time?"

The Cardinal simply said, "No."

Bishop Westin rose and gestured with an ever so slight bow of his head. He turned and left the Cardinal to his solitary task of informing the Pope.

~ ~ ~

There was a man dressed in white and sitting in an ornate chair. This was a seat for power. A seat made of gold and plush red velvet. He and his chair had held audiences with a lonely few in this inner chamber; a chamber that lay deep within the Vatican. Decisions had been made in this chair by him, and by those who had served their beloved Church before him. Yes, decisions that had guided many major events throughout history. They had been made and delivered from this chair. This was a very special chair in a very hallowed chamber.

Cardinal Mortello had just completed the telling of Max's trip and all that had been discovered. There had been an exchange of ideas on how to move forward. The conversation had ended with a question requiring this powerful man's decision. There was a very slight movement of his hand. This action sent the Cardinal to one knee. With his head bowed, he kissed the ring upon that hand. The man in white said only one word.

"Yes."

CHAPTER 8

Envoy to the Dreamer – The Preparation

A private jet was warming up on the tarmac of a secluded Italian airport. Two men in pilot's uniforms were outside the craft. One stood motionless by the open door while the other made a routine inspection pass around the tires. Headlights emerged from between two large hangars and turned in their direction. Hearing a whistle, one pilot stopped his inspection and ran to take his place on the opposite side of the open door.

The small black limousine slowed and began making a small arc towards the crew. It stopped when the rear car door was only a few feet from the steps leading into the plane. The driver hopped out quickly and ran around to open the rear passenger side door. Once open, he stepped back and waited for the occupant to emerge from the back seat. The rear door on the other side of the car also swung open, but opened by the person inside.

Similarly-dressed men exited both sides of the limousine at the same time. The only visible difference between them was that one man wore a vivid red sash around his waist. This man was ushered onto the plane first, followed by the other. The limousine driver and one pilot removed luggage from the car's trunk and placed it in a storage compartment near the plane's tail. The pilot secured the compartment door while the driver hustled around and into his car. It left immediately and disappeared into the dark. The two pilots entered the plane and the sound of the door closing was barely heard above the noise of the jet engines. With-in minutes the plane had taxied to the main runway, began to accelerate and escaped into the night sky.

~ ~ ~

Mathew was hard at work in his parish office. He patted both hands on the desk as he had just completed writing his next ser-mon. His pleasure of having finished it gave way to curiosity at the sound of footsteps coming down the hall. The sound was of several sets of feet. Who could be coming to see him at this time of day? He pushed his chair back just a little, so he could stand if it was someone important. He doubted anyone important would be coming to see him, but you never knew. They were probably just leaving the building through the back door.

To his surprise, Head Father Balgoni stepped from the dark-ened hallway into the light of the office. He was smiling, but said nothing before turning to look back into the hallway. A familiar voice came out of the dark.

"Hello Mathew, my friend."

Then Father Latanye stepped into view. Mathew was stunned and just stood frozen like a statue.

Finally, he responded. "Rick? I can't believe it? You're here?" He began to move around the desk to properly greet his old friend, but stopped short as he saw another man emerge from the hallway. His mind was racing to catch up with what was un-folding before him. Was that a red sash? It was. Was this a Car-dinal? No way! Then he heard Rick's voice.

"Mathew, allow me to introduce you to Cardinal Mortello."

Mathew's face displayed a disbelieving smile as he stepped forward to greet the Cardinal.

"Cardinal Mortello. It is a real honor to meet you in person. I've read all of your writings and based several of my sermons on them." He was interrupted by Head Father Balgoni.

"Mathew, the Cardinal has some things to discuss with you if you are available."

"Of course I'm available. Please, may I offer you a seat?" Mathew motioned toward his trusted table in the corner of the room. The Head Father stepped aside to allow the Cardinal to be seated first. Father Latanye was next to be seated. Then to

Mathew's amazement, the Head Father stepped towards the door before speaking.

"I'll be in my office, Cardinal. If you need me for anything, just have Mathew call." Before he could step out of the office, the Cardinal spoke.

"Milo, I am looking forward to that chess game you promised me. I've been practicing and I fully intend to thrash you this time, my friend."

"Antonis. I haven't been practicing. In fact, I haven't played in a very long time. You may just do it this time. I'll pray that I can still give you an interesting game." And with that, he turned and left Mathew alone with his royal guests.

The Cardinal looked at Mathew and motioned for him to join them at the table.

"Mathew, I am sorry for our rude and somewhat dramatic entrance."

"Not at all, Cardinal. Your visit here today will be the highlight of my entire year."

"You flatter me, young man. I know that you are wondering why Father Balgoni did not stay. Please do not worry that he may be offended by my wanting to speak to you alone. We spoke two days ago about this trip, and I informed him of the reason at that time. Besides, he is a personal friend of mine from when we were younger. Our families have known each other for several generations."

"I gathered that you two must have known each other for a while. I didn't even know he played chess."

"Yes he does, and he is annoyingly good at it. In the many times that we have played together over the years, I have never won. Not once." The Cardinal chuckled, and the corners of his eyes wrinkled as he did. Mathew only knew him through his Church writings, but he could already tell that he was going to like this man. More to the point, there was a lot he could learn from the Cardinal.

Mathew noticed that the Cardinal had glanced at the office door several times. He didn't know if the Cardinal was expecting somebody else, or would like it closed. With no sounds coming from the hall, he must want it closed.

"Would you like me to close the door?"

"Yes, I think that would be best. Thank you."

Mathew closed the door and quickly returned to take a seat.

"How can I be of service to you, Cardinal?"

"I apologize in advance for this straightforward approach, but time seems to be of importance. I am here seeking your help to meet a particular man."

Mathew knew the man must be John Parson, even before the Cardinal said so. That was why Rick was here. Mathew hoped that neither of his guests noticed the small twitch that rippled up his back, through his neck and caused his eyes to blink twice. He now knew that the Cardinal was the powerful person whom Rick had consulted for help finding the book. But what was the Cardinal really after here? He had many aides that he could have sent to do this. Why was the Cardinal himself here?

"Are you OK, young man?" The Cardinal asked.

"Yes, just sat down wrong or something."

"I want to be very candid with you, Mathew. May I call you Mathew?"

"Of course."

"Good, good. In order for me to do what I have come to Dallas for, I will have to share a few..." The Cardinal paused for a second. Once again, he glanced at the door, even though it was closed. "Some specific Church matters that require a very high level of secrecy." This time the Cardinal paused while looking directly into Mathew's eyes. It was obvious that he expected a reply.

"Of course, Cardinal. I understand completely and will not let you down."

"Good, good. Father Latanye has conveyed some rather startling information to me about your searching for a particular book. I think that by now, you surely realize that this book is in the possession of the Church. We, or should I say, I need to learn more about Mr. John Parson's dream."

Mathew was having a hard time holding his emotions in check. What a revelation for the Cardinal to admit the book existed, and to also acknowledge he knew of the dream.

"It is perplexing as to how he knows the name of the book. I would like for you to garner an audience for me with Mr. Parson. I very much desire to hear of this dream directly from him. To hear it in his own words. To see his expressions as he renders the telling. Please do not think I am here to discredit him in any fashion. It is an undeniable fact that he knows the name of a book that the world does not know exists. This by itself is more than enough evidence to warrant our complete acceptance that he is an instrument in one of our Lord's plans. It is our duty to learn more, so that we may learn out part in this plan. Will you help me?"

Mathew knew that a quick answer of 'Yes' was often taken as a sign of thoughtless agreement. Such a hasty agreement was usually prone to falter in the future. He hesitated so that his answer would be perceived as one coming with a deliberate commitment.

"I will, Your Eminence."

"Good, good. Ricardo had assured me that you were a man of trust. I am pleased to say that I now know that you are."

"Cardinal, I have to tell you that John Parson was reluctant to speak to me at first. And I had his wife on my side about the two of us talking. It is true that he opened up to me, but that just happened spontaneously after I rudely went to his home unannounced. I doubt that you would like to make such an entrance and hope for such an outcome."

The Cardinal sat back in his chair. His demeanor was calming, as he warmly smiled at Mathew before turning towards Rick.

"You were right, Father Ricardo. I *do* like him." He turned his gaze back towards Mathew and continued.

"He has a brilliant future ahead of him. One that will hold many chances to serve his Church from a more prestigious level. Now I have a question. When you arrange for my meeting Mr. Parson, will his wife also be present?"

"Yes she would probably be there. They do everything together. No children. But I am certain that she is trustworthy. I have no reason to doubt her discretion."

The Cardinal shifted a little in his chair before speaking. "I'm afraid that we have information of her telling others of both her husband's dream, and of a priest who is a family friend. It happened at a beauty salon. It is my opinion that this was merely her way of seeking solace from acquaintances. No sinister motive whatsoever. However, this gives us pause for concern. We cannot have her conveying a person of my stature's involvement in this matter. The mention of a Cardinal along with this book's name would trigger a flurry of historical investigators looking for it. The Church simply cannot have this level of attention brought upon it."

"I understand the delicate balance between a man and wife sharing all that they know. It is my hope that a non-abusive path can be found to allow Mr. Parson to meet us alone. A path that will not alienate him from us for his wife's sake. After all, we seek information from him. So, Mathew, how do you suggest that we proceed?"

"Well I don't know right off the top of my head, but I'm positive the Lord will provide a way for us." And with that said, his office phone rang.

Not knowing if he should answer it or not, he hesitated. The Cardinal motioned toward the phone with a nod. Mathew leapt from his chair to answer it while saying, "Excuse me".

"Hello. Yes I know it is you, Margie. She is? Oh, she is! I'm afraid that I have visitors, and..."

The Cardinal said, "Please, if you have something to do, we can wait."Mathew cupped his hand over the phone and said, "It's one of my weekly confessionals. She's up front. I could get someone else to see her this once."

The Cardinal is shaking his head. "No, no, please attend to her first. We, like you, are servants of our flock."

Mathew replaced the phone to his ear.

"It's OK, Margie. Tell her that I'll. Yes, Margie. I know you know who my visitors are. Yes we all know that you know everything that goes on inside these walls. Yes, I will tell him. Now, please tell Linda that I'll be right there. Thank you."

Mathew hung up and shook his head a little while smiling at his guests.

"Our office receptionist, Margie Pendalton. She is the sweetest 75-year old busybody you will ever meet. Thank you for understanding. If you will excuse me, gentlemen."

He turned to leave but stopped a few steps from the door. Now facing the table again, he said, "Cardinal, it is a stroke of luck that Linda has come for her confessional while you are here. She is known by all as the 'Cookin Mama' and actually has a business doing just that. Her meals are exquisite. Truly, the best food you have ever eaten. Once she knows you are here, she will practically demand to cater a meal for you. Believe me. You will want her to do this!"

Again Mathew turned and started out the door. With his head under the door jamb, he stopped again and snapped his fingers. The sound echoed up and down the hallway. He spun around and proclaimed, "I have it! Yes, God may just have provided us a way. I'll explain when I return." This time he actually cleared the door and his footsteps scurried off into the distance.

~ ~ ~

Linda was sitting in a pew adjacent to the confessional, patiently waiting for Mathew to arrive. Hearing his approach, she stood and stepped towards the booth. Mathew noticed that they were totally alone, so he softly called her name. She stopped and watched as he came to a halt only a foot from her.

"Hello, Linda. I'm sorry I'm late."

She smiles and said, "Father, you shouldn't have left them just to come see me."

Mathew was not really surprised that she knew he had visitors. It could only be one person.

"Margie?"

"Of course, Father! She knows everything. Or hasn't she told you?"

"Yes, she reminds me of it daily."

"So I think you will want to do this quickly, right? Or do you want to do it another day?"

"No, no. You are here and so am I. But first, I'd like to sit out here and talk about something." He motioned for her to move back to the pew.

He slid in next to her and she said, "You want me to cook for him, RIGHT?"

"Yes, that is one thing I'd like to discuss with you. I have already enticed him to partake of your heavenly culinary creations. I thought you might be interested in this."

"Interested in cooking for the Pope's right hand man! You bet! I'll fix something that will make him want to leave Rome for Dallas."

"So that is a yes."

"Yes, a big Texas yes! Now you said that was one thing. What else?"

"Now this is strictly between us, Linda. Ok?"

"Yes, Father."

"I have a personal favor I'd like to ask you. Please feel free to decline if you would rather not do this."

"Father, I can't imagine you asking me anything that I wouldn't do. So tell me what it is."

"Ok. I have an acquaintance. You don't know her. She and her husband are not in this Church. In fact, they are not even Catholic. However, you have met her at one of Ryan's parties many years ago. I doubt you would remember."

"Ok, so what can I do?"

"My friend's name is Barbara Parson. I found out that she has joined your cooking site and is one of your biggest new fans. She made a remark that she would love to meet you and talk about cooking. I was hoping to get you to spend some time with her tomorrow night or the night after. If you are willing, of course."

"Well Father, I would love to do this for you, but I'm leaving tomorrow morning to go on a three day cooking class event. I'd be very happy to do it when I return."

Mathew exhaled slowly and rubbed the side of his neck while he thought of how he could make this work. He doubted the Cardinal wanted to wait for three days, but it might have to be this way. Linda guessed that the Father was trying to make some puzzle pieces fit, and it probably had something to do with the Cardinal being here.

"Father, I have an idea. I can't cancel my classes. These people have all prepaid. But if your friend really wants to spend time with me, do you think she would like to be my assistant in these classes? You said she can cook, right?"

Mathew couldn't believe his ears. God truly worked in mysterious ways! It was an old cliché, but a true one.

"Linda! That would be absolutely wonderful. You sure you don't mind?"

"Mind? The truth is that I always need help in these classes. There are going to be 22 people there. If she is willing to help, tell her to come on!"

Mathew had a huge smile on his face as he fumbled for his cell phone in his cassock pocket. "Sorry, Linda. I always have it turned off, so it will take a minute to come on. Then I'll call her. She is going to be so excited. I hope."

The phone flashed to life. Several melodic tones were heard then Mathew quickly pulled up Barbara's number and hit Call.

"Hello Barbara? Yes, it's me. I am fine and you?" He looked at Linda and winked. "I have something that I hope you will be interested in. How would you like to be an assistant for the 'Cookin Mama' at one of her classes?"

Linda's eyes widened at the sound of Barbara's excitement through the phone. Mathew waited until the screech died down before putting the phone back to his ear.

"Sounds like you're interested! I thought you would be."

"Yes! Yes! Yes! I would love to do this. I can't tell you how much I would love to do this! Yes!"

"So it's a yes! I'll give her your number and you should hear from her in an hour or so."

"Thank you, Mathew. I really mean it. Thank you."

He closed his phone and smiled at Linda. "I told you she was a big fan of yours."

Linda reached into her purse and pulled out her cell phone. "I'll just put her phone number into my cell and I'll call her on my way home."

Mathew gave her the number and then she asked, "So, when can I cook for him? How about tonight? I can feed them before they have that big chess match I heard about."

Though at first he was totally surprised, he knew that it had to be one person.

"Margie again?"

"Of course, Father. She knows all and tells all!" They both laughed a little before he added, "I'll ask about the meal when I show the Cardinal to the Head Father's office. Then I'll call you, OK?"

"I'll get started the minute I get home." With that said, they headed for their respective sides of the confessional. Mathew was so happy that he found it hard to listen to what Linda was saying. But, as usual, it pertained to the same thing she always talked about and he gave his normal responses. Once done, they both exited the booths.

"Thank you, Father. See you next week."

"Go with God, my child." was his business reply. But then he leaned closer and whispered, "I owe you one, Linda."

Her eyes sparkled as she said, "It pays to have important people in your debt!" She turned and walked toward the exit. Mathew turned also and he began to hurry back to his office. He was so excited about the news he had for his guest.

Mathew flew into his office to find Rick looking over his book collection. The Cardinal was seated and appeared to have already gotten one from the shelf. At the sound of Mathew rushing back into the room, the Cardinal closed the book and looked up.

"No need to hurry, Mathew. We have been discussing your book collection. It is small but very impressive."

Mathew noticed that the Cardinal had the book that listed all of the old books known to exist. "That is my most valuable book. I use that reference book all the time."

The Cardinal pointed the book towards Mathew and said, "I have this very book in my office. I keep meaning to get the most current release so I'll be up to date, but I never do it. I just feel so comfortable with the one I have. It is a cherished gift from Ricardo."

Mathew turned to look at Rick and said, "I feel the same way about that copy. It also came from an old friend. Right, Rick?"

Both men had their eyes on Rick's back, as he appeared to be ignoring them while he continued looking at the book collection. Without even facing them, he just commented, "I know. I know. But it makes such a good gift."Then he turned around and returned to his chair empty-handed. "However, unlike you two, I always get the latest edition when it comes out."

The Cardinal motioned for Mathew to sit with them. He took his seat just as the Cardinal spoke.

"I trust your confessional went well?"

Mathew remembered why he was hurrying back, and his excitement returned to his face. "Yes, it was very productive. I have some exciting news! I've made arrangements for Mrs. Parson to be away while we visit Mr. Parson." He paused, then smiled and nodded his head just ever so slightly.

Both men raised their eyebrows in unison, but it is the Cardinal who spoke. "You have? So quickly? But how? You were only gone a few minutes."

"The parishioner that came for her confessional teaches cooking classes. Barbara, Mrs. Parson, is a big fan of Linda's cooking classes. So, I asked Linda if she would do me a favor and spend some time with Barbara. You know, as a treat for one of my friends. It just so happens that Linda is going to Austin tomorrow to teach classes over the next three days. She said she could use the help. The two of them are on the phone right now. I'll check with Barbara here in an hour or so. I was thinking about calling Mr. Parson tomorrow after Barbara leaves with Linda."

The Cardinal nodded and looked at Rick. "This is good. I like it. But one thing? How do you think he will react with you calling him right after his wife leaves on a trip that you engineered? Surely, he will know what has happened. What will you say if he asks you?"

Mathew had thought of this while walking back to his office. He didn't even hesitate. "I thought of that, too. I will be honest and explain that I have reasons. If it gets too tense, I can always remind him that he has admitted to hiding many things about this issue from his wife. I could say I was under the impression that this might be one of them. Then I could apologize for assuming such a thing and offer to wait until she returns."

Again the Cardinal nodded. "Let us hope he doesn't take you up on your offer to wait until she returns."

"He will not. He has spoken to me very openly, and we are friends now. I feel confident that he will at most, hesitate a little, but he will accept our visit."

The Cardinal seemed pleased as he addressed Rick. "Again, I have to agree with you Ricardo. Our Father Cobleir is a very resourceful individual. He obviously thinks quickly." Then he leaned towards the table as a way of accenting what he was about to add.

"I feel that God's will is moving us all. Just like pieces on a chessboard. Things are happening and falling into place so neatly. His divine hand is truly at work here." He stopped to glance at each of them, eye to eye.

Mathew rubbed his hand on the back of his head before

slowly speaking. "I think we should start discussing exactly how our conversation with Mr. Parson should unfold. What each of our roles will be? Who is going to lead the conversation? In general, what you hope to accomplish by the visit."

"Yes, I agree, Mathew." The Cardinal slowly breathed in and out before he continued. "As for what I hope to accomplish. I do not have anything in particular that I am seeking from this man. As I just said, I have no doubt that there is a divine purpose at work here and Mr. Parson is the key to whatever it is. It just seems to me, that having him speak of his dream is the place to start. We must have faith that we will recognize whatever sign is given. We all may soon experience a very profound spiritual event. The type that only comes along once in a lifetime, or maybe only once in generations."

Rick finally joined the conversation. "How are you going to explain both of us being there?"

Mathew again answered quickly. "Well, he is already aware of both of you. Let me explain. I first told his wife that I was going to ask a friend to help me look for the book. That would be you, Rick. Then I later told both of them about Rick having gone to a friend of his for help finding the book. That turns out to be the Cardinal. So I will just be introducing him to two people that I've mentioned to him before. Then the Cardinal could just ask to hear about the dream."

"This should work well for us. It's simple and straightforward. Unless you have anything more, Ricardo and I should leave you to the rest of your daily activities." As the Cardinal began to stand, Mathew quickly rose and moved his chair to clear an easier path to the door.

"I am actually done for the day. I was finishing up when you arrived. Shall I show you to the Head Father's office?"

"Yes. That would be splendid." The Cardinal spoke over his shoulder as he made his way to the door. "Ricardo, you should take this opportunity to spend time with your friend. I intend to do the same with Father Milo. We haven't spoken face to face for years. I am looking forward to reminiscing about our younger days."

Rick stood while the Cardinal prepared to leave the office. It was a sign of respect, as well as political courtesy. "I would love to sit and chat for a while with Mathew. I will be fine here until you return."

Mathew stepped into the hall and extended his arm in the direction they must go. "Cardinal, right this way please."

Rick watched as they both disappeared into the dark hallway before sitting back down. He was listening as Mathew told the Cardinal he would take him up the back way so they would not be trapped by Margie the receptionist. Their voices and footsteps gently faded into silence.

He noticed the reference book that the Cardinal had left lying on the table. After picking it up and turning to the first page, he said out loud, "Edition Three? Oh Mathew, I really must get you the current one."

~ ~ ~

"Boss? Hey, wake up boss!" Bill was pushing John Parson's shoulder in an effort to wake him up. John slowly opened his eyes and looked around, saying "What? Where am I?"

"You're in your office. You have a bad night last night or something?" Bill asked as he stepped back around to the front of the desk. John's eyes were blinking rapidly in an effort to gain focus. He shifted his weight forward so his old chair leaned upright towards his desk.

"What makes you think I had a bad night last night?"

"Well, I've been by here twice in the last 15 minutes and you were out like a light."

"I was? That long?"

"Yep, and you were mumbling something, but I couldn't understand what you were saying. Just that there were two of them."

"I said that?"

"Yes sir, you did. What were they getting on?"

"I think a plane. I was talking out loud?"

"Yes sir. You're not really awake now are you? You feelin' okay, boss?"

"Yes, Bill. You need something?"

"I just finished working on the minivan. I put the paperwork in your basket." He began to leave but stopped and said, "Oh, by the way. The white pickup needs parts. I called it in and we should have them in an hour. We're going across the street for a burger. You want one?"

"Yes, sounds good. Get me the usual. Wait a minute." John reached behind his back and fumbled to get his wallet out. He victoriously displayed it to Bill, and then looked through it. "Here is 30 dollars for all of us. Tell Lewis that lunch is on me today."

Bill snatched the money from John's hand. "Thanks, boss! Be right back."

John was completely awake now, and he felt a little foolish that Bill had caught him asleep at his desk again. Oh well, he was the owner. It's not like anyone was going to fire him. It had been a really slow day, and nobody had come in for the last two hours. Bill and the other mechanic had been steadily doing their work. John had been doing his also when he apparently fell asleep.

He didn't remember even putting his head back, but he sure remembered what he had dreamed about. It had seemed so real. But why would he dream about two guys getting on a plane? At least he's finally had a different dream. Too bad it was during the day and in his office. Why worry about it? He must have seen it on TV and just got it stuck in his head. He had paperwork to do and he needed to get to it.

He must have dropped his favorite mechanical pencil when he fell asleep. It wasn't on the desk, so he began to look on the floor when the phone rang. His right hand reached out and picked up the phone while he was still leaning over to look under the desk for the pencil.

"Hello. Auto Correct. John speaking. Can I help you?"

The sound of his wife's voice came pouring out of the phone so fast and so loud, that he almost dropped it.

"Not so loud honey, and slow down. I'm not a speed listener, babe. What cooking class?"

"A cooking class with the 'Cookin Mama'. I'm going to Austin in the morning with her. She asked me to be her assistant for the next three days. Isn't that WONDERFUL?"

"Austin? Tomorrow? This is kind of short notice, isn't it?"

"Well, maybe. Ok, it's short, but we didn't have anything planned and I didn't think that you would mind."

"No, no Barb. I don't mind. You just caught me off guard a little. Hey, it sounds like fun. You always said you wanted to meet her. You should have plenty of time to talk if you are going to be there three days. I'm happy for you."

"I am so HAPPY! You will be too. Just think how much more I'll be able to cook for you when I spend this much time with her. I can hardly wait! She is going to pick me up tomorrow morning at 8:30 and we are driving down. This is so exciting!"

"Sounds like it. What happened? Did you sign up for a drawing or something on her website? How did she pick you?"

"Oh, Mathew talked to her this morning at the Church. I guess she mentioned she needed help. I just can't believe he gave her my name. I owe him big time for this!"

"Mathew gave her your name? That's cool. He's a nice guy."

"Well I have to start getting ready for this trip. I have to go shopping for a few things. I wonder if there is time to get my hair done this afternoon. I got to go, honey. Lots to do."

"Shopping? Hair done? Didn't you just... Hello? Barb?" She had already hung up.

Knowing her, she was probably halfway out the door. He was smiling as he envisioned her flitting around a kitchen helping people do what she loved to do so much. This could be nice for him, too. Yes, he would have to make his own meals, but he could catch up on the TV shows he's recorded. There must be more than ten episodes of several of his favorite shows. He'll have nothing to do but kick back and watch TV. Besides, who's going to come see him?

~ ~ ~

Rick was still thumbing through the old reference book when he heard the sounds of someone coming down the hall. His gaze was drawn to the door as Mathew entered.

"Hey, Rick. Sorry to keep you waiting. I stopped by the break room and picked us up some tea."

"Mathew, that was thoughtful. Thank you."He reached out and took the glass. Being polite, he took a sip before placing it on the coaster that Mathew had placed on the table. "Every time I come to America, it is always nice to have ice tea again for the first time. I forget between trips, just how comforting it really is.

Did you get the Cardinal and the Head Father together?"

"Yes, and you'll be happy to know that the four of us will enjoy a delicious catered meal here in the Church tonight. Linda will have the food all up here around 6:30 this evening. Then it seems that those two will be up late tonight playing chess. I still can't believe the Head Father has never mentioned liking to play chess before."

"I think I know why, Mathew. The Cardinal didn't tell you everything about Milo's mastery of chess. When he was younger, he was a somewhat well known chess prodigy. He was undefeated for years. Then he had a vision of the Church and gave it all up to help others. He is a remarkable man. I have the utmost respect for him. He gave up something he truly loved in order to serve God. These days, he only uses his chess skills to humble the Church's hierarchy. Just as he will most definitely do to the Cardinal this evening."

"So, now that we are alone... what's going on with the Cardinal? You two almost gave me a heart attack when you just strolled into my office like that."

"Well, I'm not sure there is much to tell. You now know that it was the Cardinal I went to about the book. It seems that he has found out a lot of things these past few weeks. I can tell you this. I know for a fact that the Holy Father himself is behind this trip."

"Rick, are you saying the Cardinal confided in you that the Holy Father is also involved?"

"No, no, Mathew. I know because we flew here on a private Church aircraft. Also, everyone knows the Cardinal is the Holy Father's right hand. Since he came himself, I'm positive that he did so because the Holy Father wouldn't entrust this to anyone else." Rick turned his head slightly, lifted his eyebrows and nodded his head twice.

"Has he said anything about the book? What it is? Where it is? Anything?"

"No, he hasn't offered anything more than what you heard here today. I have to admit I am very curious now, ever more so than before. However, I get the impression that the Church doesn't really want anymore to be known about this book than is already known."

"Rick, what did I get myself into here? Seems to me that

the Church isn't too happy about any of this coming out. What could be so special about this book that the top two people in the Church are actively engaged in such secrecy?"

"Mathew, my friend. Do not worry. Did you not hear the Cardinal himself say that you would have chances for more prestigious titles? This intriguing scenario will most definitely benefit your standing with the Church in the long run. I have always known you would achieve great things in the Church. I just knew it."

"Thank you my friend. I have always felt comfort from your wisdom."

"Mathew, I have a very big request."

"Anything Rick. What can I do for you?"

Rick dipped his head like a little kid and smiled really big, as would a child about to ask something silly. "Since the Cardinal is tied up with the Head Father, could you take me to get one of those delicious flavored ice treats? I have dreamed of one since the Cardinal told me I was bound for America."

Mathew laughed out loud as he recalled the first snow cone that Rick ever had. He was like a young child who had just seen his first ice cream. "Yes, Rick. There is a snow cone stand just 30 minutes from here. Let's go, my friend. My treat!"

Rick was up and in the hall in two seconds while repeating, "Come, come, my friend. We must get there before they close."

Mathew turned out his office light and thought to himself, *This must be what it's like to have children!*

~ ~ ~

Mathew took Rick for a snow cone. They ate them at a park while watching a little league soccer game. Rick was most impressed with the American children playing a sport that was so dear to most Italians. Yes, every small Italian child had dreams of playing soccer for their beloved National team.

Later that evening, Linda lived a dream of her own. She catered a well-received meal to the second most powerful person in the Catholic Church. Rick and Mathew felt obligated to stay through most of the first chess match. Fortunately for them, it proved to be a very short match that ended in less than three minutes. Then they both excused themselves on the grounds that they were tired. Mathew volunteered to drive Rick back to his hotel.

After depositing his friend at the lobby entrance, he spent the entire ride home thinking about his impending phone call with John Parson tomorrow morning. As he locked his car and entered his house, he decided to have one glass of wine before bed. Otherwise he knew he would lay awake for hours just thinking.

The ringing of his alarm clock was proof that his plan had worked and worked well. To his surprise, he barely remembered his head falling upon his pillow. The night was gone and he felt great! Jumping up, he rushed through his morning routine. He was dressed, in his car and on the road well before the Dallas morning rush hour traffic was due to appear. His was the first car in the church parking lot. Crossing the distance from car to door, he felt unbelievably relaxed and was enjoying the fresh morning air. Down the hallway and through his door, he flipped the light switch as he tacked to the left of his desk.

He had sat down and turned on his PC when the phone rang. Who could this be? He should be the only person in the building. Lifting the phone to his ear on the second ring, he heard her voice.

"Margie? I thought I was the first. You saw me come in. No, I had forgotten that you told me you always park by the east side entrance. No, I do not believe my visitors will be in this morning. Of course, I will tell them that you missed meeting them yesterday. I'm sure they will be here again this afternoon. Yes, I'll make sure that you get to meet the Cardinal. No, I wasn't aware that he looked just like your third husband. He had a stroke just like the first. Really? That is a big coincidence. Yes, and have a good morning yourself."The woman was everywhere. Her little cubbyhole didn't even have a window. He wondered how she saw him. What an amazing little old woman. He didn't know that she had survived two previous husbands.

The rest of the morning was the usual Church business, mixed with a lot of staring at the clock on his office wall. Finally, it was 10:00. He had decided to make sure that Linda and Barbara were well on their road trip before he called John. He straightened his desk and wiped down his PC monitor. Yes, he was just stalling now and he knew it. It was time to get this done. With the number of John's business office dialed, he finally heard the sound of ringing.

"Hello. Auto Correct. John speaking. How can I help you?"

"Good morning, John. It's Mathew Cobleir."

"Good morning." John almost called him Father, but stopped short before adding "Mathew."

Mathew laughed on the inside before he said, "Am I interrupting your work? If so, I could call back later."

"No, not at all Mathew. In fact, I'd like to thank you for hooking up Barbara with that 'Cookin Mama'. Barb was bouncing off the walls all last night. She was so excited that I didn't think she would be able to get to sleep. But, she fell asleep faster than she ever has."

"So Linda picked her up and they got off OK?"

"Oh, yes! I have never seen Barb get ready and into a car so quickly. I wish you could have seen the smile on her face. It was all thanks to you, buddy. Appreciate it."

"Linda came in for her weekly confessional yesterday and one thing led to another. You know what I mean. Then she mentioned the class, and that there were 22 people signed up for it this time. It was just perfect timing."

Mathew felt like he was pretty close to the truth here. It wasn't that far off. Well, not really.

"Yes, I know exactly what you mean. So what can I do for you, Mathew?"

The moment of truth had arrived. Here goes.

"John, someone has come a long way to speak with you. I was hoping to make arrangements for a meeting."

John's head shook a little. Then he squinted as if a bright light just hit him. He didn't know why. But that dream he had in his office yesterday jumped into focus. The time he was taking to sort this out caused Mathew to feel very uneasy.

"Don't you mean there are two men who have come a long way to see me?" John couldn't believe he'd said that. What was getting into him? He couldn't believe that his dreams were starting to affect him like this.

Mathew was frozen in his chair by John's revelation that there were two men here to see him. Mathew had only said someone was here. How could John know this? Was he now having visions about current events? This was a definite item of interest to pass on to the Cardinal today.

"Well John, you are correct. There *are* two men here to see you. But, how did you know that?"

"I just know. Just like I know that one of them is wearing a big red belt made of fabric. Don't ask how I know, I just do."

"John, this is very eerie. But yes, one of them wears a red sash around his waist. He is a Cardinal in our faith. He has traveled all the way from Rome to speak with you ... if you will agree to meet him."

"Mathew, I find it rather odd that Barbara is miraculously swept out of town by a friend of yours. Right before you call to ask if I can meet someone. It kind of makes me think you, or they, didn't want Barbara around for this meeting. Why is that?"

Mathew and the Cardinal had thought this could happen. He didn't hesitate before answering, because that would sound like he had just thought this up.

"Yes, you are correct. It was my idea. I recalled that you had not told Barbara about going back to that museum display. I assumed that you were trying to shield her from certain aspects of this. I thought that THIS might be one of those things you would like to shield her from as well. I am sorry if I assumed incorrectly. I will ask them to wait until your wife returns. The important thing is that they get to talk with you. I didn't mean to offend you or slight Barbara in the least."

With that said, now Mathew had to wait for several agonizing seconds before John's voice returned to the phone.

"It's OK. I think that a meeting with your friends is a good idea. Let me assume that tonight would be good for all of you? You do plan on coming along, right?"

Mathew's heart was beating again, and he had regained a cautious smile. "Yes, I am coming along and tonight would be great. When would be a good time?"

"I'll grab a burger on the way home, you guys should eat too. I'll need to eat and clean up a bit before you get there. I'll have the coffee ready around 6:30."

"Yes, that would be wonderful. We will be there at 6:30 sharp. Thank you, John."

"See ya'll then, buddy."

With the dial tone in his ear, Mathew hung up also. Things were set for tonight. Mathew dialed the hotel where the Cardinal and Rick were staying. He asked for the Cardinal's room. This was a phone call that he did not have any anxiety about - except for the part about John already knowing there were two men here to see him. That was spooky.

CHAPTER 9

Envoy to the Dreamer – The Visit

Bill, got a minute?"

John was holding the door to the garage bay open. Bill looked up from under the hood of a car and nodded *yes*. "Be right there, boss."He slowly walked to the door while he wiped grease from his hands with a dirty red work rag.

"What's up, boss?"

"I hate to do this to you, but I need to head to the house a little early today. How close are you on that car you're working on now?"

"Be done in about 10 or 15 more minutes. You want me to watch the office and close up for ya?"

"Yes. I'll make it up to you later this week. You just pick the day."

"No need, boss. It's not a problem."

"It's only fair. Tell you what. You can just cut out an hour early on Friday and we'll call it even."

"I'd really rather take it Saturday. Kid's birthday."

"Glad you reminded me. Barb sent a present for Tommy. It's in the car. I'll get it now and put it in the office. You know we love him like he was our own. And you can just cut out two hours early Saturday. Have a good time."

"You sure?"

"Hey, I'm not just the boss. I'm the owner and you deserve it, Bill."

A huge smile spread across Bill's face before he said "Thanks!" and headed back to work.

John sprinted out to get the gift from his back seat and placed it right in the middle of his desk so Bill couldn't help but see it. He exited through the garage bay so he can render his usual, "See you guys tomorrow!"

He was in the truck and crossed the street to the burger shop. It only took three minutes to dash in, pay and pick up his order since he'd called it in ten minutes ago. He knew he should wait, but he decided to eat the onion rings right out of the sack on the way home. The burgers from that place were just way too big to eat while you drove. He would have to wait until he got home to enjoy that.

The smell of the hot food was really killing him on the drive home. It was a good thing he lived just ten minutes away. Swinging into the drive, he noticed his neighbor walking back from the mailbox. So John stuck his hand out and waved. He dashed over to his own box and grabbed what appeared to be junk mail. Once in the kitchen, he threw the mail on the table and sat down to eat. He wasn't sure if he finished so quickly out of hunger, or because he was having company in a little over an hour. Throwing the wrappings in the trash, he sprinted upstairs for a quick shower.

The hot water really felt good and relaxing. Wiping the steam from the mirror, he noticed he was smiling. Why? He actually felt excited. Yes, he was about to be visited by some high-ups from a Church. But that Church was not his church. It wasn't even his faith. Still, he felt good about tonight. Something good was going to happen here.

He was just slipping on his last shoe when the doorbell rang. He traversed the stairs just as quickly as he did coming up. John stopped short of the front door and paused to collect his thoughts. One last, slow deep breath, and he opened the door.

There stood Mathew in his full Church cassock. There were two other men still on the walk at the bottom of the steps. They were dressed in black cassocks as well. Both seem to be much older than Mathew or John. The younger of the two was helping the other one up the few steps to the porch.

Mathew said, "Hello, John. Sorry, I think we may be a little bit early. Traffic was just not there like usual."

"Yes, I saw the same thing on my way home. Please, come on in."

Mathew smiled and then stepped inside. It dawned on him that if his neighbors saw this sight, there would be questions from them the next time they talked. He stopped immediately once he was through the door, and turned to extend a hand towards the man coming next.

John assumed that since they were both so attentive to this one, he must be the highest-ranked of the three. That was when John noticed the bright red sash around his waist. This was the man he had seen in the office dream.

"Mathew, I have the coffee all set up in the breakfast nook like before."

"Great, John. But first allow me to introduce you to Cardinal Antonis Mortello."

John was not sure if proper etiquette was to shake his hand or not, but he extended his hand anyway. "Hello. I'm John Parson."

The Cardinal offered a very firm handshake himself. "It is a great pleasure to finally meet you, Mr. Parson. I want to thank you for allowing us to visit you at home on such short notice."

"It's my pleasure, sir. I understand that you both have traveled a very long way. I'm flattered by the gesture."

The Cardinal turned slightly and said, "Mr. Parson. I would like to introduce you to Father Latanye. He is a world-renowned researcher of ancient writings and documents. The Church is very fortunate to have him, and he is a dear personal friend of mine as well."

Rick stepped forward and again John extended his hand to greet the guest. John noticed that this man's grip was gentle and not as firm as the Cardinal's. He wondered if it was the byproduct of handling very fragile documents on a daily basis.

"Hello, Mr. Parson. Please call me Rick. Mathew seems fond of doing that. I've grown accustomed to it over the years."

"Rick, it is very nice to meet you. I think you are the one that Mathew told me about." John glanced at Mathew. "Right?"

"Yes. He is the friend I told you and Barbara about. The one

I had asked to help me find the book. Shall we go on and be seated, John?"

John felt embarrassed that he hadn't mentioned it first. "Oh, I'm sorry. Of course, right this way." He turned and led them into the kitchen, and over to the breakfast nook table. "Does everyone like coffee? If not, I can have some tea ready in 15 minutes. Be glad to do it."

Rick guided the Cardinal to a chair. Mathew pulled it out and the Cardinal was seated. Rick was maneuvering to take his seat and said, "Coffee sounds good."

John waited until the Cardinal looked up. He asked, "Cardinal, care for a cup?"

"May I call you John?" The Cardinal asked.

"Yes, sir. This is home. We are not very formal around here. So please, just make yourself at home."

"Thank you, John. I have felt very comfortable from the moment we arrived. You have a warm and inviting atmosphere in your home. You are to be envied. It seems so very relaxing."

While the others watched, John looked around the room as if admiring it for the first time. "You know. I've always felt comfortable here myself. But I've never really thought about how relaxing it really is in here." His eyes fell back on them and he said, "But all this was done by my wife. She is the one that makes this a home."

Rick commented, "You are a very fortunate man. I have never been any good at coordinating things like she has done in here. My small apartment in Rome is so sparsely decorated that a blind man could tell a bachelor lived there." They all laughed for just a moment. It was a good icebreaker.

With each guest's coffee in front of him, John placed his cup on the table and sat down. "So how do you want to start this off, Mathew?"

"Well, first I would like to continue something that we started in the front room. I told you who Rick was, and now I'd like to explain how the Cardinal came to be involved." He paused to sip his coffee and continued.

"If you recall the night I was here, I mentioned the friend I had called." Mathew then pointed towards Rick. "Well, he had asked for help from a friend of his." This time, Mathew turned his head and looked at the Cardinal before continuing. "The Cardinal was the friend Rick consulted. I just thought we should all know how each of us became involved."

John was sipping his coffee. He placed the cup down and said, "Ok, that makes sense. I have to admit I was curious why both of you were here. So, what next? What is it you want to hear from me?"

Mathew again looked at the Cardinal. So far, so good. The conversation had led them right to where the Cardinal wanted it to go.

"John, I am most eager to hear of your dream. In your own words, please. I have been told many things about what has been happening to you. It must be awkward for you to have complete strangers asking to hear such personal things. I truly hope that you feel comfortable talking with us."

"Sir, I feel very comfortable talking about it now. Before I met Mathew, it was different. I found it hard at times to talk to my own wife. This whole thing has been, well, really weird for me. At first, I just didn't want to talk about it at all. Then the strangest thing happened. I talked to Mathew here, and I felt so much better afterwards. Things have been better and better each day since that night he came over. I have to admit, that I've been a little apprehensive today about talking to somebody new. But now, right now. I'm amazed how calm I feel inside. I think maybe I'm accepting it more."

The Cardinal returned his cup to the coaster and slowly looked around the table before speaking. "I know that you and your wife are not Catholic. And I feel obligated to point this out, only so I can say this. There are many faiths in the world. Yes, there are differences between them. Some of these differences are considerable. However, it has always been my own personal belief that they have more in common than they are different.

"The main and above all the most important thing they all share is a belief in God our Father. He is called by many names, but the basic truths that he inspires us with are there in each of our respective faiths. To me, it is these similarities that prove He is there for us all. That He truly exists. That He is the ONE true GOD. So you see, everyone around this table is here because of His will. And His will did not create these different faiths.

Man did that on his own. You should feel comfortable talking about this, very comfortable. For you see, you are with others that share the identical basic beliefs that you have. I apologize for being so wordy. My rambling is only meant to assure you that we are friends."

Every one of them now felt an unseen presence in the room with them. They have been guided by it these past few weeks. Each of them had been directed to this fateful meeting. John could tell that the Cardinal was a very good man. Plus, John had believed the same thing since he was a teenager growing up in his church. He knew that he could talk freely, and he would.

"Cardinal, I really appreciate you saying that. I was OK with this before, and now I'm REALLY OK with it. So here goes."

John's telling of his dream was just as it was when he told Mathew. Even though Mathew had heard it that night not long ago, he was even more captivated by the dream this time. He wondered if it was because of what the Cardinal had said earlier. There were actually tingles going up his spine as John finished describing the dream. Neither the Cardinal nor Rick had uttered a word during the telling. Not a cup had been lifted from the table. Not a sound had been made other than by John. Once finished, John sipped his coffee and waited for a response from someone.

The Cardinal had moved closer to the table, and was now rubbing two fingers back and forth on his chin. He cupped his hand over his mouth and exhaled thoughtfully before speaking.

"John, may I ask you a question?"

"Please, anything."

"I am most curious of your comment about the door being round. You say it was a normal doorframe on the hall side. Then you said something about it being round on the inside."

"Yes, that is always a very vivid point in my dream. My eyes seem to, like, zoom in at that point and I see it. The original rock door or opening was round. I notice the curve of the stone. It is obvious that the doorframe on the hall side is meant to provide the normal rectangular appearance. And just so you know. In the dream, this part is always a strong image. I don't know if that is how to explain it or not. I just want you to know that it's like I'm supposed to notice this feature. Why do you ask? Do you think this is significant or something?"

"I think everything you said is significant. For some reason though, this point seemed to really hold my attention. I find it odd myself that this is the one thing that stuck in my mind. Especially when everything else you told us was as or more interesting than this. If it is something important, it will come to light in time."

Mathew leaned forward and took another sip of his coffee. With this sudden movement by him, the others all looked at him as if to say 'What?' He took this opportunity to steer the conversation towards something he had previously discussed with the Cardinal.

"John, can you tell them a little about the visions that you were having at the museum? I know that you didn't tell me much, but if you could just tell them what you told me?"

John nodded *yes* and started in at the point where he first became sick there with his wife. Again, the Cardinal and Rick were completely silent through the telling of these events. When he finished, he gulped down the last of his slightly warm coffee. He wondered if it was some type of unwritten code that made the two men wait for the Cardinal to speak first.

"John, you say that these visions are all set in old times. I was wondering how old?"

"Very," was all that John said.

"I see. I have this urge to ask if you could be referring to Biblical times?"

John hesitated while he dipped his head and rubbed his fingers on his forehead. He stopped this action and sat perfectly still for a few seconds before answering "Yes."

The Cardinal nodded his head twice.

"Again, I feel compelled to ask you something. I have no indication from your telling, but I was wondering if the visions and book might have anything to do with our savior Jesus Christ?"

It was immediately apparent to all three that the Cardinal's question struck a nerve with John. His eyebrows flew upwards and his eyes widened noticeably. Then, to their surprise, he became very excited and smiled broadly.

"Yes. I can't believe you ask that. I admit that I've intentionally tried to conceal this by choosing my words carefully. Anyway. The answer is definitely YES."

John began to shake one of his legs. He was sitting up close, and had both forearms flat on the table top. They were crossed at the wrists, and he was rapidly tapping the finger of the top hand on his other forearm.

Noticing John's more energized state, the Cardinal spoke again.

"Remember, John. You are among friends. You can say as much or as little as you wish. Please do not feel pressure to answer any question."

"No, I want to tell you something more about this. It won't be much really. But I'll tell you first why it won't be much."Leaving his elbows on the table, he raised his hands upward in front of his face. Then he rubbed his hands a few times as if trying to warm them before collapsing all his fingers into an interlocking pattern.

"I have always had the gut impulse that these visions were something for me. Just me. Again, that is one reason I kept going back to see that Roman scepter at the museum. I feel that I'm supposed to do something or find something, and these scenes from times gone by are the clues to whatever that is. The bottom line is that their meanings are for me, so I don't want to elaborate on them."

When John paused for a breath, the Cardinal interjected, "That is totally understandable. Just remember that we are here to help. Anything you divulge to us will be kept with the same respectful secrecy we apply to topics the Church holds dear."

"I know that, sir. I've known that from the first time I met Mathew here and the moment that I met both of you."

"Thank you John. It is an honor to be in your trust." If the eyes are the windows to the soul, then the Cardinal's eyes were showing that he was most sincere.

"Now, the second thing." Again, John's leg began to shake as he was visibly energized by what he was about to say. "I have always got a... What's the word? A vibe of some sort. I can't explain why, but I've always known that this has something to do with Jesus. I know this sounds weird. Hell, the whole thing is weird."

John realized that one word was not at all appropriate here. Not with these men. He rolled his eyes and started to offer an apology, but was cut off by the Cardinal raising his hand like a traffic cop.

"Please, don't give it a thought. It is a word and it conveys many meanings. Through time, this word has become far less offensive. We are all educated here, and your meaning is understood completely."

John was once again put at ease by this humble man. Yes, he really liked the Cardinal for the person he obviously was.

"Sorry anyway. The point I wanted to make is that I've felt it is about Him, but I never had anything concrete in the dream or visions that pointed to Him. That's all I really wanted to say. Told you it wouldn't be much, if anything at all. But there it is."

"John, I have one more question if I may? Mathew told me something about you having a daydream about Rick and I getting on our plane for this trip. Said you were completely positive on the phone that there were in fact, two of us. He also mentioned that you saw that one of us had a red sash."

John smiled and said, "So, Mathew, you told him that too?"

Mathew only replied, "I thought it was important. It was about current time and also very accurate."

"John. When Mathew first told me this, I did not get the significance of it at first. But after thinking about it, I agree with him that it is not a development to take lightly. Who knows what it means, but one thing is for sure. You are evolving in your divine role. Whatever that role is? You have most definitely been chosen and you are now being groomed for something. You should not fear it, but embrace it. It is an honor you should cherish and a gift that will serve God's purpose."

John replied, "Again, your reasoning makes sense. It was the first time in months that I'd had a dream other than the book. It also happened in the middle of the day. I wasn't tired. I must have fallen asleep extremely fast. In fact, I don't remember even falling asleep. And the dream was different from my cave dream."

This time Mathew asked, "Different how?"

"It felt different. It was more like I was watching it from a distance. My nightly dream is all about me being in it. I'm walking down the hall. I'm looking in the room. But the daytime dream was more like I was watching a movie. I don't really know how to explain it any better than that."

The Cardinal said, "You are doing fine. I can't imagine any of us would be able to handle this or explain these things any better than you are. You have a lot going on in your life. Though I realize that it has to be frustrating and difficult at times, I can't help but envy you. Yes, I envy you very much. I have attempted to serve my God by dedicating my life to Him. I have felt Him working in my life and many of the lives that I have come in contact with. But to experience having a part in something as unique as this ... well, I just envy you."

"Well sir, you have said some very nice things to me tonight. I really want to tell you something. I have enjoyed listening to you very much." John displayed a cocky smile before continuing. "Not enough for me to become a Catholic. So much of what you have said tonight is just good common sense. I really wish more people thought like you. You're a good man, Cardinal Mortello. I hope that I've been of some help to you tonight. I don't really see how I could have though. Didn't really tell you anything you probably hadn't already been told. But I hope it helped some."

"John. You have been very helpful. I, we, may not understand how yet. But you have been straightforward and honest. God has chosen you, my son, so I am sure what needed to happen here tonight has happened. We should all pray for the ability to correctly interpret what we have heard. For if we do, I am confident that we will see the roles and the paths He has for us."

They all shared one last cup of coffee before the Cardinal signaled that he was tired and wished to return to his hotel. There were the usual biddings of farewell, ending with a very sincere handshake between the Cardinal and John. As their car disappeared into the dark, John closed the door and knew that yet another vision of his had been fulfilled. But the realization of it, he would keep to himself. It was for him.

~ ~ ~

The Cardinal and Rick dropped by to visit at the church one last time before going to the airport. They had made their way to Mathew's office, and visited very briefly before asking to be taken to the Head Father's office. Mathew once again used the back stairs in an attempt to slip the Cardinal and Rick quietly past Margie. But she was wise now to this trick. The Cardinal was trapped in the stairwell by the ever-vigilant and all-knowing receptionist.

To Mathew's amazement, the Cardinal took it well when he learned he was the spitting image of one of her late husbands. He learned many things from her about her. How she had converted to Catholicism at the age of 62 for her current husband's sake. That she had been with the Church ever since. Even that her life now revolved around it.

The Cardinal knew from Mathew that she was well liked by everyone, but often the topic of private jokes. It was now awkwardly apparent that she had never really developed an awe of the Church hierarchy - the type found in those that have been raised as children in such an old and ritualistic religion. Even with his stature in the Church, the Cardinal was just as personable with her as he had been with John last night.

Just when Mathew thought that the Cardinal was maneuvering to extricate himself from the conversation, the totally opposite happened. He looked at Mathew and said, "Mathew, would you mind if Margie took me on a private tour of your church?"

Mathew replied, "Cardinal, I can't image a better tour guide. Rick and I will be waiting in the Head Father's office. Margie. Please bring the Cardinal to Father Milo's office after your tour."

Margie's eyes were sparkling as she authoritatively told the Cardinal, "I'm afraid we will need to go back down and start on the main floor. It will work out better, and we can end up at Father Milo's office." Rick and Mathew stepped to one side of the stairs and allowed the two to pass. Then they continued on to the Head Father's office.

Once there, they informed Father Milo that the Cardinal was being shown around by Margie. His only question was, "And you are certain that he went willingly?" They assured him that it was the Cardinal's idea. This became their topic of conversation for the entire time that it took for the Cardinal's tour.

While the three carried on their conversation, Mathew was thinking of all the times he had been told that the Cardinal was so well-liked because he was so personable with all whom he came in contact with. He was just a wonderful human being who happened to be the second-most powerful man in the Church.

Margie finally appeared and relinquished her prize to the

Head Father's office. There was a pleasant but brief conversation, followed by apologies for having to hurry off to the airport. The Head Father and Mathew waved as the small black limousine pulled out of the church parking lot and disappeared into the midday Dallas traffic.

As they turned to re-enter the church, Mathew looked up. He was not surprised to see Margie's face in the second story window. She truly did know all that happened inside these walls, and even the parking lot.

It was a beautiful day as their plane lifted off into the bright blue Texas sky. Large white wisps of clouds dotted their departure. Just as the wheels left mother earth, Rick asked, "So, Anton. Did you get what you came for?"

The answer was simply, "Yes. I believe I did."

~ ~ ~

The Cardinal found himself in that same hollowed chamber deep within the Vatican. Once again, he stood before his mentor. The very powerful man in white was listening intently from his golden chair. The story of the dream and the visions were told to him, but he showed no emotion at all. At the end of their telling, he only asked one thing of the Cardinal. He desired to know if there had been anything that stood out from the stories of Mr. John Parson?

To this, the Cardinal detailed his unexplained fascination with John's knowledge describing that the door to the cave room was actually carved as a round entrance. He had been so accurate with his visions so far, but this was not true. Having personally seen the door to the cave room, the Cardinal pointed out that the door was rectangular on both sides. Plus the wooden framework was on the inside and out. This was when the Cardinal's face went pale. For his mentor explained that the rock door was a circle. It was decided by the previous Pope to have this feature hidden beneath the wooden frame. It was felt that this attribute could have eventually led some to the true identity of the original occupant of the room.

After a little more discussion about the 'why' of this decision, the Cardinal posed the next logical question. Again, he was summoned to one knee by an ever so slight motion of his mentor's hand. The answer was simply 'Yes'. The Cardinal's head was still bowed as he inched forward to once again kiss the ring on that hand.

Before rising to leave, he said, "I will see to it, Holy Father".

CHAPTER 10
Dreamer's Invite

Mathew pulled into the church parking lot and took his usual spot. After locking the car, he began his walk to the back door. He was ever watchful of the upper story windows, as he searched for a glimpse of the church's vigilant receptionist. Once safely inside the back door, he wondered if he had actually beat her in today. Down the hallway, into his office and then hitting the light switch, these were his thoughts.

Tossing his keys into his desk lap drawer, he slowly settled into his chair. He leaned back to decide what task should be first. His head was barely on the chair back when his phone rang. No, he thinks to himself. Only one person could possibly know that he is already in his office. Without thinking, he picked up the phone and decided to shock her into thinking he saw her on his way in.

"Hello Margie. I know it's you. Oh! Uh? Cardinal Mortello!"

His mind rifled through all those nice things the Cardinal had said about him rising up through the Church. Those chances were probably flying out the window now. The one time he tried to outsmart her, THIS happens. Why is the Cardinal calling SO early? And how did he know he was in his office? MARGIE! That's how. Then he recalled them both walking off to go on that 'PRIVATE' tour. Hah! The Cardinal may be a very nice humble man, but now Mathew knew him to also be as sly as a FOX! She was his eyes in the building now. And those eyes saw EVERYTHING!

"I am so very sorry, Cardinal. That was a most improper way to answer my phone. It was my feeble attempt to get one step ahead of her. It's like a game we both play as to who beats whom in. I am so very sorry!"

The Cardinal's normal calming voice came across the phone and soothed Mathew's obviously rattled emotions.

"Good morning, Mathew. Please don't give it a thought. Every organization has its own Margie. It has been my practice to always seek them out. Once befriended, they become extremely reliable and powerful resources. I'm sure that you will agree after this morning. Oh, and by the way. I'd give up on winning that game you both play. She is older, and it's the only thing she lives for.

"Young man, a bit of advice if I may. You should continue to let her think you are trying to beat her in. But never do it. This will cultivate a bond that you can use to your advantage. Praise her for being a considerable adversary and you will find her to be your strongest supporter. Though it sounds counterintuitive, it is a simple principle that I have used successfully for many years."

"Yes, Cardinal. It sounds the same as the old saying 'Keep your friends close but your enemies closer'."

The Cardinal's laugh brought a big smile to Mathew's face.

"Well, I wouldn't really call her the enemy, but I do see the similarity in sayings."

"So, it is very nice to hear from you, Cardinal. A little bit of a shock, but very nice indeed. Is there something I can do for you?"

"Yes, Mathew. That is exactly why I am calling. This could take a few minutes to discuss. Do you have the time?"

"I would make time to speak with you, but the truth is that I was just deciding on what to do first this morning. So how can I help?"

"It has been decided that we would like very much to invite Mr. John Parson to the Vatican. This should be done as soon as possible. He will probably not want to come. So it will fall upon you to find a way to convince him. You have convinced me that you are very resourceful. I have no illusion that what I ask of you will be easy. In fact, I suspect that this will prove to be a real challenge. Please keep me informed as to your progress. I'm sure you have questions."

"Yes. Can you elaborate on the logistics of the trip? I know he will surely ask. So it would be nice to have a ready answer."

"Yes, I agree. Inform him that the entire trip will be financed by the Church. He will only be investing his time. We will bring him here on our private jet. He will be afforded a very great honor of staying here inside Vatican City. You should point out how rare an opportunity like this comes along. He should plan for at least a week. Be sure he understands that we will return him at any moment of his choosing. He merely has to say he wishes to go home. No reason will be expected. Oh, and make sure he understands that he will be considered a personal guest of the Holy Father himself."

Mathew was blown away by several of the details. The private jet? Staying inside Vatican City? The Pope's guest? This was incredible.

"What about his wife, Barbara?"

The Cardinal did not hesitate, nor did he sound hostile as he replied.

"We would prefer that Mr. Parson come alone. You should try hard to dissuade him from bringing her. However, if you see that he will not come without her then bring her. Tell him that she can meet the Holy Father as well, but only he will be involved in the real purpose of the trip. We will provide tour guides to keep her truly happy and blissfully busy for many hours each day. Also, we will provide them with a few days of joint sightseeing before their trip home. Of course, I will be most interested in any other suggestions that you may have in regards to making this happen. Please feel free to ad-lib if faced with something we have not discussed. I have complete trust in both your discretion and decisions. We will authorize anything you deem necessary."

"Your trust is most flattering. I think this will be more than enough. It will just be up to me from this point on. How do I contact you on this?"

"Margie will soon be bringing you instructions that I gave her only this morning. They will tell you how."

"Till then, Cardinal."

"Yes, Mathew, till then."

The phone went silent, except for a low hum probably from the long distance wiring. Mathew returned the phone to its cradle and then leaned back in his chair. He no longer needed to decide the first task of the day. The Cardinal had decided it for him. He began pondering a plan of action.

His first thought was to list the positive things that he could relate to John. Then he needed to create a list of negative things that he must be prepared to counter, should John bring them up. The Negative list will and should be the longer of the two. He must attempt to list all negatives, no matter how farfetched or unlikely they may seem. The more negatives he prepares for, the more likely the conversation will go his way.

He pulled a yellow writing tablet from a drawer and placed it on the desk before him. This is what he did twice a week to prepare sermons for himself and the Head Father. His eyes scanned the desk looking for his favorite mechanical pencil. Finally, it showed itself to be barely sticking out from under a closed Manila folder. Of course, it was last used to complete their sermons for this weekend.

A pad of paper, his trusted pencil and three hours of scribbling rendered a road map to John's 'Yes'. Now all that he needed to do was to rehearse, rehearse, and rehearse for what would probably be the most important phone call of his life.

Suddenly, his clarity of thought was shattered by a question. Should he have this conversation over the phone, or in person? It was true that the Cardinal called him, but he was on the other side of the globe while John was merely on the other side of town. It would be more personable to drop by, but that would definitely raise the awkward level for John. Having a Catholic priest show up and go into a closed door meeting with him ... well, that just wasn't a good idea. The phone call would be more private. The more private, the less threatening it would be for John. He heard the phone ringing as he sat back in his chair awaiting the fateful 'Hello'.

"Hello. Auto Correct. John speaking. How can we help you?"

"John. It's Mathew. Do you have a moment to talk?"

"Why? Are you wanting to send Barbara somewhere else?" John was smiling but he knew that this was a very awkward moment for Mathew, who was totally silent on the phone. "Just kidding, Mathew! Of course I have time to talk to you, buddy. What's up?"

Mathew started breathing again. He was finding out that John had a strange sense of humor. He was a nice guy, but with a little devil in him.

"You're killing me here, John. I almost stopped breathing."

"Well, I was just kidding. But you know what. It sounds like you may have taken it a little too seriously. That can only mean one thing. I must have hit a nerve. You want somebody to go somewhere for real?"

"John, before I say 'Yes', are you telling me that you already know what I'm calling about?" Mathew sounded really concerned. He now heard John laughing.

"No, no, I'm not having *visions* or anything. That was a one-shot thing. At least I hope it was. Nope, I was just jack'n with ya."

John had stopped laughing and now he was concerned. Mathew just answered 'Yes' to John's question. What do they want now? Go where? With who?

"Well, this wasn't exactly how I had thought this conversation would start out, but we are talking about a trip. So just let me blurt this out. The Cardinal called me this morning. Seems that the Holy Father has invited you to come to Vatican City."

"Where is that?"

"John, it's in Rome. You know, like Italy?"

Now John had stopped breathing. Why would they want him to come to Rome? What were they up to? He was sitting there already shaking his head 'No'.

"John. You still there?"

"Yes, I'm here. I, ah, just don't know about this going to Rome City. Italy, huh?"

"It's the Vatican City in Rome, Italy, John. It is where the Pope lives. Surely, you've heard of it?"

Of course he'd heard of it. It just took a minute to pop into his head. That was all.

"Yes. I've heard of it. Is it true that it is like a city within a city? Not governed by the Italian city of Rome?"

"Something like that. But the real issue here is that you have been offered a great honor by the head of my faith. This is a big deal, John."

"I understand that, Mathew. I didn't mean to belittle the offer at all. Of course I understand how big a deal this is. I'm not even Catholic and I've just been invited to go visit the top guy. Believe me, I get it. But why?"

"John, that I can't answer. But obviously you know what it is basically about."

"When? And how long you think they want me there?"

"Well, the first answer is easy. As soon as you are willing to go. Now the second question is totally up to you. I've been instructed to explain the following. The Church will pick up all expenses for the trip. They will send a private jet for you. If you don't have a passport, then they can make arrangements for you to have one in three days. They do this all the time. Well, they don't do this all the time, but they do get passports for people in three days fairly often. Anyway, you also would be staying inside Vatican City, not a hotel. And John, this one thing is something very rarely allowed by the Church. You need to be aware how special you are and this offer is."

"Wow. Sounds like it is a very big deal. Yeah, but I'm not sure about going over there. I'm not even Catholic. And the Pope - he is just a man to me. I understand he is a very important and obviously a very powerful man. I'm sure he is a very good man. But to me, he is just a man. Besides, I have always thought that all I needed to do was make him aware he should open the book. Why do I have to go over there? I just don't know. Hey, what about Barb? Is she invited?"

"Well, John. The Pope is like the President. He is very busy most of the time. True, this issue is garnering a lot of his attention these days, but he really only wants to talk to the man who is having these dreams. That's you, John. Please don't misinterpret this as anything bad towards Barbara. Please don't do that."

This was the second awkward pause during this phone call. Mathew was worrying about John being upset over Barbara not being invited. It also sounded like John did not really want to go himself. Finally, Mathew heard John sigh, which indicated that he was about to speak.

"I understand. Really. And so will she. We have actually discussed this very thing once, believe it or not. She would like to meet the Pope sometime, but she has said she wouldn't want to go with me this first time. Still, I just don't know. I think I'm leaning towards not going. Yeah, I just don't see me going. Sorry. Maybe he and I can just talk on the phone? Ya think that would work?"

"They really want you to come over there. John, let's give it a night or two. Please do me a favor. You and Barbara talk it over tonight and just think it over a little while. Then let me know what you decide."

"Sounds good, Mathew. I'll let you go and we'll talk it over tonight. I'll call you buddy."

"Thanks, John. Talk to you then."

Mathew hung up and then just sat there, swinging his chair from side to side. He relived the entire phone call over and over again in his mind. It seemed to have gone pretty well. Now all he can do is wait for John to call. This was going to be hard. How would he get this out of his head so he could get other things done? His mind was totally blank as to what all he needed to get done today. So, just as he had done this morning, he leaned his head back to begin deciding on the first thing to do. That afternoon, that is.

~ ~ ~

John pulled into his driveway. His usual routine completed, he was shuffling through the mail as he walked towards the house. Once inside, he walked into the kitchen. He threw the good mail onto the counter top by the coffee pot, and dropped the junk mail in the trash as he headed off to the bedroom.

Barbara was obviously not home because her purse wasn't in its usual place by the toaster. No need to wonder where she was. When she wasn't at home, she was out shopping. What she was shopping for *this* time was what he'll wonder about.

He hoped he could get cleaned up and downstairs before she got back. For some reason, a beer and some boring TV news seemed very inviting to him. That's odd. Why would he think of something as being inviting? Even his subconscious is working overtime on his impending talk with Barbara about the Vatican's offer.

His luck held. He was dry, dressed and sitting with a beer in hand while the talking heads rambled about nothing of importance. Barbara came in the front door just as he set the empty can on the coffee table. She smiled and bent down to kiss his cheek before snatching up the empty can. He heard her talking as she walked into the kitchen. Her voice grew ever louder as she got farther away, so he can hear her over the TV.

"A beer? Not like you. So, did you win the lottery, or was it just a bad day?"

"Well, it could be argued both ways. Sort of."

She immediately came back into the room.

"If you won you'd be drinking champagne and hopefully have a glass for me." She faked looking around before continuing. "No glass that I can see. Guess it was a bad day then? What happened?"

He turned off the TV and motioned for her to sit in his lap. She does. They kissed, and then he began to talk.

"Mathew called today. Seems they want me to come to Rome. As in Italy. He said the Pope himself is inviting me there."

She let out a little squeal as she playfully kicked her feet before wrapping her arms around his neck. "So when do you leave?" She gently turned his head with her hand, so she could see his eyes. "You told them yes, right? Please tell me you're going!"

"I'm kinda not wanting to."

"We talked about this before. You need to go. We agreed, remember?"

"I remember you agreeing that I needed to go. But I don't believe I ever actually said I would go."

Sliding off his lap to her feet, she stood looking down at him. "You need to go. It's the next step. Take it. Why not go and get this over with?"

"I never saw myself going. I've told you this. They don't need me over there. Besides, I've been sleeping just fine lately. Yes, sleeping like a baby ever since I talked with the Cardinal guy."

"I know that you have stopped having that dream every night. I'm happy about that too! But you still do have it once or twice a week."

"Yes, that's true, but it has not been anywhere near as intense as it was before. Plus I haven't had it at all since the Cardinal was here. Not once. That should mean something. Right?"

"Yeah, it means you haven't had it for three days. That's how long he's been gone. Three days."

"Yes, just three days. But this could mean it's over. My part in this whole thing was just to tell him to open the damn book. I don't need to go over there and do it for him. That wasn't in the dream. I never heard the voice say that."

Barbara lowered herself to her knees in front of his chair. She looked up at him briefly before settling her head in his lap. The silence was too much. John began to gently stroke her long, soft hair. His voice was soft and clear when he spoke.

"I'm sorry, baby. I feel much better now that I've been making up some of that sleep I lost. I also know I still have some serious thinking to do about what has been happening to me. I know I need to work through it. I've been feeling so much better. I just wanted to relax a little longer. Sleep a little more. You know, get more rested up before I tackle this again. I still can't believe that Cardinal came over here to see me. And now this offer? Where'd this come from? It's just too soon, maybe."

Not raising her head, she said, "I do understand. I think? It just seems to me that you should go. They did offer to pay for it, right?"

"Yes, they offered a private jet and said I'd be staying right there in Vatican City where the Pope himself stays. Said it was a big deal. A real honor that not many people ever experience."

Now she raised her head to look at him. She took his hand and cradled her chin in it. "See, honey. They think it's important enough to bring you over there. To talk with the Pope. You are important. Maybe they know something you don't. What if there is something they know you are supposed to do? That could be why they want to bring you there. You think?"

"I'd say that anything is possible after all that has happened. Maybe you're right. Tell you what. Let's not talk about it anymore tonight. What ya say about going out to eat. We can go to your favorite place. Then I was thinking we could come back, get in bed and watch that movie you love so much."

She playfully pushed his hand away, stood up and flicked her hair with her fingers. "You know you'll have to keep your hands to yourself or we *never* will get to watch that movie all the way through. Was that your first beer there, big boy?" She turned and moved quickly to the stairs. Then she looked over her shoulder at him before taking off up the stairs. "Besides, I really don't want to go out to eat. But we could try to watch that movie now!"

~ ~ ~

Barbara slowly started to move her legs, then her arms. She finally attempted to open one eye. The other eye opened a little and started to focus in the low light. Wow, she felt really relaxed. They had not had sex like that for some time now. It was really nice having her old husband back.

Her right hand snaked under the covers to his side of the bed. But he wasn't there. Her heart sank as she realized he must have had that dream again. She had so wanted it to be over. No more dreams waking him in the night. Their coupling had been such an overdue experience, and now this dream had started all over again. She thought to herself *this is just not fair.*

She found herself walking downstairs to look for him in the usual places. He was not in the house, so he must be by the pool. Heading straight for the patio door, she paused by the bay windows that overlooked the entire patio. Their neighbors had left their back yard light on again, so there was plenty of light to easily view the pool area. She stopped abruptly once she realized that John was not in the back yard. Had she missed him when she went through the house? Retracing her steps only confirmed that he was not in the house. Where was he?

With a hurried pace now, she made her way to the front door to see if his car was still in the drive. It was still there. This is odd. She was now completely awake and knew that there was only one other thing. Before this dream came along, he would occasionally walk the pathway behind the houses. When he did this, he would lock the back door before leaving through the back gate. If he was walking, the back gate would be unlatched and the lock would be hanging on the handle. This could be easily seen from the bay windows. Once back in front of the windows, the bright red lock was easily seen hanging on the handle. He's gone walking? Maybe he didn't have the dream. Maybe, like her, the evening's sexual activities had left him as revitalized as she had felt upon waking.

She was breathing easily again and the worry washed away from her consciousness with every stair step she took. Wait, was that the back door? Turning around, she hurried back into the kitchen to find John just locking the door. Her rapid approach through the dark startled him, and he instinctively raked his hand upward on the wall to find the light switch. The sudden bright light froze her in her tracks.

"Barb? You scared the HELL out of me. What are you doing up?"

"What do you think? I was looking for you, silly. You've been walking. I'm so glad that things are getting back to normal around here, finally." She had closed the gap between them, and gently pushed her body tightly against his with her head on his chest. When she began to slip her arms around him, she sensed that things were not as she was thinking. It was very slight, but he had pulled back just a little when she touched him. Why? "What's wrong, John? You OK, honey?"

He completely pulled away and leaned back against the door. He hung his head as if he was examining the floor. Moving his head from side to side, he looked up at her and said, "Something's not right here. There is just something I can't put my finger on that is totally wrong with this picture."

"What do you mean?" She stiffened her back and stood more erect as she asked, "You having that dream again? You did, didn't you? But, you don't seem like you always did before after the dream."

"It wasn't a dream this time. Not the one you are thinking of. It was something else. I don't want to talk about it." He tried to push past her, but she gently hooked his arm with hers.

"You didn't try to get away from me earlier, cutie." It was a feeble attempt to lighten the moment. It didn't work. He stopped and just stood there. She could sense that he was struggling with something very difficult. It was time to let this go.

"I'm tired too, baby. Let's go back to bed."

"Yeah, that sounds good, Barb." Her hand fell into his and they walked towards the stairs. Parting at the bottom to walk up single file, he said, "It's kinda warm outside tonight for some reason. I started sweating a little. I want to rinse off again. You go on back to bed and I'll be there in three minutes."

"I'll be waiting for you," she said as they entered the bedroom and she let her gown fall to the floor. "I'll bet I can make you forget whatever is bothering you."

Though he didn't sound as excited as he had a few hours earlier, he managed to muster a smile before disappearing into the bathroom. Once inside but before he closed the door, she heard him make a halfhearted joke. "Make that two minutes!"

They loved each other very much. It was easy for both of them to get lost in each other again. Eventually, the inevitable conclusion, and two exhausted people fell asleep in each other's arms for the second time during the same night.

~ ~ ~

The morning found Barbara up first. Her intentionally loud humming had awakened John. He could see her in the shower through the strategically open door she'd staged for him. She was so beautiful. His thoughts once again strayed along the lines of 'How did I ever get so lucky?'. He was mesmerized as he lay there, watching and listening to her. She opened the shower door and giggled upon seeing he was watching her, just as she'd planned. It was his turn to shower, so he reluctantly left the comfortable bed.

There was lighthearted jesting as they shared a quick breakfast and cup of coffee. They had almost successfully finished their morning meal when she couldn't wait any longer.

"So are you going, or not?"

He looked at her, but not in a hostile way. It was her nature and he accepted this about her. He loved her just as she was. "I don't think so. And before you start, just listen a minute." He was rubbing his fingertips on the top of his head, just like she'd seen him do a million times before. "I can't explain it. Actually, I don't understand it. And of course I just don't want to go anyway. So, FOR NOW, let's just say I'm not going. OK? Please, OK?"

From what she'd just heard him say, she didn't believe that he had made his mind up completely one way or the other. Again, she knew him well enough to just let it go for now. Besides, he would mull it over in his mind relentlessly until he decided what he was going to do, or not do. It should only take a day or two. She just nodded and said OK.

~ ~ ~

Mathew had just hung up the phone after providing the Cardinal with a status update. He had talked to John briefly. As suspected, John's first impulse was to say he didn't want to go. However, John was going to talk it over with Barbara. So the issue was still open, and Mathew was waiting for John to call back. They just had to wait maybe a day or two.

He needed to get to work, but work on what? It was going to be very difficult to focus on anything today. But he had to try. Leaning back in his trusted chair, he struggled to pick that first item of the day. He had already called the Cardinal, so that was done. Now what? Luckily, the phone rang, and he eagerly accepted the distraction.

"Hello. Father Cobleir speaking. How can... oh, Barbara! Nice to hear from you. Fine, just fine. No not busy at all. Of course, I have a minute. What's on your mind? Yes, I did talk to John yesterday. He did? Yes, that is where we left it on the phone. So you two *did* talk. That's good. Has he made up his mind yet? Still doesn't want to go. Hum. You don't? So you think he is still on the fence about going or not. Right? Good. I hope he decides to go. Yes they really want him to come over there. Of course it is an amazing offer. Yes I do think there is a good reason they want him to come. No, I just passed on the offer. He didn't tell you? It was a Cardinal named Antonis Mortello. Who is he? Yes, he is the same Cardinal that came to see John. He happens to be the Pope's right hand man, so to speak. Yes, I would say that makes him a very important man in our Church. What do you mean something different happened? A new dream. No? I don't understand. Oh, OK. You are talking about it again tonight. Good! Just let me know if there is anything I can do. But, Barbara ... we both know he really doesn't want to go. It has to be his idea to go. So, please don't try to talk him into it. We have to have faith that what needs to happen, will happen. If it is ordained for him to go, he will. Yes I do truly believe that. Ok. I'll be looking forward to your call tomorrow."

That was interesting. What was this different thing that she said happened last night? It was like a dream, but not a dream? He wondered what that meant. Oh well, at least she had promised not to try and talk him into going.

~ ~ ~

John's day went well. He was very glad they had been so busy all day long. One customer after the other just walked through the door. Yes, it was good for his business, and he was glad. But he was glad for a completely different reason than the money. He hadn't had time to think about the dilemma of go or no go. With the last set of car keys in their owner's hand, he was locking up to go home.

The drive was over before he had time to start thinking about anything at all. This was a good thing. In the drive, mail in hand and into his kitchen he strolled. The usual junk mail toss before he looked to see if Barb's purse is there, and it was. She must be upstairs. Maybe he could surprise her this time.

As he entered his bedroom, he was stopped cold by the sight of his totally naked wife lying on top of the covers and pretending to reading a book. She didn't even look up when he entered. It was one of her playful games, all right.

"What the? What are you up to, young lady?" he said as he walked around the bed so he was in front of her. His view was great! But why was the lamp on the floor in the corner?

Quickly looking at the nightstand where it should have been, he saw a bottle of wine and some raw oysters on ice. She was really pulling out all the stops this time. God, she is gorgeous!

"I have no idea what you mean, Sir," she said coyly without even looking up.

"Who's that stuff for?" he asked, while looking at the goodies on the night stand.

"I thought you might be hungry and thirsty."

He began to lean on the bed, but she pushed the book over and cut him off.

"Oh no you don't, grease monkey! You have to get cleaned up first."

"But I'm hungry."

She paused while looking at him for a second before saying, "Kneel down and I'll give you one."

"Oh really? Just one?" He was already on one knee beside the bed. She tried to give the impression that she had just noticed that she was naked. John thought to himself that she was actually a pretty good actress. He also felt it was getting kind of hot. "So am I going to get one?"

She reached over and pulled an oyster from the bowl. As she put it in his open mouth, she said, "You can have one. The rest are for clean little boys."

"But what if I'm thirsty too?"

"Shower! I could fall asleep if you don't get going."

He was up and in the shower in seconds. Practically running from the bathroom, he was again stopped by yet another amazing sight. She is now sitting very provocatively with her back against the headboard, slowly running the rim of her half-full wine glass from one breast to the other. Then she looked at him with a flirtation gleam in her eyes, "Too much?"

John laughed out loud and said, "Not for me, baby!"

His rather abrupt entrance into bed almost caused her to spill the wine. He gently took the glass from her hand and set it on the nightstand. Once again, they were in each other's eager arms as she said, "I thought you were thirsty."

"Was then, but now I'm kinda hungry. For you."

Perhaps it was her plan, perhaps it was not. The lustful hours they shared probably had come from several months of depriving themselves of each other due to that dream. Last night had been wonderful. So was tonight. But tonight was more fun. There was a lot more laughing like they used to do. It was a return to the way things had been before this dream thing had interrupted their happy routines. Again, their activities led them both into contented sleep.

~ ~ ~

Barbara was warm under the sheets, but something was missing. A quick search with her hand and she knew that he was not in bed. As she rolled over on her back, her eyes barely detected motion at the end of the bed. She knew it must be John, but what was he doing? Fortunately, the lamp was still where it was supposed to be. With a well-rehearsed movement, the room filled with light.

John was pacing very rapidly back and forth. "What are you doing? Has something else happened now?"

In a flash, he rounded the bed to her side and sat down close to her. He looked at her for a few seconds.

"No matter what angle I look at this from, I see me going. It still doesn't make any sense, but I now see me going."

She scooted a little closer and raised herself up on one elbow. Placing her other hand under his chin, she said, "Have you seen something else? Do you know why you have to go now?"

"No, not at all. It is just a feeling. A very STRONG feeling."

"So it was or wasn't another dream?"

Her hand sensed all the tension falling away from his face before he said, "Odd, but it wasn't a dream. I didn't hear anything. I just *know*. It seems so real. Just a feeling, though."

"So accept it then, dear. Just go."

"I'll need to call Mathew in the morning. I wonder when he gets in?"

"Surely he will be there by 8:00 or 8:30. Surely?"

"I'll call him from the office. Sorry I woke you up. I didn't think I was making any noise. I was really trying to be quiet. Really I was. I just suddenly had to get up. Had to move."

"Come back to bed. Come on."

~ ~ ~

Mathew flipped the light switch on in his office. It was just a little before 8:00 in the morning. He was trying to follow the Cardinal's advice about Margie. No need to get in super-early any more. Actually, there never was a reason to do it. He didn't have any real need to be in his office before 8:00 on weekdays. He found himself just standing a few feet inside his door. He was staring at the phone and wondering if it was going to ring. After a few more seconds, he concluded it is not. So he deposited his keys in the desk lap drawer as usual and eased into his chair. Maybe this would be a more typical morning. He did have some things to do today.

When the phone does ring, he just sat there looking at it. He thought to himself 'Already?'

"Hello. This is Father Cobleir. Can I help you? John! I'm glad to hear from you. Yes, and good morning to you too. You have? You are? Great! Of course, I'll call him right away. When can you be ready to go? Tomorrow? Well, that is great, but we will need to get you a passport. What? You do? I thought you didn't have one. She doesn't know you do either. What made you decide to get one? No real reason? Ok. You have a nice day, too."

Mathews immediately dialed the Cardinal's private number. He couldn't wait to tell him the good news. He had picked up his phone quicker yesterday. Maybe he was busy? Then he heard the familiar voice.

"Hello Mathew. I hope you have good news for me."

"Yes I do! John just called to say he was coming. He can leave tomorrow. And by the way, Cardinal, he just informed me that he has a passport. He didn't say why he got one, but he did say he did it last month."

"The more we learn of him, the more interesting this becomes. I'm sure you and I both are thinking the same thing."

"Yes, Cardinal. I've known for a while that he does not tell us everything. He is reluctant to tell his wife everything. It seems to me that this whole thing could be overwhelming his judgment a little. I'm sure you'd agree that it is very understandable, considering all that he is going through. "

"Of course. I couldn't agree more. As I mentioned that night, I do so envy him for having been chosen like this. But, I'm not sure that I would be faring any better under his circumstances."

"What would you like for me to do now?"

"I've already placed the plane and crew on a moment's notice. So they can be in the air within the hour. The flight time to Dallas via New York would put it landing at Addison airport near Plano this evening. The crew could rest overnight, and they could leave tomorrow afternoon at his convenience. This would put him arriving here midday the following day after sleeping on the flight over.

"There really is only one more thing for you to do. My secretary will make the same arrangements for the crew's hotel and the limo. She will call you with the details for his departure. Would you please pass them on to John? I want to thank you again, Mathew, for being so responsive to all that has been asked of you. Your service to the Church will not go unnoticed. Be safe and blessed, my friend."

"Yes, I will pass it along to him. Thank you, Cardinal. It was my pleasure completely." Again there was that humming on the line after the Cardinal hung up.

Mathew was happy and relaxed. Then a question snapped to mind. Was his role in this happening - now over? He's not sure he wants it to end. This entire affair had brought a heightened sense of excitement to his life that he had never known before. No, he does not want it to end. There was little comfort in knowing that this one last task could be the end of his envolement. He felt a little sad.

He leaned his head back on his trusty chair, but not to plan his day's tasks. He began to relive the wonderful events that, from now on, will only exist in his memory. Plus, he was stalling before calling John. He quickly realized that it was silly to try to prolong it. He pulled up John's number on his cell and hit the Call button. Soon he heard John's answer. After passing along the information and promising to call with the exact time John will be picked up, Mathew decided to do one more thing.

"John. Unless you just really want to ride in a limo, it would be my pleasure to personally drive you to the airport."

"Mathew, that's not necessary. It would be too far out of your way. Plus, you would have to bring Barbara back out here before going home. I appreciate the offer, but it is just asking too much."

"John. It really wouldn't be a problem. I'd love to do it."

"Well, if you insist, buddy. I have worked on lots of limos, and they are just cars to me. I'd just as soon ride with a friend. In fact, it might be best for Barbara."

"How so, John?"

"Well this will be the first time we've been separated by such a distance since we were married. She's going to cry. I know it. You know it. She'll deny it, but she knows it too. At least if you drive us, she'll be with a friend on that drive back home. Maybe you could even sit with her for a while, have some coffee. I think I'd feel better for her if you would do that for me."

Mathew jumped at the chance to still play a part in this. "Of course, my friend. I would be honored to do that for you. I will sit with her as long as she wants. I will clear my calendar for the evening. The two of you are very dear to me."

"Then it's settled. Look forward to your call. Later."

Again, Mathew faced the sound of a dead phone call. But this time he was more excited. This reprieve would postpone his return to the everyday life of a priest. It was only one more day, but he would cherish it.

~ ~ ~

Mathew pulled up in front of John and Barbara's house. He parked and hurried to the porch, only to see the door open before he was up the steps.

"Morning, John. Sorry I'm a little late. Wouldn't you know it? The traffic was absolutely horrid this morning. There were two wrecks a block apart on Preston. They only had one lane getting by."

"It's OK. I've been packed and ready for two hours, but she's still getting dressed. You'd think she was going to the opera. You aren't going to believe how dressed up she is."

"I'll bet she looks lovely, John."

"Well that she does. But we're just going to a little old airport. Who's going to see her?"

Mathew seemed a bit out of breath as he said, "You will, John." He patted John on the shoulder. "She's getting dressed up for you. Get it?"

By this time, they were both inside. On their way to the kitchen for one more cup of coffee, John stopped and turned to Mathew before saying, "You know, I didn't think of it that way. Thanks!"

They had barely had a sip each when Barbara rounded the corner to join them. Upon hearing her footsteps, Mathew rose and turned to greet her. She was stunningly beautiful. He had always considered her a very fashionable dresser, but she had most definitely outdone herself today. She gave him a little hug but tilted her head backward as she said, "Sorry, makeup is fresh. Don't want to get anything on that black suit of yours. It would really stick out."

John was about to pour her a cup when she coughed to get his attention. He immediately put the cup back in the cabinet when he heard her say, "Not this morning, honey. Can't risk it. How do I look?"

"You look absolutely gorgeous! But then you always do." He was smiling as he approached her and asked, "You going to let me kiss you? I saw how you treated our guest. Not very hospitable."

"No," she says, and she playfully stepped backwards with her hands stretched out to block him.

"You really mean that? I'm going away for at least a week, maybe longer and you don't want to kiss your husband?"

"Ha ha. You just wait, mister. I fully intend to smear you good at the airport right before you board. You'll see. You'll have my mark on you for a week. Those Italian beauties are going to know you belong to somebody back home."

Mathew snickered. "She's a woman with a plan, John. You don't stand a chance."

"That she is, Mathew, old buddy. Let me tell you about one of her most recent plans." He is cut off prematurely by her tapping her shoe, tilting her head and mouthing the word 'NO'.

"Mathew, it appears she doesn't want me to go there."

They shared a good laugh on their way to the front door. Mathew held it open for Barbara to step through first. She stopped on the porch and moved to one side while holding the house key in her hand. Once John passed with his one large roller bag, Mathew quickly closed the door and cleared the porch for her to lock the door. He hurried past John to get to his car first and opened the trunk. With the bag now stored, Mathew went to the driver's door while John opened Barbara's door. Anyone watching would know that somebody is traveling today, but they would probably think it was Barbara. While Barbara was wearing a high dollar designer outfit, John was dressed in a neutral colored shirt and slacks with casual loafers. It is the most dressed-up Mathew had ever seen him. They pulled away from the curb and were finally on their way.

It was easy to see that John was becoming a little nervous, since he had stopped talking and was looking out the window to avoid eye contact. Mathew decided that it was time to distract him with some small talk. "You look very sharp there, John. I've never seen you like this before. It's true that the clothes make the man, I guess."

"Hey, I didn't pick this stuff out. She did. I wanted to wear my jeans and boots, but nah. She wouldn't let me."

"Don't say that." Barbara sounded a bit hurt. "You could have worn anything you wanted. I just think this looks more appropriate for where you are going and who you are goingto see."

"I won't be seeing them wearing this. We don't get there till tomorrow. How wrinkled do you think this will look by then anyway?"

"That's right, Barbara. It's a very long flight and I'm positive they will give him time to freshen up once he gets there. He's not going straight in to meet the Pope."

"Hey! Whose side are you on?" She said lightheartedly. "Besides, I just want my husband to look important when he gets there. That's all."

"Baby, when a Texas oil baron goes to a meeting, do you think that people say 'Oh my. He's wearing jeans. He must not be important!'?"

Barbara smacked him on his shoulder. "Ok, ok. Yuk it up, you two!"

The talking and joking gave way to silence just a few blocks from the airport. John and Barbara strained to look each time the loud thunder of jet engines announced the departure of another steel bird. Mathew had fallen silent as any good friend would. He knew that these last few minutes are for them.

Leaning towards his wife, he whispered, "I'm going to hate leaving you. This is going to be harder than I thought."

"Shut up, buddy. You're not getting the smear job until you are about to get on the plane. Now stop it before I start crying and ruin my makeup."

After clearing the private gate, Mathew maneuvers his car to the waiting plane. There were two crewmen standing on opposite sides of the stair steps leading into the belly of the plane. At the top of those steps stood a young, dark-haired girl in a similar uniform as the two men.

"John, I'll get your bag. You and Barbara just take your time. They won't leave until you are good and ready."

"Thanks, buddy. I think we might just sit in here a second or two if you don't mind."

"Take all the time you need," is all that Mathew said before he closed the car door and opened the trunk to get John's bag. The second man stepped forward, accepted the bag and asks, "Tis only one?"Mathew nodded *yes* and held up one finger. After he closed the trunk, he turned and faced away from the car to give them privacy. Upon hearing the car door open, Mathew turned to see that Barbara had fulfilled her promise.

"Well John. She smeared you but good!"

"That she did, buddy. If I didn't know better, I'd think she thought I was somebody important."

Mathew couldn't help himself. "Aren't you glad you didn't wear your jeans?"

Barbara just backed up against the car and watched as the plane was buttoned up for flight. Mathew opened her door and she got in, but her eyes were locked on the plane. She was scanning each window in hopes of catching one last glimpse of John.

Mathew pulled only a short way before turning the car around so she could watch the plane taxi to the end of the runway. She cracked the window just a little to hear when the engines revved up. The roar filtered into the car as the plane hurtled down the runway towards its ultimate goal, open sky.

It was not John's first plane ride, but it would definitely be his longest. In fact, he had never been out of the country. He found his emotions confusing. He looked forward to the trip, but at the same time, he was already missing his wife and home. He thought to himself, 'Right now, I don't feel so important.'

CHAPTER II
Prelude to a Test

The first leg of the trip took John to New York. He eagerly watched from the window as they descended into air space above the city itself, captivated by the beauty of the well-known landmarks. Having only seen them in pictures or movies, it was truly breathtaking to see them from the air. How he wished he could be sharing this with Barbara. Perhaps he had been wrong to not insist that she come along. Too late now; he's here.

The landing was uneventful and one of necessity. They would refuel and be back in the air in just over an hour. As the plane once again lifted off into a perfect blue sky, his thoughts were of the wife left behind, and now his country as well.

The crew had described the onboard luxuries that were at his disposal. His personal stewardess was not only very efficient, but also full of information on his destination. She had been born and raised in Rome. She worked for the company that leased this aircraft and crew to the Church. Not knowing his real itinerary while in Rome, she entertained him with her vivid descriptions of sights and attractions he just 'MUST' see while in her homeland. Her enthusiasm for her country's cultural treasures provided many hours of interesting conversation between his two in-flight meals. They were not kidding about how long this flight was!

While talking with Gena, John learned that she was a distant cousin to the plane's captain. He had gotten her this job over six years ago and they had been crew members together ever since. This also led to the real highlight of John's flight. The captain asked if he would like to see the view from the cockpit. Of course, John jumped at the chance to do so. He was allowed to sit in the copilot's seat for almost two straight hours during the flight. It was the coolest thing he had ever gotten to do in his life. He had always had a secret desire to fly. The pilot even turned off the autopilot and let John fly the plane for 30 minutes.

He was really hyped up when he returned to his seat. The excitement of flying the plane, and then relaxing back in the cabin caused him to drift off into the best sleep he'd had in months. There had been several naps for John during the flight. But this one ended with Gena waking him to say, "Sir, we will be landing in about 20 minutes. You need to bring your seat upright please."

He watched a luscious green landscape pass beneath them as they approached the airport. Italy was really a very beautiful country from what he was seeing below. The pilot floated the plane onto the runway with no bump, just a sudden sound of tires racing to catch up with the speed of the plane. As they taxied towards the few hangars in this small, secluded airport, he saw what must be his ride. He remembered what Mathew had said to him, and John thought *So I get that limo ride after all.'*

From the plane's window, John saw two men standing by the car. By their dress, he knew that one was the driver and the other a priest of some sort. There was no red sash visible so it couldn't be the Cardinal. Wait, was that a purple sash? What was he? Once closer, he could clearly see that this was a very young looking priest.

The door was quickly opened, and Gena bid John farewell at the door. His feet were barely on the ground when the approaching priest said, "Mr. Parson? I am Bishop Turin. Regrettably, Cardinal Mortello needed to attend to Church business and he asked me to escort you to the Vatican in his stead."

The Bishop said something in Italian to the copilot who immediately recovered John's one bag from the plane's cargo hatch. The driver had the bag inside the trunk before John was settled into the back seat. With the driver in place and the Bishop having joined John in the back, the car began the trek to Vatican City.

"Mr. Parson. I hope your trip was pleasant."

"It was absolutely great. It was long, but I really had a blast." His comment had triggered a questioning look on the young priest's face. Though John's mind was still thinking about his half-hour of flying the plane, he wasn't about to risk getting anybody in trouble by talking about it.

"Good. We have almost a two-hour ride ahead of us, sir. There are many places to stop along the way, should you need to do so. Please do not hesitate to ask. We are in no hurry at all. Once we arrive, I will show you to your room. I am confident that you will be very happy with it. It does not have much of a view; however, there are many glorious things inside that I will be most happy to show you. Bishop Regalo and I have been assigned to assist you during your stay. One of us will be available day or night, should you need anything."

"Even at night?"

The young man smiled and said, "I don't mean to give you the wrong impression, sir. You are free to explore on your own at any time. I only meant for you to know that one of us will be nearby, should you have any questions or require anything during your stay. I will, of course, show you how to find us should you need us."

"Great. You know. I was worried that everyone would be speaking Italian and I'd never know what was going on. I understand you very well. You speak English better than I do."

"Thank you. I was born in a little town about 40 kilometers from Rome. However, I attended college in the United States for five years. Bishop Regalo was also schooled in the USA, and speaks English as well."

"I'll bet that's why you both were picked to babysit me."

"Babysit? Oh, I see. I wouldn't put it that way, but your point is probably valid."

"So, how many people know why I'm here?"

Again the young man squinted with a quizzical look. "Sir, I'm afraid I have no idea why you are here. I merely know that Cardinal Mortello requested we attend to you while you are here."

John now looked quizzical. "And you are OK with not know-ing?"

The young man was sincere when he responded. "Mr. Parson. When Cardinal Mortello asked me to do this, I had no reason to ask why. I'm sure that it is in the best interest of the Church, or he would not have asked. So your business here is nothing for me to be concerned about. My focus is upon fulfilling my service to my Church and its leadership."

John found the young man's answer a little unnerving, but he wasn't sure why. He concluded that it must be a cultural dif-ference of some kind. It also fell in line with something that John had always wondered about the Catholic Church. How had it managed to survive all the major world events it had seen? Like both world wars, the Nazis, and before that, the medieval times. It must have been because the leadership was able to deal with the outside world in a way that did not dilute their organiza-tional beliefs. What a balancing act.

Surely, they had been forced to make pacts with many un-savory entities through the ages. He wondered if there were any books on the subject. Yeah, right? What was he thinking? He didn't need to know anything about any more books! No thanks.

The rest of the ride proved to be as interesting as the flight. He had thoroughly enjoyed listening to Gena talk about Italy, and calling her by her first name seemed very natural. However, even if he had caught the Bishop's first name, he would not have felt comfortable calling him by it. But the young man was just as interesting to listen to. John heard stories of the little towns they passed through. Yes, this was very interesting stuff.

"Is that Rome out there?" The road they were on was just high enough so that he could tell they were close to a big city.

"Yes, Rome. We still have another 40 minutes or so."

These minutes quickly brought John's attention to bus-tling traffic. The surrounding buildings were an amazing mix of very old structures that had been continually updated with modern technology. It was so much more impressive to actu-ally see these things in person, than in a picture or on TV. The sights and sounds kept John's head turning to the left, and then to the right. The Bishop was pointing out things and offering snippets of information as they rapidly disappeared from view.

Then they were there.

They were halted at a gate guarded by men in brightly-colored costumes. The fact that they were holding long poled spears was amazing. His comments about them made the Bishop laugh. It was a very restricted laugh, but a laugh nonetheless; one that would have probably been a full, rolling laugh had he been among his closest friends.

John was so busy taking in all that he was seeing that he was shocked when the car stopped and the Bishop said, "So, we are here. If you will, Mr. Parson?" The young man opened his door. John did the same and was halfway out when he noticed the driver had come to open his door. He turned and hurried to retrieve John's bag from the trunk. A moment later, the bag was placed by the building entrance. He and the Bishop spoke briefly before the driver returned to the car and left. They had spoken Italian and of course, John was interested. But he had no clue as to what had been said.

A young boy appeared, placed his hand on John's bag and tipped it into rolling position. His attention was on the Bishop, who motioned to John to follow him. It was odd to John how the boy was watching for visual cues as to what the Bishop wanted him to do. The little guy followed them with the bag. He never spoke nor did he fall more than three paces behind them.

John was immersed in hallways that were adorned with paintings. There were scatterings of small tables with just two chairs. Just as he was wondering if anyone ever sat in them, they rounded a corner and he saw two older priests doing just that. Still following the Bishop, their travels took them down one corridor after another before the Bishop finally stopped in front of a door. Noticing how wide open John's eyes were, he asked, "Is there something wrong, Mr. Parson?"

John was still looking back down the hallway as he said, "I don't think I'm going to be exploring anywhere in here by myself. I'd get lost. You say it will be easy to find you guys, right?"

The Bishop's eyes lit up and he had a huge smile as he said, "I'm sorry, Mr. Parson. It *is* quite a maze in here. I have been here for several months now and obviously know my way around. But I do remember my own astonishment at the meandering of these corridors when I first encountered them. You must consider that these buildings have been renovated many times through the ages. There have been fires and other structural damage that prompted repairs. The buildings themselves were built in one era, using the technology and materials of that time. Then the repairs were done with more up-to-date techniques and materials. That is how it came to be this way."

He himself is now looking at the walls as he continued. "Though it adds to the mystique of the building, it has created a rather confusing mix of the new and the old."

"Well, that is very interesting. But I'm still not going to go wandering around alone. I'll only be here for a short while. Doubt I'll have time to learn my way around in here. So where are we?"

"Oh, sorry, these are your rooms."

"Rooms?"

The Bishop opened the door and entered. Still holding it, he said, "Please, come in."

John now knew why he said rooms. There was a main sitting room with three other doorways. One was on the left and two others were on the right. "All of this is for me?"

"Yes. The bedroom is through the one door on the left. The toilet is the first door on the right. There is a small study through the second door on the right. It has a very small window that overlooks a small courtyard beyond. It's not much of a scenic view, I'm afraid." He glanced at the boy who was still standing motionless in the hall. A few quick words in Italian, and the boy sprang to life. He rolled the bag into the bedroom then quickly left.

The Bishop stepped over to a small table on one side of the room. He bent to write something on a pad next to the phone. He spoke while he was writing.

"I will leave a phone number to call. Either Bishop Regalo or I will carry this cell phone for you to contact us. Again, one of us will always be only a few minutes away, should you need anything. There is a small menu next to the phone. You may request anything on it, but only during the hours listed. The menu is small, but the food is excellent. You should know that the delivery time is rather relaxed. After all, this is Italy."

"When you call, don't worry when they answer in Italian. They should immediately switch to English upon hearing you speak. If not, just be patient, for they will find someone that does. Of course if they do not, you may call the cell number and we can facilitate it for you. Also, you will find a small refrigerator in the study. There are an assortment of beverages and flavored waters as well. If you open the wooden door above it, you will find various small snacks and candies. Everything is available to you.

"Cardinal Mortello has requested that you meet him for breakfast at 8:30 tomorrow morning. I will be here around 8:15 to show you the way. Unless you have any questions, I will leave you to relax and enjoy your evening."

"I do have one quick question. How thick are these old walls?"

"I'm not sure I understand, Mr. Parson."

"At home I play the TV fairly loud. I don't want to disturb anyone else."

"Ah, I understand now. Please do not worry in the least. You are the only one here in this wing. These rooms are for very special and unique guests. There are no others."

"But I saw all those other priests and men in suits when we came in."

"Oh, yes. They are either in the other wing of the building, or in a few rooms right by the entrance. You will not be disturbed, nor is there anyone for you to disturb. You need not worry."

"Ok, then I guess I'll just see you in the morning."

"Yes, in the morning." He moved to the door but commented before he closed it behind himself. "Sleep well, Mr. Parson."

John's first thought was to visit the restroom and then he would call Barb. Boy, did he have a lot to tell her!

~ ~ ~

He thoroughly enjoyed talking to Barbara. He apologized twice for not taking into account that Dallas time was seven hours earlier than the time in Rome. This meant his call woke her up at 5:00 in the morning. They spoke for over an hour. He was glad he wasn't paying for the call.

There was no problem with ordering something to eat. They switched to English immediately, just like the Bishop had said they would. He had been right about the relaxed delivery as well.

It was over an hour before he heard the knock on his door. The delivery boy looked exactly like the one that pulled his bag to the room, only this guy was taller. Maybe they were brothers.

While John was looking for a few dollars to tip the lad, he had disappeared back down the hall. John really wanted to tip him, but he wasn't wandering off down that hall. He'd just get lost and his food would really be cold by the time he made his way back. To his surprise, the food was still very hot and very delicious. It was time to take a long, hot bath. With his belly full and every muscle completely relaxed by the hot water, he quickly fell asleep.

His nap lasted just short of two hours. The cooling of the water and the strain on his neck from the curved tub both contributed to him being fairly stiff as he rose from his bath. Earlier he had pulled his contraband blue jeans from his bag and laid them out on the bed with a well-worn Texas Longhorns sweatshirt. That's right, Barb had no idea he had secretly packed a pair of jeans into the bag while she wasn't looking. He strutted around the room with them on as a kind of victory dance. Yes, he was feeling pretty good. Just needed to get rid of this stiff neck from that tub. He thought it had to be late, but there was still light coming in from the window in the study. The rays of light were hitting the wall by the bedroom door. He found himself trying to remember what those rays of light reminded him of. Oh yeah. His dream, of course!

A quick glance at the wall clock showed it to be just a little after 5:00 in the afternoon. Hey, time for some TV. But first he went to the study and randomly grabbed a bottle of flavored water, along with a bag of chips. He found the remote by the bed and hit the POWER button before kicking back. What? Oh no! Quickly flipping from one channel to another, he began to realize a big down side to being in a foreign country. These weren't his shows, and they weren't in ENGLISH! Bummer!

What to do now? He carried his water and chips back into the study, and sat down at a little table by the window. The Bishop had been right about the view. There was nothing to write home about here. He wondered if anyone had ever hung themselves after having looked out that window? John thought that anyone staying here would have no other choice but to read one of the 50 or so books on the shelves. There were books written in English, but he was never one to just sit and read.

As he sat drinking his flavored water, he began to feel tired all over again. What was wrong with him? It wasn't even 6:00 in the evening, yet his eyelids felt like they weighed a ton. He could hardly keep them open. He began to wonder if this is what they call jet lag. He had friends who traveled all the time for work. They always talked about this, but it was the first time he'd ever felt this way. Man, he felt beat. Maybe he would just go back to the bedroom and lie down for a while.

As he drifted off to sleep, his last thought was that maybe this jet lag stuff would keep him from dreaming. That would be nice!

~ ~ ~

John's eyes began to flicker in the darkened room. As his focus grew stronger, he realized that he did not recognize this room. Where the hell was he? Along with his awakening subconscious came the realization of where he was. It was bad enough that he'd had that dream again, but he now knew that he just thought the word 'Hell', and here he is in the Vatican! Was this bad?

He slowly got up and made his way to the bathroom to splash some water on his face. He stood looking at himself in the mirror above the sink. He looked awful. The strange emotions always caused from having just experienced that dream seemed to be amplified by the unfamiliar surroundings. The urge to move, to walk, and to try to get away was unbearable. He had to get out.

He opened the door to the hallway and looked back down the way they had come in. His faculties were not all short-circuited, so he knew to place something to block the door from locking behind him. So he left and strolled down the hallway and around the corner. Then he rounded yet another corner until he came to one of those little tables with two chairs. This should do. He sat and began to sort through a dream that he knew OH so very well. Every detail and moment of it was etched so deep into his mind that he suspected he would probably remember it after he died.

He was sitting with his legs spread apart. His back was hunched over and each elbow rested on a leg. With his head hanging down, he noticed that he was barefoot. Thank God he had his jeans and sweatshirt on. Those emotions were beginning to ease up when he noticed that the tips of a pair of black shoes were in the upper edge of his field of vision. What? Those are his bare feet all right, but whose shoes are those?

The suddenness of a voice saying his name almost made him fall out of the chair. Looking up, he saw another one of those young priests.

"Are you OK, Mr. Parson? Sir? Sir?"

"Oh, hi there. Ah, yeah, I'm OK. Just need a minute to wake up a little more." Along with his mind clearing, he now felt embarrassment at how he must look to this young man.

"May I sit with you, Mr. Parson?"

"Of course. Please do. I'm sorry if this seems odd to you." He offered a little smile before adding, "It happens a lot these days."

The young man patiently sat at the table with John, not speaking or asking questions. He just waited until John came out of his trancelike state. John began feeling better and sat completely upright. This time he had enough energy for a proper smile before asking, "How long have I been here?"

"I'm not sure, sir. I've only been sitting with you for five minutes. I really can't say how long you were here before I came along. You appear to be coming out of whatever you were experiencing. I hope you are feeling better."

"Oh yes thank you. Much better. I may need you to help me find my way back to my room, if you don't mind."

"We can sit here as long as you need to, Mr. Parson. I'm here to help you in any way I can."

"You must be the other priest the Cardinal assigned to baby-sit me."

He smiled a little before saying, "Yes, sir. I am Bishop Regalo. Bishop Turin told me that you made the same reference to him. I assure you that neither of us regards you in that way. We all need help from time to time. God always leads someone to our aid when we are in need, just as I was compelled to travel this hallway in these early morning hours. "

"Ok, I feel better now. Maybe I better get started back to the room."

"Would you mind if I walked along with you?"

"I'd really appreciate it if you would. I'm not really sure

which door is mine."

They slowly made their way down this corridor and that, until a door with a shoe holding it open came into view.

"This must be my room. What time is it?"

"It is almost 3:45 in the morning. I believe that Bishop Turin is coming for you around 8:15. That doesn't leave you with much time to sleep, Mr. Parson. Would you like for me to inform Cardinal Mortello that you will need to push back your scheduled meeting time? I am certain that he will understand."

"Thanks, but I'll be fine. I've gotten by on a whole lot less sleep than this. Thanks for the offer though. I have a question. Do you have to tell anyone about this? It's kind of embarrassing, you know."

"I doubt that anyone will ask, and I am under no obligation to report your activities to anyone. Should I be asked, I could honestly say that I found you sitting alone, and we talked while walking back to your room."

"That works for me. As long as you don't mind." John stepped towards the door but stopped short and turned to face the young priest. "On second thought, I believe that everyone should feel free to tell the truth. So should you, if asked. What happens to me in the night is a matter of record. Embarrassing as it may be, it happens. Thanks, buddy."

He looked down at his bare feet and heard a metal click a second later. He made his way through the door on the left and fell back into bed. Sleep wrapped around him once again.

~ ~ ~

John had been up and ready for an hour before the knock on the door. He had been heavily tempted to wear his jeans with a nice new dress shirt. It was a struggle, but in the end he went with the new slacks his wife had purchased.

"Good morning, Mr. Parson. Did you find everything you needed last night?"

"Yes, thank you. I even took a short walk around last night."

"Good. I'm glad that you ventured out. Right this way please."

"I met the other guy. You know, ah, what's..." John struggled to remember how to refer to that priest.

"Bishop Regalo?"

"Yeah, that's the guy. Didn't he tell you?"

"I'm sure that he would have, had I asked."

They took a new corridor this morning and passed by a hall that was bustling with activity at the far end. John inquired as to what was going on down there and the priest answered while they continued to walk.

"I'm not for sure. I do know that it is a project of Cardinal Mortello. I've heard something about a book or books being delivered this morning. Perhaps they are developing a special library."

"A special library? How so?"

"I understand that there is to be a guard for that room. It stands to reason that the book or books in there must be very special."

The Bishop continued to turn first down one hall, and then down another. John was simply amazed at how big this place is. He could tell that they sometimes passed from one building to another because the walls were painted brick. He thought to himself, 'This would be no place for a drunk. You'd never get out.'

Their dizzying march finally brought them to a great room filled with elaborately decorated tables. Before the Bishop could say anything, John waved at the Cardinal seated alone in one corner. The Bishop noticed the wave, but continued to guide John to his table. Then he bid the Cardinal and John farewell before departing.

"Good morning, Mr. Parson."

"Please, first names just like at my house." He then looked around before asking, "Or would it be best for me not to call you Anton here in front of these guys?"

A friendly laugh preceded his gentle smile. "Though some here are extremely formal, I prefer your way, John. Anton will be fine."

John sat down and they began to chat about his trip and his first night here. The food was delicious and the conversation very friendly. Once the table had been cleared, two small cups of what looked like very strong coffee were set in front of them.

"Now, John. This is espresso. It is much stronger in flavor than what you are accustomed to. Please try it. If it is not to your liking, I will have them bring you some traditional coffee."

"Nah, this will be fine I'm sure. Besides, I've always wanted to try this stuff." His first sip was far more than just a little stronger than what he was used to. He tried not to show it though. Hey, when in Rome?

"So Anton, what is on the agenda today?"

"Well this is something that does require a little more privacy. Please, let's take our espresso to a private room across the hall."

Though John really didn't want to drink the rest of it, he balanced the little cup in the palm of one hand and followed the Cardinal to the little room. John allowed the Cardinal to enter first. Then he finally got to put down that little cup before closing the door.

Once seated, the Cardinal spoke immediately. "At your home, I confirmed the existence of this book from your dreams. Today, those dreams will develop substance."

"So, the special library you are having installed down the hall is where you will put the book? I take it, you intend to let me see it."

"You know of this new room?"

"We passed the hall it is in on our way here. I asked?"

"Yes, that is the purpose of the new room, and only two know the real purpose."

"So the book is there? That's why you have guards?"

"All has been prepared for you. And yes, they are there because this is no ordinary book."

John sat quietly for a moment. He thought to himself, 'No ordinary book? They have no idea what they have.'

Though the espresso was really not to his taste, John finished it quickly so he could get on with what he had come here for. He found himself rather anxious to finally see the book. Seeing John gulp down his espresso, the Cardinal did the same, but with a little less theatrics. The two men rose and John held the door. He didn't mind doing things like this for Anton; not because he was a Cardinal, but because he was actually John's senior. No need to say why. Anton could think what he wants.

John was so anxious to finally see the book that he felt like asking 'Are we there yet?' But he controlled himself and was thankful that he was walking slightly behind the Cardinal. This way, Anton couldn't see John's eager expression.

They rounded the last corner and turned down that hall. There was no longer anyone in the hallway. As they approached the only door there, the Cardinal tapped once and then pulled a key from his cassock pocket. The door swung open and revealed a familiar-looking book on a pedestal with a guard standing behind it.

Sensing that John was hesitant to enter, the Cardinal said, "You are free to enter, John. Please."

Still John was just standing and looking in without entering. The tense look on his face brought another response from the Cardinal.

"John? Is there something wrong? Please, this has all been arranged just for you."

Without even looking at the Cardinal, John asked, "How long has that guy been standing in there?"

"I would hope since the book was delivered this morning. Why?"

"So that would be at least an hour or so. Right?"

The Cardinal was staring at John, but John was staring at the guard. Finally, John turned to him and asked, "Anton, would you go in the room with me and stand by that book?"

"Of course, John. Shall we?"

The Cardinal motioned for John to enter first. To the Cardinal's total amazement, John turned suddenly and took several steps away. He stopped and stood looking at the floor.

He once again joined the Cardinal at the door. He looked him in the eye.

"Anton. I like you. I really do. And I'm sure you have your reasons. But I think it is time for me to go home. I'll find my way back to my room. I'll be packed and ready to leave in ten minutes."With that said, he began walking away, yet the Cardinal does not call to him.

John had been joking about getting lost in here. He did not really fear getting lost anywhere. He had wandered alone through the back country many times. He always found his way home. He'd have no trouble finding his way back to a room. Well, he did make one wrong turn, but he knew it after only a few steps and backtracked to the right hall.

Once back in his room, he quickly had his bag packed and ready by the door. He sat in the study waiting for a knock. He was truly disappointed. Why would they go to all this trouble and expense? What a waste of time. His and theirs! Yes, he was a little disgusted, but he still hoped that he hasn't offended the Cardinal. He liked him.

The inevitable knock came. John wished he had taken the time to put on his jeans. Crossing the floor he opened the door to find the Cardinal standing there.

"May I come in?"

There was a pause as John just stared at him. "Sure."

The Cardinal turned his head to look at the packed bag sitting upright just inside the door. "There is a small study in the back of these rooms, is there not?"

"Yes, there is." The tenseness of John's stance softened before he said, "But I'm warning you. Don't expect much of a view." This time he didn't wait for the Cardinal to go first. He walked into the small study, but waited for the Cardinal to sit first. After all, he was still his senior.

"John, I want very much to understand what just happened. Will you tell me?"

"I came here in good faith. Not to play games."

"Can you elaborate a little more, please? I must know exactly what has upset you so."

"Oh come on, you and I both know that is not the book. Yeah, it looks like it, but you know better and so do I."

The Cardinal showed his surprise at John's statement. "And what makes you so sure that it is not?"

"What? The guard! And you said you'd go into the room too! Come on. There is no way that is the book. If it were, that guy would have been out cold on the floor. Over an hour? Really?"

The Cardinal had developed a strong ability to hide his true feelings over the years. But he couldn't hide them here in front of John. John knew!

"I must apologize, John. We did not mean to offend you. We truly did not. I still would like for you to tell me something."

"What?"

"What exactly do you mean 'out cold'? Please be specific so I will understand."

"Ok. He'd be on the floor. Probably would have thrown up and passed out. The real book has a kind of aura. Like a power that protects it. If you have ever seen it up close, you'd know. You'd feel it if you were very close at all. You'd want to leave, believe me! You would feel afraid. Confused. Sick, and very nervous. All these things at once."

John began slowly waving his finger in the Cardinal's direction before he continued. "Wait a minute. You've never seen it. Have you? Oh, man, I'm so sorry I acted like that. It never dawned on me that they never let you see it. You didn't know. Did you?"

Now the bombshell exploded in John's ears as the Cardinal said, "I *have* seen it. And yes, I felt the exact things you described once when I got a little too close to it. What we really needed to know was if *you* knew – if you would recognize the book."

John's face lit up once again with his customary Texas smile. "You old fox! You did know. I'll be da... Oops! Sorry. Almost let that slip out. But you did know. Hey, this was a test wasn't it? It was all a big test!"

The Cardinal was now smiling again. The tense air had left the room and they both relaxed in their chairs.

"John, I am glad to see you smile again, my friend. I have grown to like you more with every day that I know you. You are a remarkable man. It is regrettable that this 'game', as you put it, was necessary. I trust we can put this behind us now. There will be no more games in the future. I believe we can forge ahead in complete unity. Yes?"

"Of course, buddy. I'd like that very much."

"So you are staying?"

"Yes. I'd like to. So what happens next?"

"Well you will have to excuse me for an hour or so. I must relay today's events to the Holy Father. He has expressed a great desire to know as quickly as possible of the outcome from this 'game'. Bishop Turin is available to show you around if you like. Would you like me to summon him?"

"No thanks. Not if it is only going to be an hour or two. I'll just wait here. I'd like to call my wife anyway and see what she's up to. Take your time, buddy. It's only my first day. We've got the rest of the week to work this out."

"Then I'll take my leave, John. I will contact you soon."

The Cardinal moved into the hall and plotted his path directly to the chamber where the Holy Father was anxiously waiting. As he walked, his mind went over the last statement of John's.

Did he really think that all could be settled in only six days? They have had this book for over 85 years, yet they know absolutely nothing about it. True, they were painfully aware of its ability to defend itself from man. Still, they had only been able to discern one phrase on the top of the first page. Can this man really do what they hope he can?

~ ~ ~

Once again, the Cardinal felt the awe of being in the presence of his mentor dressed in white. Upon explaining what has transpired with John this morning, the seated man said, "It seems that Mr. Parson may be what we had hoped he was. Our little test was necessary but unfortunate. I am relieved that Mr. Parson and you have recovered from it. And he is patiently waiting for you to return?"

"Yes. He said he was going to call his wife. They are probably talking now. They are fortunate to share such a loving union."

"He will be anxious to return home soon. I think you should accompany him to the villa. Time could become critical if we wait. Big things are before him and us. We must be brave and forge ahead."

The Cardinal began to kneel, but was stopped by a motion from the man in white. "You are a loyal servant of the Church, Antonis. If we are to have him share all with us, we must do the same with him. Hide nothing. Speak with him as you would me. Confide all in him. Trust him, for he is being moved by the hand of God. How else could he know of these things if not told so by our Lord?"

~ ~ ~

John had unpacked *again*. He was standing in front of the mirror and holding his jeans up to himself. It was really bugging him about whether or not to change into his jeans and boots. After looking at himself for a few minutes, he reluctantly put the faded jeans back in the drawer, and the boots back in the closet.

Besides, if Mathew found out he had worn jeans here, then Barbara would find out and there would be hell to pay for months! Not worth it. Well? Nah, she'd kill him!

He had barely closed the closet doors when he heard the knock. Hurrying over to the door, he found Bishop Turin standing there instead of the Cardinal. John smiled and stuck his head into the hall to look both ways before saying, "Oh, hi! Thought you were the Cardinal. What's up, buddy?"

The young priest was captivated by this man's lightheartedness. To serve the Church is to constantly present a reserved air, so the common people will trust and confide. This Texan was so full of life and felt free to express any emotion. How the Bishop admired and envied John.

"Mr. Parson? Cardinal Mortello has asked me to relay a message to you. It seems that the two of you are going to a villa in the countryside. He hoped that you could be ready in, say, an hour? I can help you pack if you wish."

"Go to the country? Yeah, sounds good. I won't need an hour. I'll be ready in ten minutes. Now you said the country, right? So we will like, be out of the city?"

"Yes, out of the city."

"So, I don't have to be all dressed up to go out into the country, right?"

"No. I'm sure the Cardinal would want you to dress in whatever manner you wish. Though I do not know of this villa, I am sure there is not a formal dress code there. You should dress comfortably."

"That's all I wanted to hear, buddy. Ya'll just holler and I'll be ready!"

With the door closed, the priest stood facing it for a few seconds. He smiled as he walked away, saying out loud, "Fascinating. I really must go to Texas some day."

CHAPTER 12
The Villa

Cardinal Mortello was patiently waiting in the back seat of the limousine. A young priest walked over and stood reverently just outside his window. With a push of a button, the glass slid only halfway down. The priest bent slightly at the waist to converse briefly with the Cardinal. An envelope was quickly passed inside before he retreated inside the entrance of the building. The limousine's window closed with a hum.

Bishop Turin emerged from the same entrance just moments later. He stopped and turned to watch as John appeared, wearing a dark blue long-sleeved shirt with his faded jeans and boots. He had a visibly happy strut to his walk. Could it be the boots? A small boy was pulling a bag in a hurry to keep up.

Once clear of the door, the boy took a position behind the two men. With a motion from Bishop Turin, the boy met the driver behind the car. He disappeared back into the building as the driver closed the trunk. Moving to the rear passenger door, the driver opened it and waited for John to join the Cardinal in back. At last behind the wheel, the driver slowly began to pull away from the building.

"So Anton, how long's the drive this time?"

"I'm afraid that you will not see anything new, my friend. We are returning to the airport from which you came."

"Sounds like this villa is a long ways away? How far?"

"It is only a 90-minute flight, followed by a 40-minute drive. You will find the sights interesting. That area has a very rich historical past. However, my knowledge of it is very limited. I will only be able to point out two or three sights as we pass by. "

"So the Church owns this villa? Or do you?"

"I have few earthly belongings, my friend. The villa was donated to the Church many years ago by the man who built it. Unlike your room, the view from the villa is breathtaking. It is now used as a retreat of sorts. It is a place for clergy to meditate and contemplate their relationship with God. The common man does not understand the mental toll taken on men of the cloth. We spend our lives serving others by listening to their innermost demons. It has a very profound effect on most of us, yet we manage to go on. But sometimes there are those that become very devastated by the things they see and hear. They are usually very kind men who start out to serve their fellow man through service to the Church. But their emotions are eventually overpowered by the pain and suffering of those they have been called to serve. Everyone has a breaking point. Unfortunately, these men found theirs.

"You should not pity those you see there, for the Church will not forsake them in this lifetime, and God will bless them through eternity for their service to Him."

"So your Church sends ALL of the emotionally injured priests to the villa?"

"I only wish that were the case, but it is not so. Due to finances and logistics, it is not feasible to do so. This is the ONLY facility of its kind."

"I can't wait to see it. Now just in case you were wondering. That priest named Turin, the Bishop guy. He said this villa was in the country. That's why I have on these jeans and boots. I hope you don't mind. I just feel more comfortable dressed like this."

The Cardinal chuckled. "Your attire is fine. There will only be eight of us there. There are two priests who live there full-time. Of course there are two local maids and one cook. The maids are only there during the day, and the cook leaves after cleaning up from the evening meal."

"So, are you going to tell me why we are going to this villa? Or is it a surprise?"

The Cardinal's eyes lead John's eyes toward the driver. Then he leaned towards John and softly said, "Let's just say that this will not be a test. As you put it, no more 'games', John."

"You serious?" John asked. The look on the Cardinal's face told him that he was.

"Yes. However, this is a conversation best left for this evening. Do you agree?"

John's mouth had fallen open. His gaze traveled from the Cardinal to a blank stare at the headrest in front of him. Slowly his eyes rose toward the man seated behind the wheel. The driver's eyes were visible in the rear-view mirror. The winding road had his complete attention, but obviously not his ears.

John finally understood. Being a rest and recuperation facility was just a cover for its true purpose. It was a home for the book. John nodded *yes* to the Cardinal's inquiry.

They spoke of many things throughout the remaining trip, car and plane. The Cardinal was most interested in hearing John's description of life in Texas. Curiosity of horses, cows, and of course, rodeos. John actually had the Cardinal laughing very hard at times, due to his southern style of telling tall Texas tales.

The sun was going down as the second car's engine hummed harder due to the climb to the villa. The view out of John's window was unbelievable. The valley below was rocky and barren. It reminded John of West Texas, only with larger hills. What amazed him the most were the huge brownish boulders that seemed to be everywhere. They were all sizes and shapes. It was the really large ones that he was most interested in. Where did they all come from? How were they formed? He wondered if there was some gigantic, ancient volcano nearby that had spit them out a long time ago. He could almost understand people wanting to live in West Texas ... *almost*. But here, with this terrain, what could have possessed anyone in ancient times to live here? He had always thought that the world was full of all kinds of people. He realized that the people from this area's past must have had truly hard lives.

"John, do you see it?"

Hearing the Cardinal's statement, he begins scanning the ridge top for the villa. Finally, he saw the rooftop of a very large structure. John thought to himself, "So a villa is a really BIG house." If the roof was any indication, this place must be huge! Then it was out of sight because they were once again behind a row of those super large boulders. The road kept winding around these obstacles in its pursuit of the villa at the top.

One last climbing turn, and the road leveled out right before passing through the brick arch of an open gate. They were now in a graveled courtyard that could park 20 cars if needed. The driver brought the vehicle parallel to the long covered porch. It must run at least 30 feet on both sides of the two giant, solid wood doors that loomed in the middle. The beautifully carved doors had center cuts of rose-shaded stained glass. Each glass insert heralded a solitary cross.

John, with his simplistic Texas drawl simply said, "Nice place. Looks fancy." Then he began to think. Maybe Barb had been right about dressing a little more formally. With his eyes still admiring those huge impressive doors, he said, "Anton. You sure it's OK for me to be wearing these jeans and boots?"

John's sudden lack of confidence in his wardrobe choice brought a chuckle and comment from the Cardinal. "Again, my friend. You look fine. No one will notice." With that said, the driver opened the Cardinal's door and offered him a hand out of the car. John had barely opened his door when two priests hurried towards the car. John clearly heard one say to the other something that sounded like 'Cowboy', only with a strong Italian accent.

John was still uncomfortable with other people insisting on carrying his bag for him. After a somewhat awkward tug of war with one of the priests, he gave in. After they were both escorted through those two marvelous doors, they found themselves two steps above a very large sunken sitting area. There was a stone fireplace built into the far wall that was the size of one of those small European cars. The flames from the logs must have been eight inches high. John could feel the chill from the night air falling away.

The Cardinal was occupied by his conversation with the two priests. Of course they were speaking Italian, and John had no idea what was being said. There was an occasional glance his way, first from one priest and then the other. John could only imagine what they would be saying if he had been wearing one of his cowboy hats.

He strolled over to the fire, thinking that whoever built this place really liked glass. There were large windows on both sides of the fireplace. It was still light outside, so he went over to a window to look out. The view was so nice. The winding road was still plainly visible as it appeared, then disappeared, from rock to rock. He was admiring it and wished Barb were here to see it with him. She'd have loved the atmosphere here.

Anton was right. This place *was* relaxing. As John looked around, he noticed the absence of a TV of any kind. There wasn't even a sound other than the low tone of the Cardinal's conversation. This place could cause a highly agitated person to fall to the floor asleep in 60 seconds. In fact, John found himself suddenly very tired. The flight here hadn't been anything like the one coming over from the US. Could he still be feeling that jet lag effect?

Sounds of footsteps on the wooden floor alerted him to the Cardinal's approach. Turning toward those sounds, John saw that the bully who took his bag was right behind Anton.

"John, this is Father Dosanta. He will show you to your room. There is a dining area just down the hall behind you. The evening meal will not be ready for another hour or so. I would like to retire for that hour and rest. My preference is to share the company of others at meals, but please feel free to dine in your room if you wish. Should you decide to join me, I would love to continue our conversation about the rodeo."

"Well, if you haven't noticed it by now, let me tell you. I love to talk about the rodeo. Remind me to explain what 'Cowboy Poker' is. You probably won't believe me, but it is true. I look forward to seeing you then."

The Cardinal's eyes were wide open with anticipation. "I will see you then, John."

~ ~ ~

After placing the bag on the bed, Father Dosanta tipped his head slightly before uttering something in Italian and leaving John alone in his room. It had a king size bed with a massive headboard attached to the wall. It was an elaborately carved piece of dark wood. Were those golden roses in each corner? John thought to himself that Barb would LOVE to have a bed like this. Of course it was too big to fit in their bedroom.

He walked over and sat on the large wooden trunk at the foot of the bed. The top was padded with rich leather with gold brads lining every inch of the edges. He had never been much on decorating, but he had always wanted one of these at the foot of their bed. Still, their room was too small for even this. He sat there, looking around the rest of the bedroom, thinking that he and Barbara needed a bigger house.

Seeing the phone on a table by the large windows, there was a sudden urge to call home. John moved to the bed and fell into it before crossing his legs at the ankle. One hand held the phone to his ear while the other was behind his head. It was good to talk to her, and he wondered if his laughter was being heard by anyone.

After she hung up, he just lay there and relived the day's journey. It is then that it dawned on him. He sat up, his arms behind him for support. He had forgotten why he was here. The book and that cave must be beneath the house. Though he had experienced this many times in those visions, this was real time. A new charge of energy filled him and he sprang from the bed. Freshening up quickly, he stepped out of the room and headed for the main lobby. He wondered if they referred to it as a lobby. This was a villa. Was it more house or hotel? Ah, it didn't really matter.

As he cleared the hallway and entered that huge sunken sitting area, he saw that he was alone. How odd for such a large structure to be inhabited by so few people. But then again, you didn't want too many people around this place. The object it hid was very special. The fewer people here, the less likely it would be discovered.

John was back in front of the windows by the fireplace when the Cardinal called his name. "John. I hope you are hungry. I think you will surely like this evening's meal. It is a local favorite. You do like fish?"

"Fish? Yes I love fish, but how is that local? I never saw any water of any kind on the drive up here. I do recall seeing the ocean when we landed, but we headed inland. Right?"

"Yes, you are very observant. By local, I meant a village near here that is actually on the seashore. Had we not turned up towards this villa, we would have entered the village a few minutes later. The maids and cook are all from there."

The two men strolled down the hall toward the dining area. It was a good sized room, with eight tables in all, each with four chairs. The bright red tablecloths all had sizable white crosses embroidered in each corner. They were draped over the tables so that the crosses hung flat from the center of each side.

"Well, there is no shortage of Church markings around this place. You'd have to be a blind man not to know that some religious entity owns it."

The Cardinal made his way to the table in the far corner while replying, "Though I have grown accustomed to the décor here, I admit that it may be a little loud for a layman such as you."

"Oh don't get me wrong. I like it, was just sayin'."

Again, John made a mental note that they were alone. He wondered if anybody even knew they were there. Then a small, dark-haired lady with a very pleasant smile appeared from behind them. She deposited two glasses and a large bottle of water on the table before turning to the Cardinal. John looked a little shocked and this prompted the Cardinal to explain.

"The door to the kitchen is behind those curtains, if you are wondering where she came from."

"Yeah, I was wondering just that. My room at the Vatican had those things on the walls in two places. Silly me, I looked behind them and it was just the wall. So, I figured these were the same. Just decorations. Who knew?"

"So, John. Do you want to try the fish?"

"If you say it is good, then I'll have the same."

He spoke to the lady in her native tongue, and she bowed ever so slightly before vanishing behind the drapes.

John leaned a little closer and said, "Anton. Is it safe to talk here? Obviously, nobody is out here, but...". He nodded towards the curtains that led to the kitchen.

"It is perfectly safe, as long as we speak English. None of the staff do. I am certain of that. We had the Father from the village church to help us in selecting the staff. We felt that we could easily discuss things in front of them in English that way."

John smiled again and shook his head a little before saying, "I gotta hand it to ya. You are one sly fox, Cardinal Anton Mortello." His face took on a concerned look before continuing.

"You mean that the two priests that live here don't speak English either?"

"Oh, no. They speak English fluently."

"Well, it's a good thing I didn't say anything in front of the bag dude."

"Excuse me? What is a bag dude?"

"Oh nothing. I was just being me. So after we eat, are you finally going to show it to me?"

"I am going to let you set the agenda from this point on, John. The Holy Father and I have come to believe that you are more aware of things than you allow others to know. We are confident that you have your reasons, just as we had ours for the test."

The Cardinal's face took on a very serious, and somewhat ominous appearance as he leaned toward John. "What is here is NOT to be taken lightly, my friend. It is very real, and the power that surrounds it can be extremely dangerous. This I know first-hand. I trust that your dreams or visions have impressed this fact upon you."

John slipped from his silly mood to one that matched the intensity of the Cardinal's. "Yes, Anton. I am very aware of the importance of what comes next. I also know that there are ex-tremely powerful forces at work here that actually scare me a little. I'm anxious to finally come face to face with it. But believe me. I don't want to get hurt either. I told you what happened to me the first time I came in front of that Roman scepter at the museum, remember? And it was just a relic of the past with no powers at all. But this book has power. It is guarded by it. After all it was written by..." John's hesitation raised an immediate question from the Cardinal.

"By whom? John, do you know who wrote this?"

John's demeanor was one of somebody who had just let a secret slip. His eyes darted from side to side before they focused on the ceiling, then closing as if in prayer. His eyes opened and he exhaled slowly before answering.

"I have a hunch, Anton. Just a hunch. I regret not being able to discuss this any further. For now."

The drapes erupted with sudden motion as the little lady pushed through again. She stepped to one side and reached behind the drapes. There was a sound of a rope and a pulley as the drapes split to each side. She was gone in a flash. The sound of a rolling cart preceded the delivery of their meal. She was small but efficient. The table was quickly covered with plates of food, together with baskets of bread and butter that were not purchased at a store. The smell was appetizing, and both men turned from their conversation to the delight of their palates.

John so liked the fish that he complemented the delicious flavor several times. Other than this, nothing of note was discussed by either. When only one small heel of the bread was left, and their plates clean, she appeared again to collect the dishes. A few seconds later, John was once again faced with one of those little cups filled with espresso. Remembering his last encounter with the strength of this stuff, he thought to himself that if he drank it this late in the evening, he would be bouncing off the walls. Noticing that Anton was already sipping his, John offered a smile as he did the same.

Both cups were empty and John wondered why the espresso hadn't made the Cardinal as edgy as it made him. John's inner wise guy considered two possibilities. Either Anton was simply too old for this super-caffeinated drink to speed him up, or he had developed one hell of a tolerance. As for John, he felt that he could run the mile in under three minutes flat! Well, maybe without the boots.

The two men walked side by side from the dining area back towards the front entrance of the villa. As they approached the last door on their right, the Cardinal slowed to a stop right in front of the door. John watched as he pulled a key from his cassock's pocket and inserted it into the lock. A click and turn of the wrist was all that was needed for them to gain entry to a small library. John closed the door and turned to face the Cardinal.

"Here, John." The Cardinal gave John the key. "Please take this copy. I have another. This is so that you can go down there whenever you want. Just be careful, please."

"Thanks! I will." John placed the key in his jeans' front pocket before looking at the Cardinal again.

"Are you ready, John?"

"Well, as much as I'll ever be, I suppose. Let's do it."

The Cardinal walked over and opened what appeared to be

a storage closet. He reached in and a light came on, revealing shelves with neatly stacked papers and books. He moved to the rear of the closet before motioning for John to join him. There was not much room for both of them, but there was more than John quipped about.

"Well, it's a good thing I didn't eat that last piece of bread."

"Please close the door, John."

The Cardinal reached out and moved a small pot from one shelf to another. It had been the only thing on that shelf. He then lifted the shelf, exposing a small button on the wall. Once pushed, there was a semi-loud pop that echoed in the small space.

"Will you help me, John? We must push these shelves backwards. I used to be able to do this alone, but it seems that time has robbed me of yet another youthful attribute. If you would, just put one hand here and the other above. It should swing back very easily then."

He was right. John barely placed his hands where he was instructed, and the entire wall easily swung to their left. A small bulb illuminated stairs that led to what appeared to be a hallway below. There were not that many steps, but the descent was steep and narrow. They would have to walk down single file.

"Would you like me to go first, Anton? You can just put a hand on my shoulder and I'll go down real slow-like."

"Yes. I apologize for my lack of agility."

"Don't give it a thought, buddy. I hope I'm as spry as you when I'm your age."

"Thank you, John."

John moved to the first step and stopped until he felt the Cardinal's hand upon his shoulder. John took each step very slowly. He used the Cardinal's hand to sense when Anton had shifted his weight forward before he slowly moved to the lower step. This process was repeated 11 times, until they were both standing on what looked like solid rock.

Anton again took the lead and John followed him, eagerly looking around the Cardinal's shoulders to see what lay ahead. They came to a small sitting area. John saw the bag dude sitting patiently in one of the two chairs. The Cardinal came to a stop adjacent to the two chairs.

"Do you need to sit down for a minute, Cardinal? You ok, buddy?"

"I am fine, my friend." He glanced towards the corner they are about to go around, and then back to John.

"Your quest is about to be fulfilled. What you seek is a mere seven meters around the corner. I think it is time that I follow you, John. Just be cautious when you draw near the door. Be watchful of your senses and emotions. They are the targets of the power that guard the book. If you become uneasy in any respect, I urge you to withdraw. These chairs are here for a reason. Many before you have struggled to make it back this far. That is why I have asked Father Dosanta to join us. If you have difficulty, I could not manage you alone. Now, unless you have questions, you are free to fulfill your destiny, John."

John hesitated for a moment. He noticed that Father Dosanta's eyes were open wide and looking back at him. John took one last look at his friend and smiled before turning to walk around that fateful corner.

From the corner of his eye, he saw the Cardinal motion for Father Dosanta to follow him. The priest immediately rose, yet stayed a few steps behind John. The noise of their shoes upon the stone echoed around them.

The moment he rounded the corner, he was frozen by a sight he had seen in his mind every night for many months. There were no light fixtures in this portion of the hallway. It was being lit by the rays of light that poured from a door just ahead of him. Those rays of light were intensely white, and they struck the wall on the opposite side. Just as he had always seen, he approached the door and slowed to a stop. His mind was comparing what he recalled, to what he now saw before him. Something was different. What was it?

He struggled to determine what it was. Finally, he knew. It was the doorway. The one feature that he had always been drawn to in his mind was missing. He should see the curved rock on the inside of the room. But he did not. He hesitated, because things were not playing out as he had dreamed so many times before.

In a flash, he saw men who were not there. Their dress was that of laborers, yes - carpenters from days long past. They were adding a doorframe to the inside of the room. They hastily rushed in to strike nails several times, and then stepped back into the hall. They were visibly afraid, yet they continued this until the frame was complete on the inside. No longer could the curved rock be seen.

Upon completing their task, one carpenter was shaking. He fell to his knees. The other came to his aid and lifted him to his feet. They moved towards John and passed through him before he could react to move aside. He shuddered as the cold of their souls passed through his.

Feeling a warm hand upon his elbow, John jerked around to see who it is. Father Dosanta's face was only inches from John's. "Are you okay, senor?"

John looked confused as he asked the Father, "I thought you were Italian?"

The priest smiled and replied, "I speak Italian, but I am from Spain."

John touched the Father's hand and said, "I'm okay, buddy. Just felt something cold go right through me. I'm fine. Thanks!"

The priest commented as he removed his hand from John's arm. "Yes, it is drafty in these halls."

John's attention was again focused on the door that was filled with light. He walked to its very edge, but stopped. With the exception of the book not floating transparently in the air, all that his eyes now saw was just as it should be. He always knew that the floating book was just a symbol. It was a way to show that IT was the reason for this room. He extended one arm through the doorway and into the room, as if to test what was there. He felt nothing. It was just as he had seen.

Now was the time. He turned briefly to see both men watching him intently. He smiled before entering the room. They moved quickly to a vantage point against the opposite wall. From experience, they know that they could stand and view the room safely from here, with only minor urges to flee. Father Dosanta was confused as to how John could be standing only a meter from the book and yet be so calm. Cardinal Mortello, on the other hand, now knew that John was the one that the Holy Father had been waiting for.

John's very soul was vibrating from the energy in the room. He felt compelled to touch the book, and reached out to do so.

The two men in the hall looked at each other, as if in fear. The Cardinal quickly placed one hand on the shoulder of the priest, as if preparing to push him into the room for John. Father Dosanta pulled the cross hanging around his neck to his lips and kissed it gently. Then, with a fluid motion, he made the customary cross in the air before himself, head to chest, shoulder to shoulder.

A stern and most determined look transcended his face. He was obviously prepared to charge into the room if signaled to do so by the Cardinal. John's hand was only a fraction of an inch from the book. He hesitated for several seconds with it hovering above. They noticed his eyes were closed as if he were in a trance.

Finally, John opened his eyes, pulled his hand back, took a look around and exited the room. Once in the hall he stopped and looked at the two men, now covered by his shadow. The Cardinal noticed immediately that the urge to flee was gone. But why? As he stepped from John's shadow and into the light from the room, the familiar fear slammed into him as if being hit with cold water on a hot day. He retreated to the safety of John's shadow.

"Are you okay, John? How do you feel?"

"I feel fine! A little hyped up, but fine." He knew they would be more comfortable away from this light, so he motioned for them all to walk back down the hall.

They thankfully followed him back to the small sitting area around the corner. John motioned for them both to sit down. The Cardinal sat willingly but the priest hesitated and said, "Senor, please."He pointed to the empty chair.

John stepped over to him, placed his hand on his shoulder and said, "You need it more than I do, Father Dosanta. Please, I feel fine." The priest looked to the Cardinal, who patted his open hand in a downward motion and said, "Sit, Michael, sit."

"So, my friend. You show no outward signs of feeling ill. Do you feel nothing from your experience? Nothing at all?"

"Anton, I feel GREAT! " John made two tight fists and pumped them once in the air, level with his shoulders. "Oh, I felt something in there all right! It was an energy that just made me feel so, so, HAPPY! Man, I feel GOOD!"

Father Dosanta looked at John, then the Cardinal, then John. His face was blank as if he were in total disbelief. He looked like he wanted to ask something, but he does not. He seemed content to let the Cardinal and John do the talking.

"John. I was most concerned when you reached for the book. Why did you stop?"

"Well, Anton. I had a sudden urge to open it. But I stopped because of the voice in my dreams. It said, 'Tell him it is time to open the book,' and then I saw the Pope. Not his face, just his white robes and that tall hat he wears for special occasions."

The Cardinal was sitting with one elbow on the arm of his chair. His fingers were rubbing back and forth across his lips, and his eyes gazed downward. After sitting like this for a few seconds, he looked up at John and asked, "So what are you going to do now, John? Do you know?"

"Yes. It's time for me to talk to the Pope. You really have to help me convince him to open this book." John walked over in front of the Cardinal and squatted down as if he were a catcher in a baseball game. "Anton, you must get me in to see him."

"So you want to go back to Roma? You are through here?"

"Yes, afraid so. I don't exactly understand this part. I see it, but it seems kind of out of order."

"I don't believe I follow you, John."

"Look. It seems to me that we are supposed to go back so I can talk to the Pope. Don't really know what about. But I know it will come when we start talking. No, I'm not done with this place. I don't really get it, but for some reason I will come back. This part has always been really fuzzy, if you know what I mean. It isn't as clear as the rest of it. But I bet it will happen."

John stood up and helped the Cardinal out of his seat. Seeing this, Father Dosanta stood to help the Cardinal as well. John stepped back and looked towards the end of the hall, past the room with the book.

"Why did you guys hide that big round rock?"

The Cardinal and the priest both looked at each other, and then at John. They stood there without speaking. John continued. "Come on, now. I know it's behind that fake wall at the end of the hall. It's just past the room with the book. Hey, wait a minute. You're looking like you don't know it's back there."

"John, what big rock?"

"The big round one that was in front of this cave when that guy found it. You know? That rock!"

The Cardinal's mind was reeling with questions and images of what John was describing. He knew nothing of this rock.

John stood staring down at the end of the hall. He turned to face them again before speaking.

"You know, it glows in the dark. Just like that room with the book."

"What do you mean, it glows?"

"Not the whole rock, Anton. Just the side that faced the cave. It must have absorbed all the light that it was exposed to through the years."

The Cardinal was now staring down the hall, too. John's following comment caused him to snap his attention back to John.

"You know, I think we could break through that fake wall. It's not really all that sturdy, I'll bet. Hey, you said I had permission to do whatever I wanted, remember? Does that include demolition work?"

"I'm not sure, John. Perhaps we should wait until we talk to the Holy Father first?"

John took one last look down the hall and then shook his head. "Yeah, you're probably right. Besides, I'm kinda thirsty and you look tired, my friend." John motioned with his head for Father Dosanta to help him with the Cardinal. "What do you say we call it a night?"

"Yes, John. I like that idea. I've had more activity and excitement today than I intended to. To rest would be good."

John and the bag dude helped the Cardinal back above ground and to his room. Before the Father left John, he said, "Senor. It has been a pleasure to meet you. You are most blessed by God. If you need anything during the night, please press the call button on your phone. It will sound my beeper and I will come as quickly as possible."

"Thanks, buddy. It was a real pleasure to meet you too."

~ ~ ~

John slowly moved from sleep to consciousness and lay there for a few minutes. Though it was too dark to see it, he knew that the key was on the dresser by his wallet. Why was he awake? He didn't have the dream, or any other dream for that matter. He sat up on the side of the bed. It was there in the dark nearby, and it was calling to him. Why? He knew why. He must go back down there.

As in his visions, this time he went alone. Still something seemed off. He felt unsure of the sequence of events in his head. He was here, and has that key. It must be time for this. At least he hoped it was.

He redressed in the dark like he had done a thousand times before. Shirt, jeans and then boots. His hand scooped up the key without looking as he headed for the door. The sudden brightness of the hall light made him wince.

There was no need to look around to see if anyone was there, for he knew there will not be. As if in a trance, he quickly walked to the library door and inserted the key. With it closed and locked, he entered the small storage room.

The shelves gave way as easily as before, and he soon heard the echo of his boots on the rock floor. Since he did not turn on the light, the hall was filled with an eerie haze from the book room around the corner. The hall became brighter and the haze faded away as he neared the turn. Then he saw it yet again. The pure white rays of light were spilling onto the opposite wall.

His methodical stride did not stop at the entrance this time. No, he entered right away and took a position directly behind the pedestal that held the book. Extending both hands at once, he placed them on its cover.

At first, nothing happened. He blinked, his eyes darting first this way then that, as if he were watching something play out in front of him.

Each eye closed, one at a time. Then with no warning, his body violently shook as if being electrocuted. His head was thrown back from side to side, but his hands remained on the book as though welded in place. His teeth were clenched so tightly that a small bit of blood was forced from his gums. It slowly trickled from one corner of his mouth.

As quickly as it began, so it ended. Standing motionless like a statue, his eyes POPPED open. Both hands released their hold at the same time. The sound of a muffled snap was heard as they slammed into the shape of clenched fists. His breathing consisted of regular but stunted gasps of air.

He tripped as he began to make his way to the door. Striking the frame with his shoulder, his body spun around and he stumbled backwards into the hall. His momentum continued until it was stopped by the opposite wall. Both hands were placed waist-high upon the wall and he leaned his shoulders forward as if getting ready to lunge.

This was his position as Father Dosanta ran from the corner to his side. Hurriedly placing one arm behind John's shoulders and the other grabbing John's arm, the priest pulled with all his might to drag him to the safety of the chairs. Once seated, he knelt in front of John to keep him from falling to the floor. His head was dangling motionlessly as the priest repeatedly asked, "Senor, senor. Are you okay, senor? Ok? Senor?"

The priest was relieved to see John slowly raise his head and open his eyes. Once focused and aware that it was the priest before him, John said, "I was wondering when you'd get here. In my visions, you always seemed to get here quicker. What took you so long, Michael?"

The confused look on the Father's face prompted John to add, "Hey. It's all right, buddy. I'm just glad you came to get me. In the vision, I don't remember hurting like this. It wasn't supposed to go like that." Something had changed. He couldn't put his finger on it, but something?

"You are okay now, senor? Yes?"

John stood. To the amazement of the priest, he walked just to the edge of the corner and peeked around it while speaking out loud to himself. "I guess it would be REALLY stupid to try to get to that rock now!" Then he walked back towards the priest and stopped to collect him by putting his arm around Michael's shoulders. They began their walk back to the stairs as John continued. "I'd really like to show you that rock, buddy. Did I tell you it glows?"

~ ~ ~

The following morning came to life with a brilliant sun shining on the villa. John was already dressed and packed. He was looking out his window and waiting for a call from the Cardinal at any moment. When it rang, John picked it up without taking his eyes off the scenery outside.

"Morning, Anton. Yes, you could say that. I'm sure he was. He's a good man, that Michael. Yes sir. He pulled me away just in the nick of time, that's for sure. Of course. I never turn down free food!"

Their breakfast was delicious and the little lady still as efficient as ever. The Cardinal quizzed John on his second excursion to see the book. John was delighted to hear that the Cardinal had already secured a meeting with the Pope once John returned. They were helped into the waiting limousine and Father Dosanta leaned in to shake John's hand one last time. "We will see you again, senor? Yes?"

John smiled and nodded 'Yes' before the door closed.

The return trip to the airport was quieter than the trip out to the villa. They shared some idle chitchat, but nothing of substance was discussed between them. John did feel that the Cardinal was staring at him more than usual, though he never managed to catch him in the act. John had another wise guy thought. 'I wonder if we'd be talking more, had I busted down that fake wall to show them that rock?'

CHAPTER 13
A Chat with a Pope

John's eyes were struggling to focus, but it mattered not. This time, he knew exactly where he was. Back in his familiar at the Vatican. Odd, but he actually found himself feeling at home. The events of the last two days had set the stage for him to finally meet and talk with the Pope. He and his friend Anton were scheduled to meet for lunch. That was when he would learn the time of his audience with the Pope.

John was not in a hurry to rise. He had decided to skip breakfast altogether. Back home, he only ate breakfast on weekends with Barb. On weekdays, he usually just took a cup of coffee for the drive to work. Besides, the lunch in this place was outstanding, it was free, and he intended to eat all he could.

He looked at the clock and saw that the alarm would not ring for another hour and a half. When he set it last night, he'd left himself an hour to get ready and make the short stroll to the dining hall. He fell back into a light sleep to kill the time.

The ringing of the alarm propelled him into his 'Get Ready' mode. He felt totally energized and clear headed. Yes, everything seemed to be going just great for him today. He even flipped the toothpaste twice in the air and caught it behind his back while brushing his teeth with the other hand. After this wondrous feat, he exaggeratedly slapped it onto the counter top as if he was imitating a player spiking a football after scoring a touchdown. Yeah!

He was out the door, through the hallways and entering the dining area just in time to see the Cardinal taking a seat. John was almost to the table when the Cardinal noticed him.

"Good morning, John! I trust you slept well?"

"Like a baby! Feel GREAT! And you, Anton?"

"Yes, it is always good to be back in one's normal surroundings."

Their lunch together was fun. John continued to capture the Cardinal's imagination with Texas stories about real, modern-day cowboys. After their meal, yet before the delivery of those tormenting little espresso cups, the Cardinal simply said "At 3:00 this afternoon."

John knew immediately what it pertained to. Finally, he will meet the big guy. Upon hearing this, his energy level dropped considerably. The Cardinal noticed this.

"John. You are ready for this? It is what you have been wanting, right?"

John sat looking at his friend Anton for a few moments. It was as if he was hesitant about his meeting with the Pope. Slowly John's smile returned. "Yes. Yes, it is what I've been waiting for." John's energy level began to come back, and he was once again his old self.

With lunch over and two hours to kill, John returned to his room to call Barb. They talked for well over an hour before hanging up. Their conversation had ended with a kiss being issued by each.

Afterwards, he found himself in the study, sitting at that lonely little table. Though his eyes were focused out the window, he was not seeing the boring little courtyard. No, he was replaying mental movies of his upcoming chat with the Pope. These were movies that had forced their way into his mind on a nightly basis for months now. However, unlike most of his visions, the one with the Pope was always fuzzy. This is what made him uneasy about the meeting. He didn't know exactly how it would go. There must be a reason why this one was not clear, while all the others were so very vividly clear. Oh well, whatever was going to happen would do so at 3:00 this afternoon.

There was a knock at his door at precisely 2:30. It was Bishop Turin and he was there to escort John to the meeting. This journey involved a secluded elevator that descended several levels below ground. It was an exclusive, special elevator because Bishop Turin had to use a key just to get the doors to open. Once inside, there were no buttons like a normal elevator. Instead, there was a keypad. The Bishop intentionally blocked John's view before entering a code. A very quick series of beeps were heard before the elevator came to life. John found this really odd. No buttons, and no digital numbers that showed you what floor you are on. How odd was that?

The only thing normal about this elevator was the sudden stop John felt before the doors opened. John was very curious. Where in the world is this dude taking him? There appeared to be just as big a maze of tunnels down here as there were corridors in the building above them.

Finally, their trip came to a dead end. The Bishop had taken him to another electronic door. It also had a keypad on the wall beside it. Before punching in the code, the Bishop turned to John.

"Once your meeting with the Holy Father is concluded, I will pick you up right here and escort you back to your room. I've been instructed to tell you the following. His Holiness wishes for you to feel comfortable when talking to him. It is his deepest desire that you converse with him as you would do with any of your closest friends. He made a particular request that you not give any thought to his position in the Church, or your being of another faith. His hope is that two men meet and have a truthful exchange. Nothing more, nothing less."

John said nothing. He just nodded 'yes'. The Bishop quickly blocked John's view again. There were several more beeps, and the big electronic door slowly began to open. The priest stepped to one side and motioned for John to enter. John slowly walked into the small, dimly lit entryway that flowed into a well-lit room beyond. A few steps in, he hears the sound of beeps again. He turned in time to see the Bishop's back disappearing through the closing door. It was amazing to realize how silent that door was. There was never a noise of any kind, other than the sound of the lock arming or disarming.

As John emerged into the light of the larger room, his eyes were drawn to an average-sized, elderly looking man dressed in white. There were two ornately decorated chairs of gold. Each had a small side table, with a carafe of water and a glass. These were the only objects in this room.

They faced each other. The man in white was standing in front of one of the chairs with his hands patiently folded in front of him. As John approached, he began to suffer from his usual dilemma of not knowing if he should extend his hand or not. To his relief, the man in white motioned for him to sit, thus eliminating the need for John to decide.

"Mr. Parson, please."

John stepped in front of his chair. To his own amazement, he caught himself offering an ever so slight bowing of his head. After having done so, he questioned himself about this action. Oh well, it couldn't hurt to be nice to this old guy. He *was* John's senior.

The two men sat down simultaneously. John decided to break the ice.

"Well, sir, this has to be the fanciest chair I've ever sat in."

"As with any organization that has been around as long as the Church, there are histories that accompany many of our furnishings. These two chairs are no exception to this rule. They are actually not as old as some things here. A mere few hundred years or so, but they have played witness to many historical events."

John thought to himself, 'This chair is a few hundred years old?' He found himself rubbing his hand on the velvet arm. "I can't break this or anything?"

"I assure you that it is quite sturdy, Mr. Parson."

"Well, if you say so. I'll have to take your word for it. Sure is a nice chair."

"If I may? I understand that you have been experiencing many strange, yet exciting things these past few months. Though there may be little we can offer you in guidance, I would think that you have questions about the book and other things."

John was caught off guard by how direct the Pope was, but he liked this. He had never been a man for beating around the bush himself. Yes, he could already tell that he liked this man in white. He had the same feeling about him as he had for his friend Cardinal Mortello.

"Well sir, yes I do. Where did the book come from?"

The Pope began telling the following story of the book's discovery in 1915 by a retired architect. He had been working in London when he met and married a woman from a small fishing village. They were happy together. His wife had always wanted to show him her homeland and village, but they had never found the time to do so. She unfortunately was killed in a bizarre auto accident not far from Paris. It had always been her wish to be buried in her family plot in the village. He decided to take her home and honor her wish.

Having no living family of his own, he became attached to the village and her family. It seemed only fitting that he be laid to rest beside her, so he purchased some land to build a home. He had designed his house with a basement, then added plans for a wine cellar below the basement. This is when his workmen struck solid rock. He gave up on the wine cellar, but completed the house.

One night, he was seated in his basement and contemplating how to finish it out. He began sweeping the loose sand from what he thought was a solid stone floor. His actions uncovered the edge of the rock, and then what he assumed was one small stone. The more he swept, the more sand was moved, and eventually he found that it was the curved top of what looked like a large rolling rock. The type of stone used to close off tomb entrances in Biblical times. He did not alert any authorities for fear they would confiscate his land and home to preserve the burial site.

It took him three weeks to remove an untold number of buckets of sand and finally expose what he thought to be a tombstone. Eventually his curiosity overcame his desire to respect the dead. He had an engineering degree, which made it easy for him to construct a lever and pulley mechanism to safely move the huge stone to one side. As the stone moved, he was frozen with fear as a brilliant white light began pouring from the exposed cave entrance. He fled his basement in fear, thinking it was God's punishment for having desecrated a burial site.

A week later, he massed enough confidence to return to the basement and found the light still pouring out of the small crack he had opened by moving the stone. After many prayers, he decided to open it completely no matter what the consequences. With the stone completely to one side, he slowly looked in and saw the book on the carved stone pedestal. He was relieved that there were no bodies in the cave room. As he stepped through the entrance, he felt the power of the book hit his body, and he withdrew immediately. After a few minutes of soul-searching, he walked through the entrance and straight to the book. His impulse was to touch the book, but as he extended his hand, his body was racked with uncontrollable shaking. This is when his finger barely brushed the edge of the book and sent him to his knees. He crawled out of the room and passed out in his basement.

The next morning he awoke and made his way upstairs. He began having terrible migraine headaches, combined with unbelievable nightmares. After a few months, he realized he could not live in the house any longer. He contacted a friend who worked at the Vatican and explained what he had found. Not long afterwards, the Church purchased the deed to his land and he returned to England. He suffered from the same headaches until his death only eight years later. The need for secrecy of this discovery is what led the Church to expand his humble home into what is now called The Villa.

The Pope paused to take a drink of water. John took this opportunity to ask, "So where did the book get its name?"

After setting his glass back on his table, he continued. "The Pope at that time began referring to the book by the name of the man who found it. His name was Robert Prizom. It has been called by that name ever since."

"Do you know what the inscriptions on the front cover say?"

"I'm afraid that we have only been able to translate the two lines at the top. They are in larger lettering, and it is a simple form of the early Hebrew language."

John quickly commented, "When I was looking at the book, I saw that large print at the top. So what about all those symbols on the entire bottom half of the cover? Why can't you translate it?"

"There have been many scholars selected by the Church to do just this thing. Each Pope has commissioned a group to continue the work of those before them. It is written in a language unknown to any of the world's scholars today. I know that you have met Father Latanye. He is among, if not THE, most prominent linguists of ancient languages. He has been working on those symbols for over 35 years. None have offered even an educated guess as to what those symbols mean. Considering the difficulties of obtaining a copy of that cover, it is somewhat disheartening that we have learned nothing as to their meaning."

"I'm confused, sir. What do you mean difficulties of obtaining a copy? You have the book."

"Yes, but you yourself have felt the power of it when one enters the book room. When the Church first acquired and secured the book by building the villa, three Vatican scholars of that time were handpicked to research the book. They immediately found that their assigned task had some considerable risks attached. They each tried to go in and copy by hand as many symbols as they could before becoming overwhelmed by feelings to flee. Then the next would take his turn. With each man only being able to endure one minute or less, this took two days to create a written copy of the cover.

"The one-minute exposure to the book's power required as much as an hour for each man to regain control of their emotions, and to stop shaking. Each of these men suffered for many years from what was thought to have been an easy task. They all had migraine headaches and uncontrollable shaking of their hands. The Pope at that time decided that no others were to be exposed to the book's power. It was simply too dangerous. And after all of this, we still have not been able to decipher the writings on the cover."

John took a sip of his water. "So what did the one line at the top say? You said it was Hebrew and you guys read that stuff, right?"

The Pope smiled. John was obviously feeling very comfortable asking him questions.

"Yes, Mr. Parson. We read that stuff. It may come as a shock to you. You already know what the first line says."

"I do? Why do you think that?"

"Because it is what brought you here. It says, 'Let him be told it is time to open the book.' You have known it all along, and this is how I knew you were the one."

John's eyes almost popped out of his head at hearing this. The Pope's face became a little more focused at John's response to hearing those words.

John sat motionless for a moment before hastily reaching for his glass of water. He did not drink from it, but instead sat holding it with both hands. His eyes looked past the Pope into nothingness, lost in thought. Then a quick drink, the glass returned to its table, and John spoke.

"I can't believe that it was there on the cover of the book all along." Now John leaned towards the Pope as if wanting to emphasize what he was about to say. "So, sir, why did I have to come here to ask you to open the book? You seem to already know it is time."

"May I ask you a few questions, Mr. Parson?"

"Of course."

"Why do you think you must ask me to open the book?"

"Because, I see you in your white robes and wearing that tall hat of yours. You also are holding a white staff of some kind. I've seen pictures of you with it. While looking at you, the voice speaks those words to me. So it seems to me that I am to ask you to open the book."

"One more question, if I may. I understand you had several visions when you saw the Roman Scepter of Arenia in the museum. How many, exactly?"

"Three, there were just three. Why?"

"I, too, have had a vision. It started many years ago, yet I remember it vividly. As I told you, the Church had decided not to let anyone else near the book. However, each new Pope is provided with detailed reading of all that has transpired with the book. A history, if you will. Each new Pope is given the chance to enter the room to see if they are the one to open it."

"So you have been in there with it? You've personally felt the power within?" John asked.

"I have. My encounter was short but profound. They say I collapsed and brushed it as I fell. Cardinal Mortello was the one to help me from the room. Did you know that he had once lived at the villa?"

John was shocked at this news. His friend Anton had never

mentioned this to him. "No, sir. Anton seems to have forgotten to tell me that."

"As a young priest, Father Mortello had been selected to guard the book. In the years that he lived there at the villa, he had entered the room on four occasions to help someone in distress. He was a strong man, but the repeated entries to the room seem to have aged him more rapidly than those around him. The point is that my vision had been recurring nightly. However, over the years it fell to once a week, then a month, and finally stopped occurring altogether. Until, I heard of you. It has been occurring nightly again." He paused and calmly observed John for his reaction.

John knew the Pope was waiting for something, but what?

"I'm afraid I don't follow you, sir. What was your vision? Or shouldn't I ask?"

"Please Mr. Parson. You may ask anything. To answer your question, my vision is of me telling someone to open the book. I believe that someone is YOU."

John's mind raced to process this new piece of information. At first he couldn't believe he had it wrong. No, he didn't have it wrong. Did he? Then the shock turned to acceptance, as he realized that those feelings he had been having about things being out of sync were because of this. He had interpreted the vision backwards. Now his instinct told him that the Pope was right. Then he remembered that he had touched the book just two days ago, and he could not open it. How can it be him that is to open it? He had tried and failed.

"I want to believe you, sir. It would make more sense your way, now that I think of it. You know, I've had a problem with some of the vision from this point on."

"How so, Mr. Parson?"

"Well, it's a feeling, not something I see. I just feel that some of the pieces are out of order. So I want to believe your version. But I still don't see how it can be me to open it. I touched it, and it touched me back very hard. But I couldn't, uh, it didn't open."

"I believe I know why, Mr. Parson. There was a second line at the top of the cover. Remember?"

"Yes I do. And could you just call me John? Please?"

"Of course, John."

"So, what did the second line say?"

"It said that 'A Trinity of Visions will lead the way.' Does this make sense?"

John's mind again accelerated to light speed as his visions began to realign. Finally, it made complete sense to him. The second line must be referring to the three visions he had experienced while standing in front of that Roman scepter. Maybe he IS the one to open the book. But how do these visions lead the way? John looked down at the floor, shaking his head as his thoughts raced at a dizzying pace.

"John. You seem distracted, as if something is bothering you."

"I'm sorry sir. For all these months, I thought my role in this would end when I spoke to you. I've always thought I had this thing figured out. Well, at least for my part in it. But now it's like starting all over again. And the scary part is I don't know what to do next. I'm not good at puzzles. I never have been."

John looked at this frail man in white, and he found himself wanting help for the first time. "What if I can't do it? You know, figure out what the visions mean. What if I can't open the book?"

"John, you have come a long way. Have you not? Did you think you made it this far alone? I believe you should consider that you have NEVER been alone on your journey. God Himself has chosen you to follow this amazing path. I would think that He has walked beside you from the beginning, and is at your side even now. You should resist any feelings of despair, for those are surely being used by Satan to defeat you. The Lord our Father will guide you if you remain open-minded to all possibilities before you. He will provide a way for you, John. He always provides us a way."

At this point, John noticed that the Pope's shoulders sagged just a little. So did his head. His eyes were not open as wide as they were only a minute before. There was a realization that this elderly man was not well.

"Sir? Are you not feeling well, sir?"

"I am fine, but a little tired. I have not slept well these past few nights. Perhaps we could continue this conversation again tomorrow, John. However, I would like to point out that talking to Father Mortello is just like talking to me. He and I share everything in regards to the Church's business. As I am sure you already know, he is a good man. You will find that he is also very good at puzzles."

"I have the same opinion of him myself. I like him and find him easy to talk to. I have also found you very easy to talk to. Now if you could tell me how to get out of here, I'll leave you to get some rest."

"You only need to walk towards the door you entered through. It will open automatically, and you should find Bishop Turin before you are very far along. Go with God, young man."

John turned and made his way to that big electronic door. There was a click and the door began to swing open. Once in the hall, John paused to wait for the door to start closing. It did not. Then he stepped away, and again he heard the sound of the door as it began closing. As he began to walk away, he heard the click of the door locking, and a few steps later he was face to face with Bishop Turin.

"May I show you to your room, Mr. Parson?"

"Yes, that would be great, buddy!"

They walked along in silence most of the way to the room. John had not been lying when he told the Pope he was tired, also. He was actually very tired. But why? He entered his room, kicked off his new shoes and fell backwards onto the bed. He began going over everything he had just learned. Yes, he really liked this Pope dude. He was a very nice man. John felt sad that he was ill. Then one eye slowly closed, and then the other. Sleep was upon him, and it was a very relaxing, deep sleep.

~ ~ ~

John was awakened by a light knock on his door. He moved quickly to open it.

"Anton. Come on in."

"Thank you John. I hope I didn't wake you."

"It's all right. I can't believe I feel asleep. Hey, we can sit back here and drink a soda." John turned and starts back to the little study. The Cardinal followed him and sat at the little table. "What can I get you, Anton?"

"I would like a bottle of water. Cherry flavored would be good."

"That's my favorite also."

John brought two plastic cups and the water to the table. He poured both glasses and then sat down.

"So what brings you around this way, Anton? You get lost? I know it's easy to do around here."

The Cardinal smiled at John's joking around. He really liked that about John. He seemed to be happy all the time. The Cardinal wished that more people were like John.

"I just thought I would drop by and see how your conversation with the Holy Father went. It was good?"

"Yes, it was good!" John put his elbows on the table and leaned in towards Anton. "Can I ask you something?"

"But of course, John. Anything."

"Is the Pope ill?"

The Cardinal looked out the window before saying, "He does not feel well. This is true. Why do you ask?"

"I just noticed he was talking away and then suddenly seemed to grow very weak. Then he asked if we could continue later. Is it his heart?"

The Cardinal looks a little shocked at first, but then replied, "Yes. I believe so. Of course you understand this is not common knowledge, and needs to be kept private."

"Of course. I understand that. I was just asking. Besides, who would I tell around here? You're the only one I talk to."

"I'm sure that you know I have already spoken with the Holy Father. I'm aware of your conversation, and what was discussed in general. I wanted you to know that I will make myself available to you any time you feel I could help."

"I appreciate that very much, buddy. I know that, up to now, I've kept things to myself. Nothing personal. But, now I'm going to need some help trying to understand where to go from here. I would be very happy if you and I could work together from this point on."

The Cardinal sat up in his chair. His eyes showed he was very much interested in this request. "I will try my best to be of help to you, my friend."

"Well, first of all, I found out several things that I didn't know. Seems I had the wrong idea about some of it. I think it's all falling into place now. Except, well, a few things."

"And these things are?"

"Well, for instance. It now seems that I have to figure out how these visions of mine are tied to opening that book. I told the Pope Dude that I'm not really good at figuring out puzzles. But he said you were."

John noticed that the Cardinal was smiling and shaking his head.

"What?"

"It is nothing, John."

"Come on buddy, why you laughing?"

"It is nothing, really. I truly enjoy how you phrase things. It is just that I've never heard him referred to as 'The Pope Dude'. I know enough about you to know you mean no disrespect, so please don't think that I took it that way at all. It's just that, what's the word? Oh yes. Your colloquialisms are very interesting to me sometimes."

John looked stunned. He was smiling, but thinking hard. "Did I say that? I can't believe I said it that way. Oh well, you're right. I didn't mean anything by it."

"Like I said, John, it was nothing. However, I am flattered that the Holy Father has faith in me helping you with these puzzles. Of course, to do so, you will have to share them with me."

"I know that, Anton. I have no problem telling you everything I've seen. You may even find it very interesting. I do!" John looked out the window for a second. "Can I ask you a couple of things first? About the book?"

John noticed Anton's stare. "I know, I know. Of course I can. Anyway, I was wondering about the difficulty the Pope said you guys had copying from the cover of the book. My first thought was that you could have put a mirror behind the book then just stood in the hall and looked at the cover that way. Did you guys think of that?"

"It was the first thing they tried. As hard as it is to believe, the mirrors simply didn't reflect anything. Of course this was before my time, but the reports I read said that only the pedestal was visible in the mirror. The actual comments indicated that they saw the top of the pedestal as if the book were not there."

"Wow. That is cool. Sort of like a vampire book? Just kidding, sorry. So why didn't you just take a picture of it with a camera? That would only take one second, and they could have been out of there."

"Yes, they thought of that as well. Of course there were no digital cameras back then. Everything used film. The problem was that the film always turned out extremely over-exposed after it was developed. Each frame was totally white. It was as if the lens had been pointed at something brighter than the sun! They tried several types of film and several types of cameras. The results were always the same.

"Just as a side note, John. Of course they had manually copied the cover by hand, and then made copies for the different research groups. Now, when the new digital cameras came along, we tried again. Not that we needed the pictures for translation purposes, we just wanted a photocopy for the researches. It would be more like looking at the book cover itself. However, once again, that failed. I believe the expression was that the camera's circuits were 'fried'. It meant that each of the new cameras they tried were, in fact, destroyed."

"Wow. That is interesting. How about this? I was also wondering if you have ever thought about using one of those police bomb squad robots to go into the room with a video camera. Hey, you could even use that robotic arm it has to try and open the book. Maybe you could get video of the other pages?"

The Cardinal was still smiling at John's enthusiasm with this subject. "Yes, that is also a very good idea. Unfortunately, those attempts failed as well, and once again, because the electronics were fried. I am impressed with your thinking, John. It took us a while to think of these things. You've only had a few hours, and you thought of all of this. Impressive, John, very impressive."

John's smile showed that he really liked the Cardinal's compliments. "Thanks Anton. You and I are going to figure all this out together." He stood and began to pace slowly around in a circle. The Cardinal was taking great pleasure at watching his friend get so involved.

"And before you mention this, let me tell you that they also tried touching the book from the hall with a long wooden pole. This ended very badly when the pole erupted into flames."

"No way? Really? Cool! Oh one more thing. Have you ever tried to figure out how that room has all that light? You know. I was thinking maybe the walls are that fluorescent stuff. Or maybe it's radioactive, and that is what makes everyone sick. Did you ever get one of those Geiger counter things and check it out?"

"John, please sit down. You are making me dizzy. Yes, over the years we have invited a few select scientists to investigate the light from the room. They were and still are Catholic clergy. It just so happens they, like Father Latanye, are also world-renowned scientists as well. Again, there has not been any scientific explanation offered by anyone. However John, I must say again that I am extremely impressed by you bringing these two possibilities up. Nicely done, my friend."

John stopped pacing and stared at the Cardinal for a second or two. Then he walked over and sat down again at the table.

"I just have one more question. Why didn't you tell me that you had lived at the villa before? I know about you saving the Pope from the book room. I also remember you making a statement about knowing the true power of the book. He said he touched it by accident. Though he didn't say this, I was kind of thinking that maybe you touched it, too. Am I right?"

The Cardinal's face lost its smile. Now it was his turn to quietly look out the window at that boring little courtyard. He glanced back at John before speaking.

"Yes, I did live there. That is where I first met the Pope. It was but a chance meeting that has had a rather profound effect on both my body and my position in the Church. It was shortly after that when I was reassigned to the Vatican. It has taken its toll on me, but it has also blessed me in so many more ways. It has been more than just favorable from my point of view."

"But Anton, you didn't answer my question. Did you touch the book as well? Ever?"

The Cardinal's eyes were once again cast outside that small window. They were still focused there when he answered, "Yes."

John sensed that his friend was holding back, but if they were to work together, he must share. "So? What happened?"

With his eyes still outside, he began speaking very slowly.

"It happened so quickly, and was completely accidental. After the Pope had fallen by the pedestal, I had gone to his aid. I was lifting him from the floor when he jerked and threw us off balance. I was afraid I was going to drop him and instinctively put out my hand onto the pedestal for stability. I must have just barely brushed it with the side of my hand. I remember it didn't hurt at all. Nothing like I thought it would have after seeing its effect on others. It was more a surge of consciousness than like electricity. I thought I saw ... I saw ... I guess I really don't know *what* I saw. Not really. And then we were in the hall, and it was over. Not much to tell, really."

John now joined the Cardinal in looking outside at the courtyard, but not seeing it at all. No, they were both seeing divine images placed in their heads by a book. A very special book. They continued looking outside as they spoke.

"Anton. What did you see?"

"You first, John? The other day, you started to say who wrote the book. I know you said it was just a hunch, but I would really like to know, my friend."

"Jesus. Anton. It was Him I saw standing there and writing in the book. Just a glimpse, but it was Him."

"Me too, John. Me too."

CHAPTER 14
Visions – The Ring

John and Anton were still staring out of that tiny window into the courtyard below. Twenty minutes had now passed since they confirmed each other's witness of Jesus writing in that book. They realized they were bound by more than mere friendship now; they were linked by sharing divine visions and perhaps interlocked destinies.

John was the first to speak. "I wonder what He was writing."

Anton added, "I wonder to whom He was writing? It is widely believed that Jesus never wrote anything down for Himself. It would have been left for others to chronicle for Him. If we are correct about Him having written this book, then why make the book virtually impossible to approach? Why limit the audience?"

"Well, Anton. The way to find out is for us to solve the riddle of these visions of mine. Agreed?"

"Yes, John. I agree."

They were both finally facing each other again. Both of them found it hard to move on to another topic. But in the end, they realized they must.

"So I guess it's time for me to tell you what I saw. It seems strange to talk about it. I've held these visions inside for all these months."

"Just remember, John. I am your friend. One who is traveling a similar path to yours. In fact, our paths now seem connected."

"Yes, I feel the same way. So, here goes."

John sat back in his chair before glancing out of the window one last time. Bringing his attention back inside, he was now looking in Anton's direction, but not at him.

"It always starts the same way. I'm in an ancient, Biblical-type city. From the small doorway that I'm standing in, I see people rushing past. They are all going in the same direction. There is a roaring sound coming from that direction. I always feel curious as to what it is, and why they are going there. As I lean out of the doorway to look, I am swept into the crowd and funneled along this tiny alley towards the end. It opens into a public square that is surrounded on three sides by buildings of all sorts. Most are single story, with a few two-story ones mixed in just enough to obscure your view of the skyline.

"The fourth side is a large stone structure like a palace or maybe a church. The entire front of it is made of stone steps that stretch from one side to the other. Just like the steps to a small town's courthouse.

"Above the steps is a large second story balcony with people standing on it. There are other streets like the one I came from and they are dumping hordes of people into this square. Those coming behind me are pushing all of us forward and towards those stone steps. The crowd is being stopped at the steps and nobody is being allowed any farther. It appears there are Roman soldiers all the way from side to side on the lowest four steps. They all are standing behind their huge shields. You can see the spear tips sticking out between the shields. It is obvious that they mean business. It's kind of scary as the crowd behind pushes us closer to the soldiers.

"Then there is a loud roar of noise from across the way and I look to see what is happening. I can see spear tips in the air and some plumes from helmets. There are more soldiers, and they must be marching four abreast judging by the spear heads. They do not enter the center of the crowd. They turn and march along the edge. Then another noise on the opposite side, and again I see more soldiers doing the same over there. I feel very nervous at this point, because they appear to be surrounding the crowd and here I am right up front by the steps. As it turns out though, they are simply cutting off the flow of people from the side streets by blocking off each entry point. The sound of the crowd all talking at once is just deafening, and it is hot standing in the sun while surrounded by so many bodies.

"That's when I see two trumpeters walk up behind the soldiers on the stone steps. The ends of their trumpets suddenly appear above the soldier's heads and an echoing blast is heard by us all. The crowd falls silent. I'm just frozen in place. We are all jammed so tightly together that you couldn't fall down if you fainted. Then there is motion on the balcony and we all look up.

"A man wearing a white tunic steps to the balcony's edge. He has a bright red scarf draped from behind him, over his shoulder and diagonally across his body. It is held in place by a solid gold chain being worn as a belt. He has something around the sides of his head. It's not a crown but it is made of gold because the sunlight flashes on it whenever he turns his head. The crowd starts to slowly get loud again. The man is standing with one hand grasping his chain belt and he raises the other hand in the air signaling he is about to speak. Silly me, I think I'm about to find out what is happening, but here he is speaking in a language I don't understand. I remember wondering 'Who has dreams with languages they don't understand?' Anyway, I'm actually able to follow what must be happening. He speaks for a minute then he stretches both arms straight out to each side. That's when I see soldiers on both sides of him and each group is pushing a prisoner of some kind towards the balconies edge as well. One prisoner is stocky and of a more muscular build, while the other stands with a humble air of nobility.

"The man in white lowers his arms and places them on the railing of the balcony as he continues to speak. Then he suddenly stops and takes a step towards the more noble of the two prisoners. He points towards this man, but he is watching the crowd. Though there are a few people in the crowd that shout, it appears that whatever they have been asked, they do not like this prisoner. Then the man in white steps towards the other prisoner and points at him while looking at the crowd. This is when the crowd goes nuts. They are yelling and chanting something, but I can't make it out. I just know that it is very loud!

"After a few seconds of this, the man in white moves back to the railing and raises both hands to once again silence the crowd. With a wave of his hand, a slave appears and is holding a bowl of water. There is a white towel draped over the slave's forearm. The man in white dips both hands into the water three times and raises them upwards. He then quickly snatches the white towel from the slave's arm, dries his hands and then tosses the towel in the bowl. Whatever just took place was over. The man in white spins around to leave and disappears from view.

"At this point, the dream jump thing happens. You know what I mean? I'm standing in that crowd and wondering what next, when all of a sudden I find myself on the balcony. It is as if I were walking right behind the man in white as he enters the building. I could see things as they happened, but I knew I wasn't really there. Not like when I was in that crowd. So, he is walking and yelling at everyone around him. He stops to talk with a man that seems to be in charge of the soldiers. That man motions to a guard and the guard literally runs from the room to do something. A few minutes later he returns with the muscular prisoner surrounded by his guards. The officer in charge of the soldiers barks some orders, again in this language I don't understand. The soldiers remove the prisoner's chains and the man in white walks right up in front of him. He says something to him then he removes a ring from his hand and gives it to the officer. Again there are orders barked before a soldier draws his sword and steps towards the officer. The two of them place the ring on a marble table and are attempting to cut a cross into the emblem on the ring. It must have been soft metal because they managed to do it before giving it back to the man in white. He looks at it for a few moments. He is turning it first this way then that, really looking it over. Then he tosses it to the now-released prisoner and motions for the guards to release him into the crowd below. The prisoner walks from the room with his eyes fixed on the ring that he now holds in his hands.

"Then there is the dream jump again, and I'm standing in another little street after dark. The prisoner with that ring is acting very suspicious as his eyes dart up and then back down the street. It's like he is afraid that someone is following him. He goes down one street then turns down another. I get the feeling he knows exactly where he is going, but he just isn't going straight there. Again, he keeps acting like someone is following him. He always turns a corner then stops right by it. To kind of peek back around to see if somebody is following him. It's just a really paranoid thing with him.

"Finally, he seems convinced that there is nobody there, and he takes off in a real hurry. This time he looks very determined to get somewhere in particular. After a few more turns, he stops to knock on a door. I hear a voice from behind the closed door. The prisoner responds in a low voice and then the door slowly opens. A head sticks out and looks both ways before disappearing back inside. Then I see a hand motioning for the man to come in.

"Again, the jump thing puts me inside the room. There is a man and his wife looking over the ring. They are holding it close to a candle that is sitting on a table. They must have been eating, because there are still plates of meat and bread on the table. The prisoner asks something and the other man motions to his wife without taking his eyes off the ring. The woman fetches another wooden cup and pours wine into it before handing it to the prisoner. She then pulls some meat from the tray in the center of the table and places it on a plate. Seeing this, the prisoner sits down and begins to devour the food. He pulls several large pieces of bread from a loaf near him. The way he is eating so fast makes me think that he hasn't had much to eat in a while. Though he is eating, he keeps a wary eye on the man holding the ring.

"The inspection of the ring ends with a verbal exchange between the two men. The prisoner immediately stands up and is obviously upset. The woman backs away quickly. The strange thing is that she picks up a knife when the prisoner is not looking and she holds it down behind her leg as she moves behind him. The prisoner doesn't seem to be paying any attention to her. Then the prisoner holds out his hand as if demanding the ring back. The other man says something else but the prisoner shakes his hand again. This time the man takes another look at the ring before saying something to his wife. She disappears into the adjoining room for a few seconds and then she is back at the table. She is still holding the knife behind her back. She places fifteen small silver coins on the table and backs away. The prisoner finishes his drink while standing. He quickly picks up the coins and leaves."

John stopped to take a drink before adding, "Well, what do you think so far?"

"What do you mean so far? Is there more, John?"

"More? Oh yes, there is definitely more all right." He was smiling and nipping at his upper lip while nodding his head. "There's a LOT more! But, what do you think so far?"

"Well, John. I would say that the first part is all about a common Biblical tale of Pontius Pilate who asked the crowd who he should pardon, Jesus or Barabbas. You know this story?"

"Anton, even Southern Baptists know this story. Anyone that has ever been in a Sunday school classroom knows this story. What about the rest of it? That's the part that I was asking about."

"I'm sorry, John. I did not mean anything by the question."

"I know that, buddy."

Anton was relieved to see John smiling again. Yes, he now understood what Mathew meant about John sometimes displaying a strange sense of humor.

"So what do you think about this ring? Oh, wait, don't answer that. I need to tell you this next part first."

"Ok. John, you have my complete attention, I assure you."

"Ok, so back to the vision. I again do the jump thing, and there I am back at that palace. I'm in a room watching the man in the white tunic, who we both think is Pontius Pilate. He is sitting at a table and reading some rolled up scrolls. Then he pulls a flat piece of, well I'll call it paper, but it really isn't. He writes something on it and then opens a little box on the edge of the desk. The box has two places in it. One hole is for a ring and the other for a metal stamp. But only the metal stamp is there. He reaches inside and pulls out the stamp. That is when I can clearly see that it has the exact same emblem on it as did the ring - the one he had commanded the guards to cut a cross in before he tossed it to that prisoner.

"Anyway, he picks up a candle, pours some of the melted wax on the bottom of the sheet, and then presses the stamp into it. He holds it there for a second then pulls it off. He picks up the sheet and examines the wax for some reason before placing it on the edge of the desk.

"Now what do you think, Anton?"

"I have to believe that the ring is his seal of power. A stamp he uses to authenticate documents and such. If we are to trust in your vision, then the implication would be that he had both a ring and a stamp with the same seal. It raises an interesting question though. One that I can answer for you right now."

"What question? What are you answering right now?" John had a very quizzical look on his face.

"The Church has an identical box in its archives. And yes, it was meant to hold one ring and one stamp; however, we do not have either. What we do have is a document that references the issue of Roman dignitaries as having both a ring and a stamp. They usually wore the ring so as to have it if the need arose for them to seal something."

"So what I saw was probably true. Still doesn't explain why he destroyed the ring. Any ideas?"

Anton sat thinking for just a minute, rubbing his forehead with the fingers of one hand. Then his face lit up.

"The story says that Pontius washed his hands as a symbolic sign that he was not accepting any of the responsibility for the death of Jesus. It would stand to reason that he may also have wanted to get rid of the symbol of power used to authorize it as well. What better way to do this, than to give it to a man whom he thought was responsible for the death? He would, of course, first make sure it was not usable. Thus, he had the guard cut the cross into the emblem. Giving it to the prisoner would have been one more symbolic gesture of laying the blame somewhere else. Surely, he knew the man would sell it. He may have hoped that it would have been melted down for its precious metal and gems."

"Anton, why wouldn't he just destroy it himself? He could have easily had it melted down."

"Yes he could have, but he may have felt that it would appear as if he were trying to cover up what he did. He didn't want anyone to think he felt guilty in any way for what happened. This other way he could rationalize that Barabbas destroyed it because he felt guilty for the death of Christ. I know it sounds odd, but symbolic actions in those days were practiced by everyone."

John shook his head. "I guess that could make some kind of psychological sense. Maybe?"

"John, is this all of the vision pertaining to the ring?"

"Hardly. You want to hear the rest?"

"Yes, I do."

"Ok, here we go again. This time I jump to a little workshop. There is a man sitting at a workbench. He is building a little box. It's about two inches by three inches wide, and two inches tall. It has a lid. Once he's completed it, he begins to attach jewels to it. The stones are all different shapes and colors. Then, there is a knock on his door. Guess who is standing there when he opens it?"

The Cardinal shrugged his shoulders and grins at John.

"Well, it is the guy who bought the ring from Barabbas. He is talking to the older man in the shop. I get the feeling that he is the father of the guy building the box. Anyway, the father listens to the man before he starts shaking his hands, as if he was saying 'No, go away'. But the seller keeps on talking and talking. Finally, the young man comes over and takes the ring to look at it. The father is still very upset and not wanting that ring in his shop. The son is still examining the ring, when the father grabs it and covers it with a rag as if it shouldn't be seen. The son then says something to the father and they both look at a long white staff they've been working on. Then I'm in the street, and I see the man come out shaking some coins in his hand. He obviously got them to buy the ring."

"So John, is that the end of the vision?"

"No, not yet. There are a few, like snapshot pictures, and then it ends. First there is a picture of the son cutting that white staff in half. Then comes a picture of a nice red ruby stone with a finger pushing on it. Finally there is no sight, just blackness and a loud snap. That's the end of the vision part."

The Cardinal perked up at the way John ended his statement.

"John, what do you mean the end of the vision part? There is another part?"

"Well, yeah, but it's not part of the vision that I had at the museum. I thought you only wanted to hear about what I saw there."

"Please, tell me about this other part as well. If you have experienced something else, then we should explore how it is linked to the vision."

"Ok. It's just that it is something that I occasionally see when I dream. It's not vivid like the visions at all. In fact, it is sketchy at times. Oh, well, here you go. I sometimes dream about the first part of the vision, where I am in that big crowd looking up at Pontius Pilate. When he is asking the crowd about which prisoner to release, I zoom in on his face and can tell he really wants to release Jesus. He has a look of disgust towards the crowd wanting him to release a known thief and murderer. I then see an image of God hovering above the crowd. He has a clenched fist and appears to want the crowd to yell loudest for Barabbas. At one point He glares at Pontius, who then looks up at Him before motioning for the slave to bring the water for him to wash his hands. To make this whole thing even weirder, I clearly see tears in God's eyes as He is doing this. That's all there is, and I know this doesn't make any sense at all. Why would God want it to happen? You'd think He would be hoping that the people would pick His son to be spared. Wouldn't you?"

"John, this does make sense to me. I have read many versions of this event. Each version was written by a different author at times long past the event itself. Have you ever heard the phrase 'And the Lord moved to harden their hearts against Christ'?"

"No, Anton, you got me on that one. So I now stand corrected. Guess there are some things we Baptists just don't pass along. At least, nobody told me! So, what does it mean?"

"The popular view is that God needed this to happen so that man would execute His son. Remember, even Jesus remarked that He was a lamb sent here by His father to atone for our sins. It could easily be that your dream is just confirming the fact that God made it happen as one of the final steps to fulfill a master plan. Yet, the tears show that He loved his son very much. Now, is this everything with the ring?"

"Yep, that's all on this one."

"Mathew had mentioned something about you hearing people talking, and you actually understood what they were saying. Is this true?"

"Oh, yeah, but that didn't happen in this one. I heard voices and sounds in this vision, but I never understood anything they were saying. I got feelings about what was being said, just like I get them around here when you guys speak Italian in front of me. Sometimes I can tell what you are discussing but not the actual words you are saying. There is a lot to be said for body language, buddy!"

"Yes there is, John. I agree totally, and understand exactly what you mean. It is called being observant. Not everyone is, but a lot are. I have noticed that about you."

"So where do we go from here?"

"John, I was thinking we should make our way to the dining area. I find myself being a little hungry, for some reason."

"Well I don't know about you, but I'm hungry because I always smell that meat on the table when Barabbas is selling that ring. Really!"

CHAPTER 15

Visions – The Sandals

John and Anton's dinner was enjoyable but quiet. Although they had planned to discuss John's first vision in more detail, they could not. There were others within earshot of their table. They planned to return to the small study later in the evening, so John could continue with his second vision. But as they finished dinner, they both found themselves mentally drained from the day's activities. So, on the way back to John's room, they agreed to call it a night and meet for breakfast tomorrow morning.

John took another very relaxing bath in the room's vintage bathtub. He lay there in the soothing hot water with his head back on the curved lip of the tub. However, this time he did not fall asleep. His mind was reviewing all they had talked about today - both the Pope and his friend Anton. The cooling of the bath water forced him to dry off and get ready for bed. He was in blissful sleep a few seconds after his head fell upon the pillow.

They met as agreed the next morning, and again enjoyed a delicious breakfast before making their way back to John's little study. Sharing another bottle of cherry flavored water, they were once again ready to discuss John's visions.

"Are you ready to continue, John?"

"Yes, very. Now this one is totally different. And I'm not sure that you will find any similarities between this vision and any

Biblical stories either. At least I haven't found one. So here goes. It starts with a split second view of Jesus walking with His cross, on His way to be crucified. Now I know this is a Biblical story, but this part is not really about him. It's about a woman in red who my eyes are drawn to, standing on the opposite side of the street. She stood with her hands clasped together and pressed up tightly against her chest. She was completely focused upon the suffering man dragging this cross."

"I see tears in her eyes as she watches from behind a soldier's shoulder. Then an odd thing happens. There is a man standing beside her. He is tall and stands in a manner as if to show everyone that he is important. He is better-dressed than the rest of the crowd. At one point he looks down at her, though she does not notice it. It is obvious that he does not want the likes of her standing beside him, so he steps around another man to put distance between her and himself.

"That's when I notice that she is very pretty and is wearing a nice garment herself. But I get the feeling that she is not of his station in society, or perhaps her livelihood is less than respectable. Then the dream jump takes me to the crucifixion site. Yes, I know this is a Biblical story also, but it is not the focus of the vision. As they are nailing the hands, I again see the woman in red. She is standing on the other side of the circle of people who are surrounding the soldiers doing this task. I am drawn to walk around and position myself behind her. That is when two soldiers walk behind us.

"They had been guards in the procession that brought Jesus here. One of them had a pair of well-worn sandals tied together and thrown over one shoulder. With their part of this done, they were leaving to walk back to the city.

"Now this is the part that you were asking about. I heard these men speak and I understood every word, even though it was not in English. I know, I know. This is weird stuff, but it is how this vision goes. Anyway, the one guard asks what the other intends to do with the sandals he took from the prisoner, Jesus. Upon hearing the question, the woman in red also becomes interested in hearing the answer. She slips from the crowd and falls behind them as if following them back home. Of course the soldiers pay her no mind at all. Well actually one of them does turn to look as he hears her following them. It was just a quick glance back at her before he faces forward again. Then the bigger soldier with the sandals answers 'I will know what it is like to walk in the sandals of a King tonight.' They both laugh.

"Well, she and I follow these men back to the city walls. I remember looking behind us into the distance to see what is making all the noise. It is a chariot coming rapidly towards the city. The soldiers pay absolutely no attention to it at all. We follow them through the gates and turn down a side street. They part ways at the next intersection and she makes the turn to follow the one with the sandals. For some reason at this point, I fall behind both of them by about 10 or 15 feet. Just enough distance to see them both framed by the buildings as the street crosses a larger avenue ahead. The soldier is only five or six steps ahead of her as he steps from between the buildings and into the intersection. That's when I see a flash of a chariot across the intersection and the soldier is thrown out of my view by his impact with the running horses.

"It happens so fast! I hear the sound of the chariot crashing into the building and the wood breaking. It is out of sight, but the sound is ear deafening as it rumbles down the alley to my ears. The horses are whinnying loudly but that stops very quickly. Then she is running and disappears around the corner in the direction that the soldier's body had been thrown.

"I run to the intersection and turn to see the carnage of the wrecked bodies. That is when I notice that the sky had turned blood red and there had actually been several bolts of lightning at the exact moment the man had been hit. While standing there, I see in my mind that Jesus had just died. All of this had happened at the exact same moment in time. Then my thoughts are brought back to the whimpering animals. The horses are still strapped to the remnants of the chariot, which is lying upon the soldier we had been following. These poor animals were severely injured also, and are only half-heartedly trying to get up. The driver of the chariot had been thrown clear but there was a passenger who had one leg rammed through the front of the chariot. He was alive but barely moving.

"Then I see the woman in red. She is on the other side of the horses, and tugging on something. It must have finally given way because she falls straight backwards onto the stone street. She rolls over quickly and grabs something before running right past me. I can clearly see that it is a leather strap about ½ inch wide and around 20-something inches long. She is grasping it very tightly, and the loose ends have wrapped around the wrist from swinging her arms as she runs. I don't have a clue what it was. I thought she was after those sandals because they had belonged to Jesus. Odd though, it was just this strap."

John paused to take a sip of water. He glanced out of their favorite little window overlooking nothing.

The Cardinal spoke up at this opportunity to do so. "This is very interesting. I assume there is more, right?"

"You bet ya! Lots more. So I decide to follow her, but first I glance back at the man stuck in what's left of the chariot. There is a woman in a dark blue robe, and she is kneeling down to talk to the injured guy. Anyway, I turn and follow the lady in red as she hurries down two blocks and runs inside a door. I guess it's her apartment, definitely where she lives.

"Then I jump to what appears to be a sandal shop. She is there and obviously flirting with a young man as he is making a new pair of sandals. That's when I notice that she has fashioned that leather strap into a belt, and she is wearing it around her waist. Then time speeds up and I see her marrying the shoe shop guy. Next there is a scene of her placing this old leather strap in a cloth purse and putting it gently under a baby's pillow.

"This is a very strange part here. Time jumps me a long way into the future. To some place in France. Now I don't speak French, but I can definitely tell when it is being spoken. There is a young cobbler working in a shoe shop. I just know that he is a descendant of the baby who had that strap placed beneath its pillow. Yes, a big jump in time to get to here. Then there is another jump in time, maybe just 10 years or so, but I see this man holding the leather strap so reverently that it is almost like he is worshiping it. Odd, huh? Anyway, he takes it and stuffs it into the hollow shaft of what looks like a wooden walking cane before screwing a big golden handle onto the top of it. This cane is very ornate, and has diamonds in the shape of a cross on the shaft. There is a small dark red teardrop ruby on each side of this cross. I know it was meant to represent drops of blood and it really looks like it at a distance. This was pretty cool looking. He then places it into a hardwood case, and that case into one of those old steamer trunks people used to travel with.

"I really like this next part because I've always wanted to take Barb on a cruise. This may be the closest I ever get to one, though. So there I am on the deck of this big old steamship. The cobbler is right in front of me. We are both looking up as the ship passes by the Statue of Liberty. Then there is another jump in time, and I see the cobbler as a much older man with a baby in his arms. At first I think it is his son, but a young man and woman come up to take the child. The young man smiles at him and clearly says, 'Grandpa, he is going to be a priest in this Church one day and make us all proud.'

"And this next part I really have a hard time with. It absolutely confuses the heck out of me."

"What about it confuses you, John?"

"Well, it is current time, and it is about me. I'm sitting at a rodeo there in Fort Worth Texas." John stops and smiled exceptionally big at Anton. "I bet you wished it was you at that rodeo, eh buddy?"

"John, I would love to attend a rodeo with you the next time I'm in Texas. I have always wanted to see one in person."

The Cardinal's eyes were shining with delight at just the thought of getting to do something he had dreamed of since he was a small boy.

"Well, Anton, we just need to make that happen for you. I would love to take you to one someday. Anyway, back to the vision. So I'm setting right by the railing in a ringside box of seats. I turn to see Barb walking up and there is a priest with her. They are laughing and he has on just a black suit with one of those little white collars on. Yes, he is definitely a Catholic priest. Then it is just over. Just like that, it ends.

"So what do you think about this one, master puzzler?"

Anton shook his head. "Well, John. I'm going to need a while to take in all of this vision. I don't know what to think of it right at this moment. This one is much different than the first one. It is very strange how this one jumps through time from Biblical to current. I really don't know how to take this one."

"Yeah, me either. See, I told you this one was very strange.

It obviously is showing us that leather strap through time. But I still don't get what the strap was. I've wondered if it was part of the horse's bridle or reins. But that doesn't seem to make sense to me. Why would the woman in red be pulling that off the horses? And surely she wasn't trying to get that huge animal back on its feet by pulling on such a small strap. It just doesn't make sense at all to me."

"I don't really believe the strap has anything to do with the horses. However, I am not seeing what it could be, either. John, let's go back to the priest at the rodeo. Do you think it could be Father Mathew? Have the three of you ever been to a rodeo together?"

John had not ever thought of it being Mathew. But then again, he had this vision before he ever met Mathew.

"No, Anton. Besides, Mathew is not a Texan. I'm not even sure if he has ever been to a rodeo. There really isn't a face on this priest in my vision. I kind of think with no face, it is just some kind of symbol about the Church. Of course I didn't know Mathew when I had this vision for the first time. But I have had it many times since I met him. If it was him, I would think my mind would have put his face in it. It didn't, so I doubt it is him."

The Cardinal was looking out their little window and thinking hard about something in particular. He began moving his head from side to side. Then he rolled his shoulders a little. John watched him do this, so he does it too. The small backed chairs are not that comfortable. Anton started fidgeting with the beaded belt he is wearing. Then he placed one elbow on the table, cradling his face in his open hand while rubbing his temples with the other.

John began to think that he may be getting a headache. He was just about to ask if it was so, when the Cardinal's back stiffened and he sat straight up. Looking right at John, the Cardinal spoke.

"I have an idea. You mentioned a walking cane in great detail." He began fumbling in his cassock and finally pulled out his cell phone. With a jubilant smile, he said, "Ah ha! I think I'll call my secretary and have her do a search of the Church's known artifacts."

"Oh, Judy. Yes, I am fine. I have a request. I know you would be happy to do it. Thank you. I want you to do a computer search for me. Yes, that is the screen you use. Now under search words I want you to type the following. Walking cane with cross of diamonds. One red ruby on each side of cross. Then click on the search button. Of course I'll wait. Are you sure? Nothing? No, no, that is all I needed. Thank you. So much for that thought."

"That was a good thought, Anton. It would have been nice if you guys had a cane like that. You know. I was thinking." But he was interrupted by the ringing of the Cardinal's phone.

Anton looked at the phone lying on the table.

"Oh, it's Judy. Hello, Judy? That was very thoughtful of you. Thank you."

"So why did she call you back?"

"She wanted me to know that she went to the open Internet and did a search for that cane. Nothing was found. She is very thorough."

"She sounds like it. Just so you will think I'm thorough as well, let me tell you some ideas that I've had. None of them really panned out, but maybe they could spark a thought from you."

"That is a very good idea, John. I'd be interested in hearing your thoughts."

"Well, I thought about that steamship and seeing the Statue of Liberty. I thought maybe these people were immigrating to the United States . If we could pinpoint a date or name, then we could search the Ellis Island immigration records. They would have been processed into the U.S. there on that island. I went on the Internet and you can look up names of people who came through there. But you have to have at least a last name, and we don't. I've spent hours sitting with my eyes closed, trying to look around in that vision to see if there is a name or date anywhere. It was a waste of time. I've never seen anything that would help."

"Still, that was smart thinking, John. We must remember that there will be many false leads and paths taken to nowhere. However, each failure moves us closer to the correct path and the goal we seek. We must never give up."

"You are a very inspirational man, Anton. Yes, you are."

"John, I would like to leave you for a few hours if I may. I have some pressing Church business to attend to. It is mundane in nature, but I must do it nonetheless. I only hope that I can remain focused on what I have to do and do not think about your vision, which is what I'd rather do."

The Cardinal rose and made his way to the door. As he stepped into the hall, he said, "Should I call before coming back, or would you rather be surprised?"

"Either way, Anton. I'll be here. I'm probably going to lie down in here and think through this vision a few more times. That is, if I don't fall asleep first!"

CHAPTER 16

Visions – The Message

John had planned to lie down on the bed for a little while, but not fall asleep. His failure provided him with several hours of restful sleep that ended abruptly with a knock on his door. He popped out of bed and hurried to the door, fully expecting to find his friend Anton. However, it was Bishop Turin.

"Oh, it's you. Where's Anton?"

"I'm sorry, Mr. Parson. Did I wake you?"

"Yes, but it's OK. I was expecting to be woken up by Anton. So where is he?"

"He regrets that he will be a little late due to an unscheduled meeting with some guests. I am here to escort you to the Cardinal's private office. He should be there shortly after we arrive. I will wait for you here in the hall. Please take your time getting ready."

John opened the door and motioned for him to come in. "No way I'm letting you just stand in the hall, buddy. Come on in. It won't take me a minute to get ready."

As he stepped through the door, the Bishop thanked him and then closed the door. John had already turned and disappeared into the bedroom, but he was still talking loud enough for Father Turin to hear.

"So how you been? I haven't seen you in a while." John was just tucking in his shirt while slipping one foot into a shoe. With the belt buckled, he slipped the other shoe on and took a quick look in the mirror. His hair was barely messed up. He had slept so deeply that he had not even moved.

"I have been well, Mr. Parson. Thank you for asking. I trust that you have been enjoying your time with the Cardinal?"

John was walking out of the bedroom as he answered. "Yes. Anton is a good old boy. I like him. I'm ready." He walked past the priest and opened the door. As the door shut with its usual thump, John continued, "So, how far you taking me this time?"

"We will be there in eight minutes. It is very close."

"Eight minutes, huh? That doesn't sound so close to me. I'll just follow you like always. I don't want to get lost."

Nothing else was said until they rounded a corner and saw the Cardinal hurrying across their path and disappearing through a door. John started to call out to his friend, but the echo of their shoes was loud enough to dissuade him from adding to the noise. Father Turin spoke over his shoulder to John.

"It appears that his meeting ended quicker than he thought it would."

Reaching the door, the priest quickly opened it and stood to the side for John to enter first. The lady behind the desk immediately greeted John.

"Hello, Mr. Parson. I was afraid that I would never get to meet you."

She was sitting behind her desk with a phone headset on. There was a pencil in one hand, and she was rolling it between her fingers as she smiled at them both. John stopped and smiled back at her before saying, "And you must be Judy. It is a pleasure to meet you, ma'am."

"The Cardinal just barely beat you here. He said to have you go on in when you arrive."

She motioned towards the door to the inner office. Father Turin lightly tapped on the door before opening it. He pushed it open and stood back for John to enter. With John in the office, the priest reached in to pull the door closed.

"John, I am so sorry for the inconvenience. I have postponed that meeting twice already. They simply would not wait any longer. I was thinking that we might benefit from a change of scenery for this last vision of yours. Do you mind?"

"Not at all! Hey, you have a nice place here."

John strolled over to a small table with four very plush leather chairs around it. He rubbed his hand on the top of the chair back.

"This really feels soft. Are we going to sit over here?"

The Cardinal was standing behind his desk, moving papers around on it with one hand. He didn't even look up when he spoke.

"That will be fine, John. I just want to peek at these notes from Judy. Yes, these can all wait."

He looked up and walked over to join John in the corner. They both selected chairs on opposite sides of the table, so they could face each other during their talk.

"So, are you ready to puzzle me again, John?"

John smiled as he heard Anton teasing him with the puzzle remark.

"Ah, so the master puzzler is ready, eh?"

"Yes, my friend. Puzzle me."

John sat back and began rubbing both hands on the arms of the chair. His hand movements began to slow as he started his story.

"Each of these visions is about something different. The first one was all about that ring. The second one was about that leather strap. This one is about a piece of paper. It is a message. It must be one important message, but of course it is written in a language I don't understand. Right off the bat, this third vision is very different from the others. They stand on their own, but this one is piggybacked onto the second one."

John paused because he has noticed a quizzical look on Anton's face.

"Excuse me, John. What is a piggyback?"

"Sorry, buddy. It's just an expression that means it is on top of, or.... Well, I really should have said it this way. This vision starts in the middle of the second vision. Do you remember the soldier who was run over by the chariot?"

John paused to look at Anton, who was shaking his head yes.

"Ok, when I ran around the corner to look at the crashed chariot, remember I said I saw another woman in a dark blue robe? She was kneeling down to talk to the passenger who was stuck in the chariot. I think his leg is broken up badly, and he may be dying from his injuries. Well anyway, this vision starts here. I'm looking at her bending down to talk to him.

"Then, boom, I'm right behind her, and I see he is bleeding all over the place from a piece of wood that has gone right through his leg. Oh, by the way, I also understand what is being said in this vision, even though it is not English. So, she starts to put her hand on him when he suddenly grabs her arm and pulls her down hard to just inches from his face. His other hand is reaching into a leather pouch that is strapped around his neck and one shoulder. He clearly tells her, 'I am a courier from Roma and I have an urgent message for Pilate. You must take this to the palace. You owe your sovereigns this duty.' With a blood-covered hand, he then puts this scroll into her hand, and he appears to faint.

"She starts to reach out to touch him, maybe to see if he died. Then she really freaks out about the blood on her hand and the scroll. She stands up and looks from side to side. It was as if she was looking to hand it to somebody else. But she is alone. Well, I'm behind her, but I'm like a ghost or something. You know what I mean.

"Anyway, she is just standing there looking at this bloody scroll she is holding. Then one of the horses kicks so violently that the entire chariot jerks off the ground a bit. She reacts by backing up so hard that she whacks her head on the wall of the building. Finally, she turns to walk around the corner, and I follow her down the street. She looks back once or twice but keeps going. Eventually, she is almost running to get away from there.

"Silly me. I thought maybe she was in a hurry to take it to Pilate, but no. She was headed home. I follow her down two other streets and watch her run up to a door and start to go in. That's when I notice a guy has walked up to her and is trying to put his arm around her. She pushes him away and is holding that scroll behind her back so he can't see it. He grabs her arm with one hand, and bounces a small bag of coins in front of her face with his other hand. She looks at the bag for a second before knocking it out of his hand. While he is picking up the coins that have scattered, she pushes past him and through the door. Once he has picked up the last coin, OH, is he mad and starts pounding on her door. He must have done that for five minutes before giving up and leaving.

"Then there is the dream jump again, and I'm in her room. She has placed the scroll on a table, and she is really scrubbing hard to get that blood off of her hand. Once her hand is clean, she went to wipe off the scroll. It turns out that there really wasn't any blood on the parchment after all. There was just a bit on the wax seal, so she gently wipes the blood off the wax seal. When she is finally convinced that it is all clean, she lays it back on the table and pulls up a chair. She just sits there looking at it for a few seconds.

"Now this part really blew me away the first time I had this vision. While she is staring at the scroll, I flash back in time to where and why the scroll came to be. Cool, huh?"

Anton is hanging onto every word that John says, but when he paused, the Cardinal spoke.

"It appears that this vision has several unique features as compared to the other two. The others seem to flow chronologically forward in time, while this one appears to jump backwards. This is interesting, very interesting."

"My thoughts exactly, Anton. Anyway, the jump back in time puts me here in Rome. Somewhere here in Rome, that is. I'm in a palace and there is a man sleeping in a huge bed. At first I thought he was the Caesar guy. I think his name would have been Tiberius, is that right?"

"Yes, John. He was the Caesar while Jesus was alive. However, if memory serves me well, I think he would not have been here in Roma at that time. No, I know he would not have been here in Roma. He had entrusted the running of Roma to another. I can't think of his name at the moment, but we could look that up later if it becomes important. Please, go on."

"Well, I walk over to the side of the bed to get a better look at him. Then all of a sudden he sits straight up in bed so fast that I almost wet myself. He was staring straight ahead, not at me. That's when I saw it." John's eyes were flicking from side to side as if he were watching a movie. It was obvious to Anton that John was reliving the vision again; at least this part of it.

"Saw what, John? What did you see?"

"A ghost! It was standing at the foot of his bed and pointing at him. It told him 'Thou shall not hinder the Lord's divine plan for the Son of Man. This act will surely cost thee thy life. Act not, and thy wretched life shall be ignored.' Of course this idiot doesn't pay any attention. I would have. Boy, if a ghost told me to bug off, I'd listen to him. But not this guy! When the ghost dude disappeared, he jumped out of bed, started looking behind all the drapes and called for his guards. They looked everywhere before it settled down, and he made everyone leave him alone again in his room. Then he paced back and forth in front of his bed for hours.

"Finally, the sun came up, and the light began streaming in from the balcony. He walked over to look out for a few minutes. Then he walked really fast over to a desk and wrote that message down. He lit a candle and sealed the scroll before calling for a courier. I didn't understand much of what he said except the name of Pontius Pilate."

"You saw a ghost. A ghost, John? What makes you think it was a ghost?"

"Well you could see through him. But mainly because he even called himself a ghost. He ought to know what he is, right?"

"Now John. Are you saying he said he was a ghost? A ghost?"

"Well, yes! Well, actually he said the word spirit. But that's a ghost!"

"Are you saying that he referred to himself as a spirit or THE spirit?"

John saw where Anton was going with this, and stopped to think before answering.

"Oh, well, I don't really remember. He did say something before I understood the word spirit. I just don't really know. Sorry."

"There is nothing to be sorry about, John. Visions do not come with guidebooks. They are open to interpretation by those involved. I am amazed that you have remembered such detail as you do. This is a minor thing. Please continue, John."

"Ok, so here we go again. The jump thing again takes me back to her room, and she is just sitting there staring at the little scroll. Then she stands up, wraps it in a clean cloth and leaves with it hidden in her robe. She walks slowly but with purpose, a few blocks to what looks like a church. I think it has to be a Jewish one, what do you call them? A synagogue? But she just stops a ways away from it and stands there. It's like she can't go into it, for some reason. Anyway, finally she sees this man coming out, and he sees her. It is strange, but they don't want to be seen talking together, so he nods at her as he passes right by her. She waits a second, then follows him. He goes a few blocks away and turns down a very small, I guess alley, between two buildings. There was just enough room for one person's shoulders to pass between the two. She follows him in and he stops to face her.

"They talk for a minute. I don't hear the words this time, but she is trying to get him to take the little scroll. She is obviously telling him how she came to have it. Then he nods and she pulls out the towel to show him. He covers it back up and puts it in his robe.

"Then I jump again to a room with this guy and two others. I know that I'm in that church he had come out of. I think one of the guys wants to break the seal and read it, but the other two say no. So here is what they do. They take one of their scroll books, it's pretty big, but really worn looking. I don't think they use it for anything but show now. It was a scroll that had both ends wrapped around like wooden dowel rods. So one of the dowel rods is really big around in diameter, but the other was small. There was a big brass cap on both ends of the really fat rod. It turns out that rod is hollow. They remove the cap from one end of the fat rod and try to slip the little scroll into it, but it is too big around. They try several times, but end up breaking the seal. Since it is broken now, that one guy tries again to get the other two to read it, but they still say no. So they just roll the little scroll tighter until it fits into that fat rod. Once they have it inside the rod, they put the brass cap back on it.

"Then the jump thing happens again, and I'm in like this warehouse of sorts. There are lots of shelves with all sorts of, like, really old things on them. The odd thing is that the people taking care of this stuff are all priests. Every one of them is. That's when I see this one young priest walking down this isle. He is carrying something heavy by himself, and he starts to drop it. As it begins to fall, it tips to one side and he can't stop it from hitting this shelf really hard. Guess what almost falls off the shelf? Yep, that big old scroll that those three men had put the little scroll into that fat dowel rod. Well, the young guy manages not to drop his heavy load, and he stops this big scroll from falling to the floor. But the brass knob falls off the end of the fat dowel rod and heads to the floor.

"This young guy is a real acrobat. He manages to stop the brass knob from hitting the floor by putting his shoe under it. The knob hits his shoe and rolls onto the bottom wooden shelf. He puts down what he was carrying and picks up the brass knob. He is acting really scared and is looking around to see if anybody saw what happened. Then when he is trying to put that brass knob back on the fat dowel rod, he sees that little scroll in there. He looks around again to make sure he is alone, before he fishes it out with a pencil from behind his ear. He doesn't unroll it. He just pushes it back down and puts the brass knob back on.

"Now this part still freaks me out. I see a movie. Well not the whole movie, just a few scenes. I see just enough to know that it is about the Second World War. You know the one where they bomb Pearl Harbor. Then I see a young boy's left hand all covered with blood. And that's the end of it. Bet this one really is going to puzzle the puzzle master! Eh?"

"So, John. This vision shows us a message that is sent from Roma to Pontius Pilate, but he never gets it. We don't know what it says, but we think it is hidden in a rod holding an ancient text. Now this war movie reference and the boy's bloody hand ... well, these don't make any sense at all to me. However, it may be that I'm just tired. If this is all of this vision, then I would like to quit for the evening if you don't mind. I'm really tired. I think it is because of the dizzying images that my mind has been flooded with while listening to your visions. You truly have a great deal of detail in them. I don't see how you keep it all straight!"

"Well, Anton, when you have these visions as much as I have had them in the last seven months, you tend to remember them."

"You know, John, that is exactly right! That is why you have the dream every night and these visions as often as you do. Don't you see? It is how God is giving you these clues. Yes, the detail is the result of the repetitive dreaming. If I were not so tired, I would suggest that we order some espresso and keep going."

"Nah, I'm tired too, Anton. It does take a lot out of me when I tell you these visions. They are so intense when I have them that they leave me really wired up for awhile. But I've also found that talking about them kind of jacks me up too, but not as much."

"John, let me call Father Turin and have him come take you back to you room."

John sat for a second and then asked, "How long have you known this, Father Turin?"

"Well, Father Turin has worked for me these past six months. Why?"

"Oh, no real reason. It's just that, well, I just can't put my finger on it. But from the moment I first met him... No, I better not say anything. It's nothing. Really."

"John, it must be something, or you wouldn't have brought it up. What is it that you want to say?"

"I wish I hadn't started this, but guess I'm in too deep to pull out now. This is really going to sound nuts, but every time I see him, I get this little mental image of Jesus. I know, I know. I'm nuts. But I do. Don't know why, just know I do."

Anton sat thinking for a second and then said, "Do you think he has something to do with what we are involved in?"

"Part of me wants to say 'Yes', because the mental image is Jesus and He's the one this all seems to be centered around. But you know. The rest of me doesn't see him involved at all. Oh well, let's call it a night. OK?"

~ ~ ~

Barbara was busy cleaning up the kitchen after having tried out a new recipe from 'The Cookin' Mama' website. It wasn't the best one she had tried, but it was good. She would work on it before John came home. She stopped for a second and stood with her arms crossed over her chest as if she were sadly missing something, or someone. She stared blindly out the bay window, without even seeing the pool. Yes, she is thinking about how long he has been gone. She lowered her head and looked around the kitchen. Eventually she ended up focusing on their table. The place they sat together every day. There had been many hours of great conversations shared at that table. Closing her eyes and lifting her head up towards the ceiling, she strained to hear another sound in the house besides those made by her. She was alone and now realized that she couldn't cook her loneliness away, but she had to try. The phone rang as she was picking up another recipe to try.

"Oh, Hi HONEY! I was just thinking about you. I miss you so very much. I don't want to rush you, but when do you think you're coming home? Soon?"

"Barb, hearing your voice is the highlight of my day. I really can't wait to get home. It is nice here and things are definitely interesting around here, but I really need to get this done before I come home. I hate to say it, but it could take another week or two. Has Bill ever called about the shop? I told him to call you if there were any problems, and you could tell me."

"No. I haven't heard anything from Bill. I can drive by there tomorrow and just chat with him a little if you want me too."

"No, that's all right. I trust the grease monkey totally. All I really wanted was to hear your voice, baby."

"John, you sound so tired. Have you been getting any sleep at all, or is that dream keeping you up a lot?"

"Actually, I haven't had the dream or the visions at all for days now. I guess I'm just tired from all the things we are doing and talking about during the day. It's hard to explain, but it really drains me. The Cardinal is the same way. So have you been OK?"

She hesitated just a little, then sighed before answering. "Yes. I'm fine. It just isn't the same without you here. I miss you." She looked around the room again. "The house just feels so empty. I need you, honey."

"Well, hang in there, Barb. It's getting close to the end of this thing, and then I'll be done with it. We'll have nothing to do but be with each other. God, I can't wait for that."

Then there were the usual 'I love you' comments before the phone fell silent. Again, she looked out the window and wondered what he was doing, now that he had hung up. John was lying on the bed and wondering the same thing about her.

CHAPTER 17

Quest for a Ring

The sunlight covered John's face as he began to stir under the covers. Slowly, the veil of sleep released him to fall back to his earthly consciousness. He wondered what time it was. Looking around the room, he remembered that the only wall clock was in the little study. He turned his head to look at his watch on the dresser, only to find it face down. A sudden hunger pang made him realize that it must be late in the morning.

Not wanting to miss those wonderfully delicious omelets that he had become so fond of, he jumped from bed to get dressed. He set a record for getting dressed, combing hair and arriving at the dining area. Nobody was there when he came hustling into the room. Standing there, he looked at his watch before starting to turn and leave. Barely a step was taken when he heard a voice from behind him.

"Signore. Breakfast? No?"

A quick glance behind him found his favorite waiter, and he was smiling as he motioned for John to take his usual table.

John said, "Thank you, Romano."

As he sat, the man asked, "Same? Frittata, yes?"

John smiled and nodded.

"Yes, please."

As an afterthought, John stopped the man from leaving by simply saying "Espresso, NO!"

The man looked back and quickly asked, "Succo?"

John smiled and said, "Yes, juice."

As Romano left, John was bobbing his head and thinking to himself, "Anton would be proud of me. I made it here by myself and even ordered by myself. Hey, I'm turning Italian!"

The meal was perfect and John was almost giddy for not having to deal with one of those stupid little espresso cups. How do these guys drink out of those toy cups? He thought to himself, 'I could NEVER get used to the taste, and especially those cups.'

Just as he finished his juice, Father Turin poked his head through the door as if he were looking for somebody. Seeing John, his eyebrows rose as he smiled then entered in the room. He raised both hands, palms upwards as he walked towards John's table. "Mr. Parson. I thought we had lost you."

"Well, sir. I don't have to know my way to this place. I can just follow my nose!"

Both men laughed just a bit before the priest spoke.

"I must again apologize for Cardinal Mortello. He is yet again forced to grant an audience for two more groups of visiting dignitaries. Do you have anything you would like to do until he is free?"

"Not really. I can just hang around my room. Did he say how long it might be?"

"No, he did not, Mr. Parson. However, I do know the subject of the second meeting. It is a continuation of a topic that has been going on now for several months. Regrettably, this meeting will probably last for several hours. I know that it has in the past. It would be a long wait in your room. May I make a suggestion?"

"Shoot, buddy."

No sooner had he said the words, John noticed the wide eyes of the priest, and he knew he needed to explain the expression.

"Before you ask, it is just an expression. It means 'Yes' or 'Please go on'. Something like that. Understand?"

The priest nodded as a big smile spread across his face once again. "Yes. I remember hearing that on occasion while in America. The first time I heard those words though, I thought they were warning me to duck! Of course my response caused a great laughter of my friends there. I just had not heard it for a long time. Apologies."

"So, what did you want to suggest I do?"

"Oh, yes. I was wondering. During our first meeting, I recall offering to show you around the buildings. I am certain that you have noticed the many paintings and statues that we have here. I could give you a tour of the ones that might be of the most interest."

"That's really kind of you to offer, but I don't want to put you through all that much trouble."

"Mr. Parson. I assure you it would be no trouble at all. I would be honored to show you things from our collective pasts. Please allow me to afford you this chance to view some rather lovely historical artwork."

John was already shaking his head 'no' and actually got a few words out.

"I appreciate it. Really I do. But it is just too much."

That is when John got that mental image of Jesus. John thought to himself, 'There is definitely something about this guy. Maybe I need to spend a few hours with him.'

"You know, I changed my mind. I would really like for you to show me around, if you are really sure it is not a bother."

The priest seemed truly happy at John's acceptance of his offer. "Mr. Parson. It is absolutely NO bother at all. We can start whenever you are ready."

"Well, I'm ready now." They both stood.

"Lead on, tour guide! I'll do the usual tagalong thing like always."

They moved to the hall and Father Turin took John to a corridor that he had yet to go down. This hallway was lined on both sides with pictures only a few inches apart. Many of them had little lights above them that shone down on the pictures themselves. It worked for some very nicely, but others were giving John the creeps with the shadows that formed on the edges of the frames. They moved slowly from painting to painting, and the priest was telling John very interesting things. John was really glad he accepted the tour. This one hallway took them over an hour to view. It had been so fascinating that John thought they had only been there maybe 10 minutes or so.

"Wow. I can't believe we spent that much time in that hall. It was so interesting, and you are a great tour guide. I think I could get used to looking at paintings if there was somebody like you there telling me all the nitty-gritty about each one. I really liked that, buddy. What's next?"

"Thank you for your compliment, Mr. Parson. But it was not me that you enjoyed. I think that when one knows the story of an art piece, only then can one truly see what the artist saw and what they were trying to pass on. Yes?"

John was still seeing that 'Jesus' image while he was looking at the smile on the priest's face.

"You know. I think you may be on to something there, buddy."

"Come, Mr. Parson. There is another hall, I think you will find even more interesting. It has fewer paintings, but there are several of them that are among the oldest and most beautiful in the entire collection. Please, come."

John actually had to walk quickly to keep up with the priest this time. He was so excited that he didn't realize how fast he was requiring his guest to walk. They rounded yet another corner and entered a short hallway. It was wider than the others and had the tallest ceiling he had seen. Even though the priest had stopped by the first painting and was already talking about it, John was drawn past it to the third one. It was a huge painting, almost 10 feet wide and stretching from floor to ceiling. Father Turin noticed that John had passed him and had positioned himself right in front of this massive painting. He turned and stood directly behind John before speaking.

"Ah, this is the one that I really wanted you to see. You seemed to have found it on your own. It is magnificent, but it is just a copy."

"A copy? Was the original as big as this one?"

"Well, Mr. Parson. That is a very good question. However, the answer is that the original was much larger, and not on canvas. It was a mural painted on the inside wall of a small town church."

John stood on the opposite side of the hall taking in the entire painting. It depicted a scene in a large, palatial room. There was a man seated at a flat table, and he was signing a document while several others were standing behind him watching. John felt there was something he wasn't seeing here. He sensed that there was something right in front of him that he needed to take notice of.

Father Turin noticed the intensity with which John was studying the picture. "Mr. Parson, is there something bothering you about this portrait? Mr. Parson?"

John hadn't heard a word that the priest had said. Something was right there in front of him. He could feel it. But what is it? As his eyes continued to scan the painting, he finally began to speak.

"What is this picture about? Do you know, Father? What is he signing? Was it something of historical importance?"

"Those are all very good questions, Mr. Parson. I'm afraid I know very little about this picture. However, I do know the Vatican curator very well, and he will be able to answer your questions. Would you like for me to call him and see if he is available?"

John never took his eyes from the painting. "Yes. Please do, and don't be afraid to use the Cardinal's name if he hesitates any about helping us."

He continued to study the painting, but still doesn't yet see what it could represent. All he knew is that he wasn't moving an inch from this spot until he had an answer.

Father Turin reacted to the urgency he detected in John's voice. He reached quickly into his cassock and retrieved his cell phone. Several electronic beeps are heard, and then he listened to the ringing. He noticed that John had stepped closer to the painting. Although he has done as John asked, he didn't understand what was happening, or why John was staring at the painting as if in a trance. As he continued to listen to his call ringing, he found himself now looking at the painting as well, but for what?

At last there was a voice on the line.

"Hello, Pierre. Yes, it is I. I have a question about the large painting around the corner from the 'Rose Room'. Well, I'm not sure, but there is actually more than one question, and probably going to be even more. That would be wonderful! We will wait here. Thank you, Pierre."

"You are in luck, Mr. Parson. He is on his way. It seems that this is his favorite one as well. He is not far and should be here in two minutes. By the way, it would be best not to mention the

Cardinal's name to Pierre. If your intent is to facilitate his help, using the Cardinal's name will not be to your advantage."

This comment caused John to not only shift his focus to the priest, but to step closer before asking, "You mean to tell me that Anton has an enemy here? Really?"

"Oh, no, no, nothing like that at all. It's just that they seem to, well, clash if you understand?"

John smiles. "You mean they rub each other the wrong way?"

"I'm afraid so. It's more personality differences, but they both blame each other's lack of flexibility."

John was smiling even bigger as he shook his head. "So Anton is human after all. You know everyone has that one person they just can't get along with."

"That is a very astute comment Mr. Parson, but one best left alone. Apparently, you have need of Pierre's expertise, so we should focus his attention on your questions. Agreed?"

"Agreed."

The sound of confident footsteps preceded the appearance of a rather tall and athletic priest. He walked up to John and extended his hand to deliver a very firm handshake. While shaking John's hand, he glanced at Father Turin.

"Hello, Markus. And this is Mr. Parson I'll bet."

"Yes, I'm John Parson. Please call me John."

"As you wish, sir. John it is! Now I understand you have questions about this lovely copy."

"Yes. I think it would be quicker if you told me as much as you can about it first."

"Let's do that. It was originally a mural painting in a small church. The name of the village was Tonille and the population was less than 300. The town was very old. It had a small church that housed two artifacts from the Roman Empire. It was never known how they came to be there, just that they were there. It was the pride of this little village. It was their piece of history.

"A young artist traveled there and painted this mural. It is a simple portrait of Pontius Pilate signing something towards the end of his life. What he is signing has never been known. We know this because a smaller painting was found in Jerusalem, and it was clearly noted on the back of the canvas. All that was legible was that it was Pilate signing something. Now I can see you are wondering why the artist painted this particular picture on the Church wall. It was simple. The two artifacts that the Church guarded are in this portrait of Pilate."

John immediately interrupted and asked, "So what are the two artifacts? Where are they in this painting?"

Father Marsai stepped to the center of the painting and pointed to the corner of the table that Pilate was seated at. John immediately stepped right beside him and exclaimed, "The box! It's that jeweled box, right?"

The priest turned and stared at John for just a second. He then smiled and said, "Yes, Mr. Parson. You are correct. But I thought you didn't know anything about this painting or the Church?"

"I don't."

The two priests were looking at each other when John continued. "So, what is the other artifact?"

"Well, it is being held by one of the men standing behind Pilate." The priest began to point to the man holding the item. John had already focused his eyes on the man. Again he said, very loudly, "It's the scepter. Isn't it? The Royal Roman Scepter of Arenia. Right?"

The priest gave Father Turin a very stern look before responding to John's second outburst. "Correct again, Mr. Parson. It seems that you really didn't need me at all."

Father Turin had moved a little closer to the painting now. "Pierre, may I ask you a question?"

"Of course, Markus."

"Judging by the dress of the man holding the scepter, I would guess he is a slave."

"Very good, Markus. He was, in fact, a slave."

"Then my question is this: why would Pilate allow a slave to hold such a distinguished item for him? Why wasn't Pilate holding it himself? Or why wasn't it lying on the table?"

"You are very observant, my friend. There is a rather odd reason for this. We have some documents that tell of Pilate complaining that he got dizzy or nauseous whenever he held the scepter. It seemed he had paid so much to have it made that he still wanted to be seen with it. So he made this slave carry it around behind him all the time. This is actually mentioned twice, so it must be accurate. Of course no scholar believes the scepter made Pilate sick, but they all agree he believed it. Also, there was one reference that said Pilate was upset that the slave never felt bad while holding the scepter. He was the only one it seemed to adversely affect."

"Now, before I forget. Mr. Parson, I would like to correct one thing you said though. It is a common mistake to describe the scepter as 'Royal Roman Scepter of Arenia'. However, the correct thing to say is simply 'Royal Roman Scepter'. It was not from Arenia. In fact, there never was a place called Arenia. But a lot of books still reference it that way."

John asked, "I personally looked it up on the Internet and even saw it in a museum several months ago. The museum plaque clearly described it as such! Why are you saying it is not that way?"

The priest took a deep breath before starting his explanation.

"Mr. Parson. Allow me to clarify. The items were both created by the Arenia family. They, like most artists, put their name on everything they made. They were just a little more conceited and made their names really stand out. The Church has both of these items. Their name is also very prominent on the inside of the lid of the box. They had also written it in large letters on the scepter. It was their trademark, so to speak. We have a number of items of theirs."

"The reason it has been mistakenly referred to in this manner for so many years has to do with the German Army during World War Two. The Germans were systematically stealing artwork from all over Europe. The Church set out to gather and hide everything it could get its hands on for safekeeping. These two items were taken from the village with the express promise from Roma that they would be returned after the war. However, the German Army destroyed the entire town, including the church, because the artifacts were not found there. It has never been rebuilt, so we still have them."

"As for the scepter being referred to as 'of Arenia', this was a paperwork error. The Church was forced to utilize laymen in the process of labeling and storing the hundreds of items it was collecting ahead of the Germans. Many items were erroneously labeled, and then those errors were continued when the items were put into computer databases. I've only recently gotten this scepter's writeup corrected on our own Church database. It has been wrong for decades. But as of this morning, it is correct on our site."

John was still staring at the painting. He suddenly turned to Father Marsai and extended his hand before speaking.

"I really want to thank you for telling us all this. It has been more of a help than you will ever know." John began to turn away, but he turned back towards the priest to ask one last question.

"Where is the scepter now? I saw it in the USA. Is it back here yet?"

"Yes, it is here. It may not be available for viewing for a few weeks, but with the right authorizations, you should be able to see it if you wish."

"Thank you. I may just take you up on that!"

Father Marsai bid his friend Father Turin goodbye as well, and he disappeared back around the corner. The moment he was out of sight, John motioned for Father Turin to walk with him. This time, it was John who was walking very fast and the priest was the one having to keep up.

"I want you to take me straight to where ever the Cardinal is. Right now, please. He is going to want to hear this."

"I do not know where the Cardinal's meeting is being held."

"Well then, just take me to his office. I'll wait there for him to return."

"As you wish, Mr. Parson."

"Yes, it will give me a chance to think through this a little before he gets there."

John puts his arm around the priest's shoulder. "While we are walking, I want you to tell me more about the dynamics between the Cardinal and Pierre Marsai."

Father Turin told John one story after another about conflicts between the two men. John didn't think he was going to have any problem with Father Marsai. They seemed to get along. He just wanted to hear some more stories, so he could use them to joke around with Anton.

~ ~ ~

Father Turin opened the door to Cardinal Mortello's office and allowed John to enter first. Judy looked up at them.

"Hello again, Mr. Parson! I'm afraid the Cardinal is still in his meeting. I thought Father – uh – hello, Father Turin. I'm sorry, but I thought you knew the Cardinal was in a meeting. Is something wrong?"

"Nothing is wrong, Judy. Mr. Parson has some urgent information to deliver to the Cardinal. I take it that his meeting is somewhere other than his office."

"Yes, that's right. He is not here. I would think that he would want you to wait in his office. So, please go on in. I'll let you know the moment I hear from him. Mr. Parson, but I am afraid there is no way to know how long you will have to wait."

John smiled at her and said, "No problem, Ma'am. We will just wait in the office like you said. Thanks!"

Father Turin again opened the next door and allowed John to enter first. With this door closed, John headed straight to his favorite leather chair by the table. "Come on, buddy. Let's sit over here. These are some really nice chairs." As Judy's phone rang, John added, "Busy place. Anton is not even here, and people are trying to get a hold of him."

"Yes. The Cardinal's office is always full of life these days."

They had barely sat down when a light tapping on the door drew their attention. The door opened slowly and Judy stuck her head partially into the room to say, "You two are in luck. That was the Cardinal on the phone. His meeting just ended, and he was wondering if I knew where you were. He says he will be here in three or four minutes. Would either one of you like something to drink?"

Father Turin stood and replied, "Since the Cardinal is on his way, I will take my leave of you, Mr. Parson. Please, you should try the espresso. It is very good here." He then walked through the door and commented as he passed Judy, "Please call me if the Cardinal has any further use of me. Thanks, Judy."

Judy turns to John. "So, Mr. Parson. Would you like to try our espresso?"

John was smiling and thought to himself, 'You couldn't force me to drink another one of those little cups if you were twice my size, lady.' Even with these thoughts, he still only replied "No."

There was the sound of a door being opened, a rush of soft-spoken words, and then the Cardinal burst into the room.

"John! I'm so sorry to have kept you waiting. I do think that I have fulfilled all my required meetings for the rest of the week now."

He hurried behind his desk, once again moving notes around with one hand. Picking up one of them, he crumpled it before throwing it into the trash can beside his desk. "Well, there is no need now to make that call."

He then turned his attention to John, taking a seat opposite him.

"Anton, my friend. You lead a very hectic life here. Who knew that this place could be this busy?"

"Yes, it can be rather stressing around here at times. So, I understand that you finally took Father Turin up on his offer for a tour. I trust you enjoyed it."

"Oh, you won't believe what I found out this morning. I still don't believe it." Then John told Anton everything he had found out about the jeweled box and the scepter. When he finished telling him, the Cardinal fell back in his seat and began patting his hands lightly on the arms of the chair.

"You have had a very eventful morning, my friend. So you met Father Marsai? He provides a wealth of knowledge about the artwork here. Of course, that is why he was hired."

Anton began rubbing his chin nervously with his fingers. "He said that the scepter is back here from the American tour. This may prove to be most advantageous to our efforts. Do you have any idea as to our next move or inquiry?"

"Well, actually I do. I think we need to take him up on his offer to view that scepter again. But first, can you look up the scepter in your Church database? I just have a hunch that we need to look at the pictures of it. I've seen them before. There were shots of it from different angles."

"Yes, I can. I remember seeing those same pictures once before."

They both stood and moved over to the Cardinal's large desk. Anton sat behind his desk while John took a position behind him, looking over his shoulder. After pulling his keyboard a little closer, he typed in a description of the scepter. Almost immediately, the screens began loading.

"There they are. Which one interests you first, John?"

John was busy scanning the little icons on the computer screen.

"I don't know, Anton. Maybe this one, uh, NO wait! Click on this one."

A second later, the screen was filled from edge to edge. It was a view looking straight down at the top of the scepter. This end was completely covered with jewels of all kinds, arranged in a pattern by colors: a circle of light stones alternating with a ring of darker stones. There was one large solitary stone directly on top.

Both men froze at the sight of that stone. Neither said a word for a second or two. Then they both looked at each other and uttered the same words at the same time.

"A large red ruby!"

John put his finger over the ruby on the screen, as if he were pushing it.

The Cardinal exclaimed, "We need to get our hands on this scepter!"

"The priest named Marsai told me that I could see the scepter with the proper authorizations. Would that come from you, Anton?"

"Well let's call him and find out."

The Cardinal dialed and leaned back in his chair as it began ringing.

"Hello, Pierre. Yes, I am fine. Yes, he told me you were extremely helpful this morning. Thank you. Yes, you can. Mr. Parson and I need your help with the scepter. I am aware that it just returned from tour. No, three or four days is a problem. Tomorrow would be great. Ten o'clock would be fine as well. Our plans? Well, we would just like a close inspection and perhaps to touch one of the stones set in the top."

There was a pause, then John saw the Cardinal bite his upper lip just a bit before continuing.

"And what type of problem would that present? Oil? From our hands? I see. And if that hand was gloved? Still a problem. Yes, I am very aware of the protocols for these ancient artifacts. However, sometimes there are needs that arise and require rules to be relaxed. Yes, I believe that this is one of those times. Uh, you don't agree. No, I'm not able to tell you what is so special about this time. Pierre, he is very aware of what we are doing. Yes, there is no doubt that he will authorize this. I understand your position completely. Yes, 10:00 tomorrow in the white room. We will be there. It is always nice to talk to you as well, Father."

After hanging up the phone, the Cardinal turned his head to look out the window. This was the first time that John had seen his friend appear agitated at all. Now was not the time to joke with him, but John felt compelled to let Anton air his frustrations.

"Anton. I understand that you and Marsai have a history of sorts."

Without even looking in John's direction, the Cardinal replied, "History? You could call it that if you like. That man is an insufferable stickler for rules at times when he should be flexible."

"Didn't you just tell him that the Pope would authorize this?"

"Yes, something along those lines."

"And don't you think the Pope WILL authorize this?"

"I am positive that he will. It's just that, well, to tell you the truth, John - I don't know what it is about this man that rubs me the wrong way sometimes. It has to be his attitude or tone. I just can't put my finger on it."

John was smiling as he said, "I'm glad to see you have problems like the rest of us, Anton. It means you are just human. That's all, buddy."

"John, for a young man, you are wise beyond your years. You are very right. We need to remain focused on this scepter."

"So we are supposed to meet him tomorrow morning in some white room? Isn't that what I heard you agree to?"

"Well, we are meeting at 10:00 in the morning. The white room is actually a sterile, environmentally safe room where they work with these old objects. You know, filtered air, no contaminants or chemicals present. That type of a room."

John sounded a little excited at hearing this. "Hey, are we going to get to wear one of those space suits in this room? I've always wanted to do that!"

"I'm afraid it is not that type of a room John. We just have to wear those little white booties, a white hospital-type gown, and masks like doctors wear in operating rooms. I'm sorry, my friend. You still have to join the space program to get to wear a space suit." The Cardinal was displaying his own little devilish smile at John after having said this.

John watched as the Cardinal's smirk quickly become a chuckle.

"Why Anton. Are you developing a sense of humor? Better be careful, buddy. It could keep you from becoming Pope one day."

The Cardinal's face quickly changed to a more tense expression. "Why would you say that? Have you also had any visions of my future?"

John put the brakes on his joking around. He hadn't expected this response from Anton.

"Slow down. I was joking with you. And NO! I haven't been having visions of your future. I'm not a psychic, you know. All I meant to say is that I haven't seen a single painting of any Pope with a smile. That's all."

The tension quickly faded, and the two men fell back into their usual friendly mood.

"John, I think we have done about all we can before tomorrow. As much as I would like to share conversation with you over dining tonight, I fear I must once again leave you to your own devices. There is much to discuss with the Holy Father. Also it seems we will need a note from the teacher to satisfy Father Marsai or he may not allow us to touch this relic."

Anton's eyes quickly darted to John after he realized how sarcastic his remark was. "I'm so sorry, John. I am acting very childish, and it is most unbecoming of a man of my status. Apologies again, my friend."

"Not needed, Anton. Friends don't think anything about friends getting upset. Never!"

~ ~ ~

Father Turin had collected John from his room precisely at 7:45 the next morning, and had taken him to meet the Cardinal for breakfast. They met in a small room off the main dining hall. It had only one table with six chairs around it. After John entered the little room, Father Turin closed the door before doing his well-rehearsed vanishing act. John had just sat down when the Cardinal began.

"Good morning, John! I want you to know that I feel very much better after having had a good night's sleep and some much needed prayers this morning. I am also glad to report that we did get that hall pass to show Father Marsai."

John's face took on a tense look of its own at hearing this from his friend. He couldn't believe that Anton was still worked up over his having to get the Pope to OK their activities with the scepter. With John's mind spinning on how badly this day could go if these two men squabbled, the Cardinal leaned closer to John. He smiled and said, "Gotcha!"

John's shoulders loosened as he realized that this old dog had just reached out and bit him with a joke right off the bat.

"Anton, you're becoming quite the jokester! You almost gave me a heart attack, buddy. And may I say, sir, you carried it out VERY well!"

Both men had a good laugh before ordering their usual breakfast meals. Of course John was busy the entire time trying to come up with another reason NOT to have one of those annoying little espressos that the Cardinal was so very fond of. Even though he thought he could just as easily say he didn't want one, he knew that the Cardinal now believed that he also enjoyed them. In the end, John would say yes, and then endure the humiliation he felt from drinking pure caffeine from a toy cup.

"Now John, just so you know. The Holy Father took it upon himself to personally call Father Marsai about allowing us to do whatever we felt necessary with this scepter. I believe he also instructed him to leave the two of us alone with the artifact."

"Anton, I understand you want to keep knowledge of the book from this guy. But I was thinking that whatever we find or don't find with this scepter, this Father Marsai still would not know of the connection to the book."

"So John, are you saying keep him in the room? Why?"

"Well, for two reasons really. First, with all the knowledge this guy has in dealing with these ancient artifacts, he might come in handy while we are looking at it."

"John, that makes some good sense. And you are right about there not really being anything to keep from him. Even if we find the ring, to him it is just another artifact, and he can't see a connection to a book he knows nothing of. What was the other reason?"

"Well, I know you are the type of man who really wants to win over everyone. And I applaud you for this. So, I was thinking that it would be a good way to win over this Marsai dude."

The Cardinal sat back slowly. He had a very warm look in his eyes as he said, "John, I see your point. He already knows that he is not to be included in whatever we are doing. This was conveyed to him by the Holy Father himself. This gesture would let him know that I do trust him and value his opinion. I like it. You are a very shrewd politician, Mr. John Parson. This could make all my future dealings with him much more comfortable. Again John, I must say you amaze me with your insight. I am so impressed and lucky to have you as a friend."

"Knock it off, Anton. You're going to give me a big head here and that would definitely look funny with boots!"

Again these two friends laughed together. Their unique bond was strengthened with every new twist they faced. With the meal concluded, they began their short trek to the white room.

They were met just outside the room by Father Marsai. He was sporting a much more demure attitude after having discussed today's proceedings with the Holy Father. This did not go unnoticed by either of the men.

"I have taken the liberty of having your clean room attire placed on the rack behind you. If you would like, I can help you put on those gowns. They can be difficult sometimes."

The Cardinal glanced at the rack and then faced Father Marsai. "Pierre. I would like for you to join us in the white room, so you will need to suit up also."

John watched the confused look spread across the priest's face before he stumbled, trying to speak. "Me? Uh, but I thought. I mean I was told..."

"Yes, Pierre, I am aware of what you were told. But I think it is highly likely that we are about to uncover something truly amazing, and we need a man like you to make sure we don't mess it up. Will you help us, my friend?"

John was impressed at how well the Cardinal was working this angle with the priest. Whatever it was that had divided these two men in the past disappeared. The priest became noticeably excited and said, "I would be honored to help you, Cardinal. Give me just a moment to get a few things we may need."

He then darted out the door, returning in a few minutes fully dressed in his clean room outfit and holding a small black bag.

"These are my own personal tools that I use to repair and examine the items we work with around here. You both appear ready. Shall we, gentlemen?"

He held the door open for the Cardinal.

Upon entering the room, John saw a wooden box lying on a solid white workbench. The priest walked over to the head of the table and motioned for John and the Cardinal to take positions on opposite sides. He gently lifted the top of the box while speaking.

"I have already removed the screws from the sides of this crate. Sometimes these things stick just a little, since they are fitted so tightly. You have to pull kinda hard..."

There was a sudden wooden snap, and the lid was finally free. John and the Cardinal's eyes were glued on the scepter from the moment the open lid provided them with a view.

"I'll just place this top part over here. Now, Cardinal, how do you want to proceed?"

The Cardinal looked at John and said, "Well, John. You are the one that found it?" He motioned for John to pick it up, but John hesitated because he really didn't want to be the one to do it.

"Uh, I don't like holding babies because I'm afraid I'll hurt them with these clumsy hands of mine. Anton, there is no way I'm touching that thing. Let him do it. He handles these things all the time. Besides I'm not going to be the one that breaks it."

Father Marsai looked from John to the Cardinal before speaking.

"I'll gladly handle it for you. You only need tell me what we are looking for, or what you wish me to do. I know that on the phone yesterday you expressed a desire to push on one of the stones?"

"John, again this is in your court." Anton was looking at John but nodding his head towards Father Marsai as if to say, 'So tell him what to do!'

"Ok, I can do that. Look on the top of all those jewels. You see that big red ruby in the center there. We think that if you push it, there is a secret compartment on this thing somewhere that will open up."

Father Marsai looked at John. "What? A secret compartment?"

He began to look up and down the shaft of the scepter.

"If there were a secret compartment, there would be a fine line that would show us where it is. I'm not seeing anything. No, if there is one it will not be on the shaft. It will be in the jeweled area."

With this said, the priest reached into his bag, pulled out a magnifying glass and started to examine the jewel-encrusted top of the scepter.

"I don't believe it. It can't be."

The Cardinal and John both leaned in so quickly to get a closer view that they actually bumped heads. This clumsy act doesn't faze any of the three, as they are all too enthralled with the discovery.

"What are you seeing, Pierre?" asked the Cardinal.

The priest asked, "Can the two of you hold this end right where it is? I'm going to need both of my hands for a second."

The two of them immediately grasped the scepter from both sides. They are holding it at an angle, so the jeweled end is directly in the face of the priest. He reached into his bag and pulled out a small metal pick like the one a dentist uses to examine teeth.

"Yes, this stone is the only one with a small gap between it and the stones around it. If I look at the other stones, I see at least the remnants of the glue that was used to attach them. There is no gap between any of the stones except this one." He returned both tools to his bag and looked to the Cardinal.

"You said that you wanted to push the ruby. Right?"

"Yes, we think it should be pushed."

"Then in my opinion, this stone must be on a spring device of some type. I don't see how the spring mechanism is going to be functional after these hundreds of years in a compressed position. But we can try. Hold it tightly, gentlemen, and PLEASE don't drop it."

The priest placed one hand on the shaft directly below the first circle of jewels. He grasped it so hard his fingertips turned white.

"Ready? Here goes."

He pushed the stone for several seconds but nothing happened. Then he put pressure on the stone and wiggled it from side to side to see if he could loosen it. Nothing.

They all relaxed their grip and then John said, "Wait a minute. There is supposed to be a loud wooden snap or pop when you push the stone. I mean it is a really loud pop, too. Anton, I say we have him really push it hard this time. Maybe it is supposed to break."

The priest was once again looking through his eyeglass at the end of the scepter.

"You know, John. I think I agree. There have never been any springs of any type found in items this old - at least none that I'm aware of. It makes more sense to me that an ancient craftsman would have built up a little lip of glue or carved a fine ledge on the inside that supports the stone once it is glued in place. Then you have to literally break that bond or ledge to free the stone."

He stood back and looked to the Cardinal for instructions.

"Shall I apply more pressure and see what happens?"

"I think we are committed at this point to find out, one way or the other. The answer is 'yes', Pierre."

The priest moved quickly to the other end of the table and reached under it. He pulled two clamps and a wooden board with holes along one edge from under the table. He must have done this many times, for he had the board clamped down in less than 10 seconds. Then he gently wrapped a thick soft cloth around the end of the shaft, and pushed it into the smallest hole it would fit into. Then he moved back to the head of the table and gently wrapped another thick soft cloth around the jeweled end before lowering it to the table top. Both John and the Cardinal were completely fixated on every move the priest made.

Pierre then pulled yet another device from underneath the table. It was some type of bracket with a corkscrew mechanism on one end. Once it was clamped to the table, the priest slowly turned the screw handle and a rod was pushed towards the stone. It took the priest two attempts to align this rod directly with the stone. Once it was perfectly aligned with the scepter's shaft, he placed a spongy rubber pad on the stone. Then he tightened it until the rod was holding the pad firmly against the stone.

"Well, that looks straight to me. I can turn this very slowly and increase the pressure on that stone. If we are right, then whatever is holding the stone in place will give. Before I go any further, may I ask what it is we are hoping to find?"

The Cardinal looked at John before saying, "A ring."

The priest thought for a moment, then began talking as he looked through one of the cabinets on the wall.

"Well, in that case, I would say that we are probably going to find some sand in there. They most definitely would have packed something in there to keep the ring from knocking about and alerting the owner that there was something hidden within. I've found other hidden things in objects, and they almost always use sand. Mainly, because if they put leather or cloth, it degrades over time and allows movement, but sand remains sand forever. Ah, here we go."

He has found a bowl, which he placed on the floor under the head of the scepter. Turning towards the Cardinal, he had one hand on the screw handle as he asked, "Are you sure you want to do this?"

There is another look at John before the Cardinal says, "Yes."

With that, the priest slowly began turning the handle, and the rod edged forward. At first the handle turned easily, but it grew harder with every turn. At one point, the priest stopped and rubbed his hands together as if warming them. "I always hate this part. I can feel it giving way slowly, but I hate hearing that crack when it does. I always worry that I'm going to put too much pressure on it. So I've found that when it gets really hard like this, if you just wait a second, sometimes it..."

The loud, sudden pop caught all three of them off guard. As they laughed at having jumped in unison, the room was filled with the sound of sand falling into the metal bowl on the floor. The priest held his hands poised just above the screw handle. When the sand stopped falling, he quickly unscrewed the device and the stone fell into his waiting hand. After gently replacing it on the bench, he once again snatched the metal pick from his bag. He eased the pick into the opening, and they watched him pulling something out as more sand fell into the waiting bowl. He slowly stood and walked over to the Cardinal to give it to him.

"I believe this is what you were after."

The Cardinal wouldn't raise his hands to accept it. Instead, he looked at John who immediately said, "Not me. You know what I said about holding babies!"

The other two men watched as the Cardinal took the object and held it as if it were a fragile piece of glass. There appeared to be the remnants of a leather wrapping. Grains of sand fell to the floor as he ever so gently unfolded the crumbling leather. At last, they were all silently staring at a ring.

John noticed that his friend Anton had the biggest smile he had ever seen on his face.

"How's it feel, Anton?"

The words come slowly, but they carried the weight of centuries.

"I feel closer to Christ than I have ever felt before in my life."

Hearing this, Pierre immediately asked, "Whose ring is this?"

The Cardinal looked at him. "It is the ring that Pontius Pilate wore when he condemned our Savior to the cross."

After staring at the ring for yet another few breathless seconds, the Cardinal held it out for Pierre to take. He does, but immediately asked, "Shall I put it in something for you?"

"Yes, please do that. But I want you to keep it just as it is until you show it to the Holy Father."

"The Holy Father? But shouldn't you be the one to show it to him, Cardinal?"

"I will inform him as to what we have found, and then call you as to the time of your meeting."

"Your Eminence? I don't know what to say. Why would you afford me such an honor?"

"You are a very important member of this institution, and I respect your integrity. I hope to work more closely with you in the future. Now, please tell me that you can restore this scepter so that no one will ever know of this."

"You have my word, Cardinal. When I am finished, it will be as if this never occurred."

"Good, good. Only the three of us and the Holy Father will know of this. This glorious find will be made known to the rest of the world at a time chosen by the Church.

"Now, Pierre, we will need you to have this ready for us to take on a journey at a moment's notice. I apologize for not being able to discuss this further with you, but I want you to know that it is in the best interest of the Church. Please do not take this exclusion personally. It is regrettably necessary."

"Cardinal, I have absolute trust in my Church and you."

"Come, John. We have much to discuss." He then turned one last time to Pierre and nodded as he said, "Father."

Pierre bowed his head slightly before replying "Cardinal."

Once in the hall and certain that they cannot be overheard, the Cardinal said, "John, could you see the cross cut into the emblem? It was just as in your vision. I still find these last few minutes hard to believe. I would like to go to my office and discuss our next steps."

"Anton, your office sounds good."

Then John stopped directly in front of the Cardinal and leaned closer.

"Just one thing, my friend. Please don't be offended by this. But don't offer me any more espresso or anything in those little toy cups. OK?"

The Cardinal chuckled. "It is about time you spoke up, John. I could tell you didn't like it. The truth is that I don't drink it but once every few months myself. All that caffeine was giving me heartburn. I was only doing it because I loved seeing your face every time they sat one of those little white cups in front of you. The look on your face was hilarious."

John could not believe this old gray fox had been doing this on purpose. "Ohhhh, you sly dog! I'll get you, buddy. You just wait!"

The two were laughing and as giddy as school children all the way back to the Cardinal's office. Once inside, they requested sodas from Judy and then took their regular places at the table. The conversation was slow to start because both men are still replaying the morning's events in their heads.

"So John, we have the ring. As amazing as it sounds, we have the ring. What now?"

"I'm not sure Anton. Afraid I'm blank on how to even start looking for this strap. Unfortunately, I have wanted to talk to you about going home for a while. I really need to see my wife and spend some time in the normal world again. I hope you understand?"

After the high of this morning's find, the Cardinal felt the wind drop from his sails. He knew that John had been calling his wife more frequently as the days rolled on. It was inevitable that it would happen. He just didn't think that it would happen so soon. Or was it really that he hadn't wanted it to happen so soon?

"John, I am sorry to hear this, but we both knew it was coming. You have been away from home too long, my friend. We have made some massive strides on this, and maybe it is a good point to take a break. After all, we need time to reflect on the second vision and decide what to do next. I can have the plane ready for you in the next few hours. It would put you sleeping on the plane overnight again, but you would be home tomorrow. How does that sound?"

John now wore the biggest smile the Cardinal had ever seen on him.

"Anton, my friend, that sounds absolutely GREAT! I think I want to just show up at the house and surprise the heck out of Barb. What do you think?"

"It will be the sweetest gift for her. Yes, this sounds perfect!"

Anton stood and moved to his phone.

"Hello, Markus. Yes, my office if you please. Mr. Parson will be taking the plane home to Texas this evening. Yes she will. He intends to surprise her. Thank you, Father."

"John, my friend. I want to ask you to do me a small favor if you will. Please don't think about this at all for the next few days. Spend time with your lovely wife in familiar surroundings. You should relax as long as you need. I have a hunch that things will start to happen when the time is right. We must be patient now. For these events have been in motion for centuries, and we are now on their timetable."

CHAPTER 18

Sandals of a King

S ir? Sir? Wake up, Mr. Parson. We will be landing in about 30 minutes. Would you like a warm washcloth, sir? It will help wake you."

John looked around for a few seconds before he recognized the stewardess's face. "Yes, I think so. Thanks, Gena."

He must have been sleeping very deeply for the past several hours. As he raised his seat back, the Dallas skyline slowly passed just outside his window. Home at last! He felt excitement rising in his very soul as he watched the familiar landscape beneath them. After wiping his face and hands with the warm white cloth, he felt completely refreshed and wide awake. He couldn't wait to get home and kiss Barb!

As the plane rolled to a stop, he could see his waiting limo with its driver leaning up against the trunk. John was standing just behind Gena as she swung the exterior door lever, and the door became his steps to freedom. It had to be obvious to all that he was in a hurry. John had exited the plane and was opening his own car door before the driver had time to do it for him. There was a motion from the copilot, and the driver joined him at the rear luggage compartment. They exchanged John's one roller bag and the driver hastily placed it in the trunk of the car.

There was nothing said between John and the driver during the entire ride to his house. As the limo pulled into his driveway,

John saw his car parked where it always was in the driveway. Since Barb parked her car in the garage, he wouldn't know if she was even home until he was inside the house. His anticipation grew with every step he took towards the porch. He was up the steps and slipping his key into the lock when he noticed the barking of a dog. He paused and looked around, wondering which one of his neighbors had gotten one. He then thought to himself, 'Tom must have finally given in to Peggy. She's wanted a puppy for years. I can't believe she talked him into it.'

Opening the door as quietly as possible, just in case, he soon realized that he was alone. This was a bit of a letdown, but it was still going to be a huge surprise. He had barely shut the door when he heard the garage door opening. 'OH, this is perfect!' he thought.

He stepped into the kitchen and grabbed a soda before sitting down at the breakfast table. The sound of the garage door closing was really loud when Barb opened the door to enter the house. Then it was muffled as John heard the thump of her closing it again. His anticipation grew as her footsteps got closer and then, there she was!

Walking straight past him to put her purse in its usual place by the toaster, she suddenly stopped as if frozen in place. She appeared stuck in time for a few seconds before she slowly turned her head to look at the table. John sees her eyes go from intense squinting to the size of apples as she realizes he is setting there in the kitchen. A schoolgirl squeal preceded her rushing to him. Her momentum pushed him back against the wall as her body made contact with his. Their arms intertwined like lightning, yet their lips met as gently as a soft summer rain. This is what happens when lovers are separated for weeks, and then reunite unexpectedly.

At least it was unexpected by one of them. After a few seconds, she playfully pushed away from him and slapped his shoulder. "You ass! You could have told me last night on the phone that you were coming back today. What's wrong with you, mister?"

John was standing there with his usual smirky grin. "But where's the fun in that? Now come on baby, another kiss!" He stood with his eyes closed, displaying an exaggerated lip pucker.

"You know, John, that look is good on you!"

John opened one eye to see her smiling and backing away from him slowly. He opened the other eye and started matching her steps, one for one. There was a squeal as she turned to run up the stairs. As she disappeared around the corner, he heard her say, "I'm watching that movie..."

~ ~ ~

They enjoyed several hours of joyous pleasure. Not all of it was hard core sex; there had been long minutes of touching and being touched. Now they were just lying there, basking in the simple nearness of the one they loved. John was on his back, staring up at the ceiling fan.

"You know. I really missed this fan. I don't think I saw a single ceiling fan the entire time I was over there. It's odd how different things are in other countries. I missed simple things, like ICE in my soda. You had to ask for it every time. They just don't give you ice, unless you ask for it. Oh, and that damn espresso! Not to mention those stupid little toy cups they drink it out of. I wish I could get my hands on the idiot who started making them so small. What a cheapskate he must have been! They're everywhere over there! You can't get away from them. Excuse me sir, but would you like some espresso? Here, have a tiny little cup!"

Barb was on her belly as she inched closer and put her head on his chest. The sheet has slipped from her backside, so John slid his hand down her back to her baby-soft bottom. She raised her feet and gently moved them back and forth, like scissors in the air. Then she said, "Well, if you go back over there, you could take a really BIG cup that says TEXAS on it."

At first there was silence. Then a chuckle that eventually gave way to both of them laughing together at nothing really. John rolled onto his side and began slowly running his hand from her bottom to her shoulders, and back again. Then he leaned over and whispered in her ear. "Ding Ding, Round Two!"

~ ~ ~

The next day found John still asleep. He awoke to the sound of Barbara in the shower. As always, she had left the bathroom door open, so he could see her through the shower glass. Man, it was nice to be home. Hearing the water shut off, he watched as she stepped onto the rug.

"Honey! You awake yet, baby?"

"Yes, but I don't want to get up. It's so nice in here. Come on Barb, let's just stay here."

Walking to the door while drying her hair with the towel, she looked at him and said, "You said you wanted to take me out to eat. Now get up, buddy! Get movin'!"

John reluctantly got up and headed for the shower. "So where are we going? Tell me this again. What's the big surprise?"

"Well, I think the Cardinal was right. Remember what he told you. He said you should relax in familiar surroundings. And I agree with him. So I'm planning on immersing you in the Texas experience!"

"Well Barb, our bed is in Texas. Can I have my experience here?"

She smiled and made a ticking sound with her mouth before saying "NO!"

"Ok, I get it. I'm going out. So, really, where we going?"

"We are going to go have a light brunch with Tom and Peggy. Oh, guess what they got? It's the cutest little puppy! It's so precious!"

"Yeah, I heard some PRECIOUS barking when I got home yesterday. Kinda figured that Tom wimped out and let her get a dog. You know that thing is going to bark every time we go out to the pool now, don't you? I'm going to end up shooting it!"

"You will not! How can you say that? That is so cruel! Now get your Great White Hunter's ass dressed so we won't be late. Besides, you don't own a gun!"

"Hey lady, this is Texas! We can have a light brunch, and then I'll buy a gun! What do you bet they sell 'em right there in the restaurant? Yes, I'll have a brunch with a side order of espresso; don't forget the little cup and a shotgun. Works for me."

Having just completed his little rant, John was busy combing his hair in front of the mirror when he saw Barb's reflection appear beside him. She was glaring at him with the meanest expression she could muster. He slowly turned to face her before saying, "What's the matter? Don't you like espresso?"

"John. Did they torture you over there? Did you fall on your head getting off the plane? Why are you acting like this, and WHY aren't you ready yet? I don't want to be late."

"Late? When did you make these plans? You didn't even know I was coming!"

"While you were asleep, nut boy! Have you even LOOKED at the clock? No! Now get dressed!" She began to push him out of the bathroom.

John started to get dressed, but kept talking too. "Ok, ok, so what's up after we eat?" John saw that she is completely dressed. "How'd you do that? You can't possibly be dressed yet. Hey! Are you really my wife, or did aliens swoop down and leave you here to trick me?"

"Well, after we eat, you and I are going shopping in a BIG TEXAS mall! And before you say anything, don't! You are going this time. You have been away from me for over two weeks, buddy, and now you are spending quality time with me. Your wife!"

John was completely dressed now except for one boot. He almost fell over as she pushed up against him. "Don't you want to spend time with me?"

"Well of course I do. But..."

"But what?"

"Well, I was just thinking we would be a lot less likely to get arrested here doing what I want to do!"

She smiled and pushed him away.

"Anyway, after we shop for a while, we are going to eat barbeque at your favorite place and then...well, I'll tell you that part later."

"Wait a minute, cutie. I like the barbeque part, of course, but what is this other part you are hiding?"

"It's a surprise. Now don't ask me anything else, or you are going to ruin everything."

John liked her surprises. Especially the ones she pulled at home here. He decided to stop giving her a hard time and just go with the flow. She rushed him to the car, and they arrived at the designated restaurant 10 minutes later. There was the usual chatter between two sets of neighbors who only went out together occasionally. It was fun and John continued to be in a jovial mood. He was telling them stories about what happened to him in Italy while avoiding any questions of why his auto business required him to go there. It was a weak excuse for his trip, but they weren't really interested in why. He had them laughing so loudly at times that other patrons were straining their ears to hear what was so funny.

Finally the meal was over. The neighbors parted ways after the two women touched cheeks and made kissing noises, while both men rolled their eyes at this spectacle. A firm handshake between them, and they were ready to go.

John's lighthearted mood made the rest of the day a very fun time for him and Barbara. She bought two pairs of shoes that John could not see any difference between. With hours of shopping coming to an end, they made their way to their car. All the day's bargains were deposited into the trunk before they took their seats inside. John turned the key and the engine roared to life. "So, gorgeous. Where to now?"

Barbara looked at her watch. "Make your way to the arena."

"What? The rodeo? Are you kidding me? We're going to the rodeo?"

"Yes."

She reached into her purse and pulled out her camera.

"See. I know you keep telling me about how the Cardinal really wants to go to a rodeo. I thought we could take a bunch of pictures of us there. And we can even take video with this camera, remember? So when you go back, you can play this on his computer. I thought he'd get a real kick out of it. And maybe, it will make him want to come over himself and let us take him to a real rodeo. What do you think?"

"What I think is that it is a good idea, and I like it. But I know you, Barb. You aren't telling me everything here." He was looking into her eyes, then he smiled and continued. "Ah HA! I see it in your eyes, young lady. Who's meeting us there? Don't deny it. Who?"

"You know, John? I hate it when you do that, really. But, yeah, somebody... Oh, damn it. It's Bill from the shop. I asked him to bring the family. Thought you could talk shop for a few minutes, and then we could buy some stuff for Tommy. Did I tell you that his soccer team won their division? I thought it would kinda be like a reward for him doing so good. You know, kill two birds with one rodeo."

John leaned over and kissed her. "Why didn't you just tell me? You know I like Tommy too! I like it all. Thanks Barb! It's the perfect ending of a perfect day."

She leaned over and kissed him back before whispering, "No. The perfect ending comes later. When I get you home, stud boy!"

~ ~ ~

Barbara had made reservations for the rodeo that morning while John was still sleeping. She had paid for the tickets over the phone, and Bill's tickets had already been picked up. Once inside themselves, they made their way to some box seats right in the middle and on the railing. Bill and the family were already there. Tommy ran up to give Barb and John big hugs for the rodeo tickets. John and Bill wandered off below the bleachers to talk shop. Fifteen minutes later, they reappeared and took their seats.

John noticed that Barb was not there and asked Bill's wife if she had gone to the ladies' room. Just as he was being told that Barbara had taken a cell phone call and then run to the front entrance, he heard her distinctive laugh behind him. He was smiling when he first turned to look at her, but it faded to half-mast as he saw her walking next to a priest.

John did a double-take before he sat down and stared at the arena. Barbara walked up and began introducing Father Cobleir to Bill and his family. As the discussion grew as to who would sit by whom, John decided that he really wanted to be seated next to Mathew. He mustered a big Texas smile before saying, "Hey, Mathew, sit down here between me and Barb. That way we can both tell you what's happening as it goes down."

"Sounds good, John." He stepped over to the seat that John was pointing to and extended his hand. As he sat down, he said, "I hope you don't mind. I tried to tell Barbara this morning that this really should be time for the two of you. But you know better than anyone how she is when she sets her mind to something."

"Yes I do, Mathew. She can be determined, all right."

"So, how does it feel to be home John? Good, I'll bet!"

"That it is. It's all good."

John was having a hard time making small talk with him. This was just too much. It was just like his vision. The only thing was, he never saw anything after this point. Obviously there was something linking Mathew to that leather strap, or the walking cane, or to all of it. John just didn't know. But they would be sitting beside each other for the next few hours, so he intended to find out.

"Have you ever been to a rodeo before, Mathew?"

"No. I've lived in Texas for years and always wanted to see one. This is the first time that anyone has ever asked me. I guess it wasn't all Barbara's fault that I'm here. I could have just said no, but I really wanted to come the minute she brought it up. Hope you don't mind, John."

"Don't mind at all. I'm actually very glad you are here. I always wanted a chance to just chitchat with you anyway."

Mathew turned to him and said, "I've always wanted the same thing, John. It's funny how things like this work out."

"You have no idea how true that is, buddy!"

"Huh? What do you mean?"

"Nothing, just was wondering about a few things. Like, where did you say your family came from?"

"Oh, well I'm from Boston. Born and raised there."

"Didn't you say that your family was from France? Or did I just assume that because your name sounds so French?"

"I don't remember ever saying, but it is a French name. Well, sort of."

"How do you have a 'sort of' French name?"

Mathew laughed before answering. "It's kind of a long story and I'd hate to bore you with the details."

"Things like this are not boring to me these days. I'm all ears. If you don't mind telling me."

"Well, my great-great grandfather is the one that emigrated from France to America in the late 1800s. His wife had died giving birth to his third son. The story is that he couldn't take seeing everything there because it all reminded him of her. So one day, he just up and brought both sons to America for a fresh start. Somehow he ended up in Boston, and our family has been there ever since. Not much more to really tell, I'm afraid."

"So what did your grandfather do in Boston? Was he a priest also?"

"Oh, heavens no. He was a boot maker. Just like his father

before him. The whole family has made things for people's feet for centuries. At least that's the family legend that gets passed along to each new generation. I was being trained to do it as well, when I was younger, but I took a liking to the Church. One thing led to another, and I ended up being a priest right there where I had been christened as a baby."

"I'll bet that your family was upset when you didn't go into the family business."

"You would have thought so, but it was actually just the opposite. Seems my father had told his grandfather that one day I would be a priest in the Church. It happened the day I was being christened. That's been a long time ago now. Wow, time really flies by doesn't it?"

Mathew had been talking but mostly watching the activity in the arena. He would look at John ever now and then as they spoke. This time he stayed focused on John's face.

"John, you OK?"

"Ah, yeah, I'm just kind of tired I guess. Barb forced me to walk around the mall all day before depositing me here."

John didn't need to ask Mathew anything more. He now knew that this priest either had that walking cane, or knew where it was. Now was not the time to bring it up. They really needed to be alone for that type of a conversation. But how? John just knew something would present itself out of nowhere. That is how things have been happening so far!

Barbara stood up and said, "I'm going to go get a snow cone. Anyone else?" Bill's wife stood and said she would help. Everyone ordered something. "John, what do you want, honey?"

"Nothing right now. Still full from the restaurant. Thanks anyway."

"Ok, but if you change your mind later, you have to go yourself. Those are the rules."

"Ok, ok, get me a soda." Then as an afterthought he turned towards her and yelled, "Make sure they put ice in it. LOTS OF ICE!"

~ ~ ~

Everyone had a very good time at the rodeo, especially Mathew, who actually was heard yelling loudly several times.

John watched him smiling and laughing. He could almost picture his friend the Cardinal doing the same thing.

Afterwards, it was the usual traffic jam with hundreds of cars trying to leave at the same time. They hadn't gone more than 10 feet before some highly sexual comments were being made by both John and Barbara. Of course, John started it. But once it had been mentioned, Barbara kept it going. Eventually she stayed onto Mathew's enjoying the rodeo.

"Honey, I think that Mathew had more fun than Tommy did. I'm glad I invited him. I wasn't sure he would come, but it worked out really well. I got some really good shots of all of you. I'm glad I brought the camera, aren't you? Now all you have to do is take these pictures with you and show them to the Cardinal. I'll bet he'll really enjoy seeing them."

John heard this and his first thought was "BINGO". This would be perfect! "Barb, don't you have Mathew's cell number on your cell?"

"Yes. Why? Did he forget something?"

"No, I was just thinking that I could go by his Church tomorrow and get him to email these pictures on over to the Cardinal. Besides, it would give me a chance to check in with Anton and see if anything has happened since I left. What do you think?"

"I think that would be great. Oh, but I have a hair appointment tomorrow morning, so you'll have to go without me. Sorry."

John simply said, "Works for me!"

~ ~ ~

Once again the morning found John being awakened by Barbara, but this time she was not in the shower. No, she was completely dressed and about to leave. "John. Wake up John. I'm leaving, and you need to get up if you are going to visit Mathew at the church."

Hearing the word 'Church' snapped John out of a sound sleep and right out of bed in full stride to get ready. His sudden rise caught Barbara off-guard to the point that she almost stumbled and fell.

"Hey! Watch it!"

John caught her arm and quickly apologized before letting her go so he could run to the bathroom.

"It's all that ICE you had last night, you goofball! You'll probably be peeing for a week!"

She heard his voice echo from within the tiled bathroom. "Sorry honey! I'll listen to you next time. Promise."

She mumbled to herself, "Yeah, I've heard that before."

After stepping closer to the bathroom door, she said, "I forgot to tell you. I'm having lunch with Peggy after I get my hair done. Then she wants me to go with her to get some chew toys for her new baby!"

"Hey Barb!"

"What?"

"The answer is NO!"

"What? What answer?"

John's head popped out of the bathroom door just long enough to say "No DOG! So forget it!"

Again she mumbled to herself, "As if I always listen to you, buddy. Hey, that's not a bad idea. I wonder if there are any really cute ones left?"

She was long gone when John emerged from the house and trotted over to his car. On the way there he noticed something was different about his front bumper.

"Hmmm. That's odd. Those scratches on my bumper are gone. I guess Barb finally got around to having one of the guys touch that up. It took her long enough. I bet the rodeo tickets were partial payback for Bill fixing the bumper."

The drive to the church was quick and once there, John wasn't sure where to park. He decided to drive around the building and look for Mathew's car. Once he found it, he went back to the front of the building and parked. On the walk from the car, he looked up and saw a little old lady watching his every move from one of the second floor windows.

"I wonder who she is. Ah, she looks old. She probably can't see this far and if she can, she'll probably forget it in a minute or two."

Mathew's phone rang and he picked it up. "Hello. Margie! How are... A man just parked in front? Ok? Oh, you don't recognize him. I'll be there in just a minute. NO, no, don't stop him. I'm sure it will be OK. Yes, I'm glad you called."

He hurried to the front and was surprised to see that it

is John.

"John! I wasn't expecting to see you here. Did you come to convert?"

"Oh, it's you. I thought this was a Baptist Church. Silly me!"

They both chuckled at each other's early morning wit.

"So John, what brings you my way?"

"Well, I was wondering if you could get these rodeo pictures to the Cardinal for me."

"Yes, I can! I'd be happy to do that for you. It's odd, that you bring this up. When the Cardinal was here, he had asked me if I had ever seen the rodeo. He seemed a little disappointed when I said 'no'. I bet he'll love seeing these. Please, come this way. My office is in the back."

Mathew talked about the rodeo all the way back to his office. John was smiling as he followed him. It seemed that he had been following one priest or another for weeks now. At least Mathew had more personality than Father Turin.

Ah, Father Turin. Why does that Jesus image pop up every time John thinks about him? It must mean something. John knew that there was something very special about this Father Turin. Maybe the answer will eventually be found in the reading of that book. All John had to do is solve these three visions. According to the writing on the cover of the book, they were the key. John would be able to open the book. But would he be able to read and understand it?

John noticed that Mathew was still talking about the rodeo as he led him down a dimly lit hallway. Where was he taking him? A few more steps and Mathew turned into the only open door with a light on inside.

"So, here we are John. What do you have the pictures on? I have a multi card reader attached to my PC, so I can read just about any of them."

John handed the little memory card to Mathew.

"I'm not sure what kind it is. PCs are not my thing really."

"Oh yes. I can read this one. It's the same type that my camera uses."

He began to walk behind his desk, but stopped and looked back at John when he heard his name.

"Mathew. Can we sit and talk at that table first? I have something I really need to ask you."

"Sure."

He walked over to sit down across from John, who was sitting and ready. "What's on your mind, John?"

"Bear with me a few minutes here now, buddy. I know this is about to get really weird for you. Again."

John shrugged a little and smiled before continuing.

"I don't know any other way to start this off, so I might as well just spit it out. I know you or your family, have something to do with a walking cane that has a diamond cross with ruby teardrop stones on either side of it."

Mathew's reaction was to push away from the table a little. His face instantly lost all expression and color as his mind reeled from what he just heard John say. He blinked rapidly a couple of times, then shook his head before speaking.

"What? What did you just say? How on earth can you possibly know this?"

He had fallen back in his chair and was staring at John.

"I find myself wanting to tell you that you scare the HELL out of me when you do things like this. You just know these things? How?"

John was holding his hands up, palms facing the priest and patting the air as if trying to calm him down.

"I'm sorry, buddy. I know I need to work on my delivery methods sometimes. But there wasn't any easy way to put it. Sorry."

Mathew took a deep breath before sitting up and pulling his chair back closer to the table.

"I'm sorry, John. This whole thing has to be very weird for you too. It's just that you seem to know... ah. It doesn't matter. The answer is 'yes'."

"Our family has been passing this cane down from generation to generation. My father gave it to me when I turned 21. Of course it is in storage in a very secure vault. The day after my birthday, he took me to see it for the first time. It was really an amazing day. He took me in and there was all this paperwork to fill out before they scanned my entire handprint into this machine. Then we walked back to this huge metal vault door that had these enormous steel bars about 10 feet in front of it. There was an armed guard standing by this little pedestal with this electronic pad sitting on top of it. He was smiling at my father as we walked up. He told me I had to put my hand on the pad with my fingers stretched out as far apart as I could. As soon as I put my hand on it, this light blue line swept from the top of the pad to the bottom. Then the guard told me I could remove my hand. There was this clicking sound that came from a section of those bars behind him, and he turned to push them open.

"He walked in with us and my father gave me a key and showed me which door to put it in. The guard put his key into the little lock right beside mine, and I heard another lock release. The big guy opened the door and pulled out a long wooden box. Next, my father led us to a little private room. The guard left us alone after he placed it on this table ledge along one wall. I can't tell you how impressive this all was to a 21 year old man."

"Anyway, my dad sat me down and told me a story before he let me see what was in the box. He began to tell me the story of the cane. It has been in my family for generations, and they think that it has some kind of special powers. He really believed that it was what made our family so strong in all that we do. I listened but really didn't have a clue what he was talking about until he showed it to me, and I touched it. He tried to get me to hold it in my hands, but I just didn't want to. It was strange enough just touching it. At first I thought what I was feeling was just because of how odd my father was acting. But, sitting there with my fingers touching it, I started to feel really strong and happy. It was a feeling that I can't explain. To me, the cane didn't look that old. It was really very modern looking. It had simple lines but it was very glossy looking. It just didn't look like something that you would think was hundreds of years old."

"That's when he told me that only a piece of it was that old and that the rest of it was not. We both agreed it had to be the handle. It is made of solid gold and appears to be, well ancient. It's carved like one of those heads on a Roman statue that you see in books. That has to be it because the gold is not really shiny. It's really smooth, like it was rubbed that way from being handled. The odd thing is that it has never been used to walk with. You can tell, because the tip of the cane is just wood. It is not scratched up or flattened, as it surely would have been if somebody walked with it. The tip is just as glossy as the rest of it."

Mathew saw how intently John was watching him as he told his story. But John had stopped listening altogether just a few moments before. His mind was on something from his vision. He remembered seeing a man holding that leather strap before placing it into the hollow shaft of the cane. This was the same man that John knew had brought it to America. Why didn't Mathew or his father know?

"Mathew, you said that it has been handed down for generations. It was always on a person's 21st birthday, right?"

"Oh no. Just on me and my dad's 21st. My grandfather's father died in an accident before passing it on to his son, which would have been my grandfather. He found out about the cane while his dad was dying. He was the one that started the current tradition of doing it on a 21st birthday. He wanted to make sure that the story was passed along. He only knew what his father had told him about the cane before he died in the hospital. Since he had been in and out of consciousness, my grandfather wasn't sure he got the whole story about the cane. So, we may not really know all there is to know about it. But if you saw it, you'd probably think the same thing we do."

John was looking down and tapping his fingers on the table. Mathew could tell there was something bothering John. "Ok, John. What now?"

"I have another question. Is this vault in Boston, and do you have access to it?"

"It's just outside of Boston, maybe half an hour's drive from the city center. And 'yes', I do have access to it. Actually, I'm the only one that has access to it."

"The only one? Why?"

"Well, that is one of the few things my great-grandfather was very clear about on his deathbed. He made my grandfather promise that only one person would have complete access to it at a time. So that is how it works now. I'm the only one that can get to it."

"Good."

John sighed deeply and loudly before continuing. "It's not the handle that is so old. In fact, you aren't going to believe what it is, or where it is even. But what it is will freak you out so badly you're going to shake. I think I really need to talk to the Cardinal before I tell you anything else. I'll need to do it in private if you don't mind. Sorry."

"John, you have uttered some truly amazing things to me and have known things you shouldn't have. I have known since the beginning that you are blessed, my friend. You tell me when you're ready. I have complete trust in you. Think I'll just go for a walk and stretch my legs, for say 20 minutes. That sound about right?"

"Thanks, buddy. That's plenty."

Mathew was gone is seconds, closing the door behind him as he left John in his office. He didn't stop on the steps behind the church like he usually did. Instead, he was walking and thinking. His mind was spinning with every step he took around the parking lot. It was nice weather today, and he could hear the sounds of kids yelling from a playground a few blocks away. He stayed outdoors for more than 20 minutes, because it just felt so pleasant to be outside. It crossed his mind that his rambling around the parking lot was probably driving Margie crazy. Yeah, she would most definitely be watching him from somewhere. Finally, he knew he had to go back and find out what John had up his sleeve now.

As he entered the back hall, he saw light from his office. He knew John had finished his phone call and opened the door. It was his church, his office, but he still stopped just outside the door until John looked up and saw him. "So, everything okay?"

"Sorry about that, Mathew. Yes, everything is fine. I'll bet you are about to get a phone call from the Head Father. He's going to tell you that they want you to go to Rome with me. Of course, we will have to stop by that vault of yours and pick up your cane. I hope you are willing to do that. It is extremely important that you and your cane come to Rome."

Mathew shook his head. "What? Rome? I'd ask why, but it really doesn't matter at this point. Is that where I'll find out what this is all about?"

"I'm afraid so, sorry."

"I don't know what to...". He was interrupted by the ringing of his desk phone.

"Things really happen quickly around you. I don't know how you handle all of this so well."

Mathew picked up his phone while he was still looking at John.

"Hello? Yes, Father. I'll be right there."

~ ~ ~

The evening was rather long from Mathew's point of view. He was packed and ready to go less than an hour after getting home. Why he had hurried to do this seemed beyond his control. His nervous energy drove him while packing, but haunted him the rest of the long night. He had showered, eaten, and tried to lie down to sleep more than once. Finally giving up, he sat fully-dressed in his kitchen letting cup after cup of coffee grow cold without tasting it. He was happy to finally see the clock on the wall show it was time for the limo to pick him up.

John, on the other hand, had been sexually assaulted by his wife most of the night. Barbara's female instincts had kicked into high gear after hearing that she was going to be alone once again. John never complained until his alarm clock signaled it was time to retreat. This time, he found it harder to leave the arms of his wife, but things of enormous consequences were calling him back to Rome.

He had tried to convince her to come along, but she was adamant about staying home. Initially John was curious why Barb was not going to the airport this time. The morning exercises she put him through lasted right up to the time the limo arrived. It was only then that he realized her plan, but there was never to be any objection from him. This was much better than his last departure, and her attack in the back seat of the limo.

The two limos arrived at the airfield within a few minutes of each other. Mathew lived closer and already had his bag on the plane as John boarded. With all bags on board and the door shut tightly, the plane taxied to a swift liftoff into another blue Texas sky. Mathew's sleepless night ended a few seconds after the plane's wheels had cleared the runway. He was allowed to sleep the entire three-hour flight to a small airfield just outside Boston.

It took Gena three attempts and two warm wash cloths to get Mathew to stay awake before they landed. He and John moved from plane to limo for the 30-minute ride to retrieve the cane. John was amazed that such a secure vault was housed in such a plain-looking building in a commercial industrial park. Though Mathew invited him several times, John chose to stay in the car while the cane was retrieved. There was next to no talking at all on the return trip to the airfield. John's eyes never left sight of the long wooden box that Mathew held with such a reverent grip.

With all back on board, the wooden box was secured underneath an unused row of seats. The plane once again leaped from mother earth's grasp and turned towards Europe. This time, Gena found herself quietly watching as both men slept for the first nine hours of their flight. She graciously catered food and drink to each as they awoke. Though she did not know what the wooden box held, she was very aware of the hold it had on her passengers' attention. Constant stares and short, restless conversations filled those final minutes before they landed at the secluded Italian airfield.

John fully expected to find Father Turin waiting with the limo driver, but it was not the case. The drive to Vatican City was punctuated by short naps separated by even shorter spans of sightseeing from the moving vehicle. The men finally became more animated at the security checkpoint outside the Vatican. As the limo rounded the last corner, John could see Father Turin patiently waiting for them by the entrance to the building.

"Ah, Mr. Parson! Nice to see you have returned to us. Father Cobleir? I have heard a great deal about you from the Cardinal." He then leaned closer to softly say, "You have made a very powerful ally, Father."

John heard every word and interrupted because he had urges that required attending to soon. "Am I going to be in the same room?"

"Yes, Mr. Parson. Follow me please, gentlemen."

The same little guy from before was now standing behind the car with his hands on both men's roller bags. Once again, he followed them into the building and diligently stayed only a few feet behind them as they walked to their rooms. "Father Cobleir will be in a room only ten steps around the corner from yours, Mr. Parson."

John was glad that they were walking so quickly. He really needed a private moment in his room. It was Gena's fault for being so efficient and refilling his water glass as often as she did. Maybe he shouldn't have asked for all that ice.

Finally, they were only steps away from John's old room. He bolted past the others but left the door open after disappearing from the hall. John had noticed the first smile ever from the little guy. He didn't understand English, but had no problem understanding John's situation. "Just give me a minute, and I'll catch you both in Mathew's room."

"Is this your first time to Roma, Father Cobleir?" They proceeded around the corner to the next door.

"No, I've visited several times over the years; however, this IS my first time inside the Vatican."

"Then allow me to offer my assistance to you for whatever you may need. Here is my card. The number on the back is my personal cell number. Please call at any time."

"Thank you, Father. I will." They stepped from the hall into a sitting area similar to John's. "Is this all for me?"

Father Turin performed the same little walk-through that he had with John. The little boy appeared a second later, but one bag short. He had left John's bag in his room and hurried into Mathew's room to do the same before leaving. He and John almost collided in the open doorway. The little boy looked up at John and smiled briefly once more before ducking his head to scurry on his way.

"Ah, Mr. Parson. I trust you feel more relaxed now? Yes?"

"That I do, buddy. Yes I do. Now, we need to take Father Cobleir and his package to the white room. Father Marsai is waiting for a call from you, I believe."

"That is correct. I had just spoken to him as you pulled up outside. I will call him once we start his way. I believe that the Cardinal should already be there by now. Shall we?" He motioned for the two men to move to the hall.

They had only rounded two corners when John noticed that Mathew was looking back and forth in the hall as they walked. He moved closer to his friend and said, "Just stick close to me, buddy. This place is a maze!"

"You know your way around in here, John?"

"Not really, but I can find the dining room!"

A few minutes later, they all entered the dressing area. There were the customary introductions before Father Marsai held the door open for the Cardinal and the others to enter the white room. Once inside, Mathew placed his wooden box ever so gently upon the white table. He released the little brass latch that secured the box and opened the lid. All eyes eagerly focused on a soft leather wrapping that covered a long, slender shape.

Mathew closed his eyes for just a split second, and John realized he must have said a quick prayer. Then his hands slowly pulled one fold to the side. Only the last four inches of the shiny cane shaft was visible. He looked around the room for a second as if to proudly proclaim, 'This is MY family's heirloom'. Not a breath was taken as his hand pulled aside the remaining fold of leather, and all eyes finally saw the exquisite walking cane. It had a solid gold handle that was dull from the naturally-occurring oil from the hands that had held it over the years. The most prominent feature was a cross of brilliant diamonds, flanked on both sides by a single teardrop ruby. The appearance was incredibly similar to drops of blood.

Father Marsai broke the silence. "I have seen many ancient artifacts that pale in comparison to this object's mystic beauty. It is incredible that your family has managed to keep such an object secret all these years, and to also have maintained it in such a perfectly preserved state."

Mathew didn't look up, but his smile was noticed by all. It was his acceptance of this gracious compliment to the generations of his family that were responsible. He brushed a finger along the handle before joining John on one side of the table. The Cardinal motioned for Pierre to take his appropriate place at the head of the table. Looking at Mathew, he simply asked, "Father, may we proceed?"

"Yes, Cardinal."

Father Marsai once again spoke as he began. "I understand the belief is that the handle can be unscrewed. Let's see how tightly it is... Well?" There was but a soft squeak as the handle loosened under the steady pressure. "There it goes, and it's turning freely. Here we are." The handle was off. It was a gracious gesture as he held it out for Father Cobleir to take. Then Father

Marsai fished the metal pick once more from his black bag of tools. Inserting it into the hollow end of the cane, he carefully searched for what is supposed to be inside. He obviously could not feel anything.

Once again, his free hand dove into the black bag and retrieved a small pocket flashlight that he turned on before placing in his mouth. Kneeling down now and shining the light into the cane, he moved his head slightly before saying, "AH. There it is! It has settled farther down the shaft. I have just the thing."

Without looking, his free hand felt around in the black bag as the sounds of metal clinking against metal was heard. There is a swooshing sound as he pulled a longer, pick-like object from his bag. "This ought to be long en... Yes! Got it!"

They all watched as a rather ordinary strap of leather slowly emerged from the inside of the cane. He stood up with the long piece of leather draped across both hands. They all noticed as he suddenly shuddered before saying, "Wow! How odd. There is a, ah, tingling sensation in my hands. Let me put this down." He placed it stretched out across the open wooden box.

The Cardinal inquired, "What did you feel?"

"It was, well, like pure energy." They all notice that not only was he smiling from ear to ear, his face had taken on a noticeably healthy glow. "I feel, uh, REALLY GREAT!"

Mathew extended both hands as if he were going to pick it up, but stopped short and looked around the room. "I would like to hold it, if I may?"

John said, "Buddy, you don't need to ask. This has belonged to your family for centuries."

Mathew was holding it when he closed his eyes for just a moment. "I feel it too. It is just as my father had said. Only he was referring to just holding the cane. I had wanted to hold the cane, but for some reason never had. I did touch it often and felt tingles of sorts. Before now, I thought it was just me. But I FEEL this."

His smile grew and he uttered a soft chuckle before laying it back on the box. "So what is it?"

The Cardinal said, "We are not sure at the moment."

Then John's words drew all eyes to him. "Well we didn't. But now I do." He paused before saying, "It is a leather strap from a sandal worn by Jesus." Every pair of eyes went from John to the Cardinal and back again. "Anton. I believe we need to bring these guys up to speed."

The Cardinal gently smiled at each man before simply saying, "John, I agree."

CHAPTER 19

A Message Not Delivered

The Cardinal's office was full. John, Mathew and Father Marsai had followed him back from the white room. There had been a conscious effort not to mention anything about the book in front of Father Marsai. The only focus of their discussion was John's three visions. It was obvious to all that Father Marsai was finding it hard to accept the validity of John's supposed visions.

He was guarded in his responses and comments towards John during the two hours that it took to narrate all of them. The priest was polite but his hesitation to believe was very easily seen in his eyes. He was a scientist at heart when it came to all beliefs other than his belief in God. Yes, he was a complicated individual and was struggling to buy into what the other three seemed to accept as fact. John was not fazed at all by the priest's reaction. If Father Marsai knew what they knew about the book, then all this would fall in place for him as well.

"Mr. Parson. I find this entire scenario perplexing to say the least. However, I cannot deny what I have witnessed firsthand. It is truly amazing what has occurred here. From a scientific point of view, I cannot explain how you could know where to find these things, but you did. I also have personally verified that the ring we found inside the scepter did, in fact, belong to Pilate. I found inscriptions on it and compared it to known texts that prove beyond doubt that it was his. However, I cannot explain the cross cut into the emblem. This was not mentioned in the texts that I have at my disposal.

"Now, as for the leather strap. It is old, no doubt. How old? That could be determined with scientific methods. For me, dating this piece is not the problem. The real issue is your belief that it was part of Christ's sandal. I see absolutely no way to substantiate this. I admit that I felt something unusual when I held it. I don't know how to describe it, or if I could describe it. But it was just a feeling. Nothing I can test or document.

"The believer in me wants to say you have been given these signs for the divine purpose of finding them. But the scientist in me sees no reason to speculate beyond that. I apologize for sounding skeptical, but you must understand it is the nature of my training. Being a priest came late in life for me. My calling happened long after the formations of most of my worldly views. But again, you reported these visions before they were proven true.

"Having said this, I do want you all to know that I will assist in any capacity that may help your cause. I offer my pledge of secrecy to both this group and my Church.

"Oh, and one more thing. As a man, I am excited more than you probably can tell. To be a part of a quest to find this remaining ancient document is a dream to which even a pure scientist can thoroughly commit. So, on that note, I do have some information to offer the group regarding the search for this third item.

"The Church did have an ancient Jewish Torah that fit the exact description you gave in this last vision. As unnerving as it is to me, I have to also say that it had been stored on a shelf just as you said. It had one dowel rod that was much larger in circumference than the other and both ends had ornamental brass caps. I am sure that I could find a picture of it if given a day or two."

The Cardinal interrupted. "You said the Church HAD such an object? Where is it now?"

"It was given to the Israeli Historical Archives by the Pope just 18 months ago."

Mathew spoke up, "Why would he do that?"

John added, "Why did you guys have a Jewish, whatever, anyway?" He turned his gaze from the Cardinal towards Father Marsai as the priest continued.

"Well, those are very valid questions. Once again, the answer has to do with the German Army during World War Two. When the Church was gathering objects ahead of the Nazi looting of Europe's treasures, it was approached by Jewish religious leaders suffering the same fate. Unlike the Catholic Church, these synagogues did not have the resources to transport their items to safety. We, the Church, agreed to take these items and preserve them until a safe future date for their return to the Jewish people. We have had over 100 such items in safekeeping for the past 60-odd years."

The Cardinal jumped in again. "Allow me to elaborate on this, Father. I have been actively involved with this ongoing process of repatriating these items to their rightful owners. Only last week, I had a two-hour session with another Jewish delegation concerning 22 more items that will be returned in the next few weeks. John, this was one of the meetings that held me up during your first visit, while you took your tour and first met Father Marsai. As far as the Torah, that was personally overseen by the Pope before he turned the process over to me."

Mathew commented, "So, the item we seek is apparently now being displayed somewhere in Israel. I'll bet they will not be easily convinced to let us pull the top of it and look. Also, if we did, they would rightfully claim ownership to it."

John shook his head. "You know. I just knew it was going way too easy on finding these things. This is a fairly large kink in our plans."

Father Marsai then surprised everyone around the table. With all the scientific skepticism he had voiced earlier, his following words were in stark contrast.

"Well, Mr. Parson, this is where the believer in me takes over. Though I can't explain how you know things, you do. So a logical person, a scientist even, would assume that your third vision is just as accomplishable as the first two. In other words, gentlemen, it seems to me that we should focus on the clues in this remaining vision. I think we are missing something."

Father Marsai now noticed that all three men were open-mouthed and staring at him. This lasted for a few uncomfortable seconds before he felt compelled to say, "What? I'm just saying we need not give up. That's all."

John then lightened the mood. "You know. I like you. Scientist or not. I don't understand you, but I like you. I'm just hoping you have a next step, cause I don't." His nervous chuckle helped the group break into a little laugh.

"Well, I think the next step is to list our clues. Seems we have to find a priest that would have been working in the storage area around the Torah. We also need to find the significance of a young boy's bloody hand. And of course, this whole issue surrounding an old war movie about Pearl Harbor."

John asked, "How do you spell the word you are using for this Jewish document?" After hearing the Cardinal spell it out, John said, "Oh, I was just thinking about the movie name, but that's not how it's spelled."

The Cardinal began thinking out loud. "I would think that there should be staff photos for everyone who has ever worked in the artifact storage area."

Mathew interjected. "But if we had that object in storage for over 60 years, that's going to be a lot of pictures. And you have to look at all of them because we don't have any clues to what year the vision was. Do we?"

John added, "No to the year thing, but I think we need to focus on candid pictures of the staff."

The Cardinal asks, "Why, John? What are you thinking?"

"Well Anton, I always saw this guy with a pencil behind his right ear. He was a real bean counter type dude."

Father Marsai suddenly slapped the table top and rose from his chair. "Cardinal, may I use your computer? I have an idea where we may find just the pictures we need."

"Yes Pierre, of course."

John looked at Pierre and smiled. "Hey buddy. I don't know about anyone else, but you almost gave me a heart attack. Please don't do that again." His laughter spread around the table and even caught Pierre as he walked to the desk.

"Sorry, John. I just got a little excited there. I think that somebody has been going through old office party photos and scanning them into the system by department. If we are lucky, your guy may be in one of them. I'm not sure how far back they go, but there is always a chance."

Mathew looked from the Cardinal to John before asking, "So John, is this what you've been doing these past few weeks?"

"Mostly. This whole thing just all of a sudden took on a life of its own. Right, Anton? So once again, we need to just sit back and enjoy the ride. It's been very interesting so far, and today is shaping up the same."

There is a light tapping on the door before it slowly opened and Judy's head appeared. "Could I get any of you something to drink?"

Mathew turned to John and asked with a big smile, "You want some espresso, John? I understand they have interesting dishware here."

John's face went blank, then a small smile appeared. "Barb told you, didn't she?"

"No, it was the Cardinal. Did you really let him do that to you for all those days?"

John's second blank expression focused toward the Cardinal. "I'm really going to have to get even with you, Anton! You know what they say about payback?"

The Cardinal was smiling as he answered her. "Evidently not, Judy. Thank you though."

"Oh my! John, come quick. I think I may have found your guy! Pencil and all!"

They all rushed to stand behind Pierre, who was sitting at the Cardinal's desk and pointing to the PC monitor. There was a picture of four young priests in a black and white photo. Though young, he was already balding on top of his head. And, just as John had described, there was a pencil tucked behind one ear.

"Is that your guy?"

"Well I'll be. Yep, that's the guy I saw nearly knock the rolly paper thingy to the ground."

Mathew nudged John. "It's called a Torah, John. It's like the Jewish Bible."

"There is still a problem here. These photos don't show any dates nor names. If there was anything written on the back, we'd have to find this photo and look." Father Marsai tried to push his chair back, but was blocked by everyone standing behind him.

"If you will let me up, I'll run downstairs and start looking for this photo."

The Cardinal puts his hand on Pierre's shoulder and said, "That will not be necessary, my friend. I know this man."

All eyes followed the Cardinal as he explained while walking towards the office door.

"John, you know how you have always wondered about the young priest that shows you around?"

"You mean Bishop Turin? That doesn't look like him in the photo to me."

"If you look closer at the man in the photo, you will see some facial features that are the same. He is Father Turin Senior."

"You mean to tell me that the guy in the photo is Bishop Turin's Father?"

"No. The man in the photo is his uncle. His father ownsand operates a textile company. I met him once. He is a very good man."

"So does he still work here at the Vatican? Where?"

"John, I'm sorry to say that he does not. He was here for only four years and then realized that he preferred to serve a small town. He has been at that parish for all these years. Just as a point of interest, Father Turin, Junior was brought here by me. It was a personal favor to an old friend, his uncle."

The Cardinal finally opened his office door and leaned out. "Judy, could you please ask Father Turin to join us as soon as possible?"

"But Cardinal, I left you a note. It's on your desk. You never read those, do you? Father Turin was called away on a family medical emergency. It was his father that called, I think. His uncle passed away from a stroke this morning. They found him still sitting in his chair at his Church. The Bishop left right away. Do you want me to get him on the cell phone?"

"No, no Judy! It's not that important. Uh, passed away? He has enough to deal with for now. But I do want to know if you find out any more information. His uncle was very dear to me."

The Cardinal closed the door and slowly made his way back to the table. Mathew rose quickly and pulled out his chair for him to sit down. Even Father Marsai returned to the table. The level of excitement from but a few moments ago had been replaced by this saddening news.

"I would like to have a moment for a personal prayer for my old friend."

They all bowed their heads for a silent moment. The Cardinal slowly opened his eyes and leaned back softly in his chair.

John was worried for his friend. "Anton, we should call it a day. You need time, my friend. Come on, guys. We can pick this up tomorrow morning. OK?"

"I think that I WOULD like to be alone. There are memories that need to be recalled. Tomorrow morning, say around 10:00? Here, of course."

Each man patted the Cardinal on the shoulder as they left him to his memories. They were all very solemn as they entered the hallway. Father Marsai stopped and faced them both.

"I will show you back to your rooms. I would enjoy taking you to dinner and then if you wish, I could give you a personal tour. I assure you there are sights that will interest you both."

Mathew spoke first. "I'd like that. What about you, John? Feel up for it?"

John hesitated and looked down at his feet before answering.

"I just don't really feel like getting out tonight. I think I'll just eat in my room and call Barb in a little bit. Sorry, guys. I doubt I'd be good company anyway. I need some down time myself."

The priest showed them back to their rooms and made arrangements to drop by for Mathew around 6:30 for dinner. John only repeated his apology before disappearing into his room.

"Sorry, guys. Later."

~ ~ ~

Father Marsai had timed the morning just perfectly. He was knocking on John's door at 9:45, and they were joined by Mathew one minute later. The three of them arrived at the Cardinal's door exactly one minute before the hour. John was the first to greet Judy.

"Morning Ma'am! He in?"

"Good morning Mr. Parsons. Oh, and everyone else! He is waiting inside, so go on in."

John opened and then held the door for the other two men. The Cardinal rose from behind his desk and smiled as he said,

"Morning, all! Please."

He motioned for them all to sit once again around the table. He was the last to sit, but the first to speak.

"I would like to begin by thanking you all for being so understanding yesterday. It was, well, a real shock to learn of my old friend's death. I need you to know that I spoke with Bishop Turin last night and the funeral will be tomorrow. I will be leaving this afternoon at 2:00. I would like to do as much as we can until then.

"I am at a loss as to what we can do at the moment, besides continue to brainstorm on this issue. Anyone have a thought?"

Pierre again took a methodical approach. "I think we need to refresh our facts. We know the Torah is in Israel, but we can't get at it. We now know the identity of the priest from the vision. Apologies again, Cardinal, but he is now unavailable as well. This leaves us only two clues to pursue. First, there is a reference to a war movie, and then there is the bloody hand of a boy. Both of these are extremely vague, to say the least. However, they are all that we have. I'm afraid that I am not much of a movie buff, so this one is not for me. I would like to ask John a little more about the child's hand."

"Shoot, partner."

No sooner than he had said it, he followed with "Oh, sorry. Forgot who I'm dealing with here. It is just an expression. Like saying 'OK' or 'Please continue', something like that."

The Cardinal and Pierre began nodding, smiling at each other over their newly learned slang. Pierre began his questioning of John.

"John, did you see anything on the child's hand? A ring perhaps or watch? Something like that?"

"Afraid not. No jewelry at all."

"Ok, then. Was there a sleeve showing?"

"No, just skin from the cuts down to the finger tips. It must have hurt like crazy hitting that fork like that."

Mathew asked, "It was done with a fork? How?"

"Not a table fork. The kid fell from a barn loft and hit a pitchfork on the way down. It was hanging on the wall of the barn and the tines were sticking out from the wall. It made some very bad cuts that surely needed stitches. From what I saw, it would probably have left a large Y-shaped scar."

Pierre resumed, "So we are looking for a boy, who may be a man now, that has a Y-shaped scar on his left hand."

John quickly corrected Pierre. "Well, actually the scar would be just above the wrist."

Now it was Mathew's turn to comment. "But you said the hand was bloody."

"Well of course it was. Blood runs downhill like water when you are standing up. The hand was drenched in it, but it was coming from the wrist area."

Pierre jumped on this new piece of information. "So was it on the inside or the outside of the wrist?"

Before John can answer, the Cardinal said, "It is on the inside of the wrist. Isn't it, John?"

Everyone stared at the Cardinal as John said, "Yes. It's on the inside, but how..."

The Cardinal interrupted John. "I know this story and the man with this scar. Actually, everyone here knows this man. We all work for him, so to speak."

Mathew softly said, "The Holy Father bears this scar?"

"Yes." Was the simple reply.

The Cardinal glanced at the clock on the wall before rising from his chair and saying, "Perhaps he is the proud owner of this missing message? I would like for the three of you to take a short break, please. Say 20 minutes or so?"

They all began to stand in preparation of leaving, but then John asked, "Anton? If he had this message, don't you think he would have told at least you? He knows we are looking for it, right?"

"Yes, John. He knows we are looking. If he has it and did not say, then he must have a reason. All I can do is ask."

John was the last one out of the office, and he closed the door after one final look at the Cardinal. Once in the hall, Pierre showed them to a nearby break room to wait for the completion of the Cardinal's call. Their wait was much shorter than they had expected. Judy appeared only a few minutes later and informed them that the Cardinal was ready for them to return. Only moments later, they were once again seated around the table in the Cardinal's office.

"I spoke to the Holy Father. I had seen his scar and asked him about it. He told me the same story that you rendered to us. He has confirmed that John's version of events was completely accurate. This is yet one more confirmation of the accuracies of his visions. However, he does not have nor know where this missing message is. He expressed confusion as to why he was being pointed to by the vision. I'm afraid we will find no answers here."

Again, it was Pierre who astounded them all by being the optimist in the group. "Well, I find myself thinking that this link to the Pope may be one that has not happened yet. It is the final step in John's vision. What if it is signifying where the missing message is going to be? Of course, if I am correct, then we are on hold until he is in possession of it."

John looked at Pierre. "You know, buddy. I get dizzy trying to follow your logic sometimes. But you are right when you describe that it was the last scene of my vision. Maybe you are on to something here? We really don't have any other options at this point but to wait. But for how long?"

The Cardinal brought things into perspective. "Allow me to state the obvious. I have to leave shortly and will be gone for two days. If nothing else happens, then we have at least these two days in limbo. Might I suggest that Father Marsai show the two of you around Roma while I'm gone? It would be a great opportunity for the three of you to unwind and relax. It is just a suggestion, my friends."

The Cardinal stood and headed to his desk while still talking.

"In fact, if you don't mind, I think I will just wrap up and leave now. There will be many old acquaintances arriving for these services, and I would like very much to reminisce with them."

The others took the hint and rose as well to leave. Once again in the hall, Pierre made arrangements to take them on a tour of Roma tomorrow. He then showed them back to their rooms. John and Mathew asked if he would like to join them for dinner, but he had a prior engagement to attend to. Mathew expressed a concern about getting lost on the way to the dining area. John offered some words of encouragement to soothe his fears.

"Well, buddy, I've followed my nose there twice now. No problem. I also have used that old instinct that allows a man to find his way back to his bed! We will be fine. I assure you that neither of us will lose a pound here!"

~ ~ ~

Mathew heard the knock at his door, and found both John and Pierre standing outside when he opened it.

"Good morning to you both! I was a little afraid that I'd be sore from all the walking around Roma yesterday. Pierre, again I must say you were an excellent guide. I would highly recommend you to anyone!"

"It was my pleasure. I never pass up the opportunity to share what I know about the local art and ancient sights of this beautiful city."

John pointed out, "Hey, guys. We need to get going if we are going to eat and get to the Cardinal's office by 10:00."

Pierre turned and led them towards the dining area. During breakfast, the conversation was full of comments, mainly by Mathew, about all of the statues and fountains that dotted the city. John seemed to just get a kick out of walking around and observing people in general. The walk to the Cardinal's office offered less and less talking the closer they came to it. Each man wondered how the Cardinal had fared at his friend's funeral. He had been visually shaken by the news, and it had only been a few days now.

"Morning, ma'am."

"And GOOD morning to you too, Mr. Parson. Oh, the entire group is here with you. Good morning all! He is in there waiting on you. Please go on in."

John leaned down towards Judy and whispered, "How is the old boy doing?"

She also leaned in his direction before she answered, "He hasn't said more than two words so far. I've known him for a long time now. So just act like normal, and he'll be fine once he gets started working. You know even the Holy Father himself wanted to go. They were all close friends for more than 30 years. I heard there were three other Cardinals who went with him. There were two others who wanted to go, but they both had family medical emergencies as well."

"Why didn't the Pope go if he wanted to?"

"Well, I have a friend named Betty who actually works in the office of the Archbishop who is the Pope's private secretary. She was involved in making arrangements for the Pope to attend, but was later told that he was not going. Seems the Pope was concerned that his presence there would distract from the services. He knew it would, and he really wanted the focus of the event to be totally about Father Turin."

A sudden opening of the inner office door, and the Cardinal stepped out.

"Oh. Good morning everyone. Judy, Father Turin is on his way up. Please have him come on in when he arrives. Come on in, gentlemen."

They all followed single-file into his office and headed for their usual seats at the table. They remained standing and watched as the Cardinal walked behind his desk before motioning for them to sit down. He closed the Bible that was open on his desk before joining them. Still standing himself, he spoke.

"I hope you all took Pierre up on his offer for a tour of Roma."

Mathew immediately answered. "Yes we did. He is a wonderful guide. In fact, we talked about yesterday's sights all through breakfast this morning."

John eyed the Cardinal closely, trying to determine how he was doing. With his usual habit of joking around, he tested the air. "So, Anton, I was thinking about asking Judy for some espresso. You interested, buddy?"

Mathew and Pierre glanced in John's direction, then back at the Cardinal as he replied.

He was smiling as he said, "John. I am fine. Thank you and the rest of you for worrying about me in this time of grief. However, I find myself strangely calmed today by the magnitude of the love that poured out from those at the services yesterday. He was a good man, a good Catholic, a good priest and above all a very dear friend who I will miss greatly. But life goes on, and we must have faith that he is still serving the Lord."

He stood with his hands on the back of his chair, staring blindly at the center of the table. There was a split second pause and a sigh before he returned to the present with his usual smile. He was just about to sit when there was a slight tap on the door and Father Turin stuck his head in.

"Cardinal? You asked to see me as soon as I came in. Oh, you have company. Shall I wait?"

"No, no, no, please, come in Father. I know that you have met these two men, but I would like to introduce you to one of our American brothers. This is Mathew Cobleir. Mathew, this is Father Turin."

Mathew said, "Actually, we met when I first arrived."

The Cardinal looked at Mathew for a second before replying. "Oh, yes. I knew that. I just, well, I suppose I still have things on my mind and just forgot. Good, good."

They could all tell that the Cardinal was still struggling with his memories of this young priest's uncle, who was also his dear friend. Father Turin looked at the faces of the seated men, and wondered from their expressions what was going on. Then he looked at the Cardinal.

"I would like to thank you on behalf of our family for attending my uncle's service. I know that they all appreciated it very much."

"I had to be there, Markus. He was a friend of many years."

"So Cardinal, you asked to see me. How can I be of service to you?"

"Oh, yes. The Holy Father would like to see you. He cleared his entire schedule for this morning just to sit and talk to you."

"To me? This is unexpected but good timing."

"He was also a close friend of your uncle's and wants to convey his condolences to you in person. I wanted to tell you this myself. Judy should be on the phone with Betty as we speak. Come. Let's see what is being said."

Father Turin nodded towards those seated before following the Cardinal to Judy's office. They heard her talking on the phone, then the sound of it being hung up before her voice rang out.

"He is waiting, Father."

The sound of the outer office door opening and closing signaled the return of the Cardinal.

As he sat down at the table, he saw that John was staring at the closed office door. He had that small-eyed, squinty look he got when lost in deep thought.

"John? What are you thinking so hard about? Are you

afraid someone is about to enter and give you a cup of espresso, my friend?"

John looked at the Cardinal and said with a smile, "No. But I was thinking about the good Father Turin."

He squared his shoulders with the table and placed his elbows upon it. Then, in a slow but fluid motion, he raises his clasped hands and rested his chin upon them.

All eyes were now on John as he hesitated while looking down at the table. Not even looking up, he began to speak.

"Did ya'll catch what he said when you told him the Pope wanted to see him?"

John then looked up to survey their reactions. "He said something about it being unexpected. But I wonder what he meant when he added that it was good timing? Did you not hear that part, guys?"

There was nothing said. The expressions on their faces told John that they had missed it, or it just hadn't registered with them as it did with him.

"It was like he had another purpose that was going to be fulfilled by this meeting with the Pope. And it was his uncle who had access to that Torah book while it was in storage. I was just wondering if, well, ah ... who knows?"

The men looked at each other as John's words sunk in. Though nothing is uttered, they all began to wonder if this priest was about to complete the last scene in John's vision. Slowly, they all turned and looked towards the closed door as well.

~ ~ ~

The men had anxiously been waiting while the Pope visited with Father Turin. Two hours had passed while the Cardinal spoke of memories of his friend. John was standing and looking out the Cardinal's office window while the other two sat, nervously chatting about yesterday's tour. Then came the call from the Pope. He wanted to see the Cardinal at once.

It had now been almost an hour since the Cardinal rushed off to meet the Pope. The men sat quietly at the table as they waited for his return. Each one was lost in his own thoughts of what might be happening outside the walls of this office at this very moment.

John felt confident that he was right about what had recently happened. Still, he found himself wishing for the Cardinal's return. The air in the room was filled with anxious anticipation of what was about to be revealed.

Finally, they heard the outer office door open and Judy's voice. "Cardinal. Back so soon? Yes, they are all still in there. Father Latanye? I'll call him now. Have him bring what?"

The door opened sharply, and he closed it behind him before quickly covering the short distance to take his seat.

"Well, John. Once again you were right. It seems that the village magistrate had been holding this package for Father Turin, Senior for the past few years. He had instructions for it to be given to his nephew, Bishop Turin, upon his death.

"This short note was attached to the outside of it. It says the following: 'To my dearest nephew Markus. I have followed your life and career with great interest for all these years. Your becoming a priest was the greatest pride that I have ever known. Please do not be saddened by the event that placed this package in your hands. My soul is now where I have always desired it to be. I have a final request of you. Please deliver this package, unopened, to my longtime friend who now wears the ultimate white robes of our Church. Your name will easily garner you an audience with him. I apologize for the secrecy involved here, but this must pass directly from your hand to his. Do not trust another with it. On behalf of our family, I want to express our collective pride in you and all that you do.'"

The Cardinal then reached into the large manila envelope and pulled out a few pages that were stapled together, together with a small, square box. It was about eight inches long and its sides were approximately one and a half inches tall. He held up the papers while he spoke.

"These describe the following. Father Turin Senior had always fancied the thought of transcribing an ancient text. Since he discovered the scroll in the dowel rod of the Torah, he felt that this was his opportunity to do just that. His intent was to translate it and then put it back. Unfortunately, he had been reassigned to another area before he could do so. Though it unnerved him, he chose to continue to work on translating it. He had long given up on being able to return it himself, but was still hopeful that an opportunity may arise for it to make its way home. However, when he learned that the Torah had been returned to Israel, he concluded that this was his only option.

"Though he had not been able to complete the translation, he felt he had to put it in the trust of the local magistrate while he was alive. He did not want it to be lost to humanity should he die, and for it to be boxed and stored with his personal items. These back few pages are his notes on his translation, but he did not finish it. I have instructed Judy to find Father Latanye and have him join us. He should have no problem verifying this translation, and also completing it for us."

Each man leaned forward against the table, their eyes on the small box.

John couldn't help but ask, "So, the message is in that box? Cool. Have you looked at it?"

"No. I want Father Latanye to do it. This is most definitely his area of expertise."

Mathew was staring at the box like everyone else, but he was thinking along different lines. He will finally get to see his old friend do his stuff. This was going to be very interesting.

~ ~ ~

They all heard Father Latanye arrive and chat with Judy before coming into the inner office. Father Marsai stood and offered him his seat. The scholarly-looking priest graciously accepted it and sat down after placing a small bag on the table. One of his hands rested on his bag, and the fingers were eagerly tapping while he looked around the table.

"So, what exactly is it that I have been summoned to translate? Is it in that small box, by any chance?"

The Cardinal gently pushed the small box in front of the priest. "We have not opened it. I thought that it would be best done by an expert such as yourself. You should find a scroll with a message that we desire greatly to read. Or more accurately, for you to read to us."

Though he had been listening, his hands were busy pulling several items from his bag and placing them along one edge of the table. He then turned the box first one way and then another before saying, "This box is not old at all. Let's look and see what we find inside."

He then slowly lifted off the top and set it aside. They were all mesmerized by the small roll of paper now visible inside.

"Hmmm, hello? Now this is old."

He leans down and sniffed before saying, "It hasn't been handled in a while. I would say it has been in this little box for at least a year or two. That's a good thing too. See, the edges are really beginning to degrade badly. It must have been kept in a rather damp environment."

"Yes, it was a small mountain community church. They get a lot of rain there."

He reached back in his bag and pulled out two thin metal rods, each about six inches long. Then he spread out a little white cloth on the table. After inserting one rod into each end of the scroll, he lifted it out and placed it on the cloth. He began testing the flexibility of the paper by gently pushing the little rods in opposite directions, careful not to stretch the parchment but so far. He then asked Mathew to help.

"Mathew. Please take that small spray bottle and mist this once or twice as I roll it around. Yes, that's perfect. Now as I unroll it farther each time, please mist it only when I say, and keep the bottle at least three inches away from it."

After the first spray, John wrinkled his nose and said, "Whoa. What's that smell? That's not water."

"No, it isn't. It is a resin based preservative with a little formaldehyde in it. You see. This is not paper. It is actually animal hide. It is often referred to as parchment. This is a much finer quality. That is why I use this solution that I make myself in our lab. Writings on this type of material can last thousands of years."

The others watched this exercise as more and more of the writing inside became visible. The priest finally stopped and held it open as far as he dared.

"I think that is about as far as I take this. I can read it quite easily now. It is amazing that the writing is as clear as it is. Are you ready to hear this?"

They all say 'Yes' at the same time before chuckling at their doing so in unison.

"Ok. Here we go then. It says the following."

"'To the 'Royal Governor' of Judaea?'"

The priest stopped.

"Wait, this is old. My goodness. This is, just a minute, my goodness. This is to Pontius Pilate from Sejanus. I suppose everyone here knows he was left in charge of Roma by Tiberius Caesar?"

John immediately said, "Who's Sejanus? Did I say that right? Who's he?"

The Cardinal explained. "He was left in charge of Roma when Tiberius took an extended vacation to his palace in Capri. He is the sleeping man in your vision, John. Go on, Father."

"Well it says, just a minute."

He was mumbling something to himself.

"Oh, ok. He is ordering Pilate to do the following should anything happen to the one that calls himself the 'Son of Man'. Obviously, he is referring to Jesus. Oh my. Oh, this would have changed history had it been delivered."

He lets the scroll roll shut as he looked at the Cardinal. "It basically is an order to Pilate to cremate any and all body parts of Jesus, should He die or be executed. It also goes on to say this is to be done no matter what objections come from the people or their religious leaders. The ashes were to be placed in a vase and brought back to him in Roma. Apparently, he had a vision of an angel telling him something that he refused to believe. It sounded like a threat from this spirit."

"Odd, very odd. That's all. Unfortunately, most of the seal and date have been lost due to exposure to moisture."

Seeing that everyone appeared to be at a loss for words, he asked, "So is somebody going to tell me where this came from?"

John looked at the Cardinal.

"Anton, it appears we have one more to get up to speed."

CHAPTER 20
To Read a Book

Mathew and Pierre were enjoying a delicious meal at Father Latanye's newly-found eatery. John would like to have gone, but just not tonight. Having spent 45 minutes on the phone with Barbara, he now found himself once again alone in the small study, looking out that small window into the boring little courtyard below. His bottle of cherry flavored water was emptied over an hour ago, but he noticed it not. His mind was awash with all that had happened to him both at home and here. He only hoped he would be able to complete this last task.

The knock on the door signaled it was time for a very special meeting with two very special people. Father Turin again led him to that strange elevator for his ride beneath the city. The walk to the electronic door seemed shorter than the first time. As the door closed behind him, he noticed three golden chairs in the center of the room. Two of them were occupied.

As he took his seat, John asked in his usual fashion, "So, how many of these little golden thrones do you guys have?"

The man in white answered. "As many as are required to have a conversation."

"So, what are we going to discuss tonight?"

"John, I would like to get your opinion on some things if I may?"

John's first impulse was to say 'Shoot', but he caught himself and quietly responded "Okay," instead.

"In talking with Father Mortello here, we think that only Father Cobleir need be involved any further. What do you think?"

"Well, I tend to agree with that. He is the only one who has a vested interest in what we have yet to do. That strap is an heirloom from his family, and we need it since it is one of the three keys for reading the book. Back in my room, I was thinking that maybe he should be one of those priests that live at the villa. Maybe I'm nuts, but I was just thinking. Of course he may have to learn Italian."

"This was our conclusion as well. With the exception of him needing to speak Italian, of course. So we are all in agreement with this. Now to the next point. We believe it is time for you to return to the villa."

"Oh. I guess I knew that was coming up soon. When?"

"Please do not think poorly of us, but we have already made preparations for your trip tomorrow. Cardinal Mortello will accompany both you and Mathew."

"Pope, buddy, I trust you and Anton completely. I just hope that I don't let you down. We have all jumped through a lot of hoops to get to this point. I'm just hoping it was all worth it."

"John. You have performed admirably throughout an ordeal that has taken you far from home and family. It is hard to not sound condescending when saying this. We are grateful to have been allowed to accompany you on this journey. Speaking for myself, I am most thankful to have met a man such as you."

"Well then, it sounds like we're going on a trip tomorrow. When do you plan on telling Mathew?"

"Father Mortello has volunteered to do that as soon as Mathew returns from dining in the city with Father Latanye and Pierre."

"Well then. Let's do it!"

~ ~ ~

John had volunteered to sit in front with the limo driver. Mathew and the Cardinal were off in their own world, talking about the rodeo Mathew had just been to. They had a laptop in the back with them and were looking at the pictures. It really became loud when they found the first video from Barbara's camera. During the entire trip to the airfield, there were almost non-stop comments of, 'Oh MY!' and 'My goodness!' as the Cardinal's eyes never left the laptop screen.

Once on the plane and in the air, the rodeo review continued. John was glad that they were both so caught up in it that he could sleep and stare out the window uninterrupted. The apprehension of what was coming had zapped his normal desire to kid around. Luckily, the other two were too preoccupied to notice. Just to keep up appearances, he occasionally smiled at their never-ending excitement when they looked up at him. John was sure they had viewed each picture and video clip several times.

John was surprised when Gena informed them that they would be landing in 20 minutes. Wow, what a short trip.

Once again, John volunteered to sit with the limo driver. The rodeo excitement had finally run its course, and the laptop was closed. The Cardinal had put on his tour guide hat and was going over each landmark with Mathew, just as he had done with John. They had entered the large boulder minefield which signaled that they must be getting close to the villa. John felt glad that the trip was almost over, but his anxiety was growing with every mile they grew closer to the end. Just like last time, the evening sun was fading fast as he really began thinking they must be close.

Then he saw the villa on top of the hill. But what was that flashing red light up there? He didn't remember that. Then it moved skyward, and he knew.

"Anton, isn't that the villa up there? And what is that? Is it a helicopter?"

The Cardinal and Mathew were both trying to see. Then Anton said, "Oh, I see it. Yes, John. That does appear to be a helicopter."

"Somebody must be important. I wonder if they are dropping off or picking up?"

"John. That would be both, I believe."

"Really? Who rates a helicopter ride out here?"

John heard Mathew's feeble attempt to whisper a question to the Cardinal. "Is it the Holy Father?"

"I heard that, Mathew. And why are you whispering? Anton?"

The Cardinal faked clearing his throat before answering. "I

believe it is. There were only two other guests, and they just left. We will be the only ones here for this."

They soon arrived at the front doors. John was glad to see Father Dosanta once more. They shook hands and John graciously allowed him to take the bags into the villa. Standing and looking at that big, roaring fireplace slowly brought a small amount of John's old self back. As the other two entered and walked past him, he began to think to himself, "I can do this. I've seen it. So what am I afraid of?"

The Cardinal informed both John and Mathew that the Pope desired to have the evening meal with them all. This meant they had a little over two hours to relax after the trip. It also meant that this was when the Cardinal was going to completely fill Mathew in on what to expect when they went down to the book room. John was already wondering how the Pope would manage getting down those stairs. It was hard enough on the Cardinal. But then again, Father Dosanta was a very strong man.

Of course, John used the first hour to talk to Barbara on the phone. Then he piddled around, getting freshened up before wandering down to stand and stare at the huge fire. It relaxed him for some reason, and he needed relaxation right now.

The others appeared one by one, and then the Holy Father. They all fell in line behind him like a religious parade to the dining area. John decided to bring up the rear alone. Being the last in afforded him a select view of all the robed men sitting at the largest round table. The tablecloths that John had found so loud on his first trip now seem rather fitting for these men and their attire. It just dawned on him that nobody has said a thing about his wearing jeans and boots. This was a good thing.

The meal was as light-hearted as possible, considering the big guy in white and the miraculous nature of why they were here. The Pope was the first to bring the focus of their trip to everyone's attention.

"I would like to move on to the true reason for our being here. We all are aware of the book that awaits us. We now have in our possession the three items that its cover described as the keys to it. Also, we have John - a man who has the remarkable ability to tolerate the levels of power that emanate from the book. The presence of all of these in one place is the very reason that I have also chosen to attend. I apologize for my being a physical burden, and hope that you will forgive me for wanting so desperately to attend. I hope that I am not putting you on the spot, so to speak. But John, have you given any thought to how these items are used to open the book?"

"Well, I have been giving it a lot of thought these last few days and especially on the trip here. Unfortunately, I have no feeling, one way or the other, on what to do with them. I just know that they must be with me in order to open it. I was just planning on holding them, like in one hand and trying to open it with the other. It may sound crude, but it's all I've come up with."

"And should that fail? Does anyone else have a suggestion? Anything at all could prove to be helpful here. It may not itself be the answer, but it could possibly lead to the answer. Anyone?"

There was a lengthy pause as everyone surveyed each other's expressions. Nothing was forthcoming from the group. Again, the Pope spoke. "Well, then. I have one last question, and it is definitely for the group to decide. Are we to forge ahead with this task tonight, or wait until tomorrow?"

Again, each man looked for one of the others to signal a comment, but none did. Eventually, John stepped up.

"I mean no disrespect, Sir. But you have yourself mentioned that you may find this task a physical challenge. If it were just me or one of these guys, then I'd say let's get on with it. But to be real honest here, I think you have to decide if you are up for it now, or if the morning would be better."

"I also want to add this. There are still things in my head that I do not share. Forgive me, but I have good reason for this. Now with that being said, I want to say this. I have always seen this entire group to be together on this trip to the book room.

"So, you see Sir, visiting the book room now or tomorrow morning is not the real question. You must be honest with us. Would you rather rest tonight, have a nice breakfast and then take your time getting down there for what is probably going to be a very long day?"

The Pope didn't hesitate to speak. "John. This is one of your most admirable traits. You are straightforward and honest. I would have gone tonight, at all costs, in order to be present for this event. However, with your new revelation that you see me there with everyone else, I choose to rest tonight. I can't tell you how much it means to me to hear from your lips that I am to witness this. Thank you."

"Then sir, I wish to add one more thing that I hope lifts your spirit. I am aware that you have something wrong with your heart. You fear that tomorrow will be more than it can bear. I know, for I have seen, that your participation is not hampered at all due to this. In fact, tomorrow holds something for you all. I can't be specific, but all of you are going to receive a blessing beyond your wildest dreams. Though I will not personally see, it will happen tomorrow and everyone else at this table will witness it. Now, I would like to retire myself. I suddenly feel very tired."

The Pope stood. "Let us all retire for the evening, and rejoin for breakfast in the morning." Again, they all fell in line behind him, each leaving the procession as they arrived at their room.

~ ~ ~

Breakfast at the villa was once again something to write home about. It was fresh and flavorful beyond compare. They all enjoyed the closeness of a band of brothers enjoying a moment before a hard day's toil. And then the fateful moment was upon them.

They were all standing in the small library. It was decided that John would lead the Cardinal down the stairs first. The Cardinal held his hand on John's shoulder, and they progressed slowly, one step at a time until they reached the stone floor. Then Father Dosanta did the same for the Pope. Only Mathew was directly behind the Pontiff and poised for any gesture that suggested he might fall. It was felt that between these two large men, they could easily support this frail old man.

To the great relief of all, the five men safely reached the cold stone floor without mishap. Father Dosanta dashed back up the stairs to fetch the small box with the artifacts needed to open the book. Once he had returned, the Pope immediately put his hand on John's shoulder.

"You were right, my friend. My heart beat harder when putting on my shoes this morning. I feel better than I have in years. It is truly amazing. Please, lead on."

As they came to the chairs before the last corner, John motioned for them all to stop.

"If you wouldn't mind sir, I would like to allow the only one of us that has not seen around this corner before, to do so first. I believe we all remember our first gaze around this bend."

The Pope smiled and took Mathew's elbow. "He is right. You should be the first. This is a sight that will be etched into your memories for the rest of your days."

John put his arm around Mathew as he walked him to the corner.

"Just remember what I told you about my dream. It's that hall you are about to enter." Then John stopped just short of the corner.

Mathew hesitated before stepping around to see what the others had witnessed before. He stood for a few moments, amazed at the purity of the light pouring from the door and striking the opposite wall. It was exactly as John had described it in his kitchen that night.

Mathew turned to look back at the group, and they all saw the tears that slid down his cheeks. Mathew stepped back towards them without saying a word. John commented, "It's really something to see. Isn't it buddy?"

Mathew sniffed and wiped his eyes. "That it is. It is something that I will never forget." Then he turned to face the Holy Father. "Yes, my answer is a very big YES. I want to serve here in the villa. I am available from this moment on, at your discretion."

John leaned around to look at Anton and nodded once eye contact had been made. He had known they were going to offer this to Mathew. He was glad to see that Anton had made the offer last night. He was glad to think that his friend's role in this was to continue for some time.

John said, "Now Mathew is right beside you, sir. The moment you feel anything, and I mean ANYTHING, you sing out and I'll have this chair for you in a jiffy."

The Pope wanted to get as close to the cave door as he could. His hope was to actually see inside to view what was happening. They were going to attempt to position him sitting in a chair to the area against the opposite wall that had the least effect from the light. To their amazement, the frail old gentleman made it to that spot with no problem. He was happy to have the chair, but he had made it. Once again, his eyes saw the book on the stone pedestal. He closed his eyes and they knew he was praying.

Father Dosanta opened the box and held it out for John to remove the three items. Armed with these supposed keys, he smiled one last time at each of them before touching the Pope lightly on the shoulder and entering the room.

As before, he felt nothing as he walked around to face the book. He could see them all through the door. He had the three items in his left hand, so he reached for the book with his right. There was not a tingle or anything to be felt as he tried to open the book. He pulled harder at the cover's edge, but it did not budge.

Why isn't this working? He had the three items. Something is different from the first time he touched it. What is he missing?

He looked up at them for just a second. He almost felt embarrassment at not being able to open the book. They were all looking at him, wanting him to do something. But what? He decided to adjust the balance of the items in his hand. That is when it happened.

He had been holding the scroll softly, so as not to crush the degrading parchment, and the ring began to slip from his hand. He caught the ring in his other hand, but dropped the leather strap which fell across the toes of his boots. He looked up again to look at them as if to say, "Sorry! I'm a klutz!"

Then he attempted to bend and pick up the strap. He didn't want to move his feet for fear of tearing or scuffing the leather piece. He was standing so close to the book that the only way to retrieve the strap was to place one hand on the book to steady him. With the ring in one hand, the scroll in the other and the leather strap on his feet, he did just that. The moment that the hand with the ring touched the book, he sensed that the cover was free to move.

Then, in a flash, he understood the items and their meanings. He slid the ring onto a finger to allow the hand to lift and turn the cover. It folded open as any other book would. Then he sensed something was in the room with him, and he looked to one side then the other. He felt a presence but saw nothing. What was happening? His very soul was alight with energy more abundant than the sun. Why does he not see what he felt to be there?

With panic in his eyes, he looked for help from those outside. But what was happening out there? What are they doing? Even the Pope was on his knees. They all had their hands clasped tightly in front of their chests as if in prayer. What were they staring at? It wasn't him. They were all staring to his left. He looked again, but nothing was there.

That is when he felt as if someone, or something, had just laid a gentle hand on his left shoulder. A peaceful contentment of the order had never known before flowed through his entire being, instantly calming him. Someone was there and they had their hand on him. He looked to the left one more time, but saw nothing. Confused, his eyes fell onto the open page before him.

What was happening? These symbols were not the classic Latin alphabet - the ABCs he was used to seeing. Yet he recognized them. He wondered about the symbols on the cover, so he lifted it up without closing the book. As he lowered his head, he realized that these symbols were also known to him, so he read. Could this really be happening? Or was he going crazy? Then his mind heard what his ears did not. It was a voice and he was commanded to read. So he began.

First one page, then the next, until the page would not turn. This is odd, he thought. Why can't I turn it? Then he noticed a symbol that meant that it was the end of this lesson, and his mind heard the voice again. He listened as it repeated the same phrase over and over, then silence. He was not even aware that his hand was closing the book until he felt the mysterious presence fade to nothingness.

What just happened? He tries to open the book again, but it would not budge. He looked at both of his hands. There was the ring and the scroll. Glancing down, he clearly saw the leather strap still lying upon his feet. Then he knew. The first lesson was over. Yes, over.

With a huge sigh, he looked around to see all of his companions once again standing, and the Pope back in his chair. It was over. He was drained, and it was time to leave.

He removed the ring and placed it on one corner of the book. The scroll was placed on the other corner of the book. Now able to step back, he bent and lifted the strap. He folded it in half, and then in half again, before placing it on the center of the book's cover. It was time to go.

The items were safer here than anywhere else that man could go. This was where the book was written, and where the lessons must be taught. The book and keys were safe here. They belonged here. So, here they will stay.

He walked into the hall only to have each man, the Pope as well, place their hand on his left shoulder. He sensed that they were seeking to touch something other than him, but he didn't know what it could be.

Though it didn't affect him, the light grew to an intensity that compelled the others to hurry themselves and the Pope back around the corner. John picked up the chair and followed them. The Pope had already claimed the chair that was left behind, so John places this one beside him so that the Cardinal could sit as well.

John leaned against the opposite wall and looked at the two older men seated before him. He flexed his knees and slide to a seated position on the floor. His legs were bent, each arm on a knee as he closed his eyes for just a second. Seeing John, Mathew did the same just to his right.

Father Dosanta had walked back and was looking around the corner. His head tilted first this way then that before he seemed satisfied that all was as it should be once more. He walked back to a position on John's left but remained standing. John looked up and said, "Come on, Michael, sit with us. Let's talk."

The Holy Father was first to speak. "John. You solved the riddle of the keys."

"Yes, by accident. But I now know what they represent. Shall I tell you all?"

Father Dosanta asks, "Are we allowed to know this?"

John chuckled softly. "You can know it all. This is for man. All men. The Ring is for our Father, who is in heaven. It was his plan and he made it happen. The Leather Strap is for the son who saw it through to the end. The Missing Message is for the Holy Spirit that saw to it that Sejanus did not interfere with the resurrection of our Christ. The writing on the bottom of the cover says this.

"It was amazing. I could read that stuff even though it was not the lettering on which I was schooled. As long as the book is open I can read, but when it is closed these symbols register nothing in my mind. It was as if I wasn't alone in there. Once the book was opened, I felt as if, well as if..."

The Pope spoke up. "As if there was someone standing beside you? Did you feel the hand on your shoulder?"

"Yes. That is exactly what I thought too! But there was nobody there. I looked on both sides. Then I, I, what were you guys looking at? It was as if you saw something on my left. I looked again and again, but nothing. Am I crazy?"

The Cardinal calmly said, "Did you not see us kneeling John? It was Christ Himself standing beside you. You were NOT alone. He placed His hand on your shoulder, and it was then that you began to read. So seeing Him is the blessing you spoke of last night. Right?"

John's mouth was open and his eyes moving, as if to see something in his mind.

"Honestly, I only knew that you were going to see someone. I wasn't shown who. Remember, I said only you would see it and not me. I knew there was someone in the room with me, but I couldn't see them. That is what was just freaking me out so much. I felt, well I felt, HIM."

The Pope asked, "John. Share with us what you read. Please?"

John looked at each of their faces before speaking. "There were two things that were happening at once. I know this is going to sound weird, but it was comfortable after a second or two. I was reading and seeing at the same time. I don't know where to start. Let's do this.

"It was written by Jesus to tell man the true relationship between God and us. Not like the perspective the Bible takes, no. The Bible is something inspired by God but written and interpreted by man. This book is what Jesus knows of His father. There are later lessons that will speak to our creation and several reasons why God wanted us to exist. My head is spinning with all this new information that was slammed into my mind all at once. I'm having a hard time sorting through and making sense of it at the moment. What did you just ask me? No, wait. Oh yes, it was talking about this 1,000 year dude. No, that doesn't sound right.

It referred to him as 'The Thousand Year Man'. Yeah, that's it. Sometimes there was 'The Reader'? I'm getting confused. I can't think straight here. Ok, this 'Thousand Year Man' is supposed to do, or fulfill these lessons from this book. Maybe they are just tasks that need to be done or things to be corrected. I think that only the 'Reader' is to know who this 'Thousand Year Man' is, and what he is up to. No. It's the other way around. This 'Thousand Year Man' is the only one that knows who and what he is. He knows 'The Reader'. Yeah, that's the ticket here. I think?"

It was becoming apparent to all of them that John was on the verge of passing out, or falling into a very deep sleep. Either way, they needed to get him back to his room. The Cardinal suggested that he and the Pope remain in their chairs for a chat. Mathew and Father Dosanta took John up the stairs and back to his room. They hurried back to retrieve the remaining two men.

"Please take the Holy Father next. I will be quite all right here until you return for me. How was John, Mathew?"

"He was barely moving when we made it to his room. He snapped out of it long enough to kick off his boots. Then he just fell backwards into the bed and was out. He's asleep and breathing easy."

Seeing that Father Dosanta was helping the Pope from his chair, Mathew joined him to help him walk back upstairs.

The two priests helped the Cardinal back to his room as well. They both stepped out into the cool night air for a few minutes to relax. Nothing of note was said between them, for they were very tired from the night's activities. They disappeared back inside the villa, and the lights went out one by one until none remained.

~ ~ ~

The following day was one of concern for their friend John. He had no fever, yet could hardly stay awake. He could manage to hold a thought for only a moment at a time. He did repeat one thing over and over to them; he would say very clearly, "The Thousand Year Man knows! He knows!"

John was once again sleeping soundly, and Father Dosanta was sitting by his bedside and reading his Bible. The Pope, the Cardinal and Mathew were all in a small meeting room discussing the situation. The Pope had asked for the opinions of the others, and the Cardinal was about to speak.

"I believe that John is sleeping so his mind can make sense of the torrent of information he was given rather quickly. He has been speaking of things that, well, they could answer questions that man has had for thousands of years. He mentioned something about the real reasons that God wanted Man to exist. I just cannot get this out of my mind. There are things here that could radically change the religious landscape of the entire world. All religions share common basics, so it is logical to think they would all be affected by this."

Mathew asked, "Could this information adversely affect the Church?"

The Pope calmly spoke.

"My dear Mathew. The Church is but an institution of man. It is our attempt to maintain and spread his word. But in the end, it is only the people who matter and what they believe. Truth is what man has always sought. Fears have always been based upon the lack of it. Evil could be considered ignorance. So therefore, truth would be Godly. If we are to seek God, as the Church professes, then we must embrace truth in order to glorify His wisdom. Souls navigate through life with their beliefs as a rulebook. These rules are what should guide our actions when we face the difficulties of this life. The problem has always been with man's differing interpretations of these rules."

"I have personal questions for John, once he has clearly assimilated all that he read. I also feel that since we are a very small group, we should each prepare our own personal questions without the influence of the others. These should be real questions, honest questions that mean something to us on a very personal level."

"One last thought, Mathew. I would hope that as a priest, a keeper of the faith as we are, you would not fear for the Church. If you did have such a fear, then you have it due to doubt that the Church is the truth. The buildings and rituals that we follow are not the Church. The narrow interpretations of inspired scripture are not the Church. I believe in my God. I believe that my Church stands for His truth. I see that the Church has withstood the ravages of the centuries. Yes, it has been manipulated by men. Some for their own gain, but the vast majority of the bad was done by men with good intentions. In the end, it is undeniable that the Church is still here. To have survived through time based purely on the beliefs of differing men is actually a major testament to an unseen truth that we call our Church. We support it through faith. It has always been this one act that divided man. Do you have faith or not?"

There was a tap on the door and Father Dosanta stepped in. He was somewhat out of breath. The Cardinal asked, "John - is he OK?"

"Yes, he is fine. I fell asleep for but a moment and awoke to find him gone. My first thought was the book room, but he was not there. I finally found him a few moments ago. He was sitting under the tree in the courtyard. Just sitting. He said he will be in to eat in a little while. He asked me to find out where the rest of you were. I am to tell him once I find you."

"Did he seem alert?"

"I am happy to say that he seems to be his old self again. He called me buddy and smiled."

"We will wait here until he joins us. Please let him know there is no hurry."

~ ~ ~

The door opened quickly as John's smiling face appeared. "Morning, guys! Did I miss breakfast?" He took a seat at the table. The Cardinal sat a little closer to the table before speaking.

"So, how do you feel John?"

"Well I feel great! I'm just a little hungry. No need to worry about me anymore, unless you plan on putting one of those little cups of espresso in front of me. That could cause me to relapse for sure!"

The Cardinal was most relieved to see his friend joking around again. "Espresso? It is nice to have my old friend back. You had us all very worried last night. But I can see that you feel much better, and it pleases me."

"I ordered something before coming in here. You guys don't mind if I eat and talk at the same time, do you?"

The Cardinal answered, "Not at all. If you wish, we could just meet you after you eat."

"No, that's not necessary. Besides, I bet you guys have questions."

Hearing this, the Pope asked, "Why did you stop reading the book?"

"Because I came to a page that wouldn't turn. It seems that the book is to be read in sections. I'm not sure how we are going to know when it is time to read the next one. I guess we will just have to wait and see."

"You mentioned that the book is broken into lessons."

"Yes."

"So what was the lesson you read?"

John looks at the Pope for a second, then at each other face before answering. "Well, sir. It wasn't a lesson. It told some things, basics about how this would work. And then it, I, well … there was an offer made."

They all sat closer to the table at this point. Their eyes had been on John before then, but now each pair was more intently focused than before.

Again the Pope asked, "An offer, John? An offer to who, and for what?"

"I'm fairly sure that I mentioned to you about this 'Reader'. It seems that things like this are not forced upon a man. You are given a choice to accept, or not. I guess it was a job offer of sorts."

They all looked at one another while John ate.

The Pope again asked, "And this offer was to you?"

"Yes. But I'm, I'm not really sure that I am the right person. It didn't say it, but I know that the choice is totally mine. There are no reprisals if I decline. I don't feel anything but love from, well from Him."

"It seems that you have a lot on your mind. Perhaps we should not question you any further. We should give you time to think this through. You seem to have reservations about doing this."

John smiled and put down his fork. He hadn't eaten much, but he pushed his plate away.

"No, you ask me anything you want. I really think it would be better for me to talk about this. It's just such a long time to commit to something. I'm not sure, not sure I want this."

The Pope sat upright upon hearing John's reply.

"And how long would that be, John?"

John puts his head in his hands, as if he were washing his face. Then he exhaled loudly and pushed his hands upward through his hair before leaning back in his chair.

"I love my wife. I love her with all my heart, and have since the first time I saw her. She came into my garage to have her car's oil changed. The minute I heard her voice, I just knew I wanted to spend the rest of my life with her."

He looked up at them all before continuing.

"The offer would be for the rest of my life, and the voice said that life would be long. You remember I told you that I was reading and seeing at the same time? Well, I saw things. One thing was about this. I just can't get it out of my mind."

He suddenly leans his head completely over the table. With tears welling in his eyes, his breaking voice said, "I saw me at her funeral. Oh, she was old and she had lived a very long life. We never had kids though, and it bothered us both. But, well, it was so hard to see that and know that it was going to be several lifetimes before I would be with her again."

He looked away from the table, avoiding their eyes.

"You would think that anyone offered something like this would just jump at the offer. But I, well I'm not sure I can do this. Call me crazy, but I'm just not so sure."

Then John looked up to see a table full of men all looking down at the table, as they contemplated what they would do in his place.

"Sorry, guys. I guess I'm bumming everyone out with this. Sorry."

Mathew raised his head. "John, I'm sure everyone here could easily see that you love her. I always knew that. It is so easy to see that you both share a real love. Not one of necessity or childhood fancy, but the kind that grips one's very soul forever. I don't know why I'm saying this, and I don't mean to interfere in your decision. It just seems to me, that you both share a love that will endure, well, eternity."

The Pope again spoke.

"I think it is now very obvious why you have been chosen for such an offer. You are not crazy. No, you are just one of those very rare individuals that have an enormous capacity for pure love. When most men would be thinking of immortality and power, your focus is on being separated from your mate. I agree with Mathew. A love such as yours would certainly bridge such a length of time. In fact, I would think that the very strength of that love is what would see you through it."

John again looks down, and then began to chuckle softly. This turned into a laugh as he looked around the table. It stopped as quickly as it started, and he held his eyes shut tightly for just a second.

"Have any of you ever been in an earthquake?"

Looking around the table, their faces showed confusion at the sudden change of subject change, followed by shaking heads. These expressions were about to change most abruptly to wide-eyed fear.

There came a rumble from beneath the very building they were sitting in. The objects on the table shook from a vibration that was passing through the floor. Their chairs vibrated as well. Eyes darted around the room before recognizing the calm that was on John's face. The vibrations subsided and stopped just as quickly as they had started.

The Cardinal softly asked, "John. What just happened? Was that one?"

"No. It was just something very large and heavy that was put back in place."

The men were looking at one another with questioning expressions. Then John spoke again.

"I had mentioned to you that I wasn't sure how the 'Reader' would know when it is time for the next lesson. Well, I now know. In fact, we all just found out together, but I'll explain that in a minute.

"You asked me if I had read a lesson. I told you it was an offer. It was also a bit of a table of contents, too. There were references to many things to be found in future lessons. One such reference was to reasons that God wants man to exist. I must have asked in my thoughts about this. The following was told to me.

"Since God is omnipotent, all things are known by Him. There is no wonderment or excitement to be had if one knows all, and all that will be. Also, such an entity would never be able to know more happiness than was already known.

"The concept of man and his free will to choose opens up endless possibilities for excitement and unpredictability. In layman's terms, God now has a never-ending and ever-changing subject to oversee. For a lack of a better way to say this, He now has something to do. And this leads into one question that has been asked by man, since he first conceived of this supreme power we call GOD. Some ask why does God make bad things happen.

"The answer is that he does not make them happen. But in order to have free will to choose, he must allow things to happen and deal with the aftermath. He actually WANTS us to be happy. This is when the following was explained to me. After I heard it, I didn't know why I never thought of it before. It just makes a lot of sense.

"If God can feel whatever man feels, then each man that is happy will increase the amount of happiness that God feels himself. The opposite is also true. When a man feels bad, this diminishes how happy God is. So you see, it is in God's best interest for us all to be as happy as possible.

"I only mentioned this because you had asked about the lessons. It seems to me that some wondrous revelations are to be revealed by reading that book. I just wanted to give you a sense of the things that it holds.

"Now, back to that shaking we just felt. Remember that large round stone I told you had been moved from the entrance to the book cave? The man who built this house had been allowed to move it away from the cave entrance because it was time. As the hallway was built, a fake wall was constructed just past the cave entrance. That stone has been hidden there ever since. All of that rumbling was that stone being rolled back to seal off the cave entrance. Oh, by the way, sorry about that wall. It's toast and there is a real mess from what used to be that wall. So now, when it is time to open the book and read the next lesson, it will open."

The Pope immediately asked, "So you can open this when you are to read?"

"I'm afraid I don't control it. It will control me. I will be drawn back here whenever it is time. I also believe that is why my life will be long. The times between lessons are dependent on happenings between men and within societies."

The Cardinal asked, "What of this 'Thousand Year Man'?"

"Well, that is something that is yet to be revealed. All I can say is this. There will be tragedies, trials for many, battles that we will find hard to comprehend and it all ends in LOVE. There will be a period of love like no other before it.

Mathew asked, "So why did the cave close just now?"

John smiled at each one of them before returning his gaze to his friend Mathew.

"Because, thanks to your comments..." He paused one last time.

"I accepted the JOB!"

CHAPTER 21

From Dream to LIFE

John found himself once again sitting alone by the pool in his back yard. There was the sound of the small waterfall that flowed from their hot tub into the pool. This had always been his favorite feature. The melodic sound of the water cascading over the rocks was so very relaxing. He loved sitting out here. It was nice, and he could think.

Of course, it was his dream that had placed him out here. But this time was different. He had completed the dream. Yes, he had worked through the bends and twists of this amazing trip. Now he must LIVE it.

Any second now, Barbara would find him like she always did. She would step out onto the patio and drag one of the other chairs over to sit by him. Of course he heard her coming, but he would not move or in any way acknowledge her approach. How could she possibly think that he didn't hear the racket from the chair scraping across the deck? It was 3:30 in the morning, and all was quiet out here. Half the neighborhood probably heard that chair! He was so glad there weren't any dogs barking, yet.

He would wait for her to sit down and utter those same words she did every time she found him.

"John? Are you ok, John?"

Of course he would respond just the same as he always had.

After they exchanged some small talk, they would rise and hold hands as they walked back into the house. They would slowly go up the stairs for the usual kisses and good nights.

But this time would be different. He would fake being asleep while she lay there, making plans for what she was about to do. She was restless, and he felt her moving ever so slightly. She finally came to a decision before falling fast asleep.

He would not go to sleep. It was but a few hours before he was to wake and rush off to work. He wondered if he could do things in real life in the same way he had seen in his dreams. How could he? He knew of them now. But he had noticed that if he stayed awake after the dreams, then he retained most all that he dreamt - at least, until he slept again.

This is why he had become increasingly tired as the days went by. It was also why, at times, his friends were amazed that he knew what was about to happen. No, he was NOT psychic as they believed. It just happened on days when he had not fallen asleep after having his dreams. When it became unbearable to remain awake, he would sleep and lose all that he knew of the future.

So he lay there and continued to go over all the actions that he would take. Every decision that he had made, and what it would lead to. He was okay with the decision to become this 'Reader'. He longed to know more about this 'Thousand Year Man', but was comfortable waiting, now that he had plenty of time to watch it play out.

Yes, his life was changing. It would begin today for real. The alarm sounded at 5:30 as usual, and he continued the ruse by acting as if he had just woken up as well. He sensed Barbara's excited anxiousness at the door before she kissed him goodbye. With a final look back, he saw her through the large windows in the living room. Yes, she was running, and her head disappeared from view as if she had just sat down on the couch.

He had been so lost in thought that it had happened again. He had forgotten that folder he had placed on the kitchen counter. He smiled as he realized that all he had dreamed WOULD happen the way he had seen. It would be very interesting for him to see how his dreams would fold into, and be fulfilled in real life. There was no need to waste any more energy on why or how it worked. He just knew now that it did.

He placed that call that let her know he was returning for the folder. It was hard not to snicker, as he knew why he'd waited so long for her to answer the phone. He wished he could tell her to look under the couch.

Once in the driveway, he watched as she brought it to him in the car. Again, he snickered at her trying to be coy as she glanced at those scratches on his bumper. At least he knew that she would eventually get it fixed for him, and when.

She handed it to him. They exchanged light-hearted banter, and then a kiss. He pulled out of the driveway, watching her in the rear view mirror as she turned and raced back into the house. He looked at the blue Texas sky and could only imagine at this point what it was like to fly off in a private jet. At this very moment, she was on the phone with a priest named Mathew.

John longed to finally meet this man in real time. He was the Catholic priest who would start the ball rolling with a fateful computer search. It would be this search that ultimately allowed him to lay his physical eyes upon a good friend named Anton.

Today was a day of change. It was a day that set him on his path to destiny.

It was a day that would take him from DREAM to LIFE!

A Special Thanks

I want to thank two people that read EVERY chapter as I was writing it and provided me valuable feedback. They kept me focused and wanting to complete the book.

Karrah Harasimo Bleeker– my beautiful daughter

Kenny Harasimo– my little brother

I also want to thank these people who read various numbers of my chapters and provided me valuable feedback.

Barbara Harasimo- my lovely wife

Shawn Harasimo- my handsome son

Katie Harasimo- my son's wife

Steve Harasimo- my little brother

Linda Harasimo- Steve's wife

Gerry Cerveny- co-worker at Information Services Company

Crystal Delion- co-worker at Information Services Company

I want each and every one of you to know how much I appreciated your help. You are what kept me going and helped me to finally achieve one of my life long dreams of writing a book. It was a journey that I could not have made without all of you.

I also want to thank Sarah Webb for the wonderful picture she took of me for the cover of my book. I have never liked having my picture taken but she made it seem like a natural thing to do.

With humility and appreciation I would like to say **THANK YOU!**

TABLE OF CONTENTS

SHORT STORIES

All Things Must End
Scott Edelman — 1

My-O-My
O'Neil De Noux — 15

After
Annie Reed — 41

Trigger Bill Learns About the Letter "E"
Brenda Carre — 51

Untrustworthy
Robert Jeschonek — 63

Hell's Belles
Dayle A. Dermatis — 87

Nightmare Paint
Mike Zimmerman — 103

Sharper Than a Serpent's Tooth
Christina F. York — 119

The Kids Keep Coming
David H. Hendrickson — 131

Killer Advice
Kristine Kathryn Rusch — 145

Minions at Work: Fits Like A Glove
J. Steven York — 233

Pulphouse Fiction Magazine
A WMG Publishing Magazine

Editor
Dean Wesley Smith

Executive Editor
Kristine Kathryn Rusch

Director of Operations
Stephanie Writt

FROM THE EDITOR'S DESK
WHAT IS IMPORTANT

One thing about *Pulphouse Fiction Magazine* that is very important to me as an editor is that readers will just not know what kind of story is next. Not only from story to story, but from month to month.

In one issue I will put a fairly straight-forward mystery story right next to a high fantasy followed by a space opera, all mixed with Twilight Zone like stories and stories that are just flat strange.

And then one month there is slightly more science fiction, another month slightly more mystery.

No genre and a lot of stories that just mix-up genres. That is a hallmark of this magazine.

A second element of this magazine that is critical to me as an editor is that the stories are all high quality. Very high. I have turned away many, many stories from top writers because they just didn't meet that standard.

Each story has to be a great story that holds the reader

from the very start. You may not like the plot of the story, or the content of the story, or it might not be to your taste. But it will be well-written, I can promise that every issue, every story.

And one more thing that I find very important. If a story is a great story that fits, I don't care if it was published before. So every issue is a mix of original stories (meaning first time published) and original stories that had a previous publication (meaning reprints). However, most readers find all the stories original to them.

This attitude is a 2024 attitude. Good fiction does not spoil. And no reader, no matter how well read, can read it all these days.

Now, since we have gone monthly, I have a featured story each month.

This month the featured story is by a *Pulphouse Fiction Magazine* regular, O'Neil De Noux. O'Neil was around during the last crazy year of the original Pulphouse business, and over the last 30 years has continued to improve his craft and become maybe the best writer of detective stories working.

I love having a story of his in most issues. His real-world detectives ground the readers amidst all the really crazy stories. The featured story of his this month goes back in time to 1948 New Orleans. Gripping right from the start.

So I hope you enjoy the stories in this issue. I know I sure enjoyed putting this together.

DEAN WESLEY SMITH
LAS VEGAS, NEVADA

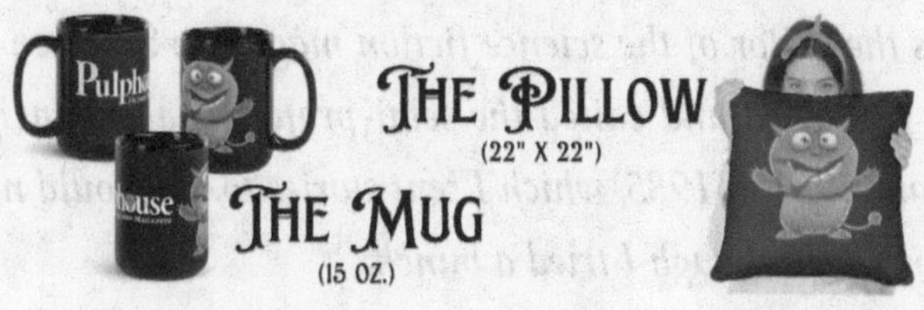

Live the Pulphouse life!

Grab your Pulphouse mug and fill it with your favorite beverage and lounge in your coziest chair with the Thumper pillow while you read the latest issue.

Want to mark off the date when your next issue will arrive? Get the Pulphouse calendar featuring some of our favorite Pulphouse cartoons!

Find all this and so much more at the Pulphouse Fiction Magazine online store at:

pulphousemagazine.com

Be cool like Thumper.

SCOTT EDELMAN

LEADING OFF THIS ISSUE *is veteran writer and editor Scott Edelman. Scott was the editor of the science fiction magazine* Science Fiction Age. *He published and edited the semi-professional magazine* Last Wave *from 1982 to 1985, which I sent stories to, but could never sell him a story even though I tried a bunch.*

Other magazines edited by Edelman over the years include Sci-Fi Universe, Sci-Fi Flix, *and* Satellite Orbit. *He became the editor of* SCI FI Magazine *(the official print magazine of* The Sci Fi Channel) *in 2002, and has edited the channel's online magazine* Science Fiction Weekly *since 2000.*

But he did write some for the early years of Pulphouse, *(yes, he has been around as long as I have) and now, his fifth story in this new incarnation is a pure Pulphouse story.*

For more information about Scott's writing and editing, go to www.scottedelman.com

ALL THINGS MUST END

SCOTT EDELMAN

We didn't know where the strings came from—they simply appeared one day, rising from where they'd suddenly looped around our wrists, necks, and ankles—and wherever we happened to be in that shared moment of their manifestation, when we raised our heads to seek out where they led—of our own volition, we believed, not tugged upward in any way by the sudden yoking—we could see no end to them.

Those five strings—thicker than thread, thinner than rope, smooth as silk, and one indistinguishable from another—shot up vertically from each of us until they at some point seemed to converge and then vanish beyond what was visible by even the sharpest human eye.

We had no idea what waited at their other ends.

We had no idea if there even *were* other ends.

That ignorance did not sit well with us, any of us, so we looked for what we could not see.

I've been speaking of the effects of that strange day as a *we* thing, as happening to us, and the reason is, I realize, so I won't have to think too much about *me*. No surprise there, as thinking that way has always been part of my nature. It long ago became clear to me—that's what led me to choose my somewhat solitary career and my mostly solitary life.

I wasn't avoiding myself in that manner during the initial longing for a cause as to what occurred that day, though. My concerns then were no different than all of our concerns. And so it was not submerging myself to say *we* looked skyward. And when we did—

Binoculars couldn't find the ends of those strings. Neither could radar. And when the military sent drones aloft to seek the source, they discovered the strings continued way outside our atmosphere and far beyond the limits of their mechanical perception. What segments could be seen of the lower portions of the strings to which we were attached, however, showed they radiated outward, parting slightly and slowly, as if the Earth were the center of the universe. Even our finest telescopes could only reveal that those ever-widening lines extended up and up...and higher still...escaping the solar system and traveling beyond the known planets seemingly forever so their ends could not at all be seen—even though all things must end.

We had no awareness the strings which bound us ever attempted to exert control. None we could perceive, anyway. We each experimented in our own ways to uncover whether that was so, and found we were allowed to move freely, without the loops which could not be loosened pulling us to the left or right, prodding us in one direction or another. We felt no tension to our connections, they were just…there… following. So we did not feel we were captives. We could live our lives on our own terms, without leading the lines along, without being led. Our momentum and inertia remained our own, our free will unsullied.

Regardless of that freedom, some attempted during that beginning to cut themselves away and back to the pre-event form of freedom which had existed throughout human history, applying scissors and fire, chainsaws and acid, and for the most desperate—their own teeth gnawing furiously. But none were successful at releasing that invasive touch. As for me, I never tried to copy their efforts, even though no punishment came for those who did. I'd spent so much of my time alone, their presence was almost welcome. I felt an odd comfort there, one similar to what I felt when considering the fish tanks in the front waiting room—a low key infectious serenity, ever present, and making few demands.

Besides, we could still go about our business. The strings did not prevent those of us who'd become tethered while out and about from returning inside, though many let fear prevent them from even making the attempt, which left them waiting until others tried and survived. Working at a mortuary as I'd been doing for five years before the strings first made their appearance had freed me of many fears, that to my surprise being one of them. Once any of us passed through a doorway, the strings would follow, continuing to hover straight above us, vanishing into whatever ceiling we were beneath, remaining taut as if a fishing line tossed into a pond hanging above our heads. And if another went outside to inspect, they'd find the strings continuing out of the roof and disappearing into the sky as usual, our homes and offices no barrier to the lines which—if the news reports were to be believed—harnessed every human being on Earth.

When it became clear the strings weren't going away any time soon, and were doing nothing (so far as we could tell) to interfere in our affairs, we did our best to move on, to live the lives we'd led before. Those of us who could, returned to our routines. As for others—some changes were unavoidable.

Our planet, for instance, became smaller. Commercial flights were halted. Not because they were impossible, but because they'd become…uncomfortable. Those who first dared to fly after the phenomenon began were unsettled by what the skies held for them. The skeins which thrust upward were inescapable even tens of thousands of feet in the air, and dodging them over all but the most desolate of areas was an impossibility for even the most skilled pilot. But after the first few times the paths of strings and planes crossed, we learned such acrobatics were not necessary to prevent damaging collisions, for the encounters caused no harm, gave no resistance whosoever. All that manifested, in fact, was a tickling within the pilots and passengers who personally passed through the strings belonging to another. It caused such a disorientation—and created so many rumors the effect might be even more terrifyingly existential—that the customer base evaporated and flights were soon grounded.

Car travel was up, though, making my life busier as a consequence, which I should have guessed would happen, considering my familiarity with the actuarial tables. That left me with little time to obsess about the new world in which we lived, a dual benefit—what was good for business was also good for my peace of mind.

Every once in a while, someone would attempt to climb their strings—which regardless of what those flying discovered up above, kept their solidity in such circumstances down below—to see whether they could learn from where they'd been cast. They believed the previous inability of seekers to find an answer via radar, telescope, and the like, was because anything but the most natural of means was inevitably doomed to fail to reach whatever was on the other end of the strings. I could have told them what they were doing was pointless, that whatever answer waited out there really didn't matter and would affect no change in their lives, but I didn't even try. That would have been pointless, too.

They'd bring food and water with them, blankets for the cold they expected would come if they successfully rose, and hammocks which would enable them to pause along the way and sleep at the end of each day. Those of us too wise to fall for such foolishness would sometimes gather below to look on each time a person mounted such a pilgrimage, which resulted in so many of our strings condensing so tightly they'd block the sun, forcing the watchers to live in shadow until we grew bored and abandoned providing an audience for the impossible. Those few who chose to remain would watch the climbers rise until they vanished out of sight, never to be seen again, which unfortunately encouraged others, who wondered if their disappearances meant they found what they'd sought.

I was never one of them.

Never one of those who felt they should follow, that is. I

was content with the new world. I did join the world in wondering, however. Just not about the same thing everyone else seemed to.

Here's the question I would often ask myself and have never been able to answer—

Were the strings truly newcomers to our existence, suddenly substantiating with no warning, giving no clue as to the event approaching, with a not there/there disconnect? Or had they always been with us, only we simply had never been able to see them before?

We all had different questions, it seems, and attempted to answer them in different ways.

Some were driven in their desperation to find the answers to their own questions by climbing the strings of others, to varying results. They would knock down strangers, then leap for their strings, feeling the less familiar tethering would give them a better chance of ascending than those who climbed their own. These unfortunate assaults seemed to happen most frequently to those who were pregnant, from whom a second set of strings rose, the theory being, I suppose, that any climb would have greater support upon ten strings than five. But whether the invaders would hurl themselves at one set of strings or two, most faced failure, for they'd pass through as if the lines weren't there at all, and hit the ground on the other side, where they'd lie dazed, sometimes unable to rise again for days, and not because of any injury, but rather...they seemed to lack the will. A few managed to maintain contact and move upward—and we never understood why those few were able when most could not. This connection to the strings of a stranger had little seeming effect on the one below, who would eventually get up from the attack and move about their day. As with all climbers, we never did find out what happened to those who rose.

Those were not the only methods the malcontents sought to break away from the world they'd been handed. There were some who leapt from tall buildings, hoping their strings would stretch like a rubber band, storing the energy needed to snap them back past where they'd begun and off into the heavens. Neither of those things ever occurred—a number of the deceased were brought to me to deal with after—so it didn't happen as often as you might suppose. Others would go deep sea diving, believing that if they descended deep enough their strings would snap. What they thought would happen next if they were to have been released, I never learned, but as it never happened, the results being more tragic than triumphant, it didn't really matter.

So most of us continued on, neither seeking answers nor seeking to be set free by them, living our lives and trying to forget the strings were even there. And after awhile, it was almost as if they weren't. On the right days, in the right moods, they were almost invisible, like those floaters in the corners of one's eye which can for the most part be forgotten except on the brightest of sunny days.

I was lucky enough to be one of those. Though perhaps it had little to do with luck, but rather the inescapable influence of my circumstances.

As I went about my work, preparing my unfortunate customers for the next world, two things happened—I saw firsthand the results of those who'd struggle to escape their fates—and by bearing witness I surrendered to whatever my own was meant to be. My job at the funeral home had me privy in a way most others were not to what came after, so I knew—not even death could cut the strings. As the bodies were laid out, the lines which bound them still rose to whatever in the sky kept them tethered. Cremation did not sever the ties, either, for I could see the strings rising from those who chose that path, so close together as to be indistinguishable, connecting the urn to the heavens. Walking the cemetery grounds every day and seeing strings leaving the grass to pierce the clouds changes a person, in a way spending one's time only around the tethered living does not, and it told me there was no escape either in this life or the next. So I knew not to try.

Unlike many industries which were either curtailed or eventually shut down entirely—such as private detectives, and the manufacturers of night vision goggles and home pregnancy tests—I remained fully and increasingly employed, the incursion having no negative effect on my life, and then not directly. It was merely ripples from those more acutely affected. People had been dying long before the strings arrived, and continued to die (albeit at a slightly higher rate) while they were here, so my skills, as mundane as they were, remained necessary. And after they left, if they left, they'd be necessary still.

But would there be an after? From time to time, I would look to the sky and wonder.

But with no answers in sight, I told myself it did not matter. As I said, I had chosen to surrender. (Or thought so.)

Accepting as I was (or told myself I was) of the new order to things, and no longer longing for release, I ignored my bonds, the ones (as I have said) I often forgot were even there, unlike those forever conscious of wanting the old ways back. Which meant my first notice that things were about to change was a slight heaviness in one of my wrists as I stretched out my hand to button the collar of a man who had passed the previous night. My fingers missed their target, colliding with the old man's chin, and when I jerked back my hand I noticed—

There was suddenly a slack to the string, as it no longer leapt straight up from the top of my wrist, but had begun to droop down below. And then I saw what wrapped around my other wrist was the same, and the strings at my ankles had already dropped so severely the curves of them now draped to the floor.

Screams erupted from outside, and I stepped to the street, for the first time feeling a resistance, and once I'd dragged myself to the sidewalk I could hear the sound of a distant whistling.

The streets around the funeral home were relatively quiet, and what few pedestrians there were had become trapped where they stood, frozen by the spirals which had begun to loop around their feet. I made to move toward the closest, but couldn't, then looked down to see my own strings gathering there. It was as if whatever had held the other end in place had let go, allowing them to fall. Or had they been cut rather than released? Whichever they had been, they continued to fall, the whistling increasing in intensity and causing an ache in my ears as they did so.

Though the mounds grew higher, the nature of the strings themselves appeared unchanged, and when I looked up, what remained above still stretched far beyond my sight, this relatively slight gathering having no change on whether I could see a beginning or end.

Someone nearby cried out for help, and when I tried to do just that, I instead pitched forward, tripping over the barrier which had by then risen past my knees. I fell on my side and rolled to my back, but when I tried to rise again, I was unable to move, for such a weight of falling strings had amassed against my chest, I was pinned. What had for so many months been ethereal and undemanding had become quicksand, and I could do no more than watch and listen while the whistling transformed into a dull rumble as if a thunderstorm were racing toward me.

I couldn't even turn my head, but what strings I was able to see still stretched to infinity. I hoped this meant, the fall by the sound of it picking up speed, that I'd soon see the end of things, but that was not to be, for the strings began to crisscross my face until my eyes were soon covered, and then I could see no more.

The darkness quickly became the least of my concerns, as the accumulated weight across my chest of what had once been weightless made it difficult to breath. I was uncertain, even as I struggled, whether we were being set free or abandoned, and my emotions vibrated between gratitude and betrayal. I no longer remember which of those feelings was strongest as I lost consciousness.

When I eventually came to, still on the sidewalk where I'd fallen, the strings were gone, the skies were clear, and I was alone. I must have been the last to rouse, for the others had all gathered themselves and gone. Many hours had clearly passed, for it was night. I could see the stars, and looking upon them could not remember having ever seen so many at once. Did that mean there were really more than there once had been, perhaps birthed by what we had endured? Or had their existence merely been blocked for so long, my memory of them could not compete with their reality? As I waited for the effects of my smothering to fully pass, I thought about those stars, and those who might live on the other planets which could be circling them. I wondered whether somewhere out there another to whom I had once been connected lay on their back as newly untethered as I was, and what their release might mean to them.

But those questions were as meaningless as any of the others, and so I rose and returned to my back office, where I completed dressing the old man for his funeral. I assumed others elsewhere were also getting on with their lives.

But not all of them, I was later to learn. Some, in response to the moment, abandoned their families and jobs, fearing the strings might return with as little warning as their initial appearance, and hoping they could outrun the inevitable and hide from what awaited them. Others never even got back to their feet, but simply lay where they had fallen and starved. Then there are the ones who longed for them back, longed for the touch which had, if not guided us, at least accompanied us. Comforted us.

I became one of those, though I was not one at first. But as I moved through the world to which we've been told we've returned, I came to realize…we've returned to nothing. I now understand the reason we never felt the weight of the strings upon us, never felt them urge us this way or that, never felt them holding us back, neither encouraging nor chastising, was that no guidance was ever necessary. It's simple, you see? All is foreordained, so what need was there to control when we always do as we are meant to do? The choices I understood to bring me here? An illusion. To believe in free will is to believe in a lie. That is what they existed to teach us, and having taught us, whether we learned their lesson or not, left.

And that is why you find me like this, with strings I myself have wrapped around my wrists and ankles, and another about my neck. They don't reach for the sky as the other hd. In fact, they exist only a few inches beyond each of the five knots I have made. But I want the universe to hear me, to know that even if no one else has listened, I at least have learned.

And if the universe does not hear, does not respond—and why would it, having said all I fear needed to be said?—I have a rope waiting, one far thicker than either the strings I've just used or the earlier five which once bound me. It's long enough—just long enough and no more—to take me where the lessons have shown me I choose to go next.

O'NEIL DE NOUX

*I*N *THIS MONTH*'*S FEATURED STORY*, *O'N*EIL *D*E *N*OUX *takes his amazing skills as one of the best writers of detective fiction working today and gives us another amazing story in the colorful past of his hometown of New Orleans.*

O'Neil has published about fifty novels with more coming regularly. His awards include The United Kingdom Short Story Prize, the Shamus Award (for best private eye fiction), the Derringer Award (for excellence in mystery short fiction) and Police Book of the Year.

Two of his stories have appeared in the prestigious Best American Mystery Stories annual anthology and I noticed he had another in the recommended reading for this last year's volume. He won the Shamus for a story in 2020. You can find out a lot more about his work at his website http://www.oneildenoux.com/

MY-O-MY

O'NEIL DE NOUX

Parents usually leave the bedroom of a deceased child unchanged but not the Vernets. The double bed lies stripped down to its sheet, pillows without pillow cases at the foot of the bed, the top of dresser and chest-of-drawers clear. The chifforobe stands open with only a few hangers in each. Nothing on the walls, the window curtains are closed to the bright sunlight outside. The room smells of lemon cleaner. I open the drawer of the small desk, find a Webster's dictionary, four pencils, a blank tablet and a pencil sharpener. The other drawers are empty. So is the lone closet, more hangers but no clothes. I go back into the hall and down the mansion's spiral staircase.

The mother, Constance Vernet, turns to me from the living room's sofa. She's in a long dark gray dress with a high collar, her brown hair in a bun, no makeup. Looks to be in her mid-forties. She waves to her right as a man in his fifties steps into the living room.

"Mr. Caye, this is my husband Zachary Vernet."

Zachary had been in his home office when I'd arrived a half hour earlier.

"So this is the Private Eye," says the balding man in the tailored dark brown suit as he sits in a stuffed chair. "I understand my wife gave you the pertinent details."

"Yes, she did."

When Mrs. Constance Vernet called me on the phone yesterday to hire me, she gave me the gist of the case—

Son Lloyd Vernet stabbed outside Club My-O-My four months ago, Sunday 2 a.m., April 4, 1948. Found in parking lot.

Mr. Vernet's voice rises, "What burns me up are two police agencies who won't even investigate the killing of my son. We've talked to New Orleans Police and the Jefferson Parish Sheriff and neither's working on the case. NOPD says the murder happened on the deck of the club, which is in Jefferson Parish. And the JP sheriff says the body was found in the parking lot in Orleans Parish, so it's an NOPD case. Meanwhile, we buried our son and no one's looking for his killer." Zachery Vernet slaps his knee. "We all know the reason. They don't give a damn about boys like my son."

Club My-O-My. Boys like my son. Haven't been to the club. The local radio ads say the club features America's most beautiful and talented female impersonators.

I take out my Moleskine notebook. "Where are Lloyd's personal effects?"

Mrs. V looks at her lap.

"What personal effects?" Mr. V asks.

"Everything that was in his bedroom."

Mrs. V says, "We gave his clothes to charity." She gives me a resigned look.

"Any notebooks? Diary? Journal? Address book?"

"What does that have to do with his murder?"

"He might have noted if someone had threatened him."

"Well, his stuff is gone."

I ask if they know of anyone who wanted to hurt Lloyd.

"Sons-a-bitches who hate boys like our son. Never figure why they get so hateful. They heckle the boys outside the club."

I nod and put that in my notes.

"Did Lloyd have any friends I can speak with?"

"No."

"Any siblings?"

"Brother at Notre Dame. Married sister in Pensacola."

Mr. V stands, pulls a white envelope from his inner coat pocket.

"Your retainer in cash. $500. I understand you charge $25 a day plus expenses."

"Yes, sir." I pull out my receipt book and he waves it away.

"Don't go over $500 without checking with me."

"Do you have a photo of your son I can borrow?"

I wait in the foyer for Mrs. V to come down with a 4"x5" photo of her smiling son. He's leaning against a tree, arms folded. Good looking guy with curly blond hair. Mrs. V nods to me, turns away and I leave the house, stepping into the thick humidity of a typical New Orleans August. I take the seven steps down to the brick walkway, look back at the three-story Greek Revival on St. Charles Avenue. The mansion looks more like a bank than a home with four ionic columns supporting a second story balcony and wide gallery above. The bricks have been painted gray and two large magnolia trees in front cast long shadows across the façade.

I CALL THE DETECTIVE BUREAU, ask for my friend Frenchy Capdeville. He isn't in so I ask for Jimmy O'Malley who also isn't in, neither is Al Francona so I leave a message for Frenchy. Head over to the coroner's office, where it's all public record to I pick up a copy of Lloyd Vernet's death certificate and autopsy report, take them back to my office.

The post mortem exam describes Lloyd Vernet as a well-nourished white male, 5'9" long (cadavers are measured in length, not height) and weighing 150 pounds with short blond hair and brown eyes. No scars, marks or tattoos listed. Toxicology report pending. The death certificate lists the cause of death as a stab wound of the heart. Manner of death —homicide. Lloyd was twenty-one years old.

The autopsy report lists six stab wounds—two in the left arm, one through the left hand, one through the right hand, one in the right shoulder and one in the chest, 2" from the sternum, which nipped the left ventricle of the heart. Wounds on the hands and arms are defensive wounds, the poor guy trying to block the knife. The pathologist lists the knife as a double-edged, 9-inch blade.

The coroner investigator's report lists the victim's personal items—clothes and an inexpensive Lancer wrist-watch with broken crystal and a leather band.

WINDBLOWN RAIN BOUNCES off my balcony's French doors and windows as I turn on the radio, find a blues station and listen to T-Bone Walker start up one of my favorites—*Call It Stormy Monday (But Tuesday Is Just as Bad)*. I turn my large cushioned chair around to watch forked lightning dance over the nighttime rooftops across Barracks Street and Cabrini Park, thunder sending a shivers through the old building. The French Quarter looks older in the rain. I take a sip of icy Falstaff and close my eyes, envisioning that boy coming out of the club at 2 a.m. and the knife impaling him, the painful, shuddering death. I see him stumble off the deck and into the parking lot to collapse, look up at the dark sky as the blackness takes him.

We know what happened. When it happened. Where it happened. But the elusive why and the more elusive who did it is out there getting drenched in the rain. The solution's always out there. I just have to find it.

The doorbell rings and I go over and hit the buzzer for the building's door, go out on the landing to look downstairs to see who I let in. Lt. Frenchy Capdeville takes off his raincoat, hangs it a hook outside my office door downstairs and looks up at me.

"You left a message?"

I wave him up and go back into my apartment for another beer.

My friend and mentor, this Zorro lookalike with curly black hair and pencil-thin moustache, raises his hand as he steps into my living room.

"Hit me."

I hand him a Falstaff and he moves to the sofa. He's in his well-worn brown suit, cigarette ashes dusting his lapel. I pull the easy chair back around to the sofa.

"So, what you need?"

"Four months ago, back in April, man killed outside the My-O-My."

He takes a drink of beer.

I go on. "Family tells me NOPD didn't handle it because they found blood on the deck of the club, which is in Jefferson, who won't handle it because the body ended up in the parking lot, which is in the city. I know the rule, wherever the body ends up works the case."

He takes another hit of beer.

"We worked that case. Came up blank."

"Worked? As in past tense."

Frenchy narrows an eye at me. "We got nothing. Midnight shift crew worked it. Det. Joe Chapman. I was busy with other cases."

"I need the reports."

He growls at me. "Victim's parents hired you?"

"Yeah."

"OK. All right. We're up to our asses in cases. If you come up with anything, I'll move on it." He takes another hit. "Man, we drop the ball so many times. Not putting in the effort. I can't be sure but Chapman probably whiffed on this one because the victim was a transvestite."

"This is New Orleans, man. We don't do whiff on cases. No matter the victim."

"We? The parents know you're not really a detective. You're a private eye." He grins.

I take a hit of my Falstaff. How many murders do I have to solve before he stops with that joke?

He takes another deep draft of Falstaff, says, "I know. Anything goes here, but not everyone's on board with that."

"Have the managers at My-O-My complained about the lack of…anything?"

"Not to me or the captain."

We both drink our beer. Frenchy's only ten years older than my twenty-seven and the years in the Homicide Division have given his face lines I don't have.

He raises his hand, says, "Another smile."

In Frenchy lingo, a smile is a beer.

PARK my pre-war DeSoto in the clam shell parking lot servicing all the restaurants, cafes and nightclubs here at West End. My Bulova reads 2 p.m., a few hours before the first show at Club My-O-My. I put on my blue suit coat to cover my .357 magnum in its holster on my right hip, glance in the sideview mirror to straighten my silver and red tie, take out my moleskine pocket notebook and a sharpened pencil before heading to the wooden steps leading up to the deck surrounding the club standing on wooden pilings covered with black creosote at the edge of Lake Pontchartrain.

A 6'5" bouncer with a crew cut, an appropriate scar on his chin, folds his arms to show me his muscles as I approach the front door My-O-My. He's in a black t-shirt and black slacks. I nod as I arrive, tell him who I am, hand him a business card.

"A private eye, huh? Like in the movies?"

"Exactly."

His upper lip curls.

"A wise guy, huh? We ain't open, yet. What you want?"

"I'm working the murder case."

"What mur…oh."

He takes in a deep breath, turns serious.

"I was here that night but I didn't see him leave."

"What did you hear about it?"

"Hell, we all talked about it but no one knows anything. It was foggy that night. He walked into the fog and ended up in the parking lot."

He makes a puff noise.

"Victim's folks hired me to look into the case. They're hurting."

He unfolds his arms, looks at my card again.

I ask for the manager and he says, "He's inside. Lou Epstein. Office in back. Left side of the room."

"Hold on to my card. If you hear anything, give me a call."

I step into the main room and pause to take it in.

Long bars line both sides of the place, padded barstools for the customers. Tables fill the center area with a dance floor in back and wide stage facing the rows of tables, an orchestra pit on the right side. Bartenders wipe down the bars as I pass. Manager Lou Epstein sits behind a large black desk, a little guy with a cigarette dangling from his mouth. Epstein is bald on top, pushing sixty and wears a light green suit.

"What are you here for?"

"The murder. I'm a detective."

He sits back, waves me to a chair in his cramped office and I introduce myself, ask if he was here that.

"Yeah. I was back here when one of my bouncers came and told me. You wanna question everyone, go ahead but don't get in the way."

"Do you remember Lloyd Vernet?"

"Barely. He was a dancer."

I ask if Lloyd had any friends at My-O-My.

"I wouldn't know."

"Y'all have problems with hecklers outside?"

"Hecklers? Yes. Bashers sometimes as well. They try to bash the performers but our bouncers run them off. Our guys who get beat up get beat up away from here."

"One more question. He left at 2 a.m. Is that when you close?"

"No. We close at 5 a.m. Different performers have different hours. He must have gotten off at two."

"He left alone?"

The manager shrugs.

I go back into the main room and watch them enter quietly—young, thin men moving to the dressing room. I follow the first ones in and they sit at a long counter in front of a wall of mirrors bathed in bright lights. I approach the first in line as he applies his make-up, introduce myself and spend the next hours talking to everyone who will talk with me in Club My-O-My—the performers—singers, dancers, musicians bartenders, waiters, bus boys, and cooks. A few remember Lloyd but did not know him well, except for his only friend, Bobbie Pulline who comes in after four, a good looking fellow with delicate features, standing a couple inches below my six feet.

I wait until he starts on his make-up and sit next to him along the counter, begin with, "I heard you were Lloyd Vernet's friend."

He blinks at me and I show him my credentials, tell him I'm working for Lloyd's folks.

"How well did you know Lloyd?"

"Only for the few months he worked here."

He turns back to the mirror and puts blush on his cheeks. "He was so young."

Pulline can't be more than twenty-five.

"He couldn't sing but was coming along as a dancer and looked great dressed up."

"He have any problems with anyone?"

"No.

"Any problems with bashers?"

"He got punched up once on Bourbon Street but two strip club bouncers ran them off."

"Any trouble from the bashers outside My-O-My?"

"Just taunts."

"Were you here the night it happened?"

"No. It was my night off." His sucks in a deep breath, shakes his head.

He tells me Lloyd was a reader. Read books. Novels. He reaches into a drawer under the make-up table and pulls out a book.

"He was reading this one."

Hemingway's *For Whom The Bell Tolls.*

"Kinda prophetic, wouldn't you say?"

Back in the main room I come across bartender Doug Jenson as he sets up a line of clean glasses. He doesn't remember Lloyd Vernet.

He tells me, "Only homo-hating basher I come across outside is a jackass I went to Fortier with. You know, high school. Dickie Barnett. Been a bully all his life. Our bouncers ran him off a couple times."

From everyone—the bashers don't mess with the customers, just the singers and dancers, the ones dressed up as women. A pretty brunette walks past me and I do a double take and Jenson snickers.

"Good lookin', huh?"

"Uh."

"Don't sweat yourself. That's a real girl. She's the head cashier. Works in the back." He nods beyond the orchestra pit.

The other bartenders know nothing about Lloyd and the killing.

I move to the office the head cashier had gone inside and she looks up at me from behind a small desk, her right hand on the handle of an adding machine.

"Sorry to interrupt." I hold up my credential pouch. "I'm a private detective. You have a minute to talk?"

She runs her free hand through her dark brown hair, blinks her large brown eyes and tells me no. She wears her hair in a long page boy, the only short haircut I like on a woman. Too bad the trend after the war has been with shorter hair on women.

"I take a break at the first intermission. At about six. I'll be at the bar on this side."

I leave a card on her desk, step out of the club, check the

nearby restaurants, all within walking distance—Fitzgerald's, Kirsch's and Brunings. Get nothing. Like My-O-My, they all stand suspended over the lake on creosote-covered pilings. Get back during the first show, watch a rollicking jazz number, dancers on stage in chiffon and sequins and feather boas and tight dresses, high heels. Three singers join them, one on each side of the stage, one in the center and they belt out Charlie Parker's *Billy Bunch* followed by the lead singer with a melodic rendering of *Do You Know What It Means To Miss New Orleans*.

A light haze begins to rise from the customer's cigarettes as they sit at the tables in front of the stage. Couples mostly, looking no different than customers at other nightclubs like The Blue Room at the Roosevelt Hotel and Starlight at the Jung Hotel. In their thirties and forties, laughing at the banter onstage, belting down cocktails. Having a good time.

The head cashier comes out of the back just as the stage show takes a brief intermission, the band switching to big band music. She moves to the bar just down from where I stand and signals the bartender who hands her a bottle of Coca-Cola. She climbs on the stool leans her back against the bar and takes a sip. She's in her mid-twenties, wears a fitted blue dress. She gives me a cocky look as I step up, the kind teenage girls used to give me when they knew they were good looking. I glance at the bartender, ask for a root beer.

"Barq's," I tell him.

"If you're investigating anyone here, you can get lost," says the head cashier.

"I'm here about the murder." My root beer arrives and I take a sip of the root beer with bite, the one with extra caffeine. I ask her name and she sips her Coke, sticks out her hand for me to shake.

"Claudia D'Amico."

D'Amico. That's Italian.

Her right eyebrow raises. "A private eye, huh?"

Her face loses the flippant look. She's not sure she remembers Lloyd Vernet, might have seen him but knows nothing about him. I show her the picture and she shakes her head.

"What have you heard about it?"

"Not much. He was stabbed outside. People think some homo-hating lunatic did it. Caught him alone in the fog." She shudders.

"Were you here that night?"

She nods, says, "Earlier. I leave at midnight most nights."

We sip our drinks and the band starts up again and couples move to the dance floor.

"Did you like the show?" Claudia asks.

"It's pretty damn good."

She raises her Coke to several of the performers talking with customers.

"A lot of our boys are heterosexual. Have wives. They just like to dress up like women."

She takes a sip of Coke, adds, "We've had Howard Hughes in here, Carmen Miranda, Alec Guinness." She presses a finger against her nose and bends it. "Mafiosi come in here on a lark, showing out-of-towners the ass-end of show business as we call it. But it is show business."

"Mafiosi?"

"Someone mentioned names like Cardone, Badalamente."

She looks at the watch on her left wrist. "Have to go back before the second floor show."

Claudia climbs off the stool, shakes my hand again and says she'll ask around, maybe someone remembers something. I watch her walk away and the bartender steps close.

"That's the most she's said to anyone since she's been here."

I tell him. "Private Eyes always get the girl. Don't you go to the movies?"

He gives me a sneer.

The second show is like a beauty contest runway with a parade of 'the world's most beautiful boys in women's clothes' as the advertising says. The songs start up and the acts come on and I go outside to watch people enter and leave. There are no hecklers and I leave before the rain comes.

THE NEXT EVENING, after a second night of getting nothing on the case, I open the French doors, as I usually do and sit and drink a Miller High Life and look at the oaks and magnolias across the street in the park and the black sky above the rooftops of the old Quarter. Frenchy shows up with the police reports at eleven and I hit him with a Falstaff. He plops on my sofa, takes a drink of beer, puts the bottle on the coffee table, leans back and closes his eyes.

"What a damn day," he says. "Guy shot to death over a parking spot. Another guy tried to hang himself because his wife left him. Tried to use the second floor pipes outside his boarding house. Guy built like a rhino. Broke the pipes. Went next door with the rope still around his neck and borrowed his buddy's 1911.

My 1911 Colt 45 semi-automatic pistol sits in a desk drawer in my office downstairs.

"Took it to the ditch behind the houses and blew his brains out. Another guy robbed the Whitney on St. Charles. Ran outside like a bat outta hell only the mask he wore messed up his vision and he ran headlong into a telephone pole. Knocked himself out."

"Whitney on St. Charles? That's my bank."

"It was your money. He went in with a Colt .38 and told the teller, 'Gimme Lucien Caye's money.'"

Cops. All frustrated stand-up comics.

"Let me rest a minute. You read the reports. You won't believe how inept we can be."

Ten 8x10 black and white photos of the scene show the blood on the deck and steps, a picture of the club lit up in the background, a dog sniffing at the blood dotting the white clam shells of the parking area, the body of Lloyd Vernet lying on his back, arms curled in front of him, legs outstretched. There's a close up of his face and the chest wound visible. I look again. Lloyd isn't wearing shoes.

The first officers on the scene checked Lloyd for vital signs, traced the blood trail to the steps and up the deck of My-O-My, talked to three people, all employees of My-O-My. Did not canvass. Didn't write down license plate numbers of the cars in the lot. Neither did the detectives when they arrived. Det. Joe Chapman who misspelled Lloyd's last name as Verget was the only detective to write a daily report on the murder.

In his follow-up report, Chapman spends most of his time describing how the stabbing occurred on the deck over the water, which means the crime occurred in Jefferson Parish. He spoke to employees—no names—and passersby outside the night after the murder. Again, no names. He says he canvassed the nearby restaurants and no one saw anything. His final follow-ups were two phone calls to the manager of My-O-My a few days later to see if any new information had surfaced.

"Pitiful, huh?" Frenchy says.

"You let him close the case."

"I was out of town. Detective Sergeant Harvey Evers signed off closing it down. I told you, it slipped through my fingers. Notice how ole Chapman didn't mention the victim was in his stocking feet?"

"Yes, I did. The killer stole his shoes?"

"Unless someone came along and took them. Happens. Had a suicide once on the river batture."

Batture—the land between the levee and the water's edge.

"Man left a suicide note in car parked nearby, had gunshot wound to the temple, contact wound. No gun on the scene. We found the gun two days later. A teenager had picked it up and was showing it to his friends when his dad caught him and called us."

"Happens? Who found Lloyd's body? Cops didn't get the name of who found him, did they?"

"Anonymous phone call."

Frenchy lets out a long breath. "Never heard of a robbery a case where someone robbed someone for their shoes."

The photos show the wristwatch with the broken crystal on Lloyd's left wrist and the wounds on the hands.

I look at the reports again, drop them on the coffee table and Frenchy's eyes blink open.

"That's all the investigation a boy who dresses like a girl gets, huh?"

Frenchy curls his lip, takes a hit of beer.

What with the lip curling?

"Got Francona and Dickens working their asses off Back-a-town. Little colored boy got strangled to death two nights ago. See anything in the newspaper?"

I shake my head.

"Course not. Colored folk are killed, not murdered. But we're working it. Chief's already cautioned me about spending too much time on the case and I reminded him he has a seven year old boy, doesn't he?"

Frenchy holds up his hand. "I can still see the little boy's hands." He takes another hit of beer. "The face was lifeless, blued tongue protruding, body contorted and his little hands looked so delicate. I touched them at the postmortem, whispered to the little fella I'd catch who did it." Frenchy looks at me.

"Can only do so much, you know."

Later, after Frenchy leaves, I go through the pictures again, look at Lloyd Vernet's hands clenched in front of his chest and wonder, like the dead little boy's mother, how many times did Lloyd's mother kiss his hands when he was a baby.

THE ONE-STORY wooden stationhouse of the Jefferson Parish Sheriff's Office stands a couple blocks from the end of Metairie Road near Causeway Boulevard with large letters JPSO printed in dark blue on the white wall facing the road. The desk sergeant asks what I want and I tell him about the case and he tells me a detective will see me.

"You're in luck," a short, thin, dark complected man in a light blue suit says as he shakes my hand. "I'm Detective Frank Castellano. I'm the one who went out there. We turned it over to NOPD. The body was theirs."

Castellano is in his early twenties with eager brown eyes.

"I wanted to work the case but our chief deputy nixed it." He raises his left hand to show me his wedding ring. "I was married right after the murder and…you married?"

"No."

"Well, it's a busy time, especially with an Italian wedding."

"Did you write a report on what you did?"

"Uh, no. But I should have my notes."

"Can I see them?"

"If I can find them. If I do, I'll call and tell you what I got. Probably just time of notification, arrival and what I saw."

"What do you remember?"

"Lotta blood."

"Do you remember speaking to anyone?"

"Uh, I spoke to the NOPD guys."

"Any witnesses? Anyone at My-O-My?"

"Don't think so."

I thank him, rise to leave, pass him a business card and he gives me his.

"No offense but you look young to be a detective."

"Twenty-three. The Chief Deputy's my uncle. You gonna keep on the case?"

"Yep."

He shakes his head. "Wish I could. We don't get many whodunits out here. We get barroom killins', husband and wife killins', people killin' people they know." He stands and walks me out. "Chief Deputy says murders like the My-O-My ain't worth a lotta effort, like mooks killin' mooks.

Black folk.

"I think that's crap, Det. Frank Castellano says. "My uncle's full of it sometimes." He leans close. "The sheriff's worse." He sticks his hand out for me to shake. "Just let me know if I can help you."

Back at My-O-My, head cashier Claudia D'Amico tells me she's confirmed Lloyd Vernet had left alone the night of the murder. She's in a cranberry colored fitted dress with a high collar.

"How do you know?"

"Couple bartenders saw him leave. They told the police."

Probably the same bartenders who didn't remember anything to me.

"Was he wearing his shoes?"

"Shoes? Why wouldn't he?"

"Do you know who found the body? Called police?

"No."

"How did he get to work?"

"That I do know. The West End bus. Most of us take it."

She points her chin to the left. "Bus stop at entrance of the parking lot."

She looks down at the papers on her desk, reaches for the adding machine and I ease out of her office.

I find the costumer in the wardrobe room and he waves me over when I ask if he has a moment. He's a heavy-set man in a pink chiffon dress and I tell him who I am and ask if he could give me Lloyd's shoe size. He checks a list and tells me, "Vernet wore a size eight."

More canvassing inside My-O-My gets me nowhere, neither does more canvassing inside and outside of Fitzgerald's, Kirsch's and Brunings, as well as two seafood places specializing in take-out orders and two small barrooms—Clearwater's and Sally's Long Tall Bar which isn't long or tall. Do learn there were a couple car burglaries in the parking lot the last few months and very little, if any, police presence in the area.

Three young guys stand at the bottom of the steps leading up to My-O-My. They separate, move out of the way as two couples go up the steps. The three reassemble and I step over to them. All three wear t-shirts and dungarees rolled up to show their high-top black tennis shoes.

"You got a cig?" The largest asks.

"Don't smoke."

I lean against a post at the bottom of the steps. The three collect at the other post, all three watching me. I watch them back, glance at my watch, have to turn my wrist to pick up the streetlight. It's ten p.m. Two more couples arrive, two come out, the men chuckling, the women chattering. The three eyeballing me take a few steps away. About fifteen minutes later, the biggest of the three—a few inches smaller than me but thicker around the middle with a crew cut—takes a step my way and calls out.

"You a cop or something?"

"Or something."

"What you waiting for?"

One of the other says, "Your boyfriend?"

The third one kisses the air.

"Any of you Dickie Barnett?"

The biggest glares at me, the other two taking a step back.

The one who blew me a kiss says, "Whaddya mean 'or somethin'?"

"I'm a private detective."

Two of the performers come out, both in dress shirts and trousers. Easy to spot as they still wear makeup. The three jerks start to follow, have to move past me and I step in their way. The biggest guy jumps back, opens his arms before balling his hands into fists.

"Don't even think about it, Dickie. I was an Army Ranger. I clean up all three of you before you can lay a hand on me. They teach you judo at Fortier?"

"We ain't doin' nothin'," The big guy says.

"We just tease them," says the smallest.

I pull out the picture of Lloyd Vernet, show it to the big guy. "Are you Dickie Barnett?"

"So what if I am?"

He doesn't look at the picture. I step closer, put it in his face. "This kid got murdered right here." I show the picture around so they can all see it. "Right here. Were you guys around that night, heckling people, bullying someone weaker than you? Did one of you jackasses stab him with a knife?"

If truth could not be easily concealed, if eye-opening looks are truthful, if the surprised looks on the faces are genuine, then these guys didn't kill Lloyd. *If.*

The shortest says, in a shaky voice, "Man, we don't know nothing about stabbing anyone."

The middle says, "We don't carry knives."

"We just tease them, man."

I pull out my small pouch of business cards and pass one to each.

"If one of y'all did it, you others should call me. Big difference in court between a witness and an accomplice. If any of you saw something that night, you can bring some relief to the dead boy's parents. They're hurting."

They look at each other, start backing away and keep going into the parking lot to climb into what looks like a 1936 Ford pickup truck. It leave a few minutes later.

———

Outside Kirsch's Restaurant the following evening a man named Joe Hanratty tells me a short guy with a knife tried to rob him on the Saturday night before Mardi Gras. That was in February. Couple months before Lloyd's murder.

"He came up on me like you did. Right out here. Pulled out a knife and told me to give him my wallet. I tried to but dropped it and he asked me my shoe size."

I look up from my notebook. "Run that by me again."

He does, adding the man scooped up his wallet and ran across the parking lot.

"What about your shoes?"

"Told him I wore a size nine and he just took my wallet."

I write the description he gives me of the robber—white male, frizzy brown hair, about 5'8", thin, wearing a pea-coat and dark slacks and dirty white shoes.

"You report it to the police?"

"Naw. I only had three bucks in the wallet. I don't want to…you know…the police."

"How big was the knife?"

"Like a Bowie knife."

The blade of a Bowie is 12-inches long with single sharp edge so I ask if the knife looked sharp on each side of the blade.

"Yeah. Like one of them stilettos."

I go back to My-O-My and run the description past the bartenders and bouncers, who don't seem to notice anyone. I had to re-introduce myself to each except bartender Doug Jenson, who remembers me but doesn't recall any frizzy-headed guy. Claudia D'Amico has not seen any frizzy-headed guys in recent memory.

"Knew one in high school, but he's a priest now in Puerto Rico or maybe Costa Rica."

On my way out, she says, "You keep working at it, Monsieur Caye. I have confidence in you."

At three p.m., the following day, I pick up the phone, call My-O-My to tell Claudia the killer's in custody.

"You solved it?"

"Not exactly, but I helped." I tell her I'll come by later with details after I tell the victim's parents about it.

A half hour earlier, Lt. Frenchy Capdeville had called me at my office and said, "We caught an armed robber with a .22 last night who asked his victim his shoe size."

"What?"

"He got the man's wallet and turned to leave only a patrol car was passing by and we caught him. Took me four hours but he copped out to your murder."

My murder.

"Can I come see him?"

"He's already booked in Parish Prison."

"Did he have frizzy hair, like I told you?"

"Yep. Floyd Hicks, 5'8", thin build with light brown frizzy hair."

A second later I come back with. "You sure he's the guy?"

"Went back to his place and he gave us five wallets, including Lloyd Vernet's. He said he killed the pretty boy by mistake, slipped on the steps. Lloyd wouldn't give him his shoes. They were new. Two tone Florsheims. Jackass was wearing them when we caught him."

"Slipped on the steps? There were six stab wounds."

Damn.

"Sometimes, murder doesn't make sense. Just hope the DA accepts the charge and doesn't send me to Jefferson Parish to file. No telling what goes on out there in the country."

"Gotta go," he says.

"Wait. The little boy," I said. "With the hands."

"Yeah. We solved that one too. It was his drunk-ass uncle. The boy was making too much noise."

Before I leave for the Vernet's, I close my eyes and think about what I'll tell them and tell everyone at My-O-My.

What do I tell them?

Murder doesn't make sense?

ANNIE REED

PROFESSIONAL WRITER ANNIE REED writes stories that span genres and are always powerful. In fact with Annie, you just never know the type of story you might be reading, but you will always know it will grab you and be a compelling read.

So far Annie has had a story in every issue of this magazine and as the editor, I hope to continue that streak.

Annie's stories have appeared in four best mystery stories of the year volumes so far. Look for so much more of Annie's work at her website https://anniereed.wordpress.com/

AFTER

ANNIE REED

The older Belle Creedy gets, the more she wonders about what happens. After.

In the mornings, when dawn's just a lick of peach in the eastern sky and she's so far into the world of her art she only knows the sun's coming up because the racket from the birds roosting in the thick pines around her house intrudes on her thoughts, she stops whatever she's working on and pads out onto the deck on the second story of her place. She watches ripples on the surface of the clear mountain lake just across the road take on the color of the pre-dawn sky, and she considers just how many coincidences go into making a world like this. Are they really coincidences after all? Or is there something more?

It's quiet this morning, so early in the day the birds have barely started their chatter. So early that Gary Weeds, another old-timer like herself, isn't even on the lake yet. Gary lives halfway up the mountain. He fishes every day he can, and since he retired in 1989, he can fish almost every day the weather lets him. He crunches down the one-lane dirt road that snakes up through the pines, rod and tackle box in his hand, and shoves off in his rowboat. Sits out on the lake half the day, the damn fool. One of these days she's gonna catch Gary peeing over the edge of his boat. Man has a cast iron bladder, but even a cast iron bladder can't stand against the ravages of time.

No one's on the lake yet. She can hear the shallow waves slapping up against Gary's boat where he moored at the end of the pier just as clear as if the boat and water were in the next room. Sound carries good out here, the air as crisp and clean as a new day should be.

Her hands ache this morning, the puffy joints of her fingers stiff and sore. "Storm blowing in," was what her mother would say. Maybe she'd be right, but this morning the sky only has a hint of clouds far to the north.

Her mother would have known the names of all the birds that live in the pines and cedars and tall birch trees. Known their names and catalogued each sound by type and volume. A good keeper of records, her mother was. Belle's not nearly as neat or concerned. She only knows that she likes the chirps and twitters, likes to imagine the conversations going on from nest to nest, punctuated with a sudden flutter of wings as effectively as she underlines words in her drawings.

This place inspires her. She produces page after page of glimpses into a whimsical world her mother never could have imagined. A place where animals talk and people are seen only from the waist down as a collection of shoes and legs and feet that stand and walk and jog, oblivious to the world they tread upon.

The animals in her drawings are smart—not book smart, but intelligent in a way that comes from observing things first-hand. Belle's had nearly three-quarters of a century doing the same thing. The animals she draws are parts of her, like she supposes writers are part and parcel of every character they write or composers leave a bit of themselves in every new song. Maybe that's the cost of living with only a small part of her head in this world of early morning quiet while most of her exists in the places she creates, worlds as real to her as old Gary's boat and tackle box.

She feels the characters in her head calling to her to come back and play, but she makes no move to leave the deck. She wraps an old fleece blanket around her shoulders to ward off the worst of the morning chill. She wants a cup of coffee, but she doesn't go inside to make that either. Soon enough she'll make the first coffee of the day, then she'll go downstairs and sink her aching fingers deep into the first dough of the day and knead it with the same enthusiasm she has for the past twenty years. She'll greet the first customer in the door of her little bakery with a smile and a nod because even in this out-of-the way spot, she has customers who appreciate things made by hand, not machine. For now, it's just her and the lake and the impending dawn, and her thoughts about what comes after.

What's upset her this morning, made her feel her mortality a little more than usual, is a memorial service for someone she never knew. Jerry Garcia's ashes were scattered the day before near the Golden Gate bridge in San Francisco.

That's a good thousand miles away from where she stands on the second story deck of her place, but she feels the loss as keenly as if she was there, standing in the shadow of that famous bridge, watching as his ashes drifted into nothingness in the damp air.

Belle was never a Deadhead. She never even went to concerts much when she was a young girl. Some of her customers call her an old hippie because she's got tie-dye shirts for sale in her place right alongside loaves of bread and fancy pastries.

Was she a hippy? She never wore flowers in her hair, never puffed much less inhaled, and her love was never free. Her life, though—her life was always less than conventional. For long years she wandered from place to place, waitressing here, typing there, and always, always drawing. Vagabond, maybe that's what she was. A vagabond who set down roots too soon. She regrets never having gone to one of Garcia's concerts now that it's certain there will never been another.

She had a radio playing yesterday. She always does when she's making food. She can't get the lyrics of one of his songs out of her head. The station played it as a tribute, a salute to surviving from a man who, like the rest of the world, ultimately hadn't.

The grey in her own hair fools people into thinking she's normal, as if the only mental affliction that happens to the elderly is senility, not the imaginary-world not-thereness of creativity. Sometimes she draws a sketch on a clean paper napkin and gives it to a child along with a muffin or a cinnamon sweet roll. Her drawings paper the walls of her place, make the children giggle and adults smile indulgently.

She wonders what will happen to the insightful animals in her world after she's gone. Will they be overlooked and trampled on by the nameless feet that shuffle and walk and march through their lives? Will they survive even if she doesn't?

She hopes someone will scatter her ashes across this lake, although she imagines after she's gone, where her remains are scattered won't matter much at all to her. Did it matter to Jerry Garcia? Maybe the animals she's spent most of her life drawing will care. She wonders what the animals in her world will say about her after she's gone, much like she wonders what they talk about while she's sleeping.

Far out across the lake, the dark shape of a bird glides close to the water. Not a pelican or a crane or one of the nesting eagles that live in the little island a quarter mile offshore. She's seen this before. Her doctor says it's just a dark spot in her vision, the harbinger of approaching blindness. She knows it's something else.

Dawn is approaching, she can feel it, see the glow in the eastern sky lighting up the glassy surface of the lake. Today the birds in the high pines aren't as chatty as they have been in days past. Maybe the dark bird on the water intimidates them. It should intimidate her, frighten her, but she's come to know it with every friend she's laid to rest, every scattering of ashes and fistful of dirt she's dropped in an open grave.

Did Jerry see the dark shape, too? Did he recognize it for what it was? She thinks it only comes for creative sorts, people who live their lives with one foot in the here and now and one in another place entirely. Maybe it's the thing that lives in the closet or under the bed in the world where her animals live, the thing that scares them, which is why they never talk to her about it, even though, lord knows, they talk to her about everything else.

She stands on the deck and watches the shape glide over the lake, closer now than it's ever been before. Her hands still ache with the early spring morning cold. Her nose is numb and her breath puffs out little clouds of mist. A bench table on her deck is decorated with a whimsical mermaid fountain she found once on a trip to Baja. The fountain doesn't work anymore, but she hadn't the heart to throw it out, so now the mermaid sits on the table and stares out across the lake much like Belle does. Do the mermaid's hands get cold? Does she long to feel herself glide beneath the surface, her strong tail propelling her far away from the unforgiving solidity of land?

And still the bird glides closer.

Belle thinks she can feel the bird now too, just like she feels the dawn, and she wonders if she'll make it until the sun comes up. Will Gary find her? Or will it be a customer, someone come for fresh bread and drawings or maybe a tie-dye shirt, and instead see Belle still up on the deck wrapped in a fleece blanket, here but not really here anymore.

She should be frightened. She's had a good long life, but when she got up from her drawing table to wander out on her deck, it wasn't with the knowledge that this would be her last dawn, the last time she looked out across the lake where she'd lived the last twenty years.

"Go on without me," she says in a voice that doesn't seem to have much substance. "Don't die with me."

A raccoon sits on its haunches on the ground below and takes notice, its sharp little nose twitching in the predawn air.

The bird glides toward shore, and the raccoon whispers to her that it will miss her.

Was that why they scattered his ashes near the bridge? So that his spirit wouldn't die? Or so that the spirits he created would live on after his was gone?

"Remember me," she says to the raccoon. It disappears on a breath of air, leaving only a cold, empty expanse of grass in its wake.

Belle sits down on a wooden plank bench on her deck, the blanket tight around her shoulders. She can't see her breath in front of her face anymore. Is she still breathing? Hard to tell. Maybe she's already gone.

She thought this transition would be the worst of all, but it's painless. She's remade herself so many times in her life—child to rebellious teenager, to wandering adult, to responsible store owner, and each transition came with its own brand of pain. Now she only feels numb and detached even from the melancholy that brought her out here on the deck to watch the dawn.

The black bird swoops low over the last of the trees standing post around her shop. It circles overhead once and then drops down to perch on the deck railing.

"Time to go," it says to her in a voice much like those of the animals she drew.

It holds out a wingtip. After hesitating only a moment, she reaches out to touch it. The feathers feel soft and as unsubstantial as a cloud to her frozen, arthritic fingers. "I'm ready," she says.

It smiles at her. It can't, of course, because it's a bird and birds don't smile, not even in the drawings and tales she's told herself, but this bird smiles. "Your friends are here," it says.

She looks over her shoulder. The sun has almost crested the mountains to the east. She can see her drawing table inside. All her animal friends are there—the raccoons and squirrels and chipmunks on the table, the brown bear and fawn standing next to each other on the floor. The regal moose, his antlers held high, stands tall on the other side. It feels good to know they haven't disappeared just because she's leaving. It's better to know that they're letting her go without tears.

"I'm ready," she says again, and smiles back at the bird.

She wanted to know what would happen. After. She imagined cold and dark and nothingness, or perhaps lifting toward an ethereal light, or maybe even drifting toward the stars. She imagined fear and sorrow at leaving everything behind. She never imagined joy.

Pain and cold and the stiffness of her body disappear as she sails off the deck on the tip of the bird's wing. Golden sunlight glints off the water beneath them, and as she looks down, she can see through the water like it was glass. She feels the water as if she was swimming through the depths of her lake rather than soaring above it.

She turns to look at the tall pines on the island where the eagles roost, and she can feel them in their nest, resting content with their bellies full of fish. She hears the trees sigh at the first light of dawn and feels the shift of gravel beneath Gary Weeds' old boots as he comes tromping down the dirt road.

"Survive," she says to the first puff of breeze across the lake. "I survive."

"Yes," the bird says. "All things do. Didn't you know?"

I'd hoped, she wants to say. "I thought I'd only be a memory," she says instead.

"The world is not that wasteful." The bird turns toward the north, leaving Belle's place behind. "Look," it says as it guides her higher. "See."

She wants to gasp at the beauty of it all. Her world, but not like she's ever seen it before. Experienced it before. She only got close in her imagination, when she glimpsed a small part of the connectedness of all things and listened when her animals talked.

This isn't After. Not the way she thought of it. Everything else was Before. This is Now, and it is absolutely where she belongs.

"Show me more," she says.

And the bird did.

BRENDA CARRE

Professional writer Brenda Carre makes her fourth appearance in this magazine with this wildly original story. Nothing is out-of-bounds when Brenda tackles it. (You might remember her last story about a very whacked-out bathroom.)

Brenda has been publishing and selling fiction for a number of decades now and we have been lucky enough to have some of her stories in Fiction River *and* The Holiday Spectacular *as well. You just can't go wrong when you find a Brenda Carre story.*

For more information about her work, go to https:// brendacarre.com/

TRIGGER BILL LEARNS ABOUT THE LETTER "E"

BRENDA CARRE

The fact that a Spirit Being had the power to end his life wasn't a part of Trigger Bill's mind set that day. He'd always had this voice in his mind he called his BS warning, but that day he'd ignored it.

He'd just dropped off groceries for Port Harry's one sorry little general store and he was headed southeast to land a bigger order in Sointula, Malcom Island. He was in no way prepared when the frozen salmon hit the sloped windshield of his De Havilland DHC-2 Beaver, turning his visibility into a kaleidoscope of cracks.

Bill heard the hard thump as the big salmon hit the floor of his cockpit. Twenty minutes out of tiny Port Harry on the northern tip of Vancouver Island, and now he couldn't see for buzzards.

Bill was the only regular source of supply to remote outposts like Port Harry and he wasn't about to feel sorry for taking a huge mark up on his deliveries. Who else owned a private float plane, huh? Who had thousands of flight hours to do that?

And now this: With no real vision forward and nothing but forest and rocks a thousand feet below, Bill reckoned he had two choices: destroy his pontoons or crash into a tree, or come around and land back at Port Harry, where he'd get razzed by Tony Joseph.

Bill banked northwest with the wind jittering under his portside pontoon. He gritted his teeth and tried to peer through his fractured windshield.

Here's when the eagle entered through the passenger side of his cockpit, like a stench of really ugly *halitosis*, and disappeared again with the stiffened fish in its talons.

Bill swore at the bird. *Haliaeetus leucocephalus.*

Bald Eagles were nothing but vultures in tuxedos. Before this, Bill had never bothered to worry if he hit one mid-air. In fact, he had his eagle kill tally up on the Black Bird's port stern.

Bill's name for his beautiful aircraft.

"You have a problem, Trigger? What's the code?" said Tony Joseph, over the com, like he was talking to some stupid kid. Bill loved to stick it to 'Get Enlightened or Die' Tony more than anyone else. Tony was the one guy in the kelp-stain community of Port Harry who owned a GPS tracker and a moss-covered A-frame on a bluff facing the Pacific Ocean.

Tony's hut now held the grandiose name of 'air traffic control'. Tony didn't like educated white guys who refused to kow-tow. The twenty dead eagles painted on Black Bird's fuselage offended the Indians. The God of Eagles (whatever unpronounceable name there was for this being) was going to come for him one day. He'd seen pictures of this critter with its red and black wing-shaped thing on the top of its head called a 'crest'.

Enough with this political-correctness, sacred-animal stuff. Tomorrow, whatever Tony's people were calling themselves was going to change yet again. Just a waste of Bill's valuable time trying to keep up.

Tony said he called Bill 'Trigger Bill' because Bill was using his airplane like a weapon. That was bull and Bill knew it. He'd seen those old cowboy and Indian movies. Trigger was the name of a horse.

"Shattered windshield's my code, Tonto," Bill retorted in kind. Tony wanted to call him a horse's A, so be it.

"I'm headed back to Port H. Get an eagle anywhere near me right now, and I'm painting a grin on my prop. My code is a frozen salmon dropped by a bot, shaped like an eagle."

"A bot?" Tony said confused. "You mean a drone?"

Bill guffawed. Messing with this idiot was just fun. "You figure it out, Tonto. Your people got drones right? Am I making sense now?"

"No, you aren't. There are spirits in the sky, and I've warned you before you should respect them," said Tony right on cue.

"Maybe in the lyrics of songs, Tonto. Go find a drum circle or something. I'm losing altitude and that's my issue."

Bill took his bearings out the door as the ground came up toward him, the tops of not-so-distant towering Douglas Firs streaking below him. A stench still clogged in his throat like an oil slick over decomposed guts.

"I can't see you," said Tony.

"Then what the bleep are you good for, hey, Red Boy? I'm over forest up the butt end of nowhere. Fifty miles from Malcom Island. Nowhere near water."

Silence from Tony to the count of ten after Bill delivered his exact co-ordinates and banked again to keep the wind from blowing him out of his shoulder restraints.

"You been drinking again, Trigger?" said Tony.

"Have *you*?" Bill snapped back. Avoiding a crash was his main desire but getting needled about his former drinking problem wasn't cool. The rotary engine's whine sounded loud in his ears as he pulled back to seventy knots. All joking was over right now.

The Black Bird's gusty drone was usually one of Bill's greatest comforts. His plane was his friend. His dependable girl. He knew every inch of his Black Bird. He'd rebuilt every part of the wreck she'd once been to make her fly. Kind of like he'd done to himself after much of a life he never talked about.

"Get enlightened or get dead, Trigger," Tony reminded him for what had to be the millionth time.

Bill snapped. "Shut up, man!"

Tony snorted at that.

"Eagle is Creator's messenger. You're at war with—"

Tony's voice cut off in the middle of some unpronounceable red man gibberish.

"Yeah, quit! See if I care," Bill said. He swore at the silent com. "Make your stupid buddies stop messing with the one means of supplies you guys got! You lose me and who'll deliver *your* groceries huh? Maybe I'm right, eh? Maybe you don't like me saying this is a drone. You got tribe out here want to mess with me, huh?"

He looked closer at the silent instrument panel "No, no, no!"

The whole panel was frozen. His altimeter, his turn coordinator. Even his GPS!

Just then a squeal like a high-pitched whistle and a bang and a scrape of talons hit the top of his cockpit. It was like being hit by a hailstorm from nowhere.

Five or six flashes of brown and white swerved away from him into clearer view.

Big ones. Real eagles. *Nope it's seven,* he counted off to himself.

Seven's a power number, Trigger, said a 'Tony' voice that wasn't there anymore. Or was it? This sounded way deeper.

"Shut up in my mind!" he growled. "You and your mystical mumbo aren't real. I gotta a plane to fly, you savvy?"

No answer.

Until just now, being tucked in his sweet aircraft's soft bucket meant safety. His comfort zone and yeah, his power. Black Bird was his ship of the air and flying was like floating. The scrape of raptor claws had just taken away that safety. He was half blind, and a frontal wind buffeting in from the west was pushing him earthward.

He screamed as the eagles stooped at him fast on wing spans of more than six feet, baring talons at least two inches long, and beaks made to tear the living meat off his bones.

They like carrion best. They'll go for the salmon only once they're done with you.

That voice again. It was Tony's and it wasn't.

Seven sets of wicked golden eyes were fixed right on Bill as they dove at him in a united squadron, their wings tucked back like guided missiles.

Bill slammed his door. This was self-preservation, man!

The whole plane bucked sideways as seven eagles hit him at once. The slam on his fuselage made him yelp like they were trying to scrape away the evidence of his eagle kill. *No way. Be sensible. Bald Eagles are stupid.*

Contrary to Indian teachings, Bill had watched crows win against eagles.

You're not a crow though are you, Bill.

"Shut up whoever you are. Shut up in my mind!" he roared. His fevered brain scrolled through what he knew and did not want to know about eagles. A mature female eagle can weigh as much as fifteen pounds. Could 150 pounds of angry eagles, knock a DeHaviland Beaver out of the air?

In a high velocity kill shot, yeah, he guessed they could.

Light refracted into his eyes from his shattered windshield. No help there. Shut both doors and he'd crash. Leave them open and he'd be shredded meat on toast. He had a whole plane full of frozen salmon. He whimpered as his Black Bird bucked sideways. They were taking him down.

Sweat iced his neck as the brown-and-white enemy streaked over and around his plane in an evil funnel of rage. Chitters of hunger sounded like conversation. *No. That's impossible.*

"Tony! Come in Port Harry!" He pounded his panel.

Pounding instruments didn't work but this was his lizard brain doing it.

"Ok, ok, just get sane, man," he whispered banking to starboard. "I can do this, I can. Please, sweet Black Bird, just get me to water. Get me down and I swear I'll never shred another eagle again."

'Too late. You should have listened to Tony,' said the voice in his head.

Bill swore, pulled back on the throttle and the Black Bird lifted fast. Relief flooded his body. The thudding had stopped. He opened his door hoping to site the ocean. Levelled out as he was at maybe five hundred feet, he should be seeing the Pacific!

The air sent a menacing hiss at him through the opening. Shadows on the thickets of forest said he was banking northwest. There was no water in sight.

What he saw was the squadron of eagles below him, following his shadow like they had a commander. His shoulders itched at the way the big birds meshed like dancing fingers and a superstitious chill washed up Bill's spine from his clenched gut. His feet went numb.

There were way more than seven. There were hundreds!

No-no-no! This isn't happening.

Convocation. The silly word for a gathering of eagles came back to him now. Like they were professors preparing to graduate students or something. It was a stupid name. There were no juveniles here. The only person here was him and the Black Bird. He didn't need teaching.

Ah, but what if they think you do, Trigger?

This Voice was way bigger than Tony.

"This isn't happening. Eagles are stu—oh god!" he said as he felt something behind him.

A screek like an un-oiled hinge sounded behind him, itching his spine bones sending chills right up into Bill's brainpan.

Bill jerked around, as his throat iced up on a gut-pinching scream. He let go of the controls in one nerveless motion.

Before this minute, you could give Bill a nice painting of an actual living heron or a hummingbird. Not supernatural or nothing. Not life threatening. Right up until this minute, he'd actually told Tony that Indian art was a bunch of fake stuff. Mumbo jumbo.

Yet here and now was the huge serrated beak of a myth looming over him. A deadly weapon long enough to tear him up and swallow him in one gulp. Beneath that beak was a body not unlike a Pterodactyl's that flowed over Bill's cargo: those ironic cases of frozen Sockeye-on-Ice that would no longer arrive anywhere in human hands.

Bill looked into a Spirit Eagles blood-rimmed eyes.

Creator's Messenger filled the whole tailpiece from side to side with his giant wings wrapping his back. Justice looked at Bill out of the vaults of outer space and devoured his wits from the inside out.

Up here in the sky, where some pilot said you can see the face of God, up and down didn't exist anymore. The saw-buzz of the engine faded. An elder god sat in his plane, and Trigger Bill understood in one terrible heartbeat that death was here.

You see how small you are now?

Bill nodded. Weirdly enough, he wasn't afraid anymore.

He felt weightless. This was inevitable in its own strange kind of poetical humour.

He was going to crash. The squadron of eagles did this. Acting as one in the name of Creator. Tony was right. Get enlightened or die.

Whole plane load of supplies. Who and what were these all going to feed?

Yet again there was humor in the mystical blackness of Spirit Eagle's blood-rimmed gaze.

As one mesmerized Bill stared into something so big it was impossible to fathom in the ocean of air. That squadron convocating down there were waiting on enough frozen salmon to feed their eaglets for months.

It would be him first though.

"I'm sorry," he said, and he meant it.

"Trigger? What's going on? I lost you…"

"I got a friend of yours here, Tony," said Bill without turning back to his instruments. "He's big and he's real and you were right."

"Yeah, I see him, man," said Tony, in a voice hushed in wonder. "Your cam came back on. Let me help you, I can…"

"Too late, Tony. It doesn't matter anymore. You were right. I was wrong. First, the eagles take you out. Not because you're bad, but because you're stupid," Bill said.

He stood up as the Black Bird went into a nose dive. There was more in the Spirit Eagle's stare than revenge.

"He's giving you transformation, Bill," Tony's voice came from the com as the fuselage dropped away from Bill.

His own spirit watched it go like a spiralling bird into a shatter of former beliefs.

He was alone now, rising on a thermal. Free and it was familiar. The talons of eagles had scraped ignorance from his awareness.

For what felt like the first time in existence Bill gave a shout of delighted laughter. Eagles and enlightenment both begin with E. I'm done! Now, that was an epic end, wasn't it huh? I have to say the only thing that I did worth anything was build the Black Bird. I just wish I'd had time to tell Tony I'm sorry," he said to the sky.

"No need, brother, you might tell him yourself."

"Yeah? You'll let me go back?" he said.

"Your choice. You could choose to rest?"

"I'm not a resting kind of guy, you should know that by now. But if you let me go back, could I finally be done with the stupid, please?" he said to Creator.

Laughter filled Bill and it was fine. The air was bright with newness around him.

"Ah, Traveler. By now you should know better than this. Have you learned nothing as yet about me."

"Yeah, I do know better. Next time I'll rest ok. This time I want to be a better Bill. How about we start with B and maybe rich and handsome or something?"

Amusement met him. "There is still the matter of restitution for all of those eagles you murdered."

"Of course," Bill said reaching his phantom arms to the bright of the sky. "Just show me how and I'll do better."

Tony Joseph looked up from his carving to the sound of wings as a raven alighted upon the padded shoulder of his plaid work jacket. The raven's talons were gentle, his bill was hooked. His feathers were soft and cold as if he'd flown at height and his eyes were bright with mischief.

"I'm sorry, Tony," clicked the Black Bird. "Feed me."

ROBERT JESCHONEK

ROBERT JESCHONEK *continues his streak of being in every issue of this magazine.*

The reason Robert has this streak is simply because his stories are often just perfect Pulphouse stories. Take this story, for example.

Robert's stories have appeared in dozens of magazines and he has published dozens of novels as well. He has even worked for DC Comics and early in his career sold me a couple stories when I was editing for Star Trek at Pocket Books. He seems to be able to do it all. And to see all the amazing projects he has done, check out his website at https://www.robertjeschonek.com/

UNTRUSTWORTHY

ROBERT JESCHONEK

One minute, I'm standing in a frozen ballroom, shivering as a giant spider-thing made of ice—a creature with the face of a little girl—skitters toward me. The spider screams and breathes fire from its lips, charging so fast there's no way I can outrun it.

The next minute, I'm back in the bathroom of a boarded-up roadhouse in the middle of a hot summer's night in rural Louisiana, flicking a little black spider off my right hand.

Bending over the filthy sink, I splash cold water on my face, trying to snap myself all the way back to reality (whatever *that* is, these days). Then I make the mistake of looking at myself in the cracked mirror, and I cringe. Even in the dim moonglow streaming between the rickety wall boards, I look awful.

Without makeup, without sleep, the creases in my dark brown face seem deeper than ever. My dark eyes are blood-shot, double bags sagging under them with the weight of worry and exhaustion. My salt-and-pepper hair, hastily hacked short on the road, is coming in frizzy and wild. It's hard to believe I was considered quite attractive all the way through my thirties.

Now I'm a haggard fugitive in my mid-forties who looks like hell warmed over.

That's what thirty-two days on the road, on the run, will do for you. That and a lifetime spent carrying other people's darkest secrets in my head.

I'm a specialist—what they call a *Secretive.* Paperwork can be stolen, computers can be hacked, but a properly trained human mind with photographic tendencies can store secrets in perfect security. God help you if the system breaks down, though; then you've got two choices: get killed or go on the run. *Then* get killed.

I've chosen option two. The fact is, there's someone I badly want to see before I get to the *killed* part.

I brush my teeth with soap residue from the ancient bulb dispenser and my index finger, then straighten my T-shirt as best I can. I'm glad it's black, so the blood spatter doesn't show up so much. My blue jeans are another story, but those are the breaks.

I have to keep moving. I needed five minutes to get my shit together here after the fight in the parking lot, but I can't afford to piss around any longer. Gotta get to where I'm going before *they* kill me...where I'm going and who I'm going to see there.

"Come on, Ashanti Virago." I take a deep breath and let it out slowly, gathering my strength. Gotta face it, gotta get out there, can't be a coward.

I flick the hook latch and turn the doorknob. Ease open the bathroom door and step outside like I own the world.

Then I walk across the parking lot, stepping over and around the bodies as if they were nothing but dog turds or speed bumps. One, two, three, five.

Six. Every last one of them beaten into unconsciousness by my hands or feet or both.

Make that seven. One last body's on the hood of my stolen silver Honda Accord. He flops off easily enough when I back up suddenly, though.

Then I bolt off into the night, leaving all those bodies like anonymous humps in the moonlit shadows of the Spanish moss-laden trees.

HALF AN HOUR UP THE ROAD, my breath turns to chilly mist, and I feel myself going away again. I barely have time to jerk the car off the road and throw it out of gear before I'm gone.

This time, I'm back in that vast, icy ballroom, feeling the freeze right through to my bones—though my shivers aren't just from the cold.

As many times as I've been to this Memory Mansion of mine, I'm still not sure what to expect next. Will it be a giant spider with a little girl's face, or something else?

I have no idea, and I'm the one who *built* this place.

"Hello?" My voice echoes in the huge chamber, but no one answers. I walk in a slow circle, gazing at the glittering ice pillars and chandeliers.

This was always my special hideaway, the core of my talent...the key to the secrets I kept.

I was a Secretive in title and practice alike, brought in to store clients' greatest secrets—the code to a vault, a password to a Swiss bank account, the location of a dead body—and keep them safe from those who covet them. I also had to make them available to their owners at a moment's notice, which is where the Memory Mansion comes in.

It was here, as required by my employer, that I constructed mnemonic devices pointing the way to each memory, giving me easy access to the voluminous library of secrets in my head. Need to recall the hiding place of some stock certificates? I just find the ice sculpture of a ticker tape machine, give it a tap, and the answer blazes into my mind like the morning sun.

At least that was how it worked before the Alzheimer's disease started. Now my mansion isn't predictable at all.

And I've never needed it more in my *life* than I do now. I've never needed to *find* someone more than I do now. At least the secrets to lead me to her, gathered during my time on the run, are still in there—though the mnemonic constructs to access them are no longer easy to control. My subconscious seems to bring them up when I need them, but I can't get all the information I need with a simple tap.

Even as I think that, a giant cobra grows out of the icy floor before me. It flickers its crystalline tongue as its head bobs from side to side, staring.

Hsssssssss.

The creature does *not* look friendly, but I need to try anyway. "Where is Serendipity Virago?"

Hsssssssss.

Just as the cobra lunges, I dart out of the way. As I sprint, I hear it slithering after me, its massive body rustling over the ice rink floor.

I'm almost to the grand staircase when something else thrusts up from the ice in front of me. This time, it's an alligator, its long, jagged maw opening wide as I slide straight for it, unable to stop.

That's when I see the same little girl's face in the gator's crystalline throat, glaring at me. She opens her mouth, too, and I see it's lined with teeth like a shark's, jutting in concentric rings.

I'm just about to plunge inside when I snap back to the real world. The Memory Mansion is gone; I'm sitting in the front seat of the Honda again, safe and sound.

I wipe the drool from my chin with the back of my hand, then grab the paper map on the seat beside me. I unfold it to the index on the back and scan the list of towns and cities.

Cobra. Gator.

When I see a name that fits the latest clues in my Memory Mansion, my hands start to shake. I find the matching location on the map, trace the route, and pull back onto the road. Then I stomp on the gas.

Somewhere out there in the darkness of the bayou, the town of Cobra's Gate awaits.

"Mother, you're fired."

This is what it's like to develop Alzheimer's after a lifetime of having a flawless photographic memory and working as a Secretive. One day, you're sitting at a café on the Isle of Capri in Italy, enjoying an espresso…

…and your son, Marcus, sits down across from you and tells you you're a dead woman.

Actually, he says you're "fired," and he's not your *biological* son—but things are a little different in Sub Rosa, the international organization I work for. *Used* to work for.

"You made The Mistake." Marcus shook his head sadly as he said it. The bright Italian sun glinted on his dark brown skin. "The dead client's wife wanted the combination to his wine cellar, and you got it wrong. Entering the wrong code tripped the security override and flash-fried millions of Euros worth of vintage wines in seconds."

What kind of employer kills you if you make a single mistake? Especially if that mistake comes after a lifetime of sterling service as an *elite* Secretive, one of the *best* in the world?

Sub Rosa, that's who. The same lovely group that strips you of any biological children you might have when they discover your potential, sending them away to limit distractions from your work…then eventually assigns other "children" (in their twenties) for you to mentor. Marcus falls in that category.

"Thanks for everything, Mother, I really—"

I didn't let him finish his sentence that day. It was clear what would happen if I didn't take immediate action.

Leaping up, I drove the table at his chin, stunning him, knocking him backward. Then I scooped up a butter knife and drove it into his rib cage with practiced ease, hitting just the right spot to disable but not kill him. I might have forgotten a few things lately, but I damn well remembered my martial arts training well enough to do the job.

Marcus howled in pain. Blood seeping from his wound, he tried to fight back, but I wouldn't give him an inch.

"Stop!" he shouted. "They'll just send someone else!"

Teeth clenched, running on instinct, I twisted the blade.

"You can't hide! You have no secrets from them!"

One more twist of the blade in his bloody chest, and I let go. "That's where you're wrong. I have a *few* secrets."

Marcus's eyes glazed over. Was he in Audit mode or just going into shock? "A few secrets? I don't know...don't remember..."

"But only one of them truly matters." I spat on my "son" and jumped up. The *polizia* would be there any minute, and Sub Rosa would not be far behind. "One secret is all *anyone* needs in this life."

THE SUN RISES as I roll into the town of Cobra's Gate. Everything looks quiet and still, but I know it won't last. In situations like this, Sub Rosa pools its Secretives to track the runner; you might be surprised how easy your movements are to predict based on the secrets from multiple sources intersecting with your life.

In other words, the name of the game here is get-in-and-get-out-*fast*.

You might not think that would be a problem. After all, Cobra's Gate is a tiny town. But the person I'm looking for—

the one who'll lead me to my final target—doesn't *want* to be found, at least by Sub Rosa's death squads.

As I drive down the main road through town, I watch the trailers and shacks for some kind of telltale marking or sign. It's a challenge. Escapees like her don't usually put out a red-and-white-striped barber pole to show you where they are.

But that's good, right? Because when you finally find her, you'll know she's the real deal and hasn't been compromised. You *hope.*

Suddenly, a skunk waddles onto the road, and I slam on the brakes. As I watch and smell it pass, I close my eyes, triggering a visit to the Memory Mansion the way I used to do before the involuntary zoning-out started.

I breathe in hot, humid air and breathe out icy mist. Just like that, I'm back in the frozen ballroom.

Before some hostile beast can rise up from the ice and attack, I focus my thoughts on harnessing the power of this place. I feel it resisting, pushing back as I fight to sink my fingers into it and make it work to my liking.

Just then, I hear a muffled growl and see the ice ripple a few feet away. Might be a clue in the form of a raging monstrosity...or might not.

But that's not a game I want to play right now. Pouring on the juice, I exert my will with all the strength I can muster.

And the growling stops. Instead of a creature, the floor extrudes a cube of ice as tall as I am.

When I touch the cube, its outer layers melt away, revealing a shape like a sculpture within a slab of marble. A ray of light streams in from one of the high windows, making the object glitter and gleam. I take a good look at it.

Then I pour on the willpower again and manage to snap myself back to reality on the road, with no sign of the skunk in sight (though the stench of it lingers).

I let out my breath and relax my tight grip on the wheel. For once, the Memory Mansion worked the way it was supposed to; I recognized the object in my vision, and it opened a secret like an oyster in my mind when I touched it.

The object was a *tire*. A tire with a big smiley face on the tread.

Jo's Tires doesn't look like much. It's just a rusty corrugated metal building with three garage bays and tires piled everywhere. If you saw it along the road on your way somewhere, you'd forget it as soon as you passed and never think of it again.

Unless you were me. Unless you knew it was part of an underground railroad for Secretives whose time is about to run out.

"Hello?" I get out of my car and walk toward one of the bays. "Is anyone here?"

No answer, though I see a light glowing dimly in a corner of the garage.

Carefully, I continue forward. "I'm a Secretive, and I understand you might be able to help me."

Looking over my shoulder, I worry that Sub Rosa will appear at any moment. I hate to think they'll ruin this place for others who need it, though I guess that's why it's—

Suddenly, I hear running footsteps and turn to see the

source. Before I can get a good look, the woman in gray coveralls sprinting toward me takes a swing at my skull with a tire iron.

I duck back away from the swing and leap into action, unleashing a vicious kick at my attacker. The kick catches her in the gut, knocking the wind out of her, and I follow it with a jab to her throat.

She reels, nearly dropping the tire iron…but it's a feint, and she comes up swinging. This time, the iron makes contact, clipping my left side hard enough to launch a bloom of pain there.

Pissed, I erupt in a flurry of moves—spinning, kicking, lunging, punching, hacking. They're some of the same moves I used to knock out seven men at the boarded-up roadhouse last night…but they don't work as well this time. The coveralled woman loses her weapon and reacts with rapid-fire moves of her own—a punishing series of blows and kicks that land more often than not.

I probe for a weakness but don't find any. She deflects everything I throw her way and responds with double the force at double the speed.

Finally, I put together a combination that has an impact, hammering her with a barrage of strikes to the upper body that are mostly just feints before a whirlwind kick to her left leg.

She goes down on that knee, and I take her the rest of the way with a single rabbit punch to the chin. Unfortunately, she takes me down with her, latching onto my sleeve and yanking me off my feet.

Next thing I know, we're on the gravel, four feet apart

with blood on our faces. It's only then that I get a good look at her—pale skin, round face, green eyes, black hair in a ponytail with a sprinkling of gray. My guess is she's Japanese or Korean, though I'm not sure.

And she's grinning.

"Good fight," she says. "Now what's the good *word*, hon?"

She wants the password that proves I'm with the underground, and I don't blame her. I think hard; a rebel Secretive gave it to me early in my journey. I locked it away in my mind…but it eludes me now, when I need it the most.

It's in there somewhere, though, I *know* it. I think back to the Memory Mansion three visits ago, and the thing that ran me down in the icy ballroom. The thought of that creature has a gravity that attracts me.

I almost say "spider" but then I catch myself. Not "tarantula," either. Something that *sounds* like it.

"Tarantella," I tell her.

"Good to meet you." She gets up on her elbow and reaches over to shake hands. "There's always help here for condemned Secretives."

"Thank you." I push myself up to a sitting position. "I'm looking for someone."

"Who's that?" asks the woman.

"My daughter," I tell her. "My baby girl."

"When was the last time you saw her?"

I wipe blood from my face with the back of my arm. "Twenty-three years ago. And God help me, I can barely remember her."

THE WOMAN, whose name is Maginot, offers me tea in a chipped white cup. Sitting on a dirty stool in one of the bays, I sip the steaming brew, relishing the hot liquid as it slides down my throat.

"How long you been on the run, Ashanti?" Maginot produces a flask and offers it to me.

I can't afford the slightest buzz to dull my senses, so I wave it off. "Thirty-three days now. All the way from Capri, Italy."

"On your own?" Maginot looks impressed. "That might be a record, hon." She sips from the flask. "So how did you find out about me?"

I scowl at the ripples in my tea. "Followed the trail through my Memory Mansion…one secret linked to another."

Maginot leans against an oil-soaked workbench, tilts her head to one side, and stares. "But where did you *first* learn about me? And the railroad?"

"Someone told me on my travels, but I don't remember who." I point at my right temple and shrug. "My memory's failing."

Maginot nods. "But not your *fighting* skills, obviously." Another swig from the flask, and she returns it to the pocket of her coveralls. "And now you want to *kill* your *child*, is that right?"

My hands clench around the cup, nearly breaking it. "I want to *find* her!"

"Same difference," says Maginot. "You know Sub Rosa's closing in, don't you? They *always* find runaways. What do you think they'll do to *her* when they catch up?"

My heart thunders in my ears as I glare at the thought of it. "I'll kill every one of them who tries."

Maginot shakes her head and pushes away from the work-bench. Grabbing a tire from a rustbucket Chevy on the lift, she throws it on a balancing rack and sets to work on it.

"This is the part where I talk sense into you," she says. "How old was your child when they took her away?"

"Three years." It's a guess. As often as I see her face in my Memory Mansion, I don't always remember much else about her.

"Assuming she's still alive..." Maginot pauses and shoots me a meaningful look. "Assuming that, she is *twenty-six years old* now. She might not even *remember* you." Again, she pauses. "So ask yourself, what do you hope to accomplish by showing up in her life all of a sudden?"

"I just..." My heart's racing. "I just want to *see* her before I...before they..."

"But is that *fair* to her? Is it any more fair than them taking her away from you in the first place?"

I get up from the stool and put the teacup down in my place. Something bends inside me, straining to give way—then straightens and stiffens again. "Are you going to help me or not?"

Maginot turns on the spin-balancer and lets it run for a moment. When numbers appear on the digital readout screen, she switches it off. "No one can truly *help* you," she says sadly. "But yes, I will do what I can to see that you reach your goal."

Relief floods through me. "Oh, thank God." My next step, I'm ashamed to say, might have been to torture her for the answers I require. "How can I ever thank you enough?"

"Shhhhh." She holds a finger to her lips. "It will be our secret, Ashanti."

JUST AS SUB ROSA uses its network of Secretives to pool their secret knowledge and track down who or what they desire, Maginot relies on a network of *ex*-Secretives. She communicates with them via secure mobile apps, tapping their collective insight in search of revelatory fractal patterns.

It's a miraculous system, and it gets results fast. Within an hour, we're in her black extended-cab pickup headed northwest, racing toward the city of Shreveport.

I'm so full of anticipation, I'm ready to burst. "Tell me about her. What's she like these days?"

Maginot's face is aloof behind her aviator sunglasses. She steers the truck with two fingers at the bottom of the wheel, texting constantly with her free hand between us. She texts so much and so energetically, I wonder how she even keeps control of the pickup. "What did you name her back in the day?"

It's on the tip of my tongue. "Why? What's her name now?"

"Married name is Delacroix."

My eyes light up. "Married? Do I have grandkids?"

Her phone warbles then, and she spots a fresh text on the screen. "Not sure yet." Then, she looks up at the rearview mirror and drops three consecutive F-bombs with a vengeance.

"What is it?"

"Hold on." She throws the pickup into higher gear. "We've got a tail."

Looking back, I see a white BMW SUV hurtling toward us, gleaming in the afternoon sun. I feel the pickup swerve and accelerate, bolting away from our pursuers.

Then my breath turns to mist, and I'm standing in the Memory Mansion again.

"No!" There's no reason for me to be here now. I focus hard, trying to regain control and jump back to the car chase.

But the icy floor just ripples and gives rise to an unexpected form. This time, it's not a giant spider, cobra, gator, or even a smiley-faced tire.

It's a *little girl*. More than that, it's *my* little girl. The one whose face inhabits so many of the constructs in this icy place.

When she speaks, her high-pitched voice echoes through the cavernous ballroom, pronouncing two words with absolute clarity:

Don't stop.

Then *whoosh*, I'm back in the cabin of Maginot's pickup, and the back window's blown out, and she's shooting over her shoulder.

The BMW behind us suddenly veers left and crashes into a speeding tractor trailer that blasts it into bits.

Maginot looks over at me. "You can't control it anymore, can you? The Memory Mansion?"

I don't answer the question. "How much farther?"

"Not far." Maginot grabs her phone and thumb-types a text like a lunatic. "But we've got another tail. We should probably abort."

I glance back. "But we're so *close*."

"I thought you'd say that." Again, Maginot rattles off a text. "That's why I've arranged for some people to meet us."

"People?"

"A few friends, that's all." Maginot stomps on the accelerator, and the pickup surges forward. "*Dependable* friends."

As much as my memory's been failing, I still get flashes of the old days now and then. I remember holding my baby sometimes, and the smell of her head. I remember changing her diaper and feeding her from a bottle. I remember her crying, and me crying too, being a single mother with no one to help me.

Sometimes, I even remember the day they came for me and took her. I remember fighting and being beaten. The last time I saw her howling face as they dragged her away.

Sometimes, it feels so real that I can't help screaming. The pain is so fresh, it's like they stole her only yesterday.

And sometimes, it seems so long ago, and the memories are so incomplete, it's as if it never happened at all. As if the Alzheimer's is taking even *that* from me.

The certainty of my own remembered pain.

Thank God no one's walking or riding a bike on the street when we barrel into the trailer park outside Shreveport.

Pretty sure Maginot would mow them down, she's driving so fast.

Not that slowing down is a good option. The sooner we get to my daughter (and grandkids?), the better chance we stand of keeping them safe from Sub Rosa.

"Which trailer is it?" I gape at each one as we fly past, as if I might recognize the daughter I haven't seen since the age of three.

"Dead ahead." Somehow, Maginot's still calm and collected, driving with the same two fingers and texting nonstop. "Good news. My gals are here already. They're all ex-Secretives I've helped in the past, so you know they've got no love for Sub Rosa."

She slams on the brakes and spins to a stop in front of a dumpy trailer with dirty white siding and decaying black trim. Another pickup and two cars are already parked in front of it, angled like barricades.

I'm out before Maginot and looking around frantically. I see six women hunkered behind the cars, all carrying assault rifles, but no twenty-six-year-old African American woman who used to go by the birth name…the birth name…

It rushes back to me, and I shout it at the trailer. "*Serendipity!* Are you in there, Serendipity?"

"Ready, people!" Maginot might only carry a tire iron, but she acts like she's in charge of the gun-toting crew. "Let's give those bastards a welcome *they'll* never forget!"

"Serendipity!" Even as my allies prepare for battle, I run to the side door of the trailer, determined to rescue my flesh and blood. "Come on out, baby!"

I try the handle of the door, but it doesn't budge. "Open

up, honey!" I pound my fist on the weathered panel. "It's Mama! Open the door!"

Just then, I hear one of the defenders shout a question. "Where the hell *are* they? I thought they were right behind you!"

"I don't know," says Maginot. "They *were* close behind."

Suddenly, the door handle moves, and the door swings inward. It takes me by surprise, and I let go, tumbling back into the stubby, unkempt yard.

That's when someone finally emerges from the trailer—but not whom I expect. I see no twenty-something black woman or beautiful grandchildren running out of there.

Instead, men in gleaming black helmets and body armor storm out of the place brandishing fully automatic rifles. They bolt down the single step from the threshold, coming up behind Maginot and her defenders, who are all looking the other way, expecting oncoming vehicles full of armed Sub Rosa killers.

It's like a shooting gallery. Before any of those women can turn and even think about getting off a shot, the armored men open fire on them. Rifles chatter, staccato bursts crackling with measured force—and the bodies of six women drop as one.

At that exact moment, against my wishes and will, my breath turns to mist in the midday Shreveport heat. The Memory Mansion takes hold again, snapping me back to the ballroom of icy desolation.

And I am faced with the ice sculpture figure of my daughter once more.

"Serendipity?" I shake my head hard, but it's full of fuzz. "I can't…I have to get back. My friends, they're…oh my God, they're…"

Bring it on in, Mommy. The ice child spreads her arms wide and waggles her fingers, inviting a hug. *Bring it on in right here.*

The thought of embracing that icy form makes me shiver…but she sounds just like my daughter. Her voice is exactly the same.

I think. Frowning, I reach deep for the memory of it, but it slips away like a fish wriggling through a murky pool.

I'm right here for you, Mommy. The ice girl glides toward me, arms still spread wide open. *I love you with all my heart and soul.*

"What's *happening?*" Panic gathers and churns in my belly. Something, *everything's* wrong, and I've known all along but only now am I able to glimpse the actual truth of it. Only now am I aware of the vaguest outline of the single most important secret that's been lurking within me all this time.

Thank you, Mommy! Serendipity continues her graceful approach. *Thank you for finding me again!*

"Again?"

Suddenly, I'm back on the ground at the trailer park, sobbing as I stare at the bloody corpses of Maginot and her friends.

Two men are talking. The barrels of their rifles dangle on either side of me.

"…the tenth cell of traitors she's rooted out so far," says the man on my right. "We ought to have a party for her or something. A cake at least."

"Why bother?" The man on my left laughs. "She'd only *forget* it in the morning!"

The man on my right chuckles, too. "That leaky memory of hers is a real *gift*, isn't it? *Ten* times she's run off in search of her kid, and it always ends up like *this*, and she *forgets* it ever happened."

"Which she blames on her 'Alzheimer's,'" says the man on my left. "As diagnosed by a doctor working for Sub Rosa, of course."

"It's a genius setup." The man on my right snaps his fingers. "Ashanti here doesn't remember shit, except she wants her little girl back. All it takes is Sub Rosa nudging her in the right direction here and there, exposing her to the right suspected Secretive subversives, and she picks up the right clues to lead us to the underground's cells and safehouses."

"Friggin' brilliant, if you ask me." The man on my left crouches beside me, smiling. "That brain damage from the accident really paid off, didn't it?"

I can't stop sobbing as I listen, and then my breath turns to frost again. This time, back in the mansion, the ice child is only inches away, smiling.

Will you always save me, Mommy? Serendipity stares up at me with ice crystal eyes. *Will you always protect your baby girl?*

"What accident?" I back away from her. "*Tell me what accident!*"

Mommy? Mommy, don't go!

Then I'm back in the steaming heat with the armored man smiling at me.

"That first time, you almost pulled it off, didn't you?" he says. "It was *your* idea back then, going AWOL to rescue your kid, and you went for it. Found a guide through the web of secrets…got her to lead you to your kid in a Sub Rosa lock-house…broke her out and ran for the hills."

I gape at him like he's speaking a language I don't understand. My mouth hangs open, pregnant with screams, but nothing comes out of it.

"Too bad you flipped the getaway car when they ran you down. But hey, things have a way of working out."

The man on my right crouches, too, and reaches over to pat my shoulder. "Your kid died, but at least the brain damage led to a second career."

Finally, the screams break free. I feel myself falling into endless clouds of frigid mist.

Only to be caught by my baby in the mansion.

Mama, she says. *I've got you. Don't worry, Mama.*

Her arms are cold around me. My tears freeze as they fall, pattering to the floor as tiny ice cubes.

At least we still have each other, Mama, she says. *Isn't that enough for you?*

I look at her crystalline face, glittering in the sunlight streaming in through the icy walls. I find a memory of her, the real her, a teenager then, sitting beside me in the car as we ran away, holding my hand tight. Blood pumping. Just before.

Just before.

We were almost free, almost safe. I remember feeling something I haven't felt since…or have I? Would I even remember what it felt like if I felt it again?

Then I wrap my arms around her and hold her tight. My skin sticks to the ice of her body, it's so cold.

"It's enough." What was her name again? "It *has* to be enough."

Then I remember, as the two of us turn slowly on the rink of the floor, propelled in little circles by the force of our hug. I remember what that feeling was, because I feel it again. It turns out it's not such a big secret after all.

Happiness. That's what it was.

DAYLE A. DERMATIS

Dayle A. Dermatis is the author or coauthor of many novels (including snarky urban fantasies Ghosted, Shaded, and Spectered) and more than a hundred short stories in multiple genres appearing in such venues as Fiction River, Alfred Hitchcock's Mystery Magazine, and DAW Books.

In this wonderful story, Dayle gives us a really twisted and fun glimpse into a world long gone. For a full rundown of all her books, check out www.dayledermatis.com

HELL'S BELLES

DAYLE A. DERMATIS

R ich Southern women have had common sense bred right out of them. What's replaced it is an overdeveloped obsession with ritual and decorum, and a fear of looking bad in society.

Which isn't a terrible thing, because it keeps me in a job.

I'm the most sought-after debutante trainer in the South. Mothers may think their daughters are perfect, having had exquisite training at exclusive finishing schools, but those girls have nothing if they haven't had my attention. And every socialite south of the Mason-Dixon Line knows it.

I had one woman faint dead away when I told her I was already booked for the season. When she came to, she offered me three times my fee (which is already considerable). I agreed only with the stipulation that she not tell my first client that I was training two girls that season.

Of course the first thing she did was blab. But it violated

her contract—it was right there, in black and white, and she'd signed it—so in the end it all worked out just fine for me.

This season, I would be responsible for the social graces and elegance of one Miss Alexandria (never to be called Alex) Pointer-Ashe. The Pointer-Ashe home was pure Antebellum, with fat white columns framing the front door. On the side porch, we would no doubt sip mint juleps while Mrs. Margaret Pointer-Ashe and her daughter signed my contract.

I handed my card to the meek-looking maid who answered the door. "Lilith D'Enfer to see Mrs. Pointer-Ashe and Miss Alexandria Pointer-Ashe," I said as she glanced at the red-scripted embossed letters. "They're expecting me."

"Please wait here, Miss D'Enfer," she said in a soft accent, leading me into a parlor tastefully decorated with floral prints and dark furniture. The huge vase of magnolia blossoms was a allergist's nightmare.

She had barely walked out when the altercation across the hall started.

"Mo-_ther_!" a voice shrieked. "I will _not_ have a curfew! You and your curfew can go to _hell_!" The final words were emphasized by the sound of shattering glass.

I couldn't help but smile. I had a real Scarlett O'Hara on my hands. Perfect.

WE SAT out on the back veranda, overlooking a lawn that looked like a golf course. A sweating pitcher of mint julep, fresh mint floating on top, and glasses were brought out by another maid. I got the important detail right, anyway.

Mrs. Pointer-Ashe frowned ever so slightly (it would be impolite to be too obvious) as she delicately paged through the substantial contract, which was longer than she no doubt had expected. She'd want her husband to look it over and tell her if it was all right for her to sign, but he'd be angry that she bothered him with it. The father's job in these situations is to pay for the coming-out ball and puff up like a proud pheasant when his daughter is presented, not be distracted with trivial details.

Mrs. Pointer-Ashe had very big blonde hair and a figure (and mannerisms) that bespoke diet pills. Her lips and nails were fuchsia, with a hint of bleed around her mouth where lines were grooving her skin. She was probably already scheduled for a facelift—she'd time it so she'd be healed just in time for the coming-out ball. ("How young she looks," she'd want the guests to say. "Can you believe her daughter is the deb? They look like sisters.")

In contrast, Alexandria was naturally slim and, although her makeup was artfully applied, it was nearly invisible. The sheer gloss that glistened on her luscious young lips probably drove boys to steal their mother's cold cream and lock themselves in their bedrooms with their computers targeted to a porn site—and she knew it. Her green eyes were heavy-lidded, like Paris Hilton's, but I could tell it was an affectation: she wasn't languid and hadn't lost all of her common sense yet.

Then again, the whole point of a debutante ball was to snag the richest, most prominent, handsome eligible young bachelor available. Only <u>then</u> could she relax, just a little.

The nuptials would be postponed, of course, until after the

deb graduated from a suitable college (Wellesley, perhaps, or U. Miss.). In this day and age, an education was considered of social import. If one was expected to serve on the board of directors of various charities, one at least needed sorority president experience.

"What does the contract say?" Alexandria asked. Her mother hadn't thought of that, was still squinting helplessly at the fine print on the first page.

"It highlights what I'll do for you and what I expect of you in return," I said. "For your part, you will refrain from drinking and smoking." I saw her eyes flicker towards the mint julep in her glass. Apparently this habit didn't bother her mother. I continued.

"I require abstinence in all areas, actually." I phrased it delicately so Mrs. Pointer-Ashe wouldn't notice, although Alexandria knew exactly what I meant, because I saw the flare of her nostrils. I estimated she'd been having sex regularly since she was fifteen. "I will not tolerate tardiness. Your full attention and participation during our sessions is of the utmost imperative.

"In return, I will teach you the etiquette for any situation you could ever encounter. You may think you know etiquette now, but I will prove you wrong and teach you what you lack. After I'm through with you, you will be able to comport yourself correctly and effortlessly with the Queen of England, the Emperor of China, the President of these fine United States, or the Lord God himself. I will ensure, finally, that your coming out will be a night you will never, ever forget."

It wasn't a promise I made lightly, and it wasn't one I'd ever broken.

Alexandria's jade-green eyes lit up at my final statement. That was the most important thing to her, of course. Later, fitting in to society would become an obsession, but now, her deb ball was the focus of her life.

It was often more important than one's own wedding. The deb ball highlighted just the girl. Even though at a wedding, the bride was the focus of attention, with the groom being more someone to inspect for adequacy, the groom was still <u>there</u>, standing next to her, taking up a tiny corner of the spotlight.

In comparison, the escorts at a deb ball were pretty much invisible.

"It has to be perfect," she said. "<u>Perfect</u>."

"In the end, that will be up to you," I said.

Of course, she was entirely incapable of fulfilling the terms of the contract.

Contrary to what everyone thinks, the mothers don't choose me. I choose the deb each season. I'm looking for someone very specific. As I said before, the Scarlett O'Hara type. Spoiled, strong-willed, prone to tantrums and bucking authority. She'll follow societal commands—at least, on the outside, and fool everybody in the process—but she won't follow parental rules, or, often, mine.

I'd laid out a full, formal dinner service on their dining room table, which was large enough on which to stage the Battle of Gettysburg. When Alexandria saw the table setting, she heaved an elaborate sigh.

"I've already <u>done</u> this," she said, her voice almost slipping into full whine mode. "At Miss Miranda's Sch—"

I slammed my hand down on the table, causing the china, and Alexandria, to jump. The china clattered; Alexandria stayed silent, although her skin may have paled every so slightly.

"Miss Miranda," I said, "is a two-bit hack. Her methods are outdated, her knowledge is several years behind the times, and she graduates every deb who goes through her school, cultivated or not, because she's terrified of being ostracized by their families. Think about that, Miss Pointer-Ashe—are you sure you received accolades because you really learned everything you needed to know?"

She pressed her lips together, but I could tell I'd struck a nerve.

After our session, she would immediately is run out and tell everyone about Miss Miranda's. By being the first, she would thus negate the fact that her own education there might have been inadequate.

I rang a small silver bell, indicating that we should sit.

I corrected the placement of her napkin across her knees, questioned her deportment with the finger bowl, and pointed out any number of miniscule errors to catch her off guard. Then I quizzed her: tell me what every utensil is used for.

She was good, but when she got a particular cocktail fork, she hesitated. Of course she did. She'd never seen it before.

Alexandria frowned, turning the fork between her fingers. It was shaped like a small pitchfork.

"An...oyster fork?" she ventured.

"No." I picked up my own oyster fork and displayed it.

She pondered it for a while longer, and then threw it on the table.

"This is <u>so</u> <u>stupid</u>!" she said. "I <u>hate</u> this! I will never, ever have to use all of this crap at a dinner!" She scraped her chair back, tossed her napkin on the floor in an even greater display of pique, and stomped towards the door.

"It is a fork," I said, "for eating hearts."

She turned, slowly, half-hypnotized by the sound of my voice, even though I hadn't raised it or changed the emotion in it.

"You're joking," she said.

"I never joke," I said.

"Then you're lying."

"Are you willing to take that chance?"

Alexandria hesitated.

I drove the final nail. "Zoe Cartwright Smith and Lucinda Matherson are coming out at a group ball."

She visibly shuddered. Coming out at a cotillion with other girls meant you didn't get the entire spotlight. It meant your father couldn't afford to throw you your own ball. It meant you and your family and your entire lineage were of substandard stock.

"You won't let that happen." She phrased it as a statement. So help me, she raised her chin and looked down her nose at me as she continued, "My father is paying you good money to ensure that doesn't happen. You <u>promised</u>."

It was all I could do not to laugh.

"I promised you that your coming out will be a night you will never forget, and I stand by that promise. But you must remember your end of the contract."

Alexandria pursed her glistening lips. I knew where those lips had been, what they had been wrapped around, just last night. She wasn't holding up her end of the contract at all, just as I expected.

"Very well," she said, falsely demure, and sat back down.

SLOWLY, Alexandria grew to trust me. Of course, that meant that she exposed even more of her true nature to me. I've ducked a lot of flying crystal and flung vases in my day, and I have to say Alexandria was a connoisseur. She had an arm like Pedro Martinez and a temper like Mike Tyson. Or Scarlett, if you held to the true Southern ways. Scarlett is a goddess to them.

And so, when it was time for Alexandria to buy a dress (pure white, as prescribed, not ivory or pearl, with no ruffles or plunging neckline), it was me she turned to for advice. Mrs. Pointer-Ashe plucked at her own white gloves and gave comment, but as Alexandria came out of the dressing room and onto the short runway (it was one of those types of stores, of course), it was my approval she sought, my face her eyes turned to.

"That one's lovely," Mrs. Pointer-Ashe murmured.

"Alexandria, darling, I'm afraid that one makes you look like a two-bit whore," I called out. "Never, ever, go for a skirt like that in a formal dress. Cocktail dress, absolutely. But evening wear…. Not unless you're planning on standing on a street corner in the hopes that Bradley Winthrop the Third comes driving by."

On one hand, she would be coming out at her own private function. The dress would be unique. On the other hand, if anyone else within three counties had the same dress, her life would be ruined. <u>Ruined</u>, you understand. She might as well wear her dress from last year's Spring Cotillion. (Insert disgusted flounce here.)

She was getting tired. The latest dress was almost right, but not quite. I pointed out the inappropriateness of the silk rosette on the left shoulder.

"Gah<u>dam</u>it!" She reached up, grasped the simple satin bodice, and ripped it cleanly down, revealing perky breasts most starlets would pay thousands for. She managed a few nicely pointed stomps on the skirt, which puddled around her new white satin pumps before she kicked it away and stormed back off to the dressing room.

Mrs. Pointer-Ashe looked stunned, or perhaps stoned, if I hadn't known her drugs of choice.

"I think this is going rather well, don't you?" I asked.

Then I sat, examining my blood-red nails, and waited.

Eventually, Alexandria came back out, looking rather meek.

"I'm sorry," she said. "That was undignified of me. I'll pay for that dress, of course."

Actually, Daddy would pay for it, but that wasn't the point.

I regarded her silently. The dress she was now wearing was ideal. Floor-length, always a requirement. No lace or elaborate beading, just a stiff satin bodice with cap sleeves and a sweetheart neckline, leading into a satin skirt overlaid with yards and yards of tulle.

"Thank you, Alexandria," I said. "A proper lady knows

when and how to apologize. Your mother and I accept your contrition."

This—the buying of the dress—was the final test. It proved I had her complete trust. She looked only to me for an opinion, never once glancing her mother's way, not even when I told her the dress was exquisite, perfect.

She would do anything I told her to do. As long as I was present. Behind my back, I knew she still had a long litany of contract violations to account for.

THE NIGHT of Alexandria's coming-out ball, I accompanied her in the limousine. Her parents would drive to the venue on their own. Once we were settled (carefully, so as to not crush her dress), I poured her a glass of champagne and toasted her success. Her dress was perfect. Her hair was exquisite. Her gloves and shoes were spotless. Her deportment was impeccable. She knew how to eat, dance, curtsy, make small talk, and gracefully remove herself from an awkward situation. She practically knew how not to sweat, even in the high summer Southern heat. That last one was going to come in particularly handy.

She hesitated, knowing she wasn't supposed to drink alcohol. I smiled encouragingly, and she took that as a sign that it was okay.

Encouraging smiles do not supercede a signed contract.

We finished the bottle (she never noticed that I never poured myself a second glass) and were down to the dregs of a second one when she passed out.

S HE AWOKE SEVERAL HOURS LATER, pressing a hand to her head and uttering a string of impressive oaths until she was coherent enough to remember I was there. She sat up and stared. The windowless bedroom was very red: wallpaper, silk sheets and bed canopy, carpet. This was not a room anywhere near the cotillion ballroom.

Then it began.

"Where am I? Where the fuck am I?" She flung herself at the door, but it was locked. She wrenched at the doorknob hard enough that even I feared it would break off. "What have you done? When my daddy finds me, he is going to—to—to fire you! And then he's going to have you thrown in jail! And he's not going to pay you anymore!"

She launched herself at me, but I stepped aside and she fell on the bed. The pillow became her next target; she screamed incoherently as she shredded it, spitting out the feathers that flurried around her.

Eventually she wore herself out, at which point I quietly said, "Alexandria."

I'd trained her well. She jumped and composed herself without thinking, then glared.

"You've made quite a mess of yourself, and we don't have much time to get you cleaned up. Luckily you haven't harmed your dress." I produced a brush and hairspray. "Hair first, then we'll touch up your makeup."

"Where am I?" she asked again.

"Hell," I said.

"You're crazy. Mother and Daddy put me in the hands of an insane person."

I pressed her down onto the stool in front of the vanity, and ran the brush through her hair.

"We had a contract, Alexandria. You signed it, openly and honestly, without coercion."

"You lied to me." Her voice was sullen.

I sprayed hairspray, then handed her some concealer. She dabbed it under her eyes.

"No, I didn't lie," I said. "The contract stipulated that you would refrain from drinking, smoking, and sexual activities. You failed on all accounts. It stated that you would comport yourself with dignity, and yet I endured tantrum after tantrum. It clearly outlined what would happen if you did not hold to the terms stated in the contract."

She stared at me in the mirror. Her mouth worked, but no sound came out. She hadn't read the contract. Neither had her parents. Alexandria and Mrs. Pointer-Ashe had signed it without checking any of the fine print.

I helped her to her feet.

"I didn't lie to you, Alexandria," I said as I opened the door. The smell of brimstone was stronger out here. "I promised you that your coming out will be a night you would never forget, and that is absolutely true."

Hand on her elbow, I guided her to the ballroom where every year, Satan held a cotillion, and charged me with obtaining him an appropriate debutante to present.

Alexandria balked in the doorway. The smell of brimstone was almost overpowering here, but like a true deb, she didn't complain—her expression didn't even change. I could sense His Fieryness near, eagerly waiting.

"I don't understand something," Alexandria said. Her gaze was on the room; her hand was poised on my arm as if I were her escort. "If a deb you've trained disappears every year, why doesn't anybody notice?"

"Honey, you're not stuck here forever," I said. "At least, not yet. When it's your time, He'll come for your soul. As far as the rest of the world will remember, you came out as the perfect deb, the most eligible young man in the county asked for your hand, and the night will be hailed as a true success."

"What will I remember?"

"Not a thing. You'll wake up tomorrow with the mother of all hangovers and—"

She whirled to face me, her dress rustling. "I won't remember?"

I shook my head.

"But…" A smile curved her glossy lips. "But you promised me a coming out I'd never forget. It was in the contract. <u>You</u> broke the contract. You never even intended to honor it."

A rumble shook the floor. Alexandria paled, but otherwise kept her composure. I recognized the sound: His laughter. I dropped to my knees.

"Your Eminence, I—"

"Too late, Lilith," He said. "She found a loophole. Absolutely delightful, my dear," He said to Alexandria. "You're the first one to catch that. Even I missed it." He held out His arm. "Come, my dear. After you're presented, we'll add a new tradition to the ball. Give you a chance to use that fork for hearts."

"You're going to kill Lilith?" she asked.

"Is that what you want?"

"Nooo…"

My head was still down, so all I saw was the hem of her skirt swish as she walked away.

"I think," Miss Alexandria Pointer-Ashe said, a charming lilt in her voice, "that it would be much more fun to do it while she's still alive."

MIKE ZIMMERMAN

In Mike Zimmerman's first appearance in these pages, he brings us a story that I bought once for a Pulphouse anthology back in 1991. The anthology was called Splatter Fairies *but we never got the book out before we shut down. (Three years later on the topic of Splatterfairies, the "Lady Cottington's Pressed Fairy Book" came out, written by Terry Jones. Not a Pulphouse book.)*

Mike asked if I would like to see the story again and I said sure, and now I remember why I bought it 30 years ago. Great fun. A perfect Pulphouse story. Welcome back to Pulphouse, Mike.

NIGHTMARE PAINT

MIKE ZIMMERMAN

for Bugs

Once upon a time, Myco the Fungus Fairy was lounging in the inverted cap of a mushroom on a sunny, magical forest Saturday. He sucked the sap out of a sassafras root, taking his own sweet time. Occasionally he scratched his white and black blotched body, from his big, juicy cherry eyes down to his sexless crotch.

"*Sexless?*" he bellowed, sitting straight up. "I'm hung like a jury! And I crap subway cars four at a time, too!"

Sorry, Myco. (He does, though).

"Righto!" He went back to sucking the root, humming "A String of Pearls."

Myco was pure fungus. Quite literally. His body was sculpted from both the most delicious and most deadly of wild fungus, thus explaining his silky, shroom-smooth flesh, as strikingly black and white as a healthy cow's. His eyes were pure, pupil-less crimson and his ears sat on the end of twin stalks coming out of his head. He lived among the magical mushrooms and paraded naked. He sang great hits. He sucked sassafras, ate rotting flesh, and drank from the nipples of the maple tree.

He was content being the Fungus Fairy, guarding the Fairy Ring, that infamous patch of mushrooms with great and secret powers, desired by all, had by none. Myco embraced their cold flesh, their rich colors, their fantastic variety. They were his family, his children. They soothed his mighty loneliness, illuminated the dark shadows of his sanity when all there was to hear was his own singing. When Myco's life was in doubt—when he needed validation—there were the mushrooms.

The first specimens of the Ring towered, fifteen-footers spreading their crowns like titanic umbrellas. When the sun struck their orange flesh, the very air became like flame, bathed in citrus color and magical warmth—if you were invited, that is. If you weren't, the lights were a ferocious psychedelic invasion.

Deeper into the Ring the mushrooms grew waist-high, the true green of Mother Nature. And as the center grew nearer, they became smaller, their coloration slowly turning over to a deep-sea blue. Almost purple in the very last ring, where they were no larger than human toenails. Once inside the ring, there was only rich loam, a substance beyond fertility where only purity of spirit grew.

Where Myco, in fairy glory, danced.

Everyone spoke of the great powers of the Ring shrooms. Everyone coveted them. But no one had yet experienced them. Myco saw to *that*.

He sighed and stretched, blowing a thick wet cloud of spores that would take root by the end of the day. The wings on his ankles fluttered contentedly as he made fists with all six toes. "Ain't life grand, perchance?"

Yeah.

Don't let on, but things were about to get shitty for Myco.

———

MYCO LEAPED to his feet when he heard the sounds. His ears cupped and pointed forward, his wings twitching nervously. Voices: male and female.

Cranky and annoying.

"God in rectum…trespassers. Do we dare investigate?" He smiled at the camera. "We dare."

Myco fired up his wings and took off towards them.

———

"DUUUH, I don't see why we couldn't just buy them off the street," said the male.

"Because last time all you got was a couple chunks of cowpie," said the female. "Besides, these are magical."

Instantly Myco was in their path. "What are magical?" he asked.

"Duh, whoda hell's this?" asked the male. He had long hair and wore patchy blue denim all over. And his ample belly dunlopped over his belt, taking attention away from the shiny, blue-steel double-barreled shotgun tucked under one arm.

"It's a marshmallow marblecake man," replied the female.

"I'm Myco."

"Duuuh…"

"*Myco*. The Fungus Fairy. Guardian of the Fairy Ring."

"Fairy?"

"That's right."

"Duh, *faggot*."

"Well, no," Myco growled. "Fairy."

"A magic fairy?" the female asked.

"The very kind."

Myco sized them up, circling and pausing, circling and pausing. These were humans, and incredibly dense ones at that. How'd they get so close to the Fairy Ring without him knowing?

"Why are you here?" asked Myco.

"Der, what's it to you?" replied the male, but the female shushed him and stepped forward with a friendly smile.

"Aloha, fairy. We're just out and about, minding our own business, living life." She wore long whip-like braids down the side of her head, ending in stained, pink ribbons. One of those free spirits he'd heard tell about, noted Myco, unrestrained party flesh under a sweat-polluted tee and denim vest.

Myco's eyes narrowed and he gestured at the shotgun. "What's with the blunderbuss?"

"Duh—"

"We're hunting rabbits," the girl blurted with a quick yellow grin.

"No hunting up here, lady," replied Myco.

"So you guard the Fairy Ring?" she asked.

"Righto."

"I've heard of it." She wore a bemused look. "I'm Sissy. This is Soanso."

"I'm Myco, the Fungus Fair—"

"Duh, you said that already," said Soanso. "Sis, let's just blow this cheesecake out of the sky and go grab the 'shrooms. They gotta be close."

"Soanso," scolded Sissy, "don't be an idiot. Maybe we can strike a deal with Myco. Maybe there's something we have that he needs…?" She cocked an eyebrow Myco's way.

"No dice, lady," replied Myco. "When left unmolested I define contentment."

"Duh, cool," said Soanso, hefting the shotgun. "Then we can harvest him."

Myco's eyes flared even redder at the threat, and he hovered back a few inches. "Be warned, lipid. My phlegm is concentrated mycobacterium."

"So?" scoffed Soanso.

"It is a non-motile aerobic acid-fast bacterium that emphasizes the pathogens causing tuberculosis and leprosy. The Fairy Ring is sacred, friends. I say it once: Don't fuck with my fungi."

Soanso smiled in reply and leveled the shotgun. "Duh, swallow some shot!"

BOOOOM!

Myco was blown back thirty feet, his midsection coming

apart like dried-out crumbcake. He slammed into the trunk of an oak tree and landed in a torn heap at its foot. Three large acorns came down on his head—*plunk, plunk, plunk!*

He slowly opened his eyes.

His chest was scorched black and ripped clear through, most of his body littered from the tree back to the rising smoke of the blastpoint. What was left of him had the consistency of egg salad way low on mayo.

Already Soanso and Sissy were loping along the path, tra-la-la, deeper into forest. They hummed to themselves, giggling, skipping along happy as can be. So close to the Ring. It was almost too much to bear.

Myco lifted himself to his elbows, rubbing clumps of himself back into place.

"Well then. Up a notch we go."

Soanso and Sissy stopped to admire the first mushrooms of the Ring, looking up the great burnt-orange trunks to the dusky underside of the massive crowns. They smelled of soil and moisture, were cold and wet to the touch. The powdery fungus stuck to their hands.

"Yucky," said Soanso, licking his fingers. "But tasty."

"These aren't the ones we want, So," replied Sissy. "We want the middle."

"Duuuuh, it was fun blowing away that little guy. Wish there were more of him. Ka-blam! Haw haw."

Suddenly Myco dropped down from one of the massive mushrooms. "Here I am, Soanso."

"Duh, cool." Soanso smiled and raised the shotgun.

"Don't…" Sissy began.

"Shush, Sis. I'm aimin'."

"Y'know, Soanso," said Myco with a sly smile. "If you put it in my mouth, you'd blow my head clean off."

Soanso chewed on that for a moment. "Duh, yeah. You're right. Open yer *boca*."

"My pleasure," replied Myco, opening a throatless mouth that was more like a mushroom-fleshed muppet's than something used for actual consumption. His lips fit snugly around the muzzle. His eyebrow ridges wiggled and teased.

"Soanso," said Sis. "Be careful…"

"Duh, shush!" Soanso smiled at Myco. "It's nothin' personal, little guy."

He pulled the trigger, and the back end of the barrel exploded in Soanso's face. But not with gunpowder. He was suddenly and violently coated with a generous helping of Mycosnot. Soanso's eyelids offered his reaction:

Blink-blink. Blink.

———

"Duh, yuck!" Soanso wiped at his coating to no avail. Sissy dabbed at him with a hanky, but the blue and red streaked stuff clung like a child.

Soanso threw her off and aimed the gun one-handed, trying to draw a bead on Myco through the phlegm dripping from his eyelids.

BOOOM-BOOOM-BOOOM!

The trunk of a nearby mushroom exploded. The ten-foot

tower came crashing down, smushing and sending chunks everywhere. A cloud of spores the thickness of Frisco fog descended on them, invading mucous membranes with savage itching, going straight down into their lungs. Sissy went to her rump, coughing violently. But Soanso developed the real problems.

"Uhhhhhuck…blehk, huuuuuuck, huuuuck, ack, duh…"

"What did you do?" asked Sissy.

Myco shrugged. "He's just having a little coffin fit."

The hacking was thunderous now, relentless and bloody, Soanso cranking up chunks of tubercular lung into his palm. It came to a spectacular crescendo as a massive fungal growth exploded from his throat, splitting him open down to his waistband. In seconds, Soanso's upper-half was a big, blood-soaked mushroom with eyes.

He swayed for a few silent moments, *blink-blink*, and pitched forward with a thick splat.

Sissy eventually found Soanso's head deep within the coagulating fungus and cleaned him off as much as she could. He bugled up one final blast of phlegm, and said, "Duuuuuh, okay."

They continued forward undaunted.

From above, Myco could only grumble.

The large mushrooms gave way to the waist-high green variety, and a humid stink resembling chewing tobacco. From here, Sissy and Soanso could see the center of the Ring. That beautiful blotch of ground surrounded by the great and secret mushrooms they coveted. Tiny and potent, the color of a pilot light, as blue as the purest sadness.

"Duuh, oh boy!"

"Easy, brainwipe," said Sissy. "I have a feeling our friend isn't done yet."

"Duh, I don't care. I'm hungry!"

Suddenly Myco hovered before them, ankle wings humming ferociously. "I'm warning you one last time. *Don't fuck with my fungi!*"

"Duuuh, you!" and Soanso began firing the shotgun in all directions while Myco dodged, parried, dove, dipped, lurched, as the blasts came one after another, *BOOOM-BOOOM-BOOOM-BOOOM-BOOOM!* The spraying triple-ought tore through tree limbs, leaves, ripped up clumps of sweet soil, vaporized a bird, orbited divots of moss, and sundered so many of Myco's children. Bits of wet fungus coated everything. Finally, Sissy grabbed Soanso's arm and forced a cease-fire.

"Duuh, he's quick—" *BOOOM!* "—lemme—"

"No! Cease fire, So!"

Untouched, Myco balled his fists from above the carnage, a deep welling of phlegm coming up his throat. But he did not fling it forth on a powerful burst of spore-breath, even though he was dying to. He merely positioned himself above the pair and clapped his hands.

Naturally, both of them looked up at the sound. Just as Myco drooled onto their faces.

"Ugggh!" moaned Soanso. "More loogie!"

Sissy gagged and spat, wiping her cheeks. "So what is it this time, fairioso? Death by sneezing?"

"I can do far better than that," replied Myco.

Within seconds, white fungal cysts appeared on their lips and fingers, on their earlobes. They spread in seconds onto their cheeks and foreheads, their necks. Soanso held up one hand and watched with bemused stupidity as his fingers went from white to green, oozing a nightmarish black sauce. "Duh, *wow*."

Sissy peeked down her spooge-soaked shirt and grinned. "Goodbye nipples."

Then the stink hit. Powerful, rich, all rot and sautéed flesh. Sissy laughed, the decay bubbling her sounds. "Eat your 'shrooms, Soanso. This ain't nothing."

"Duh, I'm rottin'."

"Yeah," she said, and bit into her left thumb, ripping it off down to the wrist and spitting it in Myco's direction. "But it's just cartoon rot. Eat your 'shrooms, Soanso. This little marshmallow man can't do a thing to us."

She shoved Myco and he buzzed back a few feet, glowering. Her nose had evaporated, but still she grinned. Meanwhile, Soanso had plowed stumps-first into the sacred soil of the Fairy Ring, gobbling several blue 'shrooms with his first bite.

Myco grimaced at the desecration…but Sissy ultimately was right. He could only watch …

Until—while chewing their second mouthfuls—they passed out cold.

Then Myco looked at the camera.

And grinned.

"Ah, look. They smooch the moist lips of bliss."

Myco hovered over their gorged, snoring forms. Fat, stained bullseyes in the center of his Ring, their bellies stuffed with everything sacred. Myco's eyes grew hot. T.B. didn't bother them. Leprosy entertained them. Myco knew he ultimately had to let them partake. So he could have them as they were now—asleep with the fungus. So he could punish them. So he could *paint*.

With a wave of his hands, his fingers became brushes. His mucous membranes began pumping. He seeped, he overflowed, he spilled his nightmare paint all over their bodies.

Then he dove head-first into their dreams.

Inside, Sissy and Soanso were sleeping before him, suspended on mattresses of plasma. Peaceful, dense dunces. Myco sized them up, labeling the important parts of their psyches with dotted lines like a cannibal's cadaver before butchering.

"What a feast to be," he said whimsically.

He was within their subconscious minds, a constricted, quiet place that was enriched beyond measure by Myco's mere presence. Misty furls of color floated through the air, evaporating off puddles of brain spew: Psycho-preserves from deep within Sissy and Soanso's gray cells. Myco folded his arms and gave the camera a glance. "So serene, so simple. But imagine the barf people like us would have to wade through every day if I let people like them continue to exist in this incarnation."

With that, 400 million Mycos suddenly flexed around the

sleeping pair, bellowing into their minds, *"It's me! The fungus is coming, hoo-ray, hoo-ray!"* as each Myco took a turn touching them with pokes, jabs, and kicks, *"the fungus is coming, hoo-ray, hoo-ray!"* Madness, 400 million points of simultaneous psychological contact, ripping them into a consciousness within their own subconscious. Trapping them under a nightmare bucket with walls of solid plasma all around them. Sissy sat with her legs spread, rubbing her eyes, bewildered.

"Duuuh WHAAAAAT?" howled Soanso, rudely awakened. He focused on the now singular Myco. *"You,* you little…" His flab rippled with rage. "I'll pound you like veal!"

Myco stomped on Soanso's foot.

"Owwww!"

And faster than dream-thought, Myco spit. The goo flew in a soft arc, churning and foaming the whole way. Becoming nightmare paint. It landed in Soanso's *owww*ing mouth, and he gagged, his eyes launching out six inches on their stalks. He made some noises like a phlegmatic jalopy and clawed his throat. He shriveled like a dehydrated testicle. His flab pulled back on him like shrink-wrap, indeed *became* shrink-wrap as his gullet opened and spewed green-gold syrup. In a matter of seconds, with only small wet sounds, Soanso was reduced to his true self—a grunting, *blink-blinking* tray of wrapped supermarket chicken parts.

"Idiocy becomes lunch," said Myco grimly. He looked at Sissy. "What's it gonna be, lady?"

Sissy snorted. "It ain't gonna *be* anything. Who the hell you think you are? You're nothing but a sexless little marshmallow."

"Sexless?" Myco blinked. He was suddenly feeling very DeNiro. "You callin' me sexless?"

"I'm calling you *dick*less!" chanted Sissy. "No dick, no dick, the little fairy has no dick!"

On the ground, Soanso's package of parts hopped in concurrence.

Myco balled up his fists. There was only so much …

Suddenly a three-foot penis the thickness of a beer can launched from his groin, its corona a polka-dotted boxing glove. It slammed right into Sissy's flapping jaw and she flew maybe ten dream-yards, bouncing off the limits of their subconscious and landing in a liquefied heap. "And if you think *that's* big, you should see the boxcars come out of my ass!"

Myco made dusting motions with his hands and retracted his member. Sissy struggled to her feet, still dazed. Soanso's package quivered and made muffled sounds. Myco sighed. "Boy, you two are narrow. You want my fungi to expand your minds, but you don't even know what the concept means."

Sissy stared. From under Soanso's shrink-wrap came a muted "Duuuh…"

"Oh, nausea's nipple," cursed Myco. He poked a finger through the plastic, allowing Soanso's head to squeeze out. "What rubes! That's it. I'm going to burst the limits of your subconsciouses myself."

"Wait!" pleaded Sissy, looking confused. "What'll that do?"

"Hell should I know?" shrugged Myco. "But you bowel-brains need something big to happen."

Myco approached the plasma wall.

"Duh, no, duuuh…you can spit on me again! All you want!"

Soanso rocked back and forth on his styrofoam tray, tears streaming and filling up gaps between his chicken parts.

"Yeah," agreed a panicky Sissy. "All you want. And you can have me over and over with that…that…*that large, manly penis of yours.*"

Myco chuckled and shook his head. "This will rebirth you as better human beings somewhere down the line. Right now you're booger-eating morons who don't know right from wrong. So, so long screwies. See you in—"

He plunged his fist through the wall, ripping a hole into the plane of least resistance: oblivion. The vacuum was immediate and violent. Soanso went in bottom-first, his styrofoam tray splitting wide to reveal chicken-skinned buttocks. He was stuck for one frozen moment of indignity. "Waaaaaaaa, noooo! I want the leprosy again! Gimme the leproseeeeee!"

And with a slick *throp*, Soanso went butt-through, squealing all the way.

The hole gaped and tore wider, revealing bright light from beyond. Slowly, like a ship lifting off into a sunset, Sissy floated towards the hole. She said nothing. Only stared into Myco's eyes, knowing in death that she was a lacking, inferior human being. And feeling it. Feeling it so hard that Myco had to look away until she cleared moorings and was gone.

"Tragic people," he whispered, but Soanso's distant howls masked it.

Myco closed his eyes, licked his lips, and stepped out of the paint.

THE FUNGUS FAIRY reappeared back home, and immediately felt better, back in the fresh loamy air. His toes grew moist and cool in the center patch of the Ring. From above the shrooms, and the trees, and the clouds, came a distant *waa-hoo!* And braying laughter. Male and female.

Myco gazed skyward and caught their trail of flotsam, flesh, and fart gas as they streaked across the sky. He followed their trajectory, his smile growing as they gently arced into the sun with a muffled *POOF!*

And everything instantly went night-night.

Myco sighed, feeling all his children secreting paint for the long night ahead, glorious nightmare paint for him to consume and unleash on the ignorant, the inhibited, and the foolish. Loogie for the ages.

"I love happy endings," said Myco with a big mugging smile for the camera. "How 'bout you?"

And with a blaring rush of orchestra, Myco unleashed himself and danced deep into the light of the rising moon. Enthralled, engorged, and free.

CHRISTINA F. YORK

CHRISTINA F. YORK RETURNS with her third story in these pages. Chris has helped me out with this magazine since the mailing parties with the first incarnation. In fact, she organized them. (Mailing parties are thankfully a thing long buried in the past.)

And as a writer, under lots of names, she has written many cozy mystery novels both for traditional publishers and indie, as well as a number of Star Trek stories for me back when I was editing Star Trek: Strange New Worlds for ten years. In fact, I have been buying Christina F. York stories now for over twenty-five years for various projects.

Chris's most recent cozy mystery novel is just out. To find out more about her work and her many mystery names, go to www.y-orkwriters.com

SHARPER THAN A SERPENT'S TOOTH

CHRISTINA F. YORK

They say that history is written by the victors. Take it from one of the vanquished, truer words were never spoken.

Seriously, if that willful little girl hadn't become the queen, don't you think the story just might have been told a little differently?

But she did marry the prince, and eventually she became the queen. The Brothers Grimm—palace apoligists, both of them—turned her story inside out and made her the heroine of the tale.

Don't get me wrong, she wasn't all bad, either, but I think it's time we set the record straight, in the name of justice for stepparents everywhere.

Being anyone's second wife isn't an easy task, and it's even harder if the first wife died tragically, surrounded by her living family. No matter what you do, you're going to spend the rest of your life in that shadow.

Not that I'm bitter, mind you, because I'm really not.

I just want a little respect, is all.

If I had known, before I married the duke, the way things would end…well, I would have married him anyway.

There weren't many career paths for a widow with two daughters, after all. The only job skills I had involved husband-catching, and when my first husband died, I tightened my corset and set about finding another.

I had my daughters to take care of.

The night I met the duke was magical. The royal palace—we met at a royal ball—was lit by thousands of candles, hanging from chandeliers. standing between the platters on the heavy wooden banquet tables, and tucked into niches cut into the stone walls. Despite the chill in the outside air, the ballroom felt warm in the candlelight.

That night I thought the musicians must be angels, their music too beautiful to be the product of mere mortals. Mutton tasted like ambrosia. The men were more handsome, the women more beautiful, than any I had seen.

Clearly, I was smitten.

I really thought I had met the partner of my dreams, and when he made me his wife, I would be his other half. He promised to consult me, to heed my advice, and to be a father to my poor, orphaned daughters, Catherine and Anne.

Not that I'm bitter, mind you. I just want people to know the truth.

He made a lot of promises.

So, I married him, and the girls and I left my late husband's family home. Just as well, since his brother had taken over.

I had gone from running the household and supervising the estate and the tenant farmers to being a barely tolerated interloper. My former in-laws were a real piece of work, I can tell you, but that's another story.

When I met my new daughter (the whole step-daughter thing came later, and it wasn't my idea, you know), I saw past her red-rimmed eyes and unkempt appearance. She had been without a mother for two years, and the duke didn't know how to care for a child.

She just needed someone to take care of her.

What I saw, underneath the tangled hair and dirty clothes, was a bright intelligence and an instinct for survival.

I should have been wary of both, but my heart went out to this little waif-child with the forlorn look. I may have been a sucker, but this kid had potential.

With the right training, she could run the kingdom.

That much, at least, I got right.

My girls, I'm afraid, suffered by comparison. Oh, they were both very pretty, just like I was at their ages. They knew how to dress well, as long as there was enough money for seamstresses and shoemakers, and how to supervise a household staff. They were graceful dancers and could carry on with the kind of pleasantries that said nothing and offended no one.

They would make very good wives someday.

WITHIN DAYS of moving into the castle, I began to see how badly things had been let go after the duke's first wife died.

Not only had Cynthia, my new daughter, been neglected, but the castle had been allowed to run down, and the servants had become a rebellious, slovenly lot.

I thought my husband could use some help.

Our first argument, prophetically enough, was about Cynthia.

"She should be better dressed," I said.

"Why? She spends most of her time with the cook in the kitchen, she'd only ruin anything better." The duke shoveled in another pile of turnips and glared at me.

I tried to appeal to his parental pride. "But she's a lovely child. She should have clothes that are as pretty as she is."

They say clothes make the man, and that goes double, of maybe triple, for women. You have to dress the part, and she was wearing servant's rags.

"Dress her as you will," the duke said, waving a hand at me. "Just be careful of your spending. I'm not made of money, you know."

I hesitated, but he had promised to heed my advice. "I'll see that she gets proper clothes. And there are ways your estate could be more profitable. Perhaps we could talk about it. Later."

I gave him what I thought was a seductive smile. We were newlyweds, after all, and that should have made him happy.

My mistake.

"I doubt I'll need the help of a woman to make my estate profitable. Tend to the household, like a good wife, and leave the rest to me."

He bent over his plate, effectively cutting off any chance of discussion. It was the first time he had dismissed me so quickly, but it was far from the last.

CYNTHIA WASN'T any easier to deal with than her father.

I called her to my chamber the next day, where I waited with a truck of clothes my older girls had outgrown.

"Cynthia, come look at what I have here."

I tried to be as nonthreatening as I could. I didn't intend to replace her mother. Really, I didn't. I just wanted to help.

But you can't help some people.

"Your father and I are going to order you some new dresses." I tried not to look at the gray rags she wore, stained with soot and God-knows-what from the kitchen.

"But the dressmakers will need some time to get them ready. In the meantime, I thought you might find something in here you would like."

My late husband had never denied his girls anything, and that truck was packed with gorgeous clothes. Silks and laces, fine brocades, in rich blues and greens. They were more suited to my fair-haired older girls than to this dark-eyed youngster, but they were beautiful clothes.

Cynthia refused to look in the trunk. She wouldn't try on any of the dresses, and she clung stubbornly to her ragged skirt and tunic. "These are my clothes," she said. "I have no need of charity."

"They aren't charity, child. They're just clothes your sisters have outgrown."

I tried to get closer, the way you try to sidle up to a wary animal, but she was having none of it.

"They aren't my sisters. And you aren't my mother!"

She ran out of my chamber and refused to leave her room for three days. Of course the servants sided with her, smuggling food in to her, and warning her every time I came by.

I know the story claims she had no clothes besides that single ragged skirt and tunic, but the truth is, there was an entire room filled with the work of seamstresses.

I think they were eventually given to charity.

So there I was. My so-called job skills had captured another husband, but he wasn't the man I thought he was. His idea of consulting me was to ask what I wanted cook to prepare for lunch. Not dinner—that was always his choice.

As for being a father to my daughters, he figured if there was food on the table and a roof overhead, he was good.

I watched my three daughters growing up.

Catherine and Anne would marry well enough and be content with their lots.

Cynthia, though, was too stubborn for her own good.

She still wouldn't wear the clothes I had made for her, and she continued to sleep in the kitchen. Not that I blamed her for that. It was the only place in the entire castle that was warm, and there were nights I would have joined her, but I didn't dare. She was the only one the cook would tolerate.

She was always the darling of the servants.

WHEN THE INVITATION came for the prince's ball, the entire household fell apart.

Catherine and Anne were absolutely convinced they would catch the prince's eye, and they fought between themselves constantly over which one would be queen.

I thought their chances were good—they had been well-trained—but I knew the competition would be fierce.

We spent long days preparing for the big night.

I invited Cynthia to join us. "You could attend the ball," I said. "We could go as a family."

Wrong thing to say.

"I'm not part of your family," she said. Like I said, she was a stubborn child, and she had long ago decided we weren't related.

The older girls were fitted for their gowns. They practiced walking and curtsying in their new shoes and fussed over their jewelry and hair. This was their chance to capture the heart of the prince.

There were times when I knew Cynthia was eavesdropping on us as we prepared.

I would hear steps outside my chamber or in the gallery above the hall where the girls practiced their dance steps. When I turned to look, all I could see was the tail of a tattered gray skirt.

But I knew she was listening.

I'm sure Catherine and Anne thought I had lost my mind, when I talked to them about ambition, since neither of them suffered from an abundance.

But they weren't my real audience.

———

THE NIGHT of the ball arrived, and Cynthia still refused to attend with us. She claimed that she had nothing fit to wear, as if that were my fault.

I considered, for just a moment, staying home with her, and trying, one last time, to get through to her. But then I looked at Catherine and Anne, dressed and waiting. At least I could help them.

Wrong again.

———

WE ARRIVED in front of the castle in the middle of a long line of carriages. Footmen, decked out in their finest livery, helped us down from our coach and onto the carpet rolled out on the broad stone steps. At the door, a herald announced each arrival.

The main ballroom was a swirl of light and color. Candles flickered everywhere, as they had the night I met the duke. The light reflected from satin gowns in every color of the rainbow and glinted off lavish displays of jewels.

Every woman of marriageable age in the land was there.

Except Cynthia, of course.

There was a feast spread across the banquet tables. The aroma of roast beef mingled with the sweet musk of mulled wine, and piles of honey-drizzled cakes added the smell of clover.

It was more spectacular than I could have imagined, and Catherine and Anne were quickly caught up in the dancing, as I watched from the edge of the room.

I had taught them all I could. Now all I could do was watch.

They were doing just fine, and Catherine was next on the prince's dance card, when trouble appeared at the door in the form of a dark-haired beauty dressed in an exquisite gown of rose-colored satin and dainty gold slippers.

The men, all of them, stared, and the herald wasn't even able to speak her name. She glided into the room on those gold slippers, and the prince abandoned Catherine to rush to her side.

He never left her side, and danced with her the rest of the evening. We all knew his search was over.

In one way, it was better for Anne. I saw her dancing with a rather dashing young count, and she was clearly practicing those husband-catching job skills. She would be fine.

The wine flowed, the music played, and the prince danced with his new-found love. The king and queen looked on, obviously pleased their son had found someone.

It looked like happily ever after was just around the corner.

Until the clock began to strike midnight.

The beautiful stranger—we never had heard her name—tore herself away from the prince and ran for the door. He ran after her, yelling for his guards to stop her, but she dodged them.

She didn't stop, didn't even say good-bye. She ran out of the castle, leaving behind one tiny gold slipper.

THE PRINCE SEARCHED the entire kingdom, looking for the woman who fit that gold slipper. It was small and delicate, and there weren't many girls who could even come close to wearing it.

No matter how they tried, neither Catherine nor Anne could fit more than a couple toes into it.

I think Anne was actually relieved, since the count she had met at the ball had already begun to court her, but Catherine was disappointed.

The search party was ready to leave our castle when Cynthia came out of the kitchen. She just stood in the corner, near the fire, but the prince caught sight of her and looked back and forth between her and the duke.

"My daughter," the duke said. "But she didn't attend the ball. She can't be the girl you're looking for."

The prince insisted, and of course the slipper fit.

I knew it would.

The prince wanted Cynthia to accompany him to the castle immediately, and she quickly agreed.

"I have searched for days to find you," he told her, "and I can't live without you another day."

Cynthia looked at me, smiling. It was the last time she spoke directly to me.

"A smart woman disguises her ambition."

———

CYNTHIA MARRIED THE PRINCE, of course. I knew all along that she would, since it was the only way she could run the kingdom. And no matter what she says, she learned a lot from me. Of course, she has the prince—he's the king now—so completely enchanted that he lets her do pretty much whatever she wants.

I like to think of that as my legacy.

As for me, I have a little place in the countryside. Her Highness takes care of the bills and leaves me alone. I think she expects me to stay her and keep her secrets, and for the most part that's what I've done.

But before I die, I wanted to tell the whole story.

I'm not bitter.

Really.

DAVID H. HENDRICKSON

FULL-TIME PROFESSIONAL WRITER DAVID H. HENDRICKSON *has been a writer for many, many years, not only as a fiction writer, but writing thousands of sports articles. He knows writing. And he knows life.*

With Dave, you never know what kind of story you will get, which as editor and fan of his work, I love. In this story, Dave gives us a perfect Twilight Zone story with a message that will smack you right between the eyes.

Dave's short fiction has appeared in Best American Mystery Stories, Ellery Queen's Mystery Magazine, Heart's Kiss, and numerous anthologies, including over a half dozen issues of Fiction River and just about every issue of this magazine so far. Check it all out at http://www.hendricksonwriter.com/

THE KIDS KEEP COMING

DAVID H. HENDRICKSON

They're all underage, of course. It's a requirement. So the hardest drink I can serve here at the *Sweet Chariot* is a lemonade or pop.

Outside, the rotted wooden sign hangs at an angle, held in place by a single remaining, rusted nail, tacked onto the weathered clapboards beside the door frame. The sign's white paint blistered and peeled long ago so the black lettering is hard to make out in the thick, wet fog that never lifts. But those who need to read it can make out its words.

COLOREDS ONLY

OVER 18 NOT WELCOME

NO EXCEPTIONS

THEY STEP inside the door looking confused and scared, even the older teenagers. They look at me with distrust or maybe anger, and who can blame them? Some step back outside to look again at the sign before returning to look at me, their skins ranging from lightest brown to darkest black but mine undeniably white.

I'm an old man, dressed in a fraying, gray, button-down shirt and dark pants, wrinkles layered upon wrinkles with liver spots on hands I can no more hold steady than a man my age can make it through the night without having to get up to pee. Some nights the shakes are so bad it's all I can do to hand over the glass or bottle of Coke without sloshing the whole damned thing all across the stained, dark wood counter top.

"What'll ya have?" I ask a youngster who's just walked in the front door. He's maybe fifteen, rail thin but close to six feet tall, skin dark as coal, wearing a gold-and-purple LA Lakers jersey and cut jeans. A purple Lakers cap, facing backwards, covers most of his close-cropped hair. His eyes are haunted, as is the case for almost all who enter here, but they also flash with anger. In his wake walks a younger boy, certainly his brother based on the strong resemblance, maybe twelve or thirteen. He wears cut jeans as well, but with only a plain, white T-shirt.

"I got Coke, Diet Coke, Dr. Pepper, Mountain Dew, and lemonade," I say.

The younger one looks like he's ready to respond, but the older one shakes his head. "Don't need nothing you got."

Maybe it's the damned sign outside. It was here when I arrived, just part of the empty building. I don't know who put it there. Over the years, I've considered putting up a new one, getting rid of the word COLOREDS. Change it to NEGROES, then BLACKS, and now AFRICAN AMERICANS. But I've never found a piece of wood, paint, nails or a hammer. Those things just aren't around.

It doesn't seem to matter. The kids find their way here no matter what. Probably would walk inside even if I put up a stop sign, or a skull-and-crossbones. But I tell myself I really need to put up a new sign even though eventually the kids always get comfortable enough to tell their stories while they sip on a nice cold pop. Or soda, as some of them call it, though back home in Detroit, it was pop and will forever remain that for me.

"It's free," I say to the two boys.

"And you white," the older one says.

I nod and grab a glass from a tray of them sitting on a shelf a foot below the bar top. I begin to polish the glasses, one by one. The three of us are alone, and the boys take in their surroundings. Quivering dark walls, barely thirty feet to both sides of us, shimmer like air atop asphalt on a hot Detroit summer day. There was a time, until about fifty or sixty years ago, this place was damned near as wide as a football field is long, its walls bulging at the seams, stretching wider and wider. But over the years the walls have contracted, like an organism finding less and less to feed on, closing in on itself till now it feels tiny.

It's a trickle of kids coming in compared to the old days. But still a steady trickle.

A damned steady trickle.

"I'll take a lemonade," the younger one says, and takes a seat on one of the seven stools, just to my right of center. He has to almost jump on top of it and wiggle himself into place, ignoring the glare of his older brother. "I'm Marcus and I'm twelve. This is my brother, Jamaal. He's fifteen."

"Don't talk to him," Jamaal says, though he sits on the middle stool as I busy myself pouring freshly squeezed lemonade with ice into the glass I've just polished. "Specially about me. Don't never talk about me. But you, too. Ain't you got no sense?"

Marcus looks downcast at the bar, eyes filled with sorrow. With my hands shaking so bad the lemonade is splashing over the edge and onto my hand and the bar top, I set the glass in front of Marcus, on a black coaster with a red center that says Coca-Cola. I grab a plain white towel off the lower shelf and wipe away the spill and dry my hands, noting that the towel is still damp from the last time and next time I need it, it'll probably be soon enough so it'll still be damp. Considering all the stains on the bar top, coasters may seem a bit silly, but to my mind they give this place the tiniest air of class. I think that's something these kids deserve.

"Ain't you got no TV?" Jamaal asks.

I think of pointing out that when I first came here in '59, most folks alive in the US had a TV, but it was black and white. No one had color TVs in those days because there wasn't no color TV programs. But I know that neither of these kids want to hear about the old days, life before color TVs, iPhones, and videogames, which I hear them talk about but still can't quite figure out what they mean. So I keep my message short.

"I'm your only entertainment," I say.

Jamaal shakes his head. "Shiiiit." He pulls from his jeans

pocket what serves as a passport of sorts in these parts. It has a grainy, stiff exterior and an interior that pops open exposing his photo as he tosses it on the bar. "Marcus, give yours to the old guy and let's get out of here."

Marcus fishes his out of his pocket, opens it to his photo, and places it beside his brother's. He takes a long drink of the lemonade.

"Doesn't work that way," I say.

"I knew it," Jamaal says with disgust.

"You have to tell me your story," I say. "How you came to be here. Then I stamp your book."

"We walked through the fog," Jamaal says. "Came to this place. Stepped inside. Now stamp our damned books and let us get the hell out of here."

"No, the *real* story," I say. "That's what you did after the real story happened. What happened so you had to come here?"

"That how you get your rocks off, old man? You some kind of perv? Must be. Your little, wrinkled white dick gets stiff hearing about black boys dying. You gotta hear every last detail?"

It takes a long time before I answer. "It breaks my heart every time."

"I bet!"

Silence hangs heavy in the air. It stretches out longer and longer and as it does I almost feel the glimmering dark walls contract ever so slightly, closing in on us the barest fraction of an inch.

"Maybe we should—" Marcus says tentatively.

"Shut up!" Jamaal says.

After a time, I say, "Stay here as long as you want. There's no hurry." I wait, then say, "But I can't stamp your book until you tell me your story."

"Says who?"

"It's the rule," I say. "And you can't move on to whatever comes next unless I stamp your book."

"What comes next?" Marcus asks, and for once Jamaal doesn't cut him off or tell him to shut up. Jamaal wants to know that answer as much as Marcus does.

Unfortunately, as much as I do, too.

"I don't know," I say. "This is where I've been ever since I crossed over. I don't know what's outside that door other than the fog you can hardly see through and the exterior of this building."

"The Man screws us from the day we born," Jamaal says, turning to Marcus. "And The Man screws us to the day we die. Then He start screwing us again all over. The Man makes all the rules, and we supposed to just say, 'Yessir.' Whitey here don't know shit, but we got to tell him our stories, else we can't move on. We stuck here with this sorry ass geezer, like he's got a gun to our heads. Like he be a cop gonna do a choke hold and make us gasp for breath we don't do what he say."

Jamaal turns to me. "Before we tell you anything about us, you gonna tell us *everything* about you. How you like that, whitebread?"

"Fair enough."

Jamaal reacts with a start. He was all set to continue arguing, but I've stolen his thunder.

I draw air through my nostrils noisily and begin. I've told the story so many, many times before.

"I was a cop," I begin, and Jamaal explodes out of his seat. "*Whaaat?*"

"In fact, that's why I'm here," I say. "You might say I'm serving a sentence."

———

I SHOT A KID. A black kid. Fourteen years old. And yet that isn't why I'm here.

It was 1955, and I was a rookie cop. Green as I could be. I'd say I was just out of the academy, but back then there were no police academies. I got paired with an Irish cop named Patrick O'Sullivan, originally from Boston. Everyone called him Sully. I wouldn't have been surprised if his paycheck was just made out to Sully. I didn't wonder, at the time, why he'd ever left his hometown for Detroit. It was only later that I'd consider that perhaps he'd been asked to leave.

One day, my second week on the job, we got a call to go into the projects. Gang problems. Sully called the projects Negro Town, although Negro wasn't really the word he used, if you know what I mean.

We went in, flying up the stairwell with its single dangling lightbulb, wooden steps half rotted out, and an eye-watering stench of urine you figured would stick with you for days. Next thing we knew, the lights went out and this kid came out of his apartment, holding a revolver pointed straight at Sully. I couldn't even see the kid, just a dark figure in the doorway.

He fired a split second after Sully ducked.

I had no choice.

I had to shoot. Had to take him down.

And as the kid went down, a beam of light suddenly turned on inside the apartment, illuminated his face. A face with a jagged, four-inch scar directly underneath the right eye.

And I saw the look of shock.

He hadn't known we were police. We hadn't had the chance to announce ourselves, and he thought it was a rival gang come to take him down. We weren't the rival gang's hit squad. We just did their work for them.

I did their work for them. I had no choice, but he didn't have a chance.

That kid's shock-filled face with that jagged, four-inch scar beneath the right eye filled my nightmares for over a year. His appearances only became less frequent because he had competition. You see, that kid isn't why I'm where I am today. I was put in a no-win situation. I had no choice. Kill or be killed. In fact, Sully screamed at me for days that if I didn't do a better job of defending him next time, he'd shoot me himself.

He used that against me.

A week later, he shot a seventeen-year-old black kid in the back who was running away from him, and then expected me to cover for him.

"What are you looking at?" Sully said. "Don't you dare get righteous on me. Your gutlessness almost got me killed a week ago. Don't you forget who your brother is. Your brother in blue."

He stood over the dead kid. "The world's better off without this piece of shit."

And so I backed him up. Signed off on the bullshit story he made up. Perjured myself for my partner, my brother in blue.

And the next time. And the time after that. I agreed to all the lies, the fabricated evidence. I looked the other way when Sully got out a throw down gun and placed it in the thin, soft brown hands of another goddamned kid.

Inevitably, a couple of them were white. Eventually an Asian or two. Sully didn't totally discriminate. But almost every last one of them was black.

When I finally couldn't take it anymore—the last time it was a sweet-looking, eleven-year-old girl who they said sang like Mahalia Jackson in her church choir, a little eleven-year-old girl for Chrissakes—I didn't rat him out to Internal Affairs. I didn't stop him.

I just asked for a new partner. Made up some story as bullshit as Sully's explanations for his growing death toll. And I stepped aside.

Didn't change a thing. Didn't stop him. I just made it easier on my conscience because it wasn't happening right in front of my eyes anymore. I could pretend it wasn't happening anymore. With Sully and the others in the department who were almost as bad.

Hey, sometimes like with the kid with a jagged scar there's nothing a cop can do. It's a tough, dangerous job. Lots of funerals on the side of the blue.

But the numbers with Sully didn't lie.

I *knew*, goddamit. I *knew*.

And I said nothing. I did nothing to stop him.

That's why I'm here. I've been sentenced to spend an eternity here, watching boys like you walk in, your lives cut so cruelly short.

And I have to listen.

Because I knew and said nothing. I fucking knew.

WHEN I FINISH, Jamaal snorts. "Poor baby." And then, "You deserve to suffer."

"When did you die?" Marcus asks.

"I stayed on the force for five years," I say. "Ate my gun when I was twenty-nine."

"Wish you had pictures," Jamaal says.

I can't blame him.

A frown forms on Marcus's brow. "Twenty-nine?"

I nod.

"But…if Jamaal still looks like he's fifteen and I still look like I'm twelve," Marcus says, cocking his head to the side. "How come you don't look like you're twenty-nine? No offense but—"

"You look like you just crawled out of a freaking grave," Jamaal says.

I nod. Another question I've heard so many times before. "You're as old as you feel."

Marcus nods thoughtfully.

When the time is right, they tell me their story. As are all the stories I hear, it involves police killing a young black boy or girl. In this case, their one story involves two boys, for they died together. I can only imagine how their parents themselves died inside that day.

Jamaal and Marcus were playing together in the park with toy guns. They rarely played together, their age difference of fifteen and twelve amounting to a Grand Canyon most of the time.

Tragically, though, not this day.

It was late on a Saturday, but still before dusk. Plenty of sunlight to see. Police shot Jamaal first, though he hadn't pointed the toy gun in their direction. A single shot in the chest.

And after Marcus whirled in the direction of the gunfire, his toy gun was pointed at them. Six bullets between the two cops ripped apart his thin, twelve-year-old chest.

"Why you?" Marcus asks. "Why are you here instead of Sully?"

I shrug. It's a question I've asked myself so many, many times, and the same answer keeps coming back. "Because I'm guilty."

"But Sully was guilty of even more," Marcus says.

"Maybe Sully and the other ones like him, the ones with no conscience, no hope of redemption, went straight to Hell." I shrug. "Although I'm not sure I really believe in Hell anymore. Maybe Hell isn't eternal fiery brimstone. It's listening to you kids and having my heart ripped open time after time. There aren't as many of you as in the old days, but sometimes I don't think I can take anymore."

Jamaal snorts. "You the victim. How white of you. You shoot a brother dead and let a psychopath kill who knows how many more and we're supposed to feel bad for you? Are you shitting me? *You're* the victim?"

"I'm no victim," I say. I can see that he feels no sympathy for my situation and I can't blame him. In a way, I feel no sympathy for myself either.

"You want me to kill you, put you out of your misery?" Jamaal asks. "Do it in a heartbeat."

It's a thought. But it's the easy way out.

I shake my head. "I did the crime. I'll do the time."

"You'll be here forever?" Marcus asks.

I remain silent for a long time even though it's a question I've heard so many times before. I sigh. "I guess I stay here until finally, some day, no more of you kids walk through that door. Maybe the day comes when I can just close up shop. Lock the doors and throw away the keys. Then I'll be able to move on myself. To whatever comes next."

"Ain't never gonna stop," Jamaal says, and slides his passport to me.

I nod and pull out the knife with a razor-sharp, six-inch blade and well-worn grip from beneath the counter. I unbutton my work shirt, exposing the old scars that populate my wrinkled skin. I slice a shallow vertical cut down my chest between the two rib cages.

The blood trickles onto my writing finger. I press it firmly onto the passport, giving a good print so it's unmistakable that it's mine.

I repeat the process for Marcus.

"You two are all set," I say. "When you're ready, step outside the door and you'll find your way to whatever comes next. I wish you the best."

Jamaal spins and leaves. Marcus lingers. "I hope someday you can join us."

But I know, deep in my heart, that this place isn't ever shutting its doors. I ain't never moving on. It's not like the old days when I had to slit my wrists to stamp all the books for those kids. But there's still a trickle.

A steady damned trickle.

The kids just keep coming.

KRISTINE KATHRYN RUSCH

KRISTINE KATHRYN RUSCH is a New York Times *and* USA Today *bestselling writer and maybe the most award-winning and prolific writer working today. She has won more awards in science fiction and mystery than just about anyone alive and she is the only person to win the Hugo Award for her writing as well as her editing.*

This science fiction short novel will hook you right from the start. Be ready to give it time to read.

You can find out a lot more about Kris's work at her publisher, WMG Publishing Inc www.wmgbooks.com or her website www.kriswrites.com.

KILLER ADVICE

KRISTINE KATHRYN RUSCH

Sixteen minutes. Sixteen minutes was simply not enough time to prepare for an onslaught. One would think with the recent breakthroughs in interstellar communication that a simple heads-up would be in order. Yet no one thought to contact Hunsaker.

Of course, the communications problem wasn't with the *Presidio*, who barely got off a single *we need help; we're docking soon* communiqué before their entire communications array went down. No, the problem was with Repair and Maintenance. Some idiot there forgot to inform Hunsaker that his resort would soon be full.

Not that the Vaadum Resort and Casino was much of a resort. It was more of a Hail Mary Pass. If you were passing through the Commons System (which was what most people did in the Commons System—pass through) and for some reason you needed to exit your luxurious spaceship for some downtime and you couldn't wait the extra day to go to

Commons Starship Resorts—which were real resorts, by the way, on full-size space stations—then you ended up at Vaadum Resort and Casino.

Hunsaker liked to think of Vaadum as a bit of a surprise. Vaadum was on the Vaadum Outpost, which predated the Commons Space Station by nearly two hundred years and looked it. Small, cramped quarters, a docking ring that couldn't accommodate most modern ships, a repair shop that was catch as catch can, a resupply warehouse that sometimes needed resupplying itself, and of course, the Resort.

Which, when Hunsaker bought it, was a seedy little rundown motel, operated by the repair crew, who learned (accidentally or so the histories said) that ships in distress often couldn't house their passengers. Better to place those passengers in a paying room than having them bunk on top of tables in the cafeteria.

Hunsaker was manning the front desk because sixteen minutes didn't make up for the six months during which he had neglected to upgrade the automatic check-in system. He hadn't cleaned the rooms in six months either—or at least, not all of them, nor had he checked the environmental systems.

He sent his entire staff—all two of them—off to dust, change linens, and ensure that each room had both oxygen and some sort of livable temperature while he scoured the entry, trying to make it somewhat presentable.

The Repair and Maintenance crew told him that the *Presidio* had twelve passengers and four crewmembers, so he would need a minimum of eight rooms, but it would be better to have sixteen.

It would be better to have all thirty rooms cleaned and livable, but really, where was the percentage in that? He had three functioning rooms at all times, and two of those were rarely full. The regulars that came through—and there were regulars, although not always the best of regulars—came for the casino, which had the only living breathing human dealer in the Commons System.

She was fifty percent fake. He didn't test the fifty percent theory or which part about her parts was rumor—although he did know that her breasts literally sparkled because she often dealt topless (hence the repeat audience).

She was a bit too vulgar for him. Vaadum Resort and Casinos was a bit vulgar for him, and quite low scale, and if someone asked him, he would have admitted that the entire enterprise had irritated him when he arrived, but didn't bother him so much now.

His standards had lowered, not because of the place, but because he didn't really deserve better.

He was just coming to terms with that.

The entry was the largest room in the Resort, not counting the restaurant or the casino. The entry had bench seats, no-die, regrow plants that he'd bought early in his tenure here and regretted ever since, and a large faux marble floor that, when he bothered to faux polish it, shined like a million bright stars.

He managed to clean the dust off the benches, prune the regrow plants so that their branches no longer took up most of the stairwell, and set up a make-shift computer system to handle the new guests, all in fifteen of his sixteen minutes. But he hadn't tried to clean the floor and he was grateful for that as the passengers of the *Presidio* pushed and shoved their way through the double doors.

All human (thank God for small blessings) and all sizes, the twelve passengers from the *Presidio* smelled—not so faintly—of burnt plastic. A few had smoke lines across their faces, and another few wore tattered clothing.

They also stank of sweat and fear and had that wild-eyed look of people Who Had Been Through It All And Weren't Yet Sure They Had Lived To Tell About It.

He had seen so many people like that over the years, and they were always distraught, always needy, and always demanding. He loathed demanding customers, even though his high-end education had prepared him for them. Once upon a time, he was the best at dealing with the most difficult of guests, back when he actually worked in a real resort that catered to the very wealthy, who, at least, were predictable in their very disagreeability.

He peered at the sea of humanity before him—well, all twelve of them anyway, which felt like a veritable sea to him, considering he probably hadn't seen twelve people all in one place since the last ship disaster nearly a year before. These people, with their untended hair and their air of complete panic, stared back at him as if he were their only savior.

He smiled unctuously—and he hadn't managed that expression in nearly a decade—and nodded his head to the first person in line.

She was a stout elderly woman, wearing a black business suit (now decorated with several rips to the right side) and matching sensible shoes. She even had a little hat perched on top of her graying curls. That hat looked like it was an afterthought—one of those things she had grabbed automatically as she fled the ship just to make herself presentable.

"Agatha Kantswinkle," she said with one of those operatic voices (complete with vibrato) that certain older persons cultivated. "I should like a single room."

She did not say please, nor did he expect her to. In fact, she raised her chin after she spoke to him.

She, at least, was a type he could handle.

"We only have a few rooms, madam," he said in his best toady voice. "You'd be more comfortable if you shared a double."

"I would not," she said. "I shall not ever room with any of these despicable people."

She leaned forward and whispered—as best an operatic voice could whisper, which was to say not at all—and confided, "There are murderers among them."

A middle-aged man in the middle, face covered with soot, rolled his eyes. A younger woman toward the back raised her gaze heavenward—if there were a heaven in space, which there was not. Still, Hunsaker didn't miss the gesture. Or the grimaces of dislike on the faces of the other passengers.

"Surely, it wasn't as bad as all that, madam," he said as he opened the file on the old-fashioned built-in screen on his desk. The comment was somewhat reflexive. He hated histrionics. But it was also geared toward the other passengers upon whom, he was becoming certain, he would have to rely to keep Agatha Kantswinkle under some kind of control.

"Not as bad as all that?" she repeated, slapping a palm on the desk, making his computer screen hiccup and nearly blip out. "Are you mad, man? When we left the Dyo System, we had fifteen. Do you think they stepped off the ship mid-flight? I think not."

Hunsaker raised his eyebrows and looked over her shoulder at the other passengers. The man with the soot-covered face shook his head slightly. The young woman had closed her eyes. A few others were looking away as if Agatha Kantswinkle's behavior embarrassed them.

He decided to ignore the woman, which meant getting her away from his desk as quickly as possible. "We have a single room, madam," he said, "but it's tiny. The entertainment system needs upgrading and the bed—"

"I'll take it," she said, handing him a card with her information coded into it, a method as old-fashioned as she was.

He charged her twice the room's usual rate and felt not a qualm about it. First (he reasoned to himself), the *Presidio's* parent company would probably pay for the extra stop. Secondly, the woman had already shown herself to be an annoyance, and he'd been a hotelier long enough (even at a disreputable place like this one) to know that customers often showed their true colors from the moment they walked in the door.

He was simply adding a surcharge for the difficulties ahead.

He finished adding her information to his file, resisted the urge to wipe his hands on the constantly sanitized towel he kept beneath the desk, and gave her his best fake smile.

"Your room, madam," he said with a nod, "is up those stairs to the left. It is the only room off the first landing."

Because it used to be a maid's room, back when the resort

had actual dreams of grandeur, in the days just after its first construction, long before he was born.

She did not thank him and mercifully did not ask him how she would unlock the door. He handed her the door's code, but it was a mere formality. The lock had broken long ago.

As she made her way toward the stairs, he processed four other passengers—real, sane, sensible people. They had all of their information coded into their fingertips like proper human beings, and they were solvent, which was good, since he debited their accounts immediately, although he didn't overcharge them (too badly) like he had Agatha Kantswinkle. People who were in a hurry to get to their rooms, relax and try to forget whatever it was that brought them to this godforsaken place.

Hunsaker was beginning to think that the rest of the check-ins would go well, when the soot-faced man approached the desk. He was taller than Hunsaker, but bent slightly, as if embarrassed by his height—which Hunsaker could well understand, since so many distance ships were not built for the egregiously tall.

"Sorry for the old lady," the man said as he extended his index finger, the only clean one on his hand. "We're really not that bad a bunch."

The finger, touching the screen, identified him as William F. Bunting, Bill for short, who began his journey in the Dyo system just like Agatha Kantswinkle. His occupation listed varied, which usually meant unemployed and searching for work, but he had nearly two dozen stellar (no pun intended) recommendations, so perhaps his occupation truly was varied and he had traveled from job to job as he traveled farther and farther from home.

"Sounds like you've had a difficult trip," Hunsaker said, offering the platitude the way another man would grunt with disinterest.

"You don't know the half of it," Bunting said. "If you had any other ship docked here, I'd request a transfer."

"Perhaps one will arrive while yours is being repaired," Hunsaker said, debiting Bunting's account, which looked full enough—especially for a man who had listed "varied" as his occupation.

"Please God," Bunting said, and sounded serious, which caught Hunsaker's attention.

For a moment, their gaze met. Then Bunting said, "I know you don't have a lot of single rooms, but you probably should give me one." He swept his hands toward his shirt. "These are the only clothes I have, and even I can smell the smoke on them. In a closed space, I'm not going to be someone people want to be around."

Even now, in a not-quite-so-closed space, Hunsaker could smell him. Hunsaker had figured the stench was the accumulated odor of all of the passengers, but maybe it wasn't. Maybe it was Bunting all by his egregiously tall self.

"We have a boutique," Hunsaker said, as if the little room stocked with clothes others had left behind really qualified as a fancy store. "I'll open it in two hours. I'm sure you'll find something to accommodate you there."

He made a note to go to that little room and run the clothing through the automatic cleaning equipment yet again. He had no idea when someone had last picked through the material. At least he'd figured out that he should display it all, and that no one would know that it had been previously worn.

"Thank you," Bunting said, and pulled forward a slightly pudgy balding man. "In that case, we'll share a room."

The slightly pudgy balding man didn't seem disconcerted by this. He looked grateful, in fact. Hunsaker took his information, also stored properly on his index finger—Rutherford J. Nasten—and sent both men to the best-ventilated room in the entire wing.

Hunsaker kept processing until he got to the young woman in the back, who, luck would have it, got a single room simply because Agatha Kantswinkle had demanded a single room and there were only twelve passengers.

"All I have is a room we call the Crow's Nest," Hunsaker said. "It's small, but it's at the top of this part of the station and it has portals on all four walls."

"That sounds good," the woman said tiredly.

"Sounds like the trip from hell so far," he said, actually interested for once, partly because she was so reticent and partly because she had been so expressive earlier.

"You don't know the half of it," the woman said, touching his screen with her left thumb. She was security conscious, then, not willing to follow the norms on how to behave.

It took a moment for the screen to display her information, almost as if it were tired of doing all the hard work, and for a moment everything blurred. Or maybe that was his eyes. He was unaccustomed to dealing with people any more, and even less accustomed to the level of tension he had felt since the passengers had arrived.

"Breakdowns can be stressful," he said, as he monitored the information in front of him. The light above hit her face just right so that it reflected into the screen, making it seem like her information had come up superimposed over her image.

Susan G. Carmichael, daughter of Vice Admiral Willis Carmichael of the Dyo system. Hunsaker tried not to raise his eyebrows at her pedigree. A woman like this should have been upset at the meager nature of his resort, yet she didn't make a single complaint. Maybe she would make up for Agatha Kantswinkle.

"The breakdown *was* terrifying," Susan G. Carmichael said, her voice soft. "There was actually a fire."

That caught his attention. Ships had come here that had suffered melting in the systems, ships that had filled with smoke in an instant, ships that had lost power, but none had suffered from a fire. Fires were relatively easy to kill. All it would take was a momentary shutdown of the environmental system. No oxygen, no fuel; no fuel, no fire.

"A bad one?" he asked.

Her gaze met his. Her eyes were a shade of goldish brown that he hadn't seen before. He wasn't sure if it was natural.

"They didn't catch it right away," she said.

He stopped processing her information. "How could they miss that?"

"Apparently systems were already malfunctioning." She swallowed visibly. She was clearly still terrified and covering it up by pretending to be calm. "We were lucky that you were so close."

He hadn't realized—well, how could he have realized

anyway, when he only had sixteen minutes to take a nearly empty (neglected) resort and turn it into a place where people could sleep somewhat comfortably.

"Do they know what caused the fire?" he asked.

"I'm not sure they know anything about anything," she said as she squared her shoulders. "What do I need to get into my room?"

Finally, someone asked the logical question. Perhaps the others had been too traumatized to think of it, or too overwhelmed to care.

"Just touch the door," he said. "I keyed it to your fingerprint."

Not that it mattered. He really did have to get the locks fixed first.

"Thank you." She slipped away from the desk, then stopped. "I heard you mention a boutique...?"

He shrugged, feeling honest for the first time that day (maybe the first time that year). "It's more of a whatnot shop. But we do have clothing."

"Anything is better than what I have," she said, and gifted him with a small smile before heading up to her room.

He stayed in the reception area for another few minutes, staring up the stairs. The hotel felt different with people in it. He'd often thought of the hotel as a chameleon, coloring itself with the attitude of its guests.

Which meant that the hotel was shaken, terrified, and a little bit relieved. He made himself take a deep breath. The air down here still smelled acrid. He set the environmental controls on scrub, not wanting to smell smoke and sweat for the next week.

Then he tallied up his single day's intake. More than he'd made in the last three months. If the repairs took another two days, which was the average time for repairs on this station, he would make most of his year's operating expenses. If the repairs took longer (and it sounded like they might), he might make a significant profit for the first time in nearly a decade.

But he would have to endure the mood, and he would have to stay one step ahead of these people. He had to get the clothes ready, open the boutique (such as it was), roust his one remaining chef to work the restaurant, and get the staff to clean a few more rooms just in case the living arrangements didn't quite work out.

Not to mention the fact that the ship's crew had yet to arrive and take their rooms.

He sighed. He had become even more cantankerous than he had been during the last big shipping disaster nearly three years before. It wasn't good for him to be so isolated.

Or maybe it was. Imagine how cantankerous he'd be if he had to deal with these types of personalities each and every day.

The thought made him smile. Then he continued planning his evening, realizing that to do things properly, he would get very little sleep.

THE BOUTIQUE WASN'T A BOUTIQUE, anymore than this resort was a resort. It was barely a hotel, although it did have private rooms, which was good enough.

Or so Susan Carmichael figured. She had hung back after

Agatha Kantswinkle had shoved her way to the front of the line, after repeatedly announcing her intentions to have a room of her own as the group fled the ship for the safety of this little bitty place.

Susan hadn't been on an outpost this small in years, and certainly not one this old. She was relieved to hear that it had maintenance facilities, but worried that they wouldn't be up to the task. The *Presidio* was nearly ruined. It had suffered a catastrophic failure of most of its systems, and that fire had destroyed a section of the ship.

Destroyed was probably too grand a word. Made that section of the ship unusable, maybe for the rest of the trip.

Which she would not think about, at least for the next twenty-four hours.

She had waited the two hours the prissy little man at the front desk had told Bunting to wait for the boutique to open. She knew as well as anyone that the boutique wasn't a regular store, stocked with purchased merchandise, but a shop stocked with castoffs, leftovers and discards from hotel guests.

She didn't care. She had left her own wardrobe on board the ship, and she had instructed the crew to discard most items, even the most personal ones. Although "instructed" wasn't truly accurate. One of the crewmen—Richard Ilykova —had stopped her in the somewhat disorderly exit off the ship (hell, everyone was pushing, shoving, jostling, trying to get out), and told her that her cabin had been closest to the fire.

We won't be able to save your stuff, he said, clearly worried that she'd be angry. *But you might find a way to clean it on the station. You want me to set it aside?*

No, she'd said curtly and continued jostling her own way out of the ship.

She should probably have been more polite. Ilykova hadn't needed to say that to her. He hadn't needed to say anything. He'd kept a protective eye on her the entire time she'd been on the ship, and she wasn't sure if he was attracted or if he thought she was the one who had sabotaged the ship. She had found him attractive if a bit bland—one of those pale blue-eyed blonds who could vanish into the walls because he seemed so colorless. When she'd seen him watching her, she'd decided to keep an eye on him. Maybe he saw that as flirting, or maybe he had just been doing his job. She wasn't sure, and she wasn't sure she cared.

All she knew was that now, she needed new everything, from undergarments to blouses. She didn't like the idea of wearing someone's cast-off underclothes, but she didn't see much of a choice. She would have to ask about guest laundry facilities here, although she doubted there would be any.

The prissy little man from the front desk had done the best he could to make this small room seem like a store. Some of the clothes hung on racks, with others stacked on shelves along the walls. There were old entertainment pads, some with their contents listed on the back like a directory, and blankets, which surprised her. The blankets looked inviting, even though she was warm, which told her just how tired she was.

The prissy little man was hovering near the door, checking a portable pad as he kept an eye on her. He had already helped Bunting. Bunting had gone in and out in the time it had taken Susan to look for a single shirt.

At first, she'd thought the prissy little man a mere employee. He gave off that appearance, a man beaten down by his supervisors, afraid to make decisions on his own.

But once she got into her room, she'd accessed the resort's information logs and discovered that the prissy man actually owned the place. He had the kind of pedigree that upscale resorts usually paid excessive amounts to hire—degrees from prestigious business schools and exclusive resort management programs.

The fact that he was here, and he owned the place, suggested some kind of problem, probably personal. He seemed unimaginative enough to remain in the same business, and not quite bright enough to realize that a resort this far away from habitable planets wasn't really a resort at all.

Or maybe he did realize it and fled here on purpose.

She glanced at him. Dapper, small, furtive, the kind of man (like Ilykova) who could blend into the walls if necessary. Only the prissy little man had another trait—the ability to outsnob anyone in the room. That powerful ability to judge was as important to running a real resort as it was to governance. It made the weak cower.

It just didn't bother her.

She went to the rack holding women's clothes. She found black pants with no obvious problems, blue pants that needed just a bit of care, a fawn-colored skirt, and a very old white blouse that appeared to have real lace trim. She added four other tops and found undergarments on a back shelf.

She piled all the items on a nearby table, and beckoned the prissy little man.

"I know you have a corner on the market," she said in her most polite voice, "but this trip is turning out to be inadvertently expensive, and so I was wondering if I could get some kind of volume discount...?"

He didn't even look up. "The ship's parent company should reimburse you."

Meaning they'll deal with the much too-high prices. They might not even notice.

She thought of bargaining more, then decided against it. She wasn't going to charge the ship for the disaster, but she would take money if the parent company decided to offer it.

She clutched the clothing, which smelled strongly of some kind of cleaner, and headed toward the door. He said, almost as an afterthought, "The restaurant will be open shortly. Spread the word, would you?"

As if she wanted to see the other passengers. As if she were responsible for them.

But she was hungry, and she knew they were too, and all of their rooms were on her way back to the accurately named Crow's Nest.

"Sure," she said, "if you give me something to carry these clothes in."

He sighed and reached under a pile of men's shirts. As she walked back to him, he pulled out a cloth sack—something that looked like a cleaning bag, a low-rent version of a laundry bag that offered to do the cleaning all by itself.

She was long past caring what it actually was. She put the

clothes in the sack, wrapped its drawstrings around her hand, and carried the entire thing to the stairs.

Dinner, restaurant, the damn passengers. Calling attention to herself all over again.

She wasn't entirely sure she cared. But one thing she did know.

She wasn't going to knock on Agatha Kantswinkle's door.

Agatha would want Susan to keep her company.

Susan wasn't ever going to do that, again.

THE SCREAM ECHOED through the stairwell. A woman's scream, sharp, high-pitched, startled. Cut off in the middle.

For a moment, Richard Ilykova bowed his head. The last thing he wanted to do was deal with another crisis. He stood in the lobby of the hotel, which was cleaner than some he'd seen on makeshift starbases. The owner, Grissan Hunsaker, looked up from the work he was doing behind the desk, his features contorted with fear.

No help from that quarter.

Richard sighed, then bounded up the stairs, feeling his exhaustion in every step.

The scream didn't sound again, but he heard footsteps other than his own. Doors squealed open, slammed shut, and voices started.

He found a group of people clustered on one of the landings—the B Team, he privately called them. The people who had paid lower fares, filling out the ship's rooms, people who wouldn't even have gotten on the ship had the owners managed to sell all the tickets.

In the middle of them, a woman—Lysa Lamphere—lay prostrate on the floor.

He remembered her only because she was so pretty. Easily the prettiest woman on the ship this trip. But she didn't have the brains or the personality to match her beauty, which disappointed him.

Not that anyone who booked passage on the *Presidio* would look at him. They were all too important for that. Except Ms. Carmichael. She had smiled at him, which surprised him.

She had noticed him watching her, which had surprised him even more.

The group stepped back as he approached. Even though they weren't on a ship any longer, they seemed to think he was in charge.

Maybe he was.

"What happened?" he asked.

"Dunno," someone said.

One of the men—Bunting? Richard almost didn't recognize him in the new set of clothes he wore—added, "I was in my room when I heard the screaming. Sounded pretty awful, so I came directly here."

Richard had no reason to doubt it. Bunting had the unfortunate ability to arrive first in any crisis. Unfortunate only because he didn't have the compatible ability to know the right thing to do once he had arrived.

Richard was of the private opinion that Bunting had made the fire on the ship worse by trying to fan it out rather than hit the controls for the room's environmental system. But Richard was number four man on the crew, the lowest of the low, and he didn't dare criticize anyone.

He crouched beside Lysa. She was sprawled on her back, her arms up as if they had been near her face when she had fallen. Her hands were clenched into tight fists, and her legs were twisted sideways.

He touched her face. The skin was soft, silky, the way that skin should be, the way that enhanced skin often wasn't. Her beauty was natural, then, and even more pronounced when that mousy personality wasn't front and center.

She had no fever, and she didn't look injured.

Richard glanced up, saw Hunsaker lurking near the stairs, said, "Do you have a doctor?"

"More or less," Hunsaker said.

"What is it?" Richard snapped. "More? Less?"

"More if she's sober," Hunsaker said.

Richard cursed. "I assume you have basic medical equipment."

"Yes," Hunsaker said.

"Then get it," Richard snapped.

Hunsaker fled.

The group remained, staring down. These were the people who irritated him. The ones who had wanted the lighting in their room changed and didn't know how to do it themselves, the ones who woke him from a sound sleep to ask how to work the automatic cafeteria, the ones who thought he was at their beck and call even though, technically, he wasn't.

Right now, they were content to let him see if the woman was all right.

Hunsaker came back with a handheld medical scanner and a tray of medical pens, each with some kind of magical function. Magical because Richard didn't know much about medicine, at least this kind. He had some knowledge, but on the other end—how to turn the body against itself, not how to make it function again.

Hunsaker crouched near him and ran the scanner over her, clearly not trusting Richard with the device, which suited him just fine.

"I think she simply fainted," Hunsaker said with surprise.

"And hit her head?" Richard asked.

"Oh, she'll be bruised, but there doesn't appear to be much else wrong with her," Hunsaker said.

Then his gaze met Richard's, and Richard could tell what the other man was thinking. They both worked service in not-the-best conditions. They both knew that people rarely fainted without a reason.

"You think, perhaps, she's finally having a reaction to the trauma on the ship?" There was a hopeful note in Hunsaker's voice, a note that said, *Please, don't make this my problem.*

"I doubt it," Bunting said before Richard got a chance to reply. "I mean, she screamed first."

Richard closed his eyes for just a second. A brief indulgence, a moment to himself before it all started up again. He'd hoped for an interlude, a bit of quiet, a chance to rest, but it clearly wasn't going to happen.

He stood, eyes open now, and looked at the door.

It didn't look latched.

"Is this her room?" he asked, already suspecting the answer.

"Oh, no," Hunsaker said. "Miss Lamphere is rooming upstairs with—"

"Me," said one of the women behind Richard. He turned slightly. A slender woman with buckteeth stared back at him. He remembered her, because she had propositioned him late one night back on the ship. She'd been drunk, and in her drunkenness she assumed that the ship's promotion line, which said that the crew was there to serve her every need, apparently understood "every need" to mean *every* need.

Her dark eyes met his and a spot of color appeared on her cheeks. She remembered the encounter too.

"Miss Potsworth," he said, not using her first name—Janet—because he didn't want her to get the wrong impression, even now. "I take it Lysa was not in her room?"

"She'd just left a few minutes ago," Janet said. "We'd just been told there was going to be dinner and she was famished."

Famished. That was a word he hadn't heard in a very long time.

"So what was she doing here?" he asked, more to himself than to anyone else. The room was all by itself on this level, and it was a bit out of the way of the stairs.

"Oh, probably letting Miss Kantswinkle know about the meal," Janet Potsworth said. "Lysa was the only person—I think—"

And she looked around for confirmation. A few others nodded, as if she already knew what Janet was going to say.

"—who still liked Miss Kantswinkle. Although I would say that 'liked' is probably too strong a word. She felt that Miss Kantswinkle deserved our respect, given all her work with the children—"

"Right," Richard said, having heard Agatha Kantswinkle's long diatribe about her years of service with orphaned children a dozen too many times. "Miss Kantswinkle is in this room?"

"Yes." This from Hunsaker who was doing his best to revive Lysa.

"Then why isn't she out here?" Richard asked. After all, she was the nosiest women he had ever met.

He stepped over Lysa's arm, and rapped on the door with a half-closed fist. The sound echoed through the stairwell, rather like her scream had. No one answered, but the door swung open slowly.

Richard peered inside, but did not go in. A slightly metallic smell greeted him. The room was tiny, the bed pushed against one wall. There were no windows. A chair and a tiny desk pushed against the other wall.

And in the center of the room, on the floor, lay Agatha Kantswinkle, black shoes pointing toward the door, frumpy skirt slightly askew, meaty thighs pressed together.

She had not fallen decorously, like Lysa had. Agatha Kantswinkle had toppled like a tree. He half expected to see a dent in the floor. He wondered why no one had heard the fall from below, then wondered if there was a room below. He tried to remember the layout, and couldn't.

He could feel someone else peering over his shoulder, but he effectively blocked the door so no one else could see inside. Then he pulled the door closed and stood in front of it

"She's not there, huh?" Bunting asked.

"You could say that," Richard said, his gaze meeting

Hunsaker's. Hunsaker was still crouched over Lysa. He didn't seem sure how to revive her.

Richard knew a few tricks—none of which used technology—but he didn't want to try them in front of the small group. Instead, he said to Hunsaker, "Let's take her back to her room."

Hunsaker looked relieved at the suggestion.

They enlisted the help of Bunting who was one of the strongest men that Richard had ever met. Unfortunately, Richard knew this because he'd had Bunting's help carrying dead weight before. Only that weight had been really and truly dead, not unconscious like Lysa.

Richard helped Bunting get her upright, then Bunting scooped her in his arms as if she were no more than a pile of clothes.

"Which way?" he asked.

"I'll show you," Janet said, and Richard bit his tongue. Better to remain silent than to warn the man she might show him more than her room.

Together they went up the stairs. Richard followed, mostly because he didn't want to be alone with the small group on the landing—and he really didn't want to talk to Hunsaker. At least not right away.

Instead, Richard would supervise the two in Janet's room and probably help Bunting make his escape.

Or Bunting would help him.

Richard frowned. This damn nightmare trip wasn't over yet.

HUNSAKER LOOKED at the medical equipment, then moved his gaze toward the closed door. The look that crewman, Richard Ilykova, had given him had sent a chill through him. As had his response when asked if Agatha Kantswinkle was inside her room.

Ilykova was one of those men Hunsaker had seen hundreds of times over the years on Vaadum. Working some kind of spaceship, going from one place to another because the previous place didn't suit.

After he'd checked in, on the company's money (unlike the passengers), he had moved away from the desk, so that he didn't see Hunsaker move all his information to the handheld pad. Hunsaker usually did that with crew, because so many of them traveled under false names, with very thin personal identification documentation.

Ilykova's was better than most. In fact, that was what caught Hunsaker's attention. Hunsaker had expected a tissue-thin biography, something that showed Ilykova wasn't who he seemed and seemed to ask the technological question *Really, this man is so unimportant. Who cares?*

But the identification looked real at first, so real that it nearly fooled Hunsaker. In fact, it would have fooled Hunsaker if it weren't for the fact that Hunsaker expected crew to be a bit dodgy.

So he'd looked a little deeper, saw a ripple in one bit of biography and followed it, finding another layer of biography under yet another name. Usually that meant someone was traveling on some government mission, and while he couldn't rule that out, he also couldn't rule out the fact that Ilykova was dodgier than most.

"Well," Hunsaker said to the people around him to get rid of them. "There's nothing we can do now. Did Miss Carmichael let you know that we're serving dinner?"

"She did," one of the women said.

"Then perhaps you'd best move along. My chef, while excellent, doesn't like an empty restaurant and will close if no one shows up."

"I'm not really hungry," the other woman said. "But I suppose I could eat."

"You never know when you'll get another chance," the first woman said to her.

Hunsaker watched through a slat in the railing as the women made their way to the bottom of the stairs. He waited until they were out of sight before he moved. Then he peered up the stairwell to make sure no one was coming down.

No one was. He was alone, for which he was quite relieved. Although that sense of relief didn't last long. His heart was pounding and his palms had grown damp.

He hated this part of the job. Back when he was training, they had called it "crisis management," but really, it was more like surprise roulette. Which bad thing would happen today?

He wiped his hands on his pants, then stepped toward the door. He pushed hard with his shoulder, knowing that the latch didn't work, knowing that he would regret that in the hours, days, maybe weeks to come.

The door creaked open. He made himself look down.

There she was, just as he expected, Agatha Kantswinkle, dead on the floor. In a room without a functioning lock or any kind of portal or any other way out.

She had placed her small bag of items on the bed—and he

hoped it was that bag that gave off the slightly metallic smell that was now filtering out of the room. Because he could only think of two other things that could cause such an odor. One was a surplus of blood. The other—

He sighed.

He would check the other after he made certain the woman was dead.

He made himself walk into the room, hoping he wasn't stepping on anything important. He crouched beside her like he had done with Lysa, but with Agatha Kantswinkle, he didn't touch her.

There was no need. She was dead. He didn't need a doctor or any kind of expert to tell him that. Truth be told, he was probably the expert on the outpost, given how many dead bodies he'd dealt with in the past few decades. Really, it was one of his pet peeves—one of his major pet peeves—one of his major pet peeves that he could never admit to anyone—the habit that people had of dying away from home.

He'd known when that woman cut to the front of the line that she would be trouble, and here she was, being trouble.

He bit his lip so that he wouldn't curse her. He was just superstitious enough to think that might be bad luck. Instead, he sighed. Now he was going to have to call the base doctor and have her preside over this mess, even though he really didn't want to.

Not because he didn't want a doctor overseeing a corpse, but because he didn't want *this* doctor overseeing a corpse.

He left the room and pulled the door closed, hoping no one else would try to get in, since it was so damn easy. This time, he did curse, but he cursed himself. And shook his head.

And headed to the bar to fetch Anne Marie Devlin before she got too drunk to walk.

"A BODY," said Anne Marie Devlin with great relish. She hadn't had a body to deal with in at least six months, maybe even a year. She slapped her hands on the bar and slid out of the bar stool, hoping that Hunsaker didn't know how much she needed the leverage just to move.

She was drunk, but not as drunk as she got by the end of the day. She would remember this, even if she didn't sober up, which she might have to, considering.

She grabbed her bar napkin—some lowly piece of cloth that Hunsaker believed necessary for cleanliness—and wiped the beer foam off her chin. She didn't know if she had beer foam on her chin, but she always thought it was better to wipe off the imaginary beer foam than leave the real stuff to cake.

Then she grinned to herself. Oh, sober, she probably wouldn't think that funny but it was funny as hell at the moment.

"How much have you had to drink?" Hunsaker asked in that precise snotty tone of his, the one that showed all of his expensive education and his breeding and his superiority. Of course, her education had cost twice as much as his, and she probably came from a better family, and she should've felt superior, but she'd left that behind, along with her dignity.

She just wished Hunsaker would remember that. No,

better. She wished he would honor it. He remembered it and snotted down to her each and every time he saw her.

"Natural causes?" she asked, blinking hard. The bar felt smoky, even though it wasn't. The fog was just in her eyes.

"Isn't it your job to figure that out?" he snapped, and that got her attention. Usually—if you could cite a usually, considering they'd only had three deaths together (and didn't that sound romantic? Only three deaths)—Hunsaker told her what the cause of death was, when it happened, and how she should fill out the death certificate. Usually, she got irritated that he told her how to do her job, and even more irritated when it turned out that he was right.

The fact that he was unwilling to say how the guest died was a revelation in and of itself.

"Excuse me," Anne Marie muttered and headed to the side of the bar. This place was ridiculously small, considering it was the outpost's only bar. People could drink in the restaurant and the casino, but they couldn't drink *comfortably* in either place.

She leaned against the bar and looked around. A few of the guests from that damaged spaceship had gone into the restaurant for dinner. She could smell roast pheasant or whatever the hell tonight's meal was called. It was always the same, some dish made of parts from unidentified meat or maybe synthetic meat or maybe even (oh, don't go there, but of course she did) corpses, mixed with some kind of gravy or sauce, and actual vegetables grown on the only really nice part of the station, the hydroponic garden.

She'd become a vegetarian a long time ago, mostly in self defense. She didn't want to think about the source of the meaty protein, so she didn't. Except when she dealt with corpses or illnesses or both.

Her stomach lurched. Served her right for drinking beer on an empty stomach. Beer made with real hops because she had insisted long ago. Sometimes she drank the whiskey brought in by ships or the wine imported from various faraway places, but at least she knew how the beer was made.

She had been hired to make it.

She had been the station's bartender, way back when. Before they realized that by the end of the evening she was too drunk to serve drinks. Before Hunsaker, even, because he felt that an automatic drink mixer was better than a human one any day.

Hunsaker had ferreted out her secret, that she actually had a medical license and she kept it current. She had to. She didn't want to be sued by some passenger that she had to save because really, underneath the alcohol, she was the noble sort and felt that the Hippocratic oath had nothing to do with hypocrisy and everything to do with nobility.

Not that she could be hypocritical or noble with a corpse. She grabbed the breathalyzer and took a hit from it, feeling it clear her alcohol haze like a slap to the face. She hated this thing, not just because it cleared the buzz and made her sober in an instant, but because it would give her one motherfucker of a headache in 24 hours, and she wouldn't be able to do anything about that.

Except drink, of course.

She took a second hit for good measure, then turned to Hunsaker. He stood at attention, shoulders back, hands folded before him, mouth in a very thin line.

"Ready?" he asked in that damned tone.

She was thirsty, her eyes ached, and she could feel the depression that always lurked ready to crash down on her.

"As I'll ever be," she said, and let him lead her out of the bar.

RICHARD MANAGED to escape Janet Potsworth's room just as Lysa woke up from what Janet was calling Lysa's faint. It wasn't a faint, because Lysa had enough time to scream before passing out, but she had slipped into unconsciousness very quickly, and he had a few ideas as to why.

But he wanted to think about them first, and that required him to get away from the conversation, and from Janet Potsworth who had grabbed his ass when he bent over to make sure Lysa was comfortable. Potsworth was a menace, and he would be glad to get rid of her—although he wasn't sure when that would happen, especially now that Agatha Kantswinkle was dead.

He hadn't expected her to die, probably because she had always been the first person on the scene of the other deaths aboard the *Presidio*. He'd come to see her as a stout little angel of death, and had found himself wondering more than once if she hadn't done something to cause them.

He still hadn't ruled that out even though she had clearly been murdered herself. Maybe her death was in retaliation for one of the others…?

He sighed. He had no idea. And he was going to need one,

because it was clear—at least to him—that a murderer lurked on this station.

He tread lightly as he hurried down the stairs—he didn't want to call any more attention to himself than he already had. He'd shown a bit more expertise in these matters than he wanted to, and someone had noticed.

That someone was the hotelier, Hunsaker. Hunsaker was refined and organized, not the kind of man you'd normally find in this shabby place at the edge of nowhere. Usually the proprietors of places like this were down-on-their luck drunks who couldn't be bothered to wait on a customer even if the customer offered five times the normal room rate. Or the proprietors were well-meaning spouses of someone on staff in maintenance, some handy person with cooking skills and an ability to take the drabbest room and make it just a tad gaudy.

Hunsaker seemed like he had training in hotel management. He certainly took his time checking everyone in, which meant that he looked up their identification as well as debiting their accounts.

He'd noticed Richard and he'd understood what Richard had said when Richard had closed the door on Agatha Kantswinkle's corpse. Often Richard made those snide little comments for his own edification, knowing that no one else would catch his meaning. But Hunsaker had and Hunsaker had looked momentarily put out. Not panicked. Put out. Like any good hotelier.

Richard passed the landing where Lysa had passed out. The door to Agatha Kantswinkle's room was closed and no one stood outside of it. He wondered if anyone were inside, and if Hunsaker had dealt with the corpse yet.

He almost stopped—he had a few suspicions he wanted to confirm—but he didn't. He was afraid that if the old lady's body hadn't been removed, then he would make himself even more of a suspect than he already was.

And he knew he was a suspect. Everyone from the *Presidio* was.

The first death had occurred two days out, when they were in the deepest of deep space—an area the captain had called no man's land because there were no settlements within landing range and no outposts. The trip from the Dyo System through the Commons System was dicey no matter what, but there was a section that was just plain empty. Humans weren't welcome at any of the stops for two full days of the trip. The captain had warned the crew—all three of them—that the first part of the run had nowhere safe to stop until Vaadum Station, and even then he liked to avoid the place because it was so small and so rundown. He preferred the extra day to Commons Space Station, where everyone could get off the ship and relax in style.

Richard braced himself for the extended run on a relatively small ship. He was particularly susceptible to cabin fever because he'd been the only survivor of a murderous rampage on a cruise ship as a boy. He'd been taking a trip with his father, who had died right in front of him. Everyone on that ship had died except Richard and the shooter, who had left in an escape pod before the ship docked at one of the many Starbase Alphas, this one nicknamed the NetherRealm

And that had been just the beginning, of course. He'd seen

a lot of death on small ships. Just never in quite such an odd manner as the three deaths on the *Presidio*.

He had argued that the *Presidio* shouldn't stop until it got to Commons Space Station, which had a security team and was in a sector with a real government, one that would actually look into the killings. There was no government here, even though technically, Vaadum was in the same sector as Commons. Vaadum was too far off the beaten path and too small to have so much as a leader, let alone some kind of official who would report back to the various governments presiding over the Commons System.

The captain had listened too, even though the three murders had terrified him—nothing like that had ever happened to the man, and of course Richard hadn't confessed his own history. Richard was only working the *Presidio* to gain passage across the sector. He was out of money and out of options, something that hadn't happened to him before. So he took one of his identities and used it to get work on the first ship that would take him.

Of course, that ship had to be the *Presidio*.

If the fire hadn't happened, if the ship hadn't had to stop here, Richard would've quit when they reached the Commons Station. He would have cited the killings as a hostile work environment and no one would have had second thoughts about his departure.

He couldn't leave here, now. There was no reason to stay on this station, since ships rarely stopped here, and he did need to keep moving. But he really didn't want to get back on that ship, provided the people in maintenance could actually fix the thing.

He let himself out of the "resort," through the double doors, past the restaurant. The smell of simmering beef—or was it lamb?—made his stomach growl. He wasn't sure when he last had a real meal.

Although he wasn't sure how anyone could serve real food here, either. He doubted supply ships made a huge profit coming in and out of Vaadum. But they probably got paid well to stop.

He hurried down the corridor toward the maintenance area. Clearly, the maintenance area had once been the entire station. The corridor proved it. The corridor was grafted on, little more than a tube with an environmental system, leading to the second part of the station, the resort, which someone had built on at least a century ago—and not from the best materials.

This part of the station felt very fragile. He could almost feel the corridor bounce with each of his footsteps, even though he knew that the thing wasn't built that way. It was his very active imagination, something he had failed to shut off for years now.

Finally, he got out of the corridor and into the maintenance area. It seemed huge, although it wasn't. He knew the sense of vastness was an optical illusion caused by the emptiness. The maintenance area was the oldest part of Vaadum, built two centuries ago to house at least six large ships in various states of disrepair.

Apparently, the station's owners throughout the years hadn't wanted to chop up the area, imagining, probably, that there might come a time when all seven repair bays were being used.

The *Presidio* had the center bay. It looked odd in here, since the ship wasn't built to be inside any kind of bay. Once it had been assembled, it remained outside buildings. But the station's tiny ring made it impossible to repair ships docked to it.

Richard was glad he hadn't been onboard when the captain had had to maneuver the *Presidio* in here. That must've taken some white-knuckle flying, particularly since the ship was so damaged.

Richard could see the damage from the entry. The fire had burned its way through one entire wing of the ship. The wing had remained intact, but here someone had knocked the exterior off. Through the hole—large enough to hold at least five men—he could see the scorch marked interior.

He shuddered.

He'd been afraid on ships before, starting with that cruise with his father, when the assassin had stood up, a laser rifle in his hands. He'd aimed it at Richard, and Richard hadn't cringed. He'd been twelve, too young to understand—too sheltered to understand—that the man who aimed the laser rifle at him meant to kill him.

Only the assassin hadn't meant to kill him. He'd left Richard—who was then known as Misha—alive, as a warning to Richard's mother, who had worked as some kind of double agent. Richard had never tried to understand the politics of it. All he ever knew was that his father and so many others had died because one government hired an assassin to warn his mother away from some job.

He wasn't even sure she had felt guilty about it, although she had been angry. And angrier at him when he had gotten his revenge on the assassin. She had wanted the assassin alive —for what reason Richard never knew.

He never tried to understand his mother. But her life, her decisions, had caused him to be here now, decades later, on the run for half a dozen killings, all of them he could say—he would have once said—justified.

Especially that first one.

"Help you?"

One of the maintenance guys came over. He was holding some fancy tools that Richard had never seen before. The maintenance guy was the first person that Richard had seen on this station who looked like he belonged. Whip thin, angular, sharp dark eyes and hair cropped close to the skull. He had a smudge along one cheek.

"I work on the *Presidio*," Richard said. "I was wondering if you'd found a cause for the fire yet."

"Why?" the maintenance guy asked.

Richard studied him for a moment. The maintenance guy seemed solid enough, although Richard wasn't the kind of man who trusted easily. Hell, Richard wasn't the kind of man who trusted at all.

But the maintenance guy had been on this station for a long time, and he would have had no involvement in the fire or the deaths. Not even Agatha Kantswinkle's death.

"I want to know if it was deliberately set," Richard said.

"What's it to you?" the maintenance guy asked.

Richard blinked at him, and nearly snapped, *What's it to me? If this outpost hadn't been nearby, I would have died on that ship. Murdered, if the fire was set. No one would have survived.*

"Three passengers were murdered on that ship," Richard said, "and another just died here."

The maintenance guy started. He hadn't heard about Kantswinkle then.

"So I want to know if that fire was a coincidence or deliberately set. Because I'm not getting back on that ship with someone who sets fires in space."

"But you'd get back on the ship if it had design flaws that made it catch fire?" the maintenance guy asked.

Richard almost smiled. He hadn't thought of that. Which showed that he was someone who didn't know much about ship mechanics, and knew too much about killers.

"Does it have design flaws?" Richard asked.

"All ships have design flaws," the maintenance guy said. "Some are deadlier than others."

"And this ship?" Richard asked, beginning to feel annoyed.

"This ship had some weaknesses that were easy to exploit," the maintenance guy said. "If you asked me to prove that someone deliberately set a fire, I can't. At least, not right now. If you asked me to guess how the fire started, I'd say that someone encouraged it. And I'd say you all were damn lucky to survive."

Richard felt a shiver run down his back. Two lucky survivals. If he were superstitious, he'd think that there was a third in his future.

"Can the ship be repaired?"

"It'll take us a few days," the maintenance guy said. "We have to rebuild a few things, replace even more, and then make sure that it's strong enough to handle space again. When we're done, it should be better than new."

He sounded confident. He actually sounded excited about the prospect of reviving the ship, of making it worthy to fly again. He probably didn't get challenges like this one often.

Or maybe he did. Maybe his job was all about cobbling ships together so that they would survive to the next port.

"Can you make it tamperproof?" Richard asked.

The maintenance guy gave him a sad look. "No ship is tamperproof," he said. "Especially not a ship as old as this one."

Richard must've looked unsettled, because the maintenance guy added, "We'll make it better than it was. If you have a problem out there, it won't be because of the ship."

"Yeah," Richard said, "I'm beginning to figure that out."

———

Anne Marie Devlin still smelled of beer. Hunsaker wrinkled his nose as he stood inside Kantswinkle's room. Anne Marie had crouched over the body for only a moment, and then she started walking the parameter of the room as if the room were big enough to have a perimeter. She inspected every little thing. The walls, the chair, the bed, the floor.

Everything except Kantswinkle.

Finally, Hunsaker couldn't take it any longer. "What *are* you doing?"

Anne Marie didn't answer him. She stood on her toes, and peered at the small control panel he'd installed for the guests. The control panel didn't give them much control over anything, just the illusion of control.

You let them operate the heating and cooling in their tiny space, and they thought they had charge of the universe.

"Anne Marie," he snapped. "I asked you a question."

"You did, didn't you," she said, her back to him. He had never met such an aggravating woman. She'd be a marvel if she didn't drink.

"What. Are. You. Doing." He enunciated each word so that she would know just how annoyed he was.

"I. Am. Investigating," she said, mimicking his tone exactly.

His cheeks heated. Did he really sound that obnoxious? Not to his own ears, certainly. "Investigating what?"

Anne Marie turned. She looked at the door first, and then at him. He pulled the door again to make sure it was pulled tight.

"Don't do that," she said.

"Why not?" he asked.

She walked to the door and cracked it open just a little. "It's better this way."

"Don't tell me you're getting claustrophobic now," he said. He'd heard about her other ailments. The alcoholism she refused to treat aggravated the depression she refused to acknowledge which was caused by something in her past she refused to talk about.

All in all, the most infuriating woman he had ever met. And one of the most brilliant.

"I have a hunch I'll always be claustrophobic in this room from now on." She peered through the crack in the door as she clearly checked the hallway, then pushed the door open just a bit wider. "We're alone."

He had to check on that himself. Not that he didn't trust her, but he really didn't trust her.

"What's going on?" he said when he was satisfied no one lurked in the hall or the stairwell.

"This poor dear woman," Anne Marie said, thereby proving she had never met Agatha Kantswinkle, "suffocated."

He glanced at Agatha Kantswinkle's neck. No mottled marks, no sign of a struggle. If this woman had suffocated, she had done so without hands around her neck or something pressed against her nose and mouth.

He swallowed hard. "Even if the environmental system had shut down," he said, "she wouldn't have died this quickly."

"Yes, I know," Anne Marie said. "The problem is the environmental system hadn't shut down."

"Then how did she die?" he asked.

"I told you," Anne Marie said. "She suffocated."

"You can tell that from eyeballing her?" he asked.

Anne Marie smiled just a little. "I'll confirm with an autopsy," she said. "But I will confirm."

"No one touched her," he said. "And if it wasn't the environmental system, then what was it?"

"Oh, it was the environmental system," Anne Marie said. "That's why your other guest fainted. The door opened, she saw the body, she screamed, took in what she thought was a lungful of air to continue her scream, and passed out. Lucky girl. Had she been closer to the door inside the room, she would have died too."

Hunsaker was feeling dizzy. He realized he wasn't breathing either. He made himself take a breath, but it felt odd. He hadn't thought of breathing before. Maybe, like Anne

Marie, he wouldn't want to be in this room alone with the door closed either.

"What did she breathe?" he asked.

"It wasn't pure carbon dioxide," Anne Marie said, "or her skin would be bright red. More likely a cocktail of gases, something that created the faint bitter odor that was in the room when we arrived."

He had been here earlier. The smell had been stronger. He didn't tell her that.

"How do you know?" he asked.

She held up one of her portable scanners. "I've been taking readings from various areas of the room. I'm getting a mixture of things that should never be in a residential area of a space station. I have the behavior of both women. I have the smell. And then there's the controls themselves."

She swept a hand toward them.

He walked past her and peered at them.

Someone had hit the override. The damn thing was blinking, asking for a manual code to confirm the oxygen mix, which was purer than it should have been.

Not only had someone tampered with the controls, but someone had tampered with them *twice*—once when Agatha Kantswinkle entered the room, and then again after she died.

"I would assume that these systems keep track of who touches them when?" Anne Marie asked.

He had no idea. The last time he'd used an override had been a decade ago. Since then, he'd replaced most of the guest room environmental controls, going to a simpler system— one that gave the guests two options—hotter or colder. Nothing as fancy as this little box, which even allowed the guests—with the override code—to mix their oxygen from thin to thick.

"I don't know," he said, feeling absolutely helpless.

"Well." Anne Marie smiled, clearly liking his discomfort. "I guess you'd better find out."

————————

POUNDING, pounding, pounding.

Susan sat up, filled with adrenaline. She'd been dreaming. Not dreaming so much as trapped in a memory.

The slight banging noise, rhythmic, feet against the thin wall.

Her mouth tasted of bile. She got off the bed, rubbed her hand over her face, and went to her door.

Janet Potsworth stood outside. She looked more disheveled than Susan had ever seen her.

"Oh, you're all right then," Janet said with obvious relief.

Susan frowned. "Of course I'm all right. Why wouldn't I be?"

"Because you didn't come for dinner," Janet said.

Susan rolled her eyes. She had asked the chef—if that man could be called a chef—to give her a meal for her room. He had obliged, serving her some kind of stew that wasn't on the menu.

The staff will eat this, he said. *You will like it better.*

She had carried it upstairs herself, and she had liked it. She ate alone for the first time in a week. No angst, no speculation, no fear.

Just a quiet meal in her quiet room. Then she let her exhaustion take her, and she had fallen into a blissful sleep.

Until she dreamed of Remy's death. The man had hanged himself in his room—which had taken some doing. The sheet wrapped around his neck, dangling off some fixture. She hadn't seen it, but she had heard his feet, banging, banging, banging, which she hadn't thought odd until later.

He wasn't bumping against the wall when they found him. She must have been hearing him die.

In fact, no one thought he had done anything except kill himself. He was the first, after all. They'd said some words over him, looked at his traveler's contract, saw that his body didn't have to be returned to anyone, and slipped him into the darkness of space, along with a few of his possessions.

An act they all regretted when the second body turned up. By then, it had become clear that Remy hadn't killed himself and that banging she had heard was his attempt to get her attention. Or to kick his way free. Or to find purchase for his feet. Or to get to his killer.

She hated thinking about it, but she did think about it. Often.

As did everyone else, it seemed. Including the killer. Who had to be laughing at them all.

She wasn't getting back on that ship. Not now, not ever. And she shouldn't have opened her door to Janet either. Janet was one of those obnoxious women who thought every man was a conquest and every woman was competition.

So there had to be another reason she was here.

"I'm fine," Susan said, and started to close the door.

"You can understand why we were concerned," Janet said, "considering what happened to poor Agatha."

Susan sighed. She was now supposed to ask, *What happened to Agatha?*...as if she cared. Agatha was the most obnoxious woman she had ever met. And that was saying something.

She didn't want to know what happened to Agatha. And if she took the verbal bait, she'd be regaled with some horrifying story of someone's rudeness to the most obnoxious woman she had ever met.

"Yes, I can understand," Susan lied. "Thank you for thinking of me."

And then she pushed the door closed.

"IT STARTED IN THIS PANEL," said the maintenance guy. His name was Larry and he had been on the station for more than a decade. Larry loved his work. *Out here*, he said when Richard asked, *my job is a real challenge. You gotta be creative, you know? And you gotta be right. We've never lost any ship that's left here, and we've never gotten any complaints about our work later on. It's the best job I've ever had.*

Richard somehow found that enthusiasm reassuring. Reassuring enough to join Larry inside the burned out section of the *Presidio*. It smelled of smoke and melted plastic. His nose itched with a constant urge to sneeze. He breathed shallowly through his mouth because he had a hunch if he started sneezing, he wouldn't stop.

"See right here," Larry said, pointing at a mass of blackened something-or-other, "there's one of those design flaws I mentioned. Nothing that would trigger on its own, but something that could be taken advantage of."

He explained it in rather technical language that Richard was surprised he understood. It sounded so simple, and yet he wouldn't have been able to do it.

"But this thing had been burning for hours when we found it," Richard said. "All the warning systems had been shut down."

"And the environmental system tampered with," Larry said. "The oxygen mix had to have been low here. There wasn't a lot of fuel for this fire, and there should have been. Also, this ship has a built-in system for putting out fires. It would have vented the atmosphere, and isolated the area. It did none of those things."

"Is that easy to tamper with?" Richard asked.

"For me, sure," Larry said. "For you, not so much."

"So someone who knew the ship's systems," Richard said.

"Most ships' systems," Larry said. "You have to know what's standard, what's unusual, what's expected, and what's normal."

"So someone who worked on the ship," Richard said.

Larry smiled. "Probably not. You guys were a week out, right?"

Richard nodded.

"That's plenty of time for someone to study the specs and figure out how this ship worked. Provided that he already had a base of knowledge on how ships in general worked."

"Could they time it?" Richard asked.

"Meaning what?"

"So that we were close to Vaadum when it happened?"

"Sure," Larry said. "That was the only smart way to do it. Unless your saboteur wanted to die along with everybody else. Or planned to take an escape pod. Of course, no one did. They're all here. I assume all your passengers are accounted for too."

"Yeah," Richard said. "They're all here. On the station. With us."

NOTHING LIKE MURDER TO make a man stop procrastinating. After Hunsaker watched Anne Marie Devlin use one of the robotic carts to take Kantswinkle's body to the infirmary, he got his tools and finally fixed the lock on Kantswinkle's room. He couldn't shake the feeling that if he had done this before Kantswinkle had arrived, he would have prevented her death.

Then he would have had to deal with her the next two days while the *Presidio* was being prepared. That thought made him shudder—and made him feel guilty. It wasn't her fault that she was dead...

Except that no one seemed to like her, she was difficult to deal with, and if he had to pick someone to murder in this small group of stranded passengers, he would have chosen her.

Which made him shudder even more.

Had she died because of who she was?

Or because of how she acted?

Or because of the room he assigned her?

That last thought got him to find his staff (all two of them) and have them clean some of the other rooms, the ones with the limited environmental controls. Then he moved five of the passengers—Bunting and his roommate, Janet Potsworth and Lysa Lamphere, and Susan Carmichael.

The first four had left their rooms willingly. Then he had gone to see Carmichael.

He knocked, and she didn't answer. So he knocked again, harder. The door flew open, and Carmichael stood there, looking bleary.

She had struck him as the kind of woman whose hair was never out of place, and yet all the strands stood at odd angles with some kind of violent looking red mark on the side of her face. It took him a moment to realize that she had a pillow impression on her cheek, and her hair was mussed from the blankets. Clearly, Susan G. Carmichael was a messy sleeper, even if she never was messy awake.

She didn't want to be moved. She nearly slammed the door in his face, but he stopped her, and told her that if she stayed here, there was a good chance she'd end up like Agatha Kantswinkle.

Then Carmichael frowned.

"What happened to Agatha?" she asked.

He peered at her. She really and truly did not know.

"She's dead," he said.

Carmichael closed her eyes for a minute, sighed, and leaned against the door jamb. "I suppose she was murdered," she said tiredly.

"Yes," he said.

Carmichael opened her eyes. They were a vivid blue. "I

suppose it was too much to ask the murderer to stop killing once we got off that damn ship."

"I suppose," Hunsaker said, not knowing quite how to respond.

"He's going to run out of victims, and that will call attention to him," she said. She sounded angry, as if it personally affronted her that the murderer kept killing even though she didn't think it wise.

"I don't think he minds the attention," Hunsaker said. "Can I help you get your things?"

"There's not much," she said, indicating the purchases she had made earlier sitting on top of the chair. "I can get them."

Still, he took a pair of shoes and a blanket, just because he suddenly felt that he needed to be useful. Not that he hadn't been useful. He'd been more useful today than he had been in weeks, maybe months. He'd repaired locks on four doors, including Agatha Kantswinkle's (and then he sealed off that damn room, maybe forever), he'd gotten a whole bunch of rooms cleaned, he'd gotten the kitchen staff up and running again, and he actually had people in his hotel.

Until they murdered each other off, of course.

He left the door to her room open, since someone on his staff would be up here shortly to clean, fix this lock, and close off this room. No one was going to be in the older rooms, not while there were murderers on board.

"Did she suffer?" Carmichael asked as he led her down a flight of stairs, through a corridor, and into the newer—and, once upon a time, more hopeful—wing of his hotel.

He looked at her. She actually seemed concerned. No one had asked this question before. He hadn't even asked it when he'd been talking with Anne Marie, and he probably should have.

"I don't know," he said honestly—or as honestly as he dared. It took time to suffocate. If the death was merciful, she would have passed out like Lysa and then stopped breathing, but if it wasn't, she would have been gasping for air—

Although, he realized, had she had trouble breathing, all she had to do was step into the corridor and get far enough away from her door. She would have been able to clear her lungs, and maybe even get help.

"I suspect she didn't suffer at all," he added, now that he'd thought about it.

Carmichael grunted, which surprised him. He would have expected a "thank heavens" or some other kind of reassuring remark. Instead, she sounded almost displeased.

"Did you know her well?" he asked.

"No one knew her well," Carmichael said. "No one wanted to."

"Oh." He would have suspected as much. "What about the other people who died? Were they unpopular too?"

"What's it to you?" she asked.

He flushed. He usually wasn't that nosy.

"I'm sorry," he said. "I didn't mean to pry. I was just wondering."

"Murder really shouldn't be the subject of casual conversation, now should it?" Carmichael asked.

"I guess not," he said, refraining from pointing out that right now, the conversation wasn't as casual as she seemed to think. After all, three people had died on the ship, there was a fire, and now another person had died. Not that casual a conversation. Maybe even relevant.

They stopped at Carmichael's new room. He unlocked it for her and went in first, feeling a slight surge of adrenaline as he took his first breath. Would he always feel that now in his guest rooms? Would he always be afraid that a single breath could kill him?

"Well," Carmichael said following him in, "it's not quite as pretty as the other room, but it does look newer."

He hadn't thought of the other room as pretty, although it had personality which this one lacked. This one was like all the other rooms in this wing, big enough for a large bed, a table and two chairs, as well as an entire wall dedicated to in-room entertainment, if someone wanted to pay a premium price.

He didn't ask Carmichael what she wanted. He figured she could charge it to her bill if she decided she needed entertaining. He didn't want to be near her any longer.

He set her shoes and blanket on the floor, then backed out of the room. She didn't seem to notice. She was putting her clothing on top of the table as he left, as oblivious to his presence as a rich woman was to a robotic cleaner.

He hurried down the steps and back to the front desk, feeling unsettled. This group of people was beginning to frighten him. He had no idea when he'd be rid of them either. The ship had to be repaired or some other ship had to come here and get them out of his hotel.

For the first time in a very long time, he missed having some kind of security on the station. Someone other than the burliest member of his staff threatening the guests with increased fees—which was usually enough to calm them down, since Hunsaker already had control of their accounts.

But he didn't want to threaten anyone here, because who knew how they would react?

He didn't want to think about it—any of it. Instead, he focused on a cleaning schedule for the vacated rooms. A cleaning schedule and a repair schedule. Time to make sure all the locks worked properly and all the equipment was tamper-proof.

Time he started doing his job.

Again.

HIDEOUS MAN. Odious, actually. Who did he think he was to discuss other people's deaths as if they were entertainments?

Susan Carmichael sat on the bed in her new room, wide awake now, wondering if she would ever sleep again.

Agatha dead, here and not on the ship. That had shaken Susan as much as figuring out that Remy's death hadn't been suicide. Not that the thought of a suicide in the room next to her hadn't disturbed her too. Any death would have bothered her.

But the murders, the fire—somehow she had gotten it into her head as they fled onto Vaadum that they would be safe here, that their long nightmare was over.

She propped her pillows against the headboard and leaned her head back. She could feel the muscles in her back, so tight that any movement hurt.

She didn't like this room. The other one had the illusion of safety. She had gotten that room when she still believed that the outpost would be much better than the ship.

Now she knew it was no different. A limited group of people trapped in a limited amount of space.

There was nowhere to run, no way to escape. The ship was incapacitated, and—so far as she could tell—the *Presidio* was the only ship on the station.

Did the locals (what should she call them? Station rats?)—did they have a way to leave? She wasn't sure about that either, but she should probably find out.

She had been under the impression that Vaadum was one of the only safe stops between here and Commons Space Station.

But she didn't even know how far Commons Space Station was from here. Maybe she could convince someone to take her there. Or to hire a ship and have it arrive, getting her out of here.

Of course, some of the others would want to come, and that wouldn't work, because one of those others might be the killer.

She needed a way to defend herself. She didn't have one, at least not yet. And now she wouldn't be able to sleep again. She needed to stay awake, stay vigilant, should anyone try anything.

Susan pulled her knees to her chest. She needed a plan.

She just wasn't sure where to begin.

THE CAPTAIN HAD FOUND a spot in the bar, toward the back under the dim lights. Richard had to cross most of the room—which smelled of beer and sweat and spilled whiskey—to realize that the captain had five empty glasses in front of him.

Richard sighed.

The captain was a small man, former military—but with which army in what war, Richard had never asked (it was none of his business—and he'd learned, through his mother, politics was the most deadly business in the entire sector). The captain had run his ship on a tight schedule. He and the other two pilots had separate eight-hour shifts in the cockpit.

Richard had been hired on to do the menial work that had nothing to with flying the ship—keeping the passengers happy, making sure that the lower decks were spotless, maintaining the robotic cleaners and cooks. The food on the ship wasn't spectacular, but it hadn't been advertised that way. There were ships that made this run that were all about food, food every few hours, food from every culture in the sector, food as rich and varied as the passengers themselves.

But this ship hadn't been a cruise so much as a passenger vehicle. It took people from here to there in a modicum of comfort, with as little fuss as necessary.

Until the first death, Richard had mostly dealt with trivial complaints—broken entertainment sectors, malfunctioning avatars in the gaming area, the occasional sudden (and he thought humorous) switch to zero-g in a toilet. Agatha Kantswinkle had tried his patience—her bed was too soft, the equipment near her room too loud, the cooking smell from the galley too strong—but he'd had the leeway to move her twice, and her final cabin seemed to suit her more than the others, which had cut the complaints to about half of what they had been.

He'd settled in for a flight filled with irritations and hard work, but he knew once he got to Ansary, he'd be done with real work and he'd have money for the first time in months.

He had vowed not to get that low on funds ever again.

Now, here he was, unpaid and trapped on a space station that had at least one killer on board.

He peered at the captain. The man was staring blearily into his glass, as if he could read information written on the bottom of it. The captain was the one man Richard knew wasn't behind any of this, for two reasons.

The first was circumstantial—the captain had been with Richard during the first two killings. If the captain had been involved he would have had to have had a collaborator, and the captain never consulted with anyone.

The second reason was more practical—the captain owned his ship. It was part of a franchise operation, and he got paid per passenger for the entire trip. If the ship was full, he made a hefty profit. Half full, he made some money. Empty, and he'd go bankrupt or have to get out of the business.

Richard could understand someone who wanted out so badly that he would destroy his own ship. But he couldn't understand doing it while paying customers were on board, nor could he imagine doing it with fire. There were so many other, much simpler ways.

Richard sat down across from the captain, jiggling the tabletop. The glasses clanked together, but it still took a moment for the captain to notice him.

Or at least to acknowledge him.

"Care to toast the end of my career?" the captain asked, lifting a glass.

"It's not as bad as all that," Richard lied.

"Ship's not reparable," the captain said.

"Yes, it is," Richard said. "I talked to them."

The captain shook his head. "Not flying that thing anywhere. Half the lower deck'd be unusable, it'd smell, and the environmental systems are whacked. Not safe. Least not by our standards."

By that, he meant the standards of the company he worked for.

"So are they sending a replacement ship?"

"Two weeks," the captain said. "Maybe. Or we can hire onto someone else's ship. Have to ask the passengers. What's left of them."

"Two weeks?" Richard asked.

"Coming from Ansary We'd go back to the Dyo System. We'd be back where we started. Not that it matters. I get to have a hearing. Like it's my fault they let some murderous nutcase onto my ship."

"You didn't check the manifest?" Richard asked.

The captain glared at him. Or tried to. It wasn't that effective a look, considering how wobbly his head was and how bloodshot his eyes were.

"What'm I supposed to? Turn away paying customers with spotless records? Of course, I checked. Not an idiot. Or didn't think I was."

The captain sighed.

"Someone's trying to destroy me," he muttered.

Which was a distinct possibility, one Richard hadn't thought of.

"Does someone hate you that much?" Richard asked.

"You mean besides me?" the captain asked. "Oh, hell, I don't know."

"You didn't do anything wrong," Richard said.

"Sent that first body into space," the captain said. "Didn't turn around then and there. Shoulda brought everyone back."

"We thought it was a suicide," Richard said. "And when the other two deaths happened, we were closer to Commons Space Station than to the Dyo System. It would've taken a week to go back to Ynchyn."

This nightmare trip started in Ynchyn.

"Seems logical, doesn't it? They don't train you for this kinda thing, you know. Maybe I shoulda confined everyone to quarters."

Richard nodded. After all, that had been his initial suggestion—or at least, his suggestion after the second murder. Ignatius Grove, a professor, heading to a new job at some prestigious university in the largest city on Ansary. The man taught mathematics of all things, and he had died when the skin in his throat had a growth spurt, shutting off both sides.

Everyone would've thought that a freak death as well, particularly since Ignatius Grove and Agatha Kantswinkle spent each meal complaining about their various food allergies, if Richard hadn't seen that particular form of murder before. He knew that there were little nanosomethings that could activate the growth mechanism in the skin. If swallowed, the nanosomethings invaded the throat. No one had ever done studies to see if any of them made it to the stomach or if that would've made a difference if the throat hadn't closed first.

Ignatius Grove had died a particularly hideous death. So had Remy Demaupin, the first victim. In fact, all three victims had died terribly. The third, Trista Jordan, had died when someone had sealed her mouth and nose with some kind of bonding adhesive. Richard wasn't sure what was used—some kind of liquid glue. She should've been able to use her call button to ask for help—and she probably would have, if she hadn't also been glued to the chair in her room.

The killer hadn't tried to hide that death, not that it would've mattered. There was no time to investigate it, because shortly after they found Trista, the fire had started.

Or at least had been discovered.

"Confining people to quarters," Richard said, "probably wouldn't have helped. We had a pretty determined killer on board. Still do, actually. Have any ideas who it is?"

"I'd've shot the bastard if I knew." The captain picked up one of the other glasses and downed its contents. "Hell, maybe I should shoot everyone now. That'd take care of the problem. What do you think?"

"It's one solution," Richard said.

"It's as good as any," the captain said, and picked up the remaining full glass. "If I could just get my butt outta this chair. Which I'm not going to do. If someone wants to kill me, so be it. They might be doing me a favor. You want to kill me, Richard?"

The captain's gaze met Richard's. For the first time, the captain seemed sober. His expression was very serious.

Richard had the sense that the captain knew more about him than Richard thought.

Richard had waited too long to pretend shock at the question. And he couldn't just wave it off, not considering the look the captain just gave him.

"If I kill you, what do I get out of it?" Richard asked.

The captain grinned and his head bobbled, that moment of clarity seemingly gone. "My eternal gratitude, my friend," he said, just before he finished the third drink. "My eternal gratitude."

HUNSAKER SAT behind the desk and dug through the files. He had his back to the wall and, out of the corner of his eye, he watched the entrances and the stairway. He didn't want anyone to surprise him for any reason.

He had a pad propped up on his thighs. His personal screen, not the one tied into the resort proper. He had upgraded the pad dozens of times, sometimes illegally. More than once, he'd stolen programs from his guests, and from one—a well connected gambler who liked the odds (and the breasts) in the casino—he had stolen an entire database of shady characters throughout the sector.

He didn't expect to see any familiar names in that database, but he found one.

Richard Ilykova, aka Yuri Flynn Doyle, Edward Michael Adams, and Misha Yurivich Orlinskaya, Mercenary and Assassin for Hire, believed to be responsible for more than two dozen deaths system wide.

Hunsaker shivered. He had known that Richard Ilykova hadn't been a common worker on a passenger ship. The man was too competent for that—not too mechanically competent, but too competent in the ways of death. He hadn't flinched when he had seen Kantswinkle's body, nor had he seemed too upset by this whole ordeal.

Yet all those deaths—the three on the ship and the fourth here, seemed awfully sloppy for a man who made his living killing people.

Hunsaker sighed softly and exited the illegal database. He felt dirty just thinking about Ilykova's job. About the man himself, actually. Ilykova hadn't seemed harmless—Hunsaker wasn't that naïve—but he had seemed...more efficient than deadly.

A movement caught his eye. Ilykova approached the desk. Hunsaker hadn't even seen him enter the room.

Hunsaker let out a little squeak. Ilykova raised an eyebrow in amusement. He'd clearly caught Hunsaker's moment of fear. Ilykova smiled—one of those knowing smiles—and then proceeded as if he had seen nothing out of the ordinary.

"Looking up the guests, are we?" he asked.

"So?" Hunsaker asked, then realized that probably wasn't the smartest response. Neither, he supposed, would be *What's it to you?* Or *Get the hell away from me.*

"So, does anyone have a history with lack of oxygen?"

"What?" Hunsaker asked, mostly because he hadn't been expecting that question.

"I realized when I was talking with the captain that all of our victims suffocated in one way or another. The fire would have caused the rest of us to suffocate as well. I was just wondering if we have some sort of revenge scenario going on here." Ilykova put his elbows on the desk.

"You tell me," Hunsaker said, his voice wobbling a little.

Ilykova frowned. "I don't have access to a deep database. You do."

Then his eyes widened just a little.

"Oh," he said. "You decided to research me first."

Hunsaker's heart was pounding. He had nothing to lose here—if Ilykova were going to kill him, it would happen here, now. So he called up the earlier screen, with Ilykova's history and pushed it across the desk at him.

"These things are so poorly done," Ilykova said. "It doesn't tell you much, does it?"

He looked up, his pale blue eyes twinkling. How could a man laugh about murder?

It made Hunsaker think of Carmichael: *Murder really shouldn't be the subject of casual conversation, now should it?*

Nor should it be something to smile about.

Apparently, Hunsaker's silence caught Ilykova's attention.

"We all have a past, Grissan," Ilykova said. "Yours involves embezzlement from every single resort you worked for. Quite creative embezzlement, I might add, the kind that would've made you very, very rich if you had kept to your original plan."

Hunsaker felt a warmth rise in his cheeks. No one knew about this. No one. How did Ilykova find it?

"The problem was, in your profession, that the younger, less experienced members moved from resort to resort, while the older ones got a well-deserved sinecure. That's the word, right? Sinecure?"

"Sinecure implies a job with little work. That's not true. To rise to the top of my profession, you must be willing to work at all times." Hunsaker's words were curt, showing his annoyance. He felt his face grow even warmer. He had let Ilykova irritate him.

Ilykova smiled slightly. "My mistake. I simply meant that you hit the top of your profession and remained in one place, a resort that became 'yours,' even if you didn't own it. You became the eyes and ears of the place, the face that everyone recognized. The person they associated with the resort. Which was why they bought you this place instead of prosecuting you. Did you know what a dive they got for you? It was the perfect revenge on their part, wasn't it? An effective banishment away from the populated areas of the sector. Did it embarrass you?"

Embarrassed, humiliated, *angered*. Hunsaker didn't say anything, though, although he expected all of the emotions ran across his face.

"Still," Ilykova said, "you got to keep the money you stole from the other resorts. You could've vanished. You just chose not to."

Too ashamed to leave. Hunsaker simply couldn't face any of his old colleagues ever again. Ever, ever, ever again.

"We all have a bit of history," Ilykova said. "I'm sure you had a reason for your sticky fingers. I have a reason for my history as well. My mother was Halina Layla Orlinskaya. Look her up in your little database."

Hunsaker took the pad back, his fingers shaking, dammit all to hell. He wasn't as practiced at controlling his physical reactions to his emotions, not like he used to be.

He looked up Halina Layla Orlinskaya. She had half a dozen aliases as well. A high level spy, who defected with some devastating knowledge that changed the course of one of the border wars, she survived her last few years by hiring herself out as a mercenary to various governments.

"What it doesn't say there, I'm sure," Ilykova said, "is that she hired me out as well, as an assassin. She thought I had the personality for it."

"Did you?" Hunsaker wished he could take the words back.

But Ilykova didn't seem to notice. "Not really. I think one should feel passionate about his work. An assassin's job requires no passion at all. Don't you think that one should put his heart and soul into his job?"

"I used to," Hunsaker said.

"And I'll bet you miss that emotion," Ilykova said. "I did. I wanted to *do* something with my life. Ah, to *do* something. Of course, now I'm broke and hiring onto ships as a lower level employee just to get across the sector."

He leaned across the desk. Hunsaker couldn't lean away. His back was already pressed against the wall.

"So you see, I had no reason to kill those people," Ilykova said. "I didn't know them. And I'm certainly smart enough not to set a fire on a spaceship far from the nearest port."

"But," Hunsaker said, his voice smaller than he wanted it to be, "you knew Agatha Kantswinkle."

Ilykova smiled, a real smile, genuinely amused. "Didn't like her either, huh? No one did, so far as I can tell. But I didn't have to kill her. She would've gotten off the ship at Ansary. And here, on Vaadum, she was your problem, not mine."

Hunsaker swallowed. "So you're saying you didn't do it."

"That's right," Ilykova said. "Why would I?"

"Someone paid you?" Hunsaker asked.

Ilykova shook his head. "If someone paid me, I would've been a passenger. I wouldn't have signed on for *work*."

It sounded logical. It all sounded very logical. Hunsaker just didn't know if he should believe it.

"So what's this about suffocation?" he asked.

"Oh, just a theory," Ilykova said. "Everyone suffocated in one way or another. So if you think of these crimes as related, then maybe the manner of death came as a form of revenge for a death by suffocation…?"

"I wouldn't even know how to look for that," Hunsaker said.

"I would," Ilykova said, and took the pad away from Hunsaker.

———

RICHARD WAS FINDING a whole lot of nothing as he dug through Hunsaker's database. The database wasn't that good. It was old, for one thing, and the updates hadn't been meshed into the system all that well. They had been grafted on and not efficiently, certainly not efficiently enough for a proper search.

He would have to get onto the *Presidio*. It had a good database and he might be able to find what he was looking for there.

Because, in this cursory exploration, he couldn't find

anyone with any links to any suffocation deaths, murdered, accidental, or even natural.

He was about to hand the pad back to Hunsaker, when someone screamed.

"Oh, not again," Hunsaker muttered.

Richard tossed him the pad and ran up the steps, half expecting to hear a thump. He didn't though. But he did hear another scream and, he realized, these screams were male.

They weren't frightened screams or startled screams (except maybe the first one), more likely horrified screams, end-of-the-world screams, the kind you emit when everything was hopeless and all was lost.

Another scream, and then another. Doors slammed as people left their rooms. He was joining quite a crowd as he ran up the stairs.

The screams came from the top floor.

He arrived, along with three other passengers from the ship (Janet Powell, Lysa Lamphere, and William Bunting) to find a man he'd never seen before on his knees, hands over his face, screaming like a stuck alarm.

Another body lay on the floor, this one a woman, also someone he'd never seen before either. Her eyes were open and glassy, her tongue protruding slightly.

She was clearly dead.

Someone sighed behind him.

Richard turned slightly. Hunsaker stood near his shoulder, and stared at the woman on the floor.

"Now what the hell am I going to do?" Hunsaker said with great annoyance. "I mean, really."

Judging from the look on Ilykova's face, Hunsaker had spoken out loud. He felt that warmth returning to his cheeks. He kept his head down, so that he didn't have to look Ilykova in the eyes, and moved into the room.

He put his hand on Fergus's shoulders. Fergus had worked for Hunsaker since Hunsaker came to the resort. Fergus and his wife, Dillith, who now doubled as a corpse. Not that she was ever much livelier than a corpse. But for what Dillith lacked in energy, she made up for in precision.

She could find a speck of dust the robotic cleaners left behind. She could turn bed sheet corners perfectly. She was slow, but she was anal.

And in Hunsaker's "resort," precision mattered more than speed.

Fergus stopped screaming when Hunsaker touched him. Fergus looked up, eyes sunken into his face, and said, "What am I going to do?"

His use of the sentence was plaintive. Hunsaker's had been self-involved. He had jumped from corpse/murder/crisis to *who the hell was going to work for me in this godforsaken place?* in less than a minute. He wasn't proud of that, but he really wasn't a man who developed much affection for his employees.

In fact, he believed affection got in the way of work. He didn't know much about Dillith and Fergus besides their names, their work methods, and the fact that they both preferred late hours rather than getting up early.

"Stand up," Hunsaker said with as much sympathy as he

could muster, which probably wasn't enough. "We'll figure something out."

Fergus stood. He was a slight man, and he fell into Hunsaker's arms, much to Hunsaker's chagrin. He hadn't invited the man to hug him. He certainly didn't want the man to touch him. But Fergus was beyond noticing subtleties. He was sobbing. Hunsaker could already feel his shirt getting wet.

He patted Fergus on the back and maneuvered him out of the room. Then he looked at Ilykova who was watching him with that look of amusement again.

"Do me a favor," Hunsaker said to Ilykova. "Get Anne Marie Devlin, would you?"

"Who?" Ilykova said.

"The base doctor," Hunsaker said.

"I think this woman is beyond a doctor—"

"Just do it," Hunsaker said, resisting the urge to move Fergus toward Ilykova. That would show him passion, all right.

Ilykova nodded, then hurried down the stairs. Three passengers from the ship stood around as if this were a theatrical event.

"Go back to your rooms," Hunsaker said. "There's nothing to see."

As if a woman wasn't already dead on the floor. There was plenty to see. He just didn't want them gawking at it.

They, of course, didn't move. He glared at them and tried to look tough, which was hard to do when you had a member of the staff sobbing in your arms.

"Go," he said, and that seemed to work. Maybe it was his tone, his clear disgust at everyone around him.

The three left slowly. He watched them go down the stairs, patting Fergus on the back the entire time as if he were a baby who needed to be burped.

Then Hunsaker peered at the room. It didn't look that much different than it had two hours ago.

When he'd helped Susan Carmichael move out of it.

SHE HEARD THE SCREAMING, of course. How could she have missed it? And she resisted her first instinct, which was to burrow deep under the covers of this new room, and pretend like she couldn't hear anything.

But Susan Carmichael wasn't a hider. She wasn't the kind of person who ran to the scene of a crime either, although she couldn't be entirely certain what she heard was a crime.

But someone didn't scream with that level of grief—and that was grief, wasn't it?—without a precipitating event, and considering Agatha's murder, the best assumption—the only assumption, really—was that a crime had occurred.

Again.

Which meant she had to get the hell off this station.

Somehow.

She changed clothes, slowly and deliberately, putting on the ivory blouse over the black pants. She slipped on her shoes, smoothed her hair, grabbed her personal information, and left this room as well.

The screaming had stopped, but she could hear faint voices in the distance. She glanced at the stairs, to ensure that no one was on them, and then she quietly made her way down.

It was time she stopped all of this. She gave up. She had been fleeing her family, but really, life out here was much, much worse than life with them could ever be.

Besides, her father had the capability of getting a ship here within twenty-four hours. He had ships all over the sector. One of them had to be nearby.

She just had to contact him.

She made her way down the stairs toward the main desk. Surely, there was some kind of interstellar communications node. Or maybe just a sector-wide node.

Or worse case—which was a case she'd put up with, after all—she would simply contact the nearest ship and have them contact her father.

And then she would wait.

Although she probably needed some kind of guard.

There wasn't a lot of choice. Everyone from the ship was a possible murderer, and there weren't a lot of people on the station.

But all of the murders she knew of took place while the victim was alone.

So the next key was to be with someone at all times.

Except right now.

Right now, she needed to contact Daddy.

After that, she would find a companion—and find a way to stay awake until help arrived.

ANNE MARIE DEVLIN was no longer drunk. She wasn't even under-the-surface drugged-sober drunk. She was so far past drunk that she felt giddy.

Actually, the excitement made her feel giddy. She felt useful for the first time in months.

If she didn't know herself better—and she knew herself quite well, thank you—she would say she had become a drunk because she was bored.

But she had been a drunk long before life ceased to be a challenge. She knew that excitement was just a temporary high, while alcohol numbed the senses, which was usually what she preferred.

Right now, however, she needed all the senses that she had. She was inside yet another room—this one a favorite of hers—standing over yet another corpse that had been murdered by yet another tampered environmental system.

The question was, how had it been tampered with? And why?

She was peering at the system itself, noting something off, when she realized one of the ship's passengers was also in the room. A tallish white-blond man with pale blue eyes.

The man who had fetched her. Richard Something-Or-Other.

"I prefer to work alone," she said.

"So do I," he said.

They stared at each other for a moment. Hunsaker, who also preferred to work alone (she knew that because he had told her half a dozen times) stood near the doorway, his shirt soaked with Fergus's tears. She'd managed to get Fergus out of the room and down to the kitchen where the chef could watch him. Fergus was quite pliable most of the time. Right now, he was damn near catatonic.

Perhaps anyone would be after crying that much.

She turned toward Hunsaker. "What the hell were you thinking? Sending those two to work in these rooms with a murderer on the loose?"

"Who knew that the killer would come after one of us?" he said.

"I don't think the killer did," Richard Something-Or-Other said. "If you'll allow me."

He shoved—*shoved!*—Anne Marie out of the way, and peered at the control panel himself.

"You do realize if this man is the killer, he now has access to the evidence," she said to Hunsaker.

"You do realize if this man is the killer," Hunsaker said, mimicking her tone, "then you just gave him a reason to kill us."

They glared at each other again.

"I'm not the killer," Richard Something-Or-Other said, "but whoever is has some serious engineering skills."

She couldn't resist: she peered into the controls as well. These older models had digital readouts and mechanisms attached to mechanisms. She had just looked at the one in the room where Agatha Kantswinkle died—and that control did not have a secondary digital readout. This one did.

She looked at Richard Something-Or-Other. He raised his eyebrows at her, as if he were surprised as well. Then he touched the whole thing with a single fingernail. The second readout was loose, but had been attached into the control's mechanism. She peered at the mix. When Dillith had been in here, the atmosphere's mix had been the same as it had been when Agatha Kantswinkle died.

Anne Marie frowned. She glanced over her shoulder at the door. Hunsaker was still leaning on the jamb, glaring at her. He seemed to disapprove of what she was doing.

Or maybe he disapproved of Richard Something-Or-Other.

Or maybe he always disapproved of everything.

She sighed and walked to the door.

"Move," she said.

Hunsaker didn't.

"I mean it. Move. I need to see something."

"What?" he asked.

"It's easier to look than it is to explain," she said pushing him aside. Then she peered inside the locking mechanism. Another small digital readout had been attached.

"This door was closed when Fergus got here, wasn't it?" she asked.

"I don't know," Hunsaker said. "I didn't ask."

"You didn't bother to tell them to keep the doors open?"

Hunsaker's glare changed to something filled with a kind of fury. "Of course I did. It's part of the general instructions, anyway. The door should always be open when the staff is inside, even if no one else is."

"Hmm," she said.

"What?" Richard Something-Or-Other asked from his position near the environmental controls.

"This is a timer," she said. "It closes the door."

"And this timer," he said, "changes the environmental mix."

"It couldn't have been put in here when Dillith was here," Anne Marie said.

"Someone set it up earlier than that," Richard Something-Or-Other said.

"Which means that the killer wasn't after Dillith," Anne Marie said.

"He was after Susan Carmichael." Hunsaker said that last, breathed it in fact. Anne Marie could hear the shock in his voice. "If I'd gotten here just a little too late, then—"

"You would've died too," Anne Marie said. "We have to brace this door open."

"I doubt the room will kill again," Richard Something-Or-Other said.

"But the other rooms might," Anne Marie said.

"I moved everyone out of the older rooms," Hunsaker said.

"Let's hope that's enough," Anne Marie said. She actually felt a little chill. She liked the chill. Excitement—she had missed it so much. "Maybe he'll start coming after the rest of us too."

"Oh, don't get your hopes up," Hunsaker snapped and left the room.

Richard Something-Or-Other raised his eyebrows again. "What was that all about?"

Anne Marie shrugged. "I guess he's upset by all of this."

Richard nodded. "I think it would be surprising if he were not."

HUNSAKER STOMPED DOWN THE STAIRS. Now he didn't know what to do. Did he warn Carmichael? Did he put all the guests in the same room and let them duke it out until a ship arrived and got them out of his resort?

He stopped halfway down the stairs and leaned his head against the wall. All of his training, all of his long and fancy education, all of his experience good and bad did not train him for any of this. He could just imagine the lecture titled *How to Handle a Murderer Loose in Your Resort.*

Simple: Call the local authorities.

And if there were none?

He banged his head against the metal just once. If he rounded them up, where would he take them? The restaurant? The casino?

The casino at least covered a big area. It would be hard to tamper with the environmental system.

Maybe he should just force them all back to their ship, and if they killed each other, so be it. Hell, if they died from smoke inhalation, so be it. It wasn't his concern.

While they were here, they bothered him.

While they were on their ship, they had nothing to do with him.

That's what he'd do. He'd get the maintenance guys and make them act as security guards. Even the chef and the blackjack dealer could work security (so long as she put her shirt on). They'd round up these horrible people and put them back on their own ship and if they died, they died.

His stomach turned.

Maybe if they all died, he could just jettison the ship into deepest darkest space. He'd set it on autopilot and get it the hell out of here.

For a moment, his spirits rose.

Then he remembered he'd already charged their accounts. There was a record he couldn't tamper with of them being on his station.

Dammit.

He had no idea what to do.

RICHARD HELPED Anne Marie get the corpse down to the medical wing. He'd had enough of carrying bodies. By his count, this was the fifth this trip, and the only one he hadn't met while she was still alive.

The medical wing was in the farthest part of the station, and certainly didn't deserve the appellation "wing." It was a medical suite at best, a smallish group of rooms set up as an afterthought.

Agatha Kantswinkle lay on one table, naked—which was an image he'd never get out of his mind again—and, to his surprise, the other two bodies from the ship lay in clear refrigeration units, looking no worse for being dead the last few days.

He set Dillith on the closest table, and stretched his muscles with relief.

"Thank you," the doctor said in that tone all professionals used which actually meant *you're done, now get the hell out.*

Which he did.

And as he stepped into the corridor, he realized he'd been

going about this investigation all wrong. He'd been looking for common ties, for suffocation deaths, for *motive*, and he, of all people, should know that motive mattered a lot less than the entertainments said it did.

His motive for most of his early killings had been because his mother had hired him out to do the job. The later killings had been because he could make money at it. Only the first killing had had a real motive: the man had murdered his father and ruined Richard's life.

Richard didn't need to look at motive.

He needed to look for experience. Technical experience.

With environmental systems.

He scurried back to the hotel's main entrance, and hoped that Hunsaker's horrible aging database had at least enough information to solve all of this.

———

SHE WASN'T HYSTERICAL. Hunsaker could've dealt with her if she had been hysterical. He had training in hysterical. High-end hotel guests often got hysterical about nothing. And here, which was decidedly *not* high-end, people got hysterical because…well, because they were here.

Susan G. Carmichael had every reason to be hysterical. She could've died in her room had he not taken her out of it. But she had already figured out that she might die and she was calmer than he was.

She had even found a way to contact her father, who was such a famous Vice Admiral that Hunsaker had even heard of him, and he was sending a ship that would be here in 18 hours sharp, along with some kind of back-up that would take care of the problem.

Whatever that meant.

But she wasn't returning to her room.

To any room, really.

She wanted to remain with Hunsaker, thinking that some-how, Hunsaker would be safe.

He sat on his chair with his back against the wall, no longer sure what safe was. She was sitting on the edge of his desk, surveying the area as if she ran it instead of him.

He was still debating whether to get everyone else out of their rooms when Ilykova burst through the doors.

"I need your database," he said.

"Whatever happened to please and thank you?" Hunsaker muttered, knowing he was being a complete ass, as he handed over the pad.

Ilykova ignored that, although he did glance at Carmichael. He didn't seem that surprised to see her. Then he leaned against the desk and started trolling the database, his fingers moving faster than Hunsaker's ever could.

The three of them didn't say a word as Ilykova worked. Carmichael watched him. Hunsaker kept an eye on the doors and the stairs, not that it had made any difference in the past.

Then Ilykova looked over at Carmichael. "Were you and Agatha Kantswinkle ever alone?"

"Here?" she asked.

"On the ship," he said.

She looked down. "I talked to her once. After that incident —you know. I felt so sorry for her that—"

"What incident?" Hunsaker interrupted. It wouldn't have

been his business had everything happened on the ship, but the ship's problems had spilled into his little resort, and he felt he had a right to know.

She looked at him. "We had a dinner hour on the ship. We all got fed at the same time, and the room wasn't that big. We got to know each other better than you usually got to know people on passenger ships, which wasn't necessarily a good thing."

Ilykova nodded, although he kept his head down, still searching the database as he listened.

"Anyway, just after Professor Grove died, we were all on edge, and Agatha started into how we needed someone to take charge, to make sure things wouldn't get worse, and Mr. Bunting had enough. He told her she was a nosy snobbish old woman who wouldn't know how to treat other human beings even if she had special training, and she certainly couldn't be in charge of anything, and he didn't believe anything she said about herself and—." Carmichael shook her head. "I was agreeing with him at first, she was an unpleasant woman, and I would've given anything to avoid her as much as possible, but he didn't stop, and by the end, she looked just devastated."

Ilykova was looking up now. Hunsaker was surprised as well. He couldn't quite imagine Kantswinkle looking devastated.

"I waited until everyone left," Carmichael said, "and told her that we were all on edge and that he had no right to lay into her like that, and she started to cry, which made me very uncomfortable. I walked her to her room, and told her to get some rest, that it would all seem better in the morning, and then I left."

"Then what?" Hunsaker asked, expecting more to the story.

"Then we found Trista's body and the fire and we barely made it here," Carmichael said.

"I got the distinct impression you wanted nothing to do with Ms. Kantswinkle," Hunsaker said.

Carmichael looked at him in surprise. "I thought I hid that."

"You avoided her in the lobby, checking in," Hunsaker said.

Carmichael looked down, sighed. "She was clingy. Halfway through our discussion, I realized she was bombastic because she was lonely and needy and I'd made a huge mistake trying to comfort her. If this had been some kind of normal flight, I wouldn't have been able to shake her for the rest of the trip."

"If it had been a normal flight," Ilykova said, "you wouldn't have spoken to her in the first place."

"True enough," Carmichael said. Then she frowned at him. "Why did you ask about us?"

"I have a theory," he said.

But he didn't say any more. And he continued to tap on the pad, which annoyed Hunsaker.

"Are you going to share the theory?" Hunsaker asked.

"I think someone thinks you saw something," Ilykova said. "Did you?"

Carmichael shrugged and shook her head.

"It would've been when you two were alone together."

She shook her head again. "Nothing."

He grunted as if he didn't believe her. He continued to work.

After a long moment, he said softly, "Well, I think I found something."

"WHAT DID YOU FIND?" Hunsaker asked. Carmichael crowded close. Richard didn't answer right away. First he made certain no one else could hear. He checked the doors, and looked up the stairwell.

When he came back to the desk, he spoke as softly as he could. He explained his idea—that he search for expertise, not motive. He didn't discuss how he feared the database would be limited (it was, but it didn't matter, he'd found enough).

"When I searched for expertise in environmental systems, I got two names. I expected at least one from the crew, but that was wrong."

"Which names?" Carmichael sounded panicked for the first time since he saw her down here.

"William Bunting and Lysa Lamphere."

"Bunting," Hunsaker said. "He was the one who yelled at Agatha Kantswinkle, you said."

Carmichael nodded.

"But," Richard said, "whoever killed Agatha and went after you, Susan, had a short window to do so. You had your room assignments already. Did you let anyone in your room?"

"Janet Powell," Carmichael said. "But I never left her alone and she never went near the controls."

"Anyone else?"

She shook her head.

"Where were you after we found Agatha's body?"

"I didn't leave the room," Carmichael said.

"Except to buy clothing," Hunsaker said.

"Yes," Carmichael said. "I bought clothing. But Bunting couldn't've done it then. He was in the boutique with me."

She used the word boutique with a touch of sarcasm. Richard frowned for a moment. Bunting had yelled at Agatha Kantswinkle, and made her cry. She wouldn't have let him near her. But another woman…?

"Did she have any troubles with Lysa?" Richard asked.

Carmichael shrugged. "I have no idea. I'm not even sure they spoke."

He didn't want to push her too hard. "Did you see either William Bunting or Lysa Lamphere that night you were alone with Agatha?"

"Lysa," Carmichael said. "But it was no big deal. She had forgotten something in the dining area. She went past us, looking a bit concerned. It wasn't important."

"Past you from where?" he asked.

"I assume she came from her room," Carmichael said.

"But you were walking Agatha to her room."

"Yes," Carmichael said.

"From the dining area."

"Yes."

"Which was nowhere near Lysa's room."

Carmichael looked at him.

"Her room was in a whole different area of the ship."

"And the fire started not too far from Agatha's room," Carmichael said.

Richard nodded. He felt certain they knew who the killer was now. Lysa Lamphere had killed Agatha and gone after Carmichael because they could tie her to the entire event.

"It all sounds so nice and pretty," Hunsaker said, "until you remember that Lysa nearly died from inhaling the same toxic air that Agatha died from."

"Did she?" Richard asked. "She went into the room, made the switch with the environmental controls, maybe even watched Agatha die, and then switched them back. She waited until everything cleared a bit, and then went through her charade. I have a hunch if we search her room, we'll find some small breathing equipment, something she hid before going back to 'discover' Agatha."

"Why would she do that?" Carmichael asked.

They were all so naïve. Or maybe he wasn't naïve enough. It seemed obvious to him. Once he had Lysa's name, he understood how everything happened. And a little bit of why.

"So that no one would ever suspect her. You ruled her out even after I discovered her expertise because she had suffered as well."

He almost added, any good professional would've done that. But he didn't. Still, he saw the way Hunsaker looked at him. Hunsaker knew that.

"May I have the pad?" Hunsaker asked.

Richard handed him the pad, bracing for the next question, which came with predictable swiftness.

"I don't suppose you have expertise in environmental systems?" Hunsaker asked.

Richard resisted the urge to smile. "No, I don't."

"I will check," Hunsaker said.

"Do," Richard said. "But remember what I told you before.

I wouldn't have started the fire. If you want to scuttle a ship, there are better and quicker ways to do it. She didn't want us all to die. She knew we were close."

"But why kill five people?" Carmichael asked.

"That's what I mean to find out," Richard said.

IT TOOK A BIT OF WORK. Buried deep in all the information was one single tie. To the mathematician. His new job was a promotion, one she didn't feel he deserved. She had studied under him, and he had refused to grant her a degree, saying she was sloppy. She moved to engineering, and graduated, although not with honors, and not in a way that gave her any currency in any job. She would've needed more education for that.

She had boarded that ship with a plan to follow him to Ansary, maybe destroy his career there. Or maybe kill him. But she didn't.

Trista died because she had seen the murder, and she planned to do something about it. Lysa had never planned for Trista's body to be discovered. She probably thought the fire would've been found sooner. By the time someone had found it, the entire ship went into a panic. Which, if Richard thought about it, meant that her calculations had been off.

Professor Grove, the mathematician had been right about her after all. Her math skills hadn't been up to the task.

Then Agatha Kantswinkle and Susan Carmichael had seen Lysa in that area, and if there were an investigation, they might've mentioned her. She didn't want to risk it. So she planned the last two murders, and might've gotten away with all of it, if Hunsaker hadn't moved Carmichael out of her room.

What Richard couldn't figure out was why she killed Remy Demaupin.

"I didn't," Lysa snarled. They had tied her up and moved her to the bar, along with all the other passengers. No one wanted to be alone any longer. They all worried that Richard and Hunsaker and Carmichael had caught the wrong person, even though Lysa had made it pretty clear from the moment she got tied up that they hadn't.

"What do you mean you didn't kill Remy," Carmichael said. "We know you did."

Lysa shook her head. "He killed himself," she said. "In fact, he inspired me. I figured everyone would look for a connection between him and Professor Grove. Then we would have the emergency and everyone would forget and…"

She lowered her head. Richard watched her, realized he'd met her type before. The type that imagined what they'd do, then did it, and wondered why nothing quite worked the way they'd planned.

"You should've just shoved him out of an airlock," Richard said.

Everyone looked at him. He realized he'd said too much.

He shrugged, pretending a nonchalance he didn't entirely feel.

"What I mean is that had you done something simple, no one would've thought twice about it. All this elaborate stuff was your downfall."

That still sounded bad. He sounded like one killer giving advice to another. Which, in fact, he was.

Hunsaker crossed his arms, watching Richard, a slight frown on his face. Anne Marie stood in the back of the room, listening. The captain was still at his table, drowning himself in drink. Carmichael kept checking the time, hoping that her father's ship would get here soon.

Everyone else sat very far away from Lysa, as if her particular brand of insanity was catching.

Richard didn't stay that far away though. For all her brand of insanity, her elaborate kills, and her mistakes, she was what a murderer should be.

Someone who had a reason to do what she did—not a bloodless reason. A personal reason. An important reason. Something that was, to her, life and death. So she acted in a life-or-death manner.

And he found that both inspirational and appropriate.

He didn't ask her any more. Carmichael's father could take them all in his various ships. Somewhere Lysa would get prosecuted for what she had done. Not that this was a happy ending for anyone.

The captain would probably lose his job. Carmichael was going back to a situation that she clearly didn't want to be in.

And Richard would have no way to get to Ansary.

Not to mention all the people who had died. Their families would never be the same.

He walked back to Anne Marie Devlin. Pretty woman. Or she would've been if she weren't a depressive and a drunk. She was sober right now, but he could see the tendencies. She was the kind who didn't want to change because she saw no point in it.

Besides, change was hard. That was becoming clearer to him, each and every day.

THE SHIPS ARRIVED in fifteen hours, not eighteen, and they took everyone away. Once Hunsaker realized who Carmichael's father was—he truly was a mucky-muck of high muck who had a lot of mucking money—he made noises about the damage to his resort and how embarrassing it would be if it ever came out that his daughter had been a target.

When that hadn't moved her father, Hunsaker added that it would also be embarrassing for people to know that his daughter had been fleeing from him when all of this occurred.

Hunsaker got a tidy payout, enough to renovate the entire resort if he felt like it. And he felt like it. He wanted this place as tamper proof as possible. He didn't ever want to be in this situation again.

Ilykova hadn't left with the rest. He wasn't going to testify either, no matter how much everyone pleaded with him. He sat in the bar these days and watched Anne Marie drink, which was a sight to behold. He didn't seem miserable, but he didn't seem happy either.

He was waiting for the next ship, for a way out. Although he clearly didn't know where he was going.

And Hunsaker had been thinking about it. The station was a world unto itself. Technically, anything that happened here was prosecuted in the Commons System, but no prosecution had ever happened.

Hunsaker wasn't sure what he would've done if Ilykova hadn't been here. Ilykova wasn't big or burly and he didn't seem tough. But he had experience.

And he had no qualms about doing what it took to keep the peace.

You should've just shoved him out of an airlock.

Hunsaker couldn't've done that to anyone. Ever. But he could pay someone to do it while he looked the other way.

That wouldn't've worked in this circumstance, of course. But it might in future circumstances.

And if Hunsaker had learned anything from this experience, he had learned it was better to be prepared.

If he had been prepared, none of this would've happened.

The doors would've locked properly, the environmental controls would've been up-to-date, and all the rooms would've been cleaned.

Woulda coulda shoulda

He wasn't going to have any regrets. He was going to move forward.

He squared his shoulders and walked to the bar. He paused for a brief jealous moment when he saw how close Ilykova was sitting to Anne Marie. Then he saw the look of disgust on Ilykova's face, and realized that the man would never be interested in her.

So Hunsaker sat down at their table, and offered Ilykova a job.

No one was surprised when Ilykova said yes.

Minions at Work: Fits Like a Glove

Love Pulphouse? Become a subscriber!

Electronic Subscription:
Six months, 6 Issues... $29.99
Twelve months, 12 Issues...$59.99

Paper Subscription:
Six months, 6 Issues... $99.99 (free shipping)
Twelve months, 12 Issues... $199.99 (free shipping)

Subscribing is easy at the Pulphouse Store. And while you're there, check out the fun merchandise (Thumper pillow anyone?), previously published issues and much more. The Pulphouse Store is the place to go for full immersion into all things Pulphouse!

pulphousemagazine.com